This Certificate issued under the seal of the C...
Office in accordance with title 17, *United Sta*...
attests that registration has been made for th...
identified below. The information on this ce...
been made a part of the Copyright Office re...

*Marie Strong*

Acting United States Register of Copyrights and Director

MW00565609

**Effective Date of Registration:**
February 20, 2020
**Registration Decision Date:**
October 07, 2020

## Title

**Title of Work:** The Big Fall

## Completion/Publication

**Year of Completion:** 2019

## Author

- **Author:** Frank A. Aloi
  **Author Created:** 339 page novel, about Attorney with legal troubles who represents a mob kingpin
  **Work made for hire:** No
  **Citizen of:** United States
  **Anonymous:** No
  **Pseudonymous:** No

## Copyright Claimant

**Copyright Claimant:** Frank A. Aloi
51 Lac Kine Dr, Rochester, NY, 14618

## Limitation of copyright claim

**Previously registered:** No
**Basis of current registration:** This is the first application submitted by this author as claimant.

## Certification

**Name:** Frank A. Aloi
**Date:** February 16, 2020

**Correspondence:** Yes

# P R O L O G U E

Four in the morning. The Sunday before the Fourth of July. The rag top was down on the Vette convertible as it accelerated south on Alameda through old Chinatown. Geologists had just published their findings that enormous fissures ten miles down undermined the Wilshire Boulevard Corridor, Beverly Hills, Santa Monica, and most of the refineries and tank farms down the coast to San Pedro. Doom and gloom and inevitability warnings really weren't necessary from the scientists to bring home the tenuous quality of paradise in the Pacific.

Everyone knew it was too good to be true and surely must end in the cataclysmic quake. But the geologic time bomb seemed to attract people similarly faulted. And most of them were more edgy than usual in the run of strange weather that had blanketed the Southlands. Storms had been lashing the coast. It had cleared earlier but then an oppressive low settled in to choke the basin. The City groaned a vast empty lament, the petrified melody of wind scrambling to escape the walls of a ruined cathedral. Sirens crisscrossed in the distance. The bad weather had kept the loonies inside. Now they were out in the twenty-four-hour heat, their lives nothing more than an accelerated grimace, and the City of Angels would pay. You could almost reach out and grab a fistful of the hot humid air. The driver fought the dizziness, steadying himself by hanging on to the wheel for dear life. He swerved erratically. The wet lash of the fiery air stung him back. Perspiration beaded on his forehead and rolled in rivulets down his cheeks. Then he fought the wheel with his right hand as he desperately clasped his left over the wound in his side that was again oozing blood. They were tempting him with that one-way ticket again, over the edge and into the black. He was drifting. There it was! The brilliant red ball, concentric black lines spiraling to its core. He strained to make out its innermost circle. The innermost circle? A train whistle sounded, lonesome and true. Drifting the road markers now an indistinguishable blur.

It was snowing, a million miles back. He crossed the acres of track in the switching yard. The blizzard had closed his High School and shut down the City. The wet snow waffled down glistening in the moonlight like a tossed fistful of diamonds. The plough rumbled, drawn by four horses, lanterns clanging against the boards on its ends and middle. A plough almost as wide as the street, and the ploughman riding the skids, the reins in one hand and a bagged bottle in the other. He waved at them and shouted that it was always good to be back.

They kept coming as if he wasn't really there. He groaned "but why" as they rolled through him. His face was buried in the wet snow. The wet? Johnny Fixx shook his head and blinked at reality. He'd shut down the Vette in the middle of Alameda under a blinking red traffic signal. His face was wet with spray from the water truck that had brushed past. Steam slithered up from the hot tarmac. The pain ripping at his side doubled him up. Malevolent dragon gargoyles leered out from just beneath the gutters of pagoda styled roofs - ancient guardians for the endless blocks of buttoned up storefronts in Chinatown. Lights were pinging around in his skull, then a cloud of smoke seemed to settle into his eyes as he nodded off to the rush of equatorial heat.

The drive into the City from Tan Son Nhut airport, past the homes of the departed French, white and cream villas trimmed in green with red tiled roofs, flanked by broad shade trees. There were courtyard walls painted with purple bougainvillea, and boulevards bounded by hedgerows delicately manicured. Groves of palms and tamarind trees, and flame trees shaded the streets. Hotels with enclosed mezzanine terraces, continental shelfs, and sidewalk cafes - the Continental Palace, the Majestic, the Rex, and the Caravelle.

Thousands of mopeds and bicycles, pedicabs, their collective pedals the electric swarm of locusts, controlled, but barely, the ominous undercurrent of the place. Heavier transport rumbled, jitney buses and Lambrettas spewed clouds of noxious fumes, and jeeps and trucks by the hundred danced the stutter step of brake and accelerate on the busy thoroughfares. There were hawkers in every doorway, an oriental bazaar, silks and scimitars, cinnamon, and ginger, then endless sandbagging, sand filled oil drum barriers, concertina wire, and wire mesh window coverings, sights and sounds of two worlds colliding in the marathon moment before Salome's final veil floated down.

The streets were jammed with people, the military riding to the front, spit and polish of unblooded ARVN's bright eyed in the rumble of their transport, peasants in carts drawn by water buffalo, children riding their hindquarters urging them on with bamboo switches, whole families trudging in the heat and humidity, their pajama clad women balancing poles on their shoulders, woven baskets at either end holding their earthly possessions, their heads shaded by conical straw hats, and cork sun helmets. Ladies in flowing Ao Dai's, Indians in turbans selling souvenirs and changing money, and cadaverous old women spitting blackish-red betel nut juice into the dust.

Flesh for sale.

"Boom, boom? You numma one jai?"

Johnny Fixx sat a table at a sidewalk cafe, Dancer beside him, just then more interested in the "goods" being offered for sale. "Short time? Numma one jai?" smiled lasciviously the jade statuettes at the next table.

The sappers broke from a line of mopeds and buzzed at them their mouths thinned in a one way look that declared their intention to kill or die trying. Fixx dove across the table and shouldered his friend to the curb. The sappers heaved in two grenades. The ladies at the next table who had held Dancer's attention were torn apart, and neither he nor Dancer suffered even a scratch. Who lived, who died, the lifeline was that thin.

Joey Dancer!

A painful pounding raged inside Fixx' head. He was in a twisted jungle forest, its trees naked from defoliants, bony branches reaching accusingly. And then the skeleton forest was flattened by an avenging comet, its ravenous tail switching at serpentine mangrove vines, bone gray roots of mahogany trees, and broad leafed jungle plants that wetly hissed each in their turn before succumbing to the fiery scythe.

His vision cleared. It was the City of Angels, the only forest within sight the distant ranks of praying mantis oil derricks, monotonously unearthing subterranean black gold.

He was bleeding like a faucet. The bleeding must stop if he was to have any chance. Fixer pulled over and struggled to pick himself out of the car. He squared his shoulders and forced deep breaths into his trembling middle. He clasped the rearview mirror, caught sight of the blocky face, deeply lined, with dark nearly dead eyes, and wildly unkempt hair, and gasped at the stranger who barely could focus to answer his stare.

His pockets were stuffed with bandages and he laid out the gauze pads and wide ace bandages on the hood of the Vette, then tightened up in preparation for what he knew he must do. His shirt had come undone and he dabbed at the wound with a pad. He peeled off another, rolled it into a plug, and twisted its end into the hole in his side. The pain was a white hot tear across his middle that abruptly changed direction to bludgeon his brain in triphammer blows. Waves of nausea doubled him over. He swiped at his tearing eyes and tightened up his behind so as not to void.

"No matter how bad the pain that rips at a part of you, it will inevitably become more generalized and thus be more bearable," said the sensei. The old man was always right. This time was no exception. Fixer plastered another pad over the plug and held it all in place with the ace bandage he wrapped and tied around his middle. It was then that he finally noticed that he'd pulled over beside an old neighborhood theatre, a bleached dry boarded up debacle clothed in cracked tile and shattered glass. An ancient poster display had somehow survived. "High Sierra" probably a fifties revival after Bogie's passing. The print was nearly bleached out. Johnny Fixx leaned in close to make it out.

"Higher he went than man has ever climbed . . . but he couldn't escape his destiny! . . . 'Mad Dog' Earle. . . Sentenced to die alone."

Alameda, across Sepulveda to the Terminal Freeway, heading toward the sea. Fog billowed up through the bridge superstructure, patchy sticky looking stuff, tasting of oil slicks in the harbor. Spotlights played over the cadaverous gray walls of truck terminals. A freight rumbled through the switching yards, shrieking its whistle for the right of way. He raced through the grade crossing weaving around the blocking gates as the freight barreled on through, a split second behind. Every muscle, every pore screamed to shut down. The Vette careened

iv

wildly across the double solid line narrowly missing a wildly honking van coming the other way.

"Bear down," he screamed. Persistent rivulets of perspiration rolled down his face.

"Almost there," he whispered hopefully.

A hundred eighty-five feet over the channel now on the giant mile long green suspension bridge - the Vincent Thomas - that would carry him onto the San Pedro peninsula. The packet of C-4 rested on the passenger seat, the stainless push button detonator catching the dappled light from far above in the bridge superstructure - cold plated reality. Then onto the Harbor Freeway meandering south to the sea on Gaffney Street.

"Did it have to come down to the final play?"

The tops of Royal palms slapped at him accusingly, their trunks bending in the breeze twenty five feet below on the embankment. And beyond, the weird landscape of San Pedro. Oil tank farms, pipes and flame capped cracking towers row on endless row, the hiss of dragons disturbed in their repose. Acres of cranes and derricks, power line towers, menacing prehistoric sentinels, he imagined - then rank upon rank of Japanese imports in the car lots by the piers, a sea of ants on the march not to be denied their daily feeding of the dollars of Greater Los Angeles.

"Dollars," he muttered, running it again - one last time. It was unthinkable that he had been drawn in beyond his ability to extricate himself. Living on the edge had built a kind of arrogance that no corner was too tight or back street too dark for his matchless talent to maneuver around the tentacles.

Time to pay up," he thought, rolling back onto the highway. The front wheels slammed into a rut and the jolt opened the tear in his middle. He squeezed the wheel for all he was worth, just then his balancing bar on a tightrope that figured to be a foot too long.

The streets registered - a final roll call. Left on Sixth to Pacific, then right towards lands end - Point Fermin. He shut down his lights as he topped the final rise on Pacific where the Palos Verde peninsula began its drop off to the sea. The jetty was at the end of the track beyond the barricade at the cul de sac that closed off Pacific. Arc lights sputtered in the fog and in the haze the old freighter tiredly heaved in the swells as deck cranes whirred and clanged against the night, hoisting nets and pallets of cargo aboard.

Johnny Fixx held in place, seconds, then minutes. He'd complained that his chronic bad luck had been his undoing, but Samantha had always seen through him.

"Everything you do, you want to do Johnny," she'd said, "but then you don't want to be reminded of it."

Her kisses had sealed off his world and for precious moments made a better one. But there hadn't been nearly enough time. What was done couldn't be undone. He'd made damned certain of that. There was a certain inevitability to it almost a feeling of relief, as he put her in gear to roll down the grade. Traffic barriers blocked the right of way to the cul de sac, their twin red beacons flashing to warn strangers away. Red lights, concentric black circles within! Caution to the unwary, but to Fixx, an invitation, and suddenly Fixer knew where he'd been heading for so many years.

The detonator was set for ten seconds. He hit the switch and floored the accelerator. Rubber burned on tarmac and the Vette fishtailed in the wet. There was an instant of cover in a fog bank. Fixer burst through, and then they made him. They'd been expecting company. Two cars pulled out from behind stacked crates, nose to nose to block the road. Small arms fire cracked and they zeroed in riddling the hood and shattering the windshield. They should have nailed him. An icy calm put out the fire in his gut. He'd made it - they just didn't have his number, not quite yet.

He slammed through the car barricade, the Vette leaping the final yards to the gangplank. Harry Lang was there at the foot of the gangplank screaming obscenities, methodically firing an automatic in a two hand hold. The Vette lurched forward a few feet more before its wheels roared futilely for the ground that was no longer there. The C-4 went up in a blood red ball. The Vette was incinerated. An instant of deathly silence, as a breeze whipped away the smoke and flames. The debris of the Vette dropped into the water and a gaping hole showed in the freighter's water line.Then a massive explosion lifted the freighter breaking its back on a cushion of water. Flames roared up from the broken hull consuming the superstructure. Crewmen scrambled off where they could, jumping wildly to safety. Mortally wounded, the freighter slowly heeled over and sank in pieces in the murky water. The last of the fire sizzled out as all but the top most section of the stack slid under. Then a final massive explosion as cold sea water reached the boilers, and a tongue of flame leaped skyward from the stack. The last air bubbles gurgled to the surface and then it was quiet, the only sound the generator clicking for the still blinking reds on the traffic barrier.

It had all begun thirteen months before.

# C H A P T E R   O N E

Rudy Kutter was in an expansive mood. Two terms as District Attorney of Los Angeles County brought him a reputation as a crusader against organized crime and the drug lords that were its lifeblood in the Southlands. That record paved the way for the inside track for the nomination to make the run for the seat of retiring Senator Lawrence Logan. Kutter paced before the wall length mirror in the washroom. He ran two fingers over his chin checking whether his shave had been close enough. Broad cheeked, high forehead, hair thinning but still enough if combed from the side across to cover the bald spot in the center of his scalp, Kutter was a beefy six footer who looked younger than his fifty years.

Kutter grinned back at himself in the mirror. What was it in his expression that they latched onto? "IBM" he chuckled. "Corporate confidence" was the tag the TV anchor had laid on him. Kutter tugged at his vest. The blue pinstripes were smartly tailored to cover the beginnings of the paunch. Kutter ran the comb through his hair one last time before retracing his steps back through the corridor into his office.

Mary Donlan, his first assistant, sat before his desk, her head buried in the briefing book, the duplicate of which she'd placed on his blotter.

"Hi, boss," she smiled. Blonde and pale complected, Mary Donlan styled her hair short and brushed severely back off her face and worked hard at hiding her voluptuous figure in primly tailored business suits. She was bright and tireless, but more than that, unashamedly ambitious, a quality which made the DA and his first assistant a hand and glove fit and which Kutter exploited to the fullest.

Kutter muttered "mornin' Mary" and dropped into his chair to begin leafing through the matters in the briefing book. "Mary, what time is that TV reporter due?"

Mary Donlan checked her wrist watch. "You've got a half hour. She said 10:30 a.m."

1

Kutter continued his attention to the case details on the pages before him then abruptly slammed shut the looseleaf binder. "I'm not into this today," he smiled. "You can handle these things - can't you?"

"All but one Rudy."

"Which one is that?"

"Harry Lang". . . Her voice trailed off and Kutter's color instantly purpled.

"Is that bastard giving us trouble again?"

Harry Lang was a twenty-two year veteran of every major war LAPD had ever waged. With a zeal that Rudy Kutter characterized as increasingly bordering on the psychotic, Harry Lang didn't simply investigate. He literally tore at cases, ripping away the lies and half-truths without regard to who was run over in the process until the solution was finally unearthed. And it seemed to be getting worse. His wife had a history of mental illness and Lang finally was forced to institutionalize her. In the aftermath of that trauma, the Lieutenant was again losing ground in his lifelong battle with the bottle. He had made Lieutenant eight years before. The Chief, at Kutter's prodding, had offered Lang a Captaincy if he'd come inside. Harry Lang on the street in Kutter's view was an explosion waiting for a match - an intolerable circumstance in a most important year for the DA. The situation had most recently been exacerbated with charges of brutality lodged against Lang in the Escobar narcotics case the Lieutenant allegedly had personally taken a hand in strong arm tactics during the interrogation of Juan Escobar, a nineteen year old suspected drug smuggler, who also happened to be the sibling of a prominent Chicano family. The barrio was up in arms and the clock was ticking on a resolution of the confrontation before it became a full blown political crisis.

At one point a deal had been worked with the Chicanos - the issue would be diffused if Lang moved upstairs and off the street. But again the Lieutenant refused. There was one more scumbag to take down. Tony Persia - reputed consigliere to the local organization - a man with whom Kutter was obsessed.

"Not Persia again," blurted Kutter, thinking aloud.

"I'm not sure boss. Harry wants us to get an order for a tap on Jimmy Doyle."

"That's bullshit," snapped Kutter. "There isn't a Judge in the County who'd write that Order. Doyle's a booster. He's a dead end - a bush leaguer."

"That's not how Lang sees it. He says Doyle is into some major league stuff and if he catches him dirty, he'll . . . The remainder of Mary Donlan's statement died in her open mouthed amazement. Harry Lang burst into Kutter's office. Lang was wild eyed and unshaven. Red haired, his complexion beet red, Lang even running on empty projected wiry, energized and unpredictable.

"What the hell," snapped Rudy Kutter.

"Sorry," Lang barely articulated the word.

"Unfamiliar with that one, eh," quipped Mary Donlan.

Lang ignored her and spoke directly to the DA. "I heard you were leaving for two days on a speaking tour. I couldn't chance you not going to bat for me on that Order."

"Look Harry," said Kutter with as much control in his tone as he could muster, "this Jimmy Doyle thing is a wild goose chase. He's a punk."

"Was," answered Lang. "I hear he finally graduated. Even taking some post graduate courses."

"Facts," snapped Kutter. "If I go to a Judge I've got to show probable cause that Doyle is into a major felony. What have you got beside some penny ante break ins and hijackings?"

3

The intercom buzzed. Kutter's secretary announced, "Crystal Lee is here from Channel 6."

Kutter answered her, working at leveling his tone, "tell her I'll be with her shortly and apologize for any delay."

"What the hell does that smart assed dame want?" groused Lang.

Mary Donlan smiled, "never did attend that sensitivity training, eh, Harry?"

Lang frowned and bit back the retort that would vent his suspicions that Mary Donlan had designs on her married boss that went above and beyond the ambit of things legitimate for a loyal gal Friday.

Kutter prompted, "facts, Harry. I'll be here for a couple of hours. You want Doyle's ass, give me facts."

Lang glared at the DA and his first assistant thinking that Kutter would be the first to take the bows if he turned the pinch of the booster into a front page roll over on a big name crook.

"Okay, okay - facts you want. I'll get you facts."

Lang abruptly wheeled and walked out of the office and in his distraction barely avoided walking over Crystal Lee who was impatiently pacing the outer office. Surprise showed in her expression. Slender and lithesome, Crystal shrugged her trademark ebony mane that fell to her waist.

"Sorry," gruffly alibied Lang as he sidestepped her.

"Beaten any Chicano kids lately," taunted Crystal Lee.

Lang stopped squarely in his tracks and turned to menace the Channel 6 anchor.

4

"Maybe if your slant relatives stopped producing the shit, there wouldn't be any reason for us to bust the pushers who are crippling our kids with junk!"

Crystal Lee gestured at her cameraman.

"How 'bout we do this on camera, Lieutenant?"

Lang mouthed the word 'cunt' and brushed aside the cameraman as he exited the office.

Rudy Kutter emerged from his office, sized up the scene, surmised what had occurred and immediately moved to disarm Crystal Lee.

"We're trying to get him to retire gracefully."

Crystal's frown voiced her conviction that Lang would never know how.

Kutter shrugged, flashed as winning a smile as he could, and said, "well, sorry to keep you waiting. Come on in."

Crystal Lee barely stifled her anger and instantly reverted to form, flashing a plastic smile.

Kutter thought 'nice caps' and ushered the anchorperson and her cameraman into his office.

Crystal eyed Mary Donlan and Kutter explained "Mary may have background information that will help us."

"In a pig's eye" thought Crystal Lee. Rudy Kutter was a wily pro who probably more than once had been sandbagged by a member of the press taking liberties with a confidence. Mary Donlan was his personal fail safe to ensure that what he talked about "off the record" stayed that way.

Crystal positioned her cameraman and asked, "ready, Mr. Kutter?"

5

Mary Donlan moved to a corner safely off camera.

Rudy Kutter dropped into an overstuffed chair. Crystal Lee pulled another chair into his sight line but a bit off center. She fancied her left side most photogenic.Her camera was positioned to capture the bosses' best angle. As they settled into the chairs, she repeated, "are you ready, Mr. Kutter?"

"As I'll ever be" grinned the DA. "Just keep 'em above the belt." Crystal gestured to her cameraman.

"Set?" He nodded. The telltale red orb flashed on as he hit the trigger.

"We're with Rudy Kutter, the DA of Los Angeles County. Mr. Kutter, do you have the nomination?"

"The State Committee is meeting in Sacramento before the end of this week. As you know there are at least two other announced candidates. So until the Committee expresses its preference there is no nominee."

"But we've been told that you practically have a lock on the nomination?"

Kutter chuckled. "I don't think any of us can say that. The Committee will state the party's choice, but as you know, the losers can challenge that designation in a primary. So, no, I don't think there's any lock on the 'nod' - but I will say this. I do expect to be given very serious consideration."

Crystal smiled, interjecting, "and you do expect to be the nominee?"

Kutter nodded. "At the risk of sounding trite, I wouldn't have declared if I didn't believe I was the most qualified person for the job."

"What about the Escobar scandal?" asked the anchorwoman.

Kutter had expected Crystal to change tacks and probe the police brutality issue.

"'Scandal' is, I think, an improper designation. There have been guilty pleas to the narcotics sale indictments. Questions were raised as to police tactics during the investigation and arrests. As you know, the police categorically denied any wrong doing. Their internal affairs people are investigating. I've got a Grand Jury looking into the case. I can assure you that we will carefully investigate every allegation."

"But isn't it true, Mr. Kutter, that attorneys for Juan Escobar have made a Motion in Superior Court to re-open their client's plea? And they've filed a Notice of Intention to sue the City - haven't they?"

"'Yes' to both of your questions, Miss Lee. But neither event amounts to any corroboration of the charges. I think it's important that we keep things in perspective. Internal Affairs is doing its job and when we have their report, I can assure you that this office will take whatever action is called for, regardless of consequence."

"Is any officer in particular being investigated?"

"Every person involved in the investigation and arrests is being looked at. I don't think it's appropriate to tell you more than that while Internal Affairs is still investigating, and a Grand Jury is sitting."

Crystal Lee persisted. "Isn't Lieutenant Harry Lang a target of the investigation?"

Kutter suppressed a frown. The woman could be irritating. She was on the money with Lang. But Rudy Kutter wasn't about to make the mercurial Harry Lang for better or worse a campaign issue.

"Again, Miss Lee, I simply can't get into the course of the Grand Jury investigation, and I don't want this answer to be misconstrued. I'm not saying directly or indirectly that any officer or officers in particular are targets of the Grand Jury."

Crystal Lee waved to her cameraman who dutifully shut down his equipment. She smiled - a half smart assed grin that said "gottcha pal." Rudy Kutter guffawed. "You're really something Crystal."

Kutter moved to rise from his chair - a necessary move to break the confinement of the interview.

Crystal directed. "Sit tight please while we get a reversal."

Kutter slumped back in his chair, saying facetiously "anything for the fourth estate."

\*   \*   \*   \*   \*

Harry Lang was in a foul mood as he walked through the detective ward room, pointing to first one man, then another, and finally a third - assembling his troops, detectives he had brought along in the Department, hard nosed coppers made in his image whose greatest virtue was their "no questions asked" loyalty to Harry Lang. Sam Turre, still sporting the crew cut and spring steel hungry demeanor of a marine even though it had been twelve years since he'd been mustered out. Dave Hendricks, the thinker of the bunch, a man who looked the horn rimmed glasses campus lifer stereotype and always figured every angle. Steve Dawes, a pudgy, balding pleasant man, who just happened to be the Department's weapons expert.

Lang paced before his troops.

"Kutter is figuring the angles. He won't commit just yet on the Jimmy Doyle tap. I'm not gonna' wait. We're gonna' tap him anyway. See to it Davey."

Dave Hendricks nodded that he would and then asked the question even though he knew exactly what Lang would say.

8

"Anything we find from the tap can't be used . . . ." Lang cut him off.

"Bullshit Davey." His manner softened. It was just Hendricks' way of telling the boss to think it through - to go slow - and not shoot himself in the foot.

"Look, Davey, I got this hunch. It's gonna' pan out. I know this piece of shit is dirty - if he's dirty enough - that's it. We've got him and maybe more. If the tap lifts some rocks we'll just say it was 'surveillance' that gave us the leads. Keep logs."

Lang chuckled, "even for the ghost stake outs. And besides, maybe I just might persuade the DA to open his eyes to where his bread is buttered with a little reminder that we covered his action with that douche bag assistant of his after they both got loaded and bedded down after the Sheriff's banquet last month."

The Lieutenant shifted gears.

"What have we got currently on Tony Persia?"

It was a standing marching order for Harry Lang's crew that they spend any spare time between assignments surveilling old line mob boss, Tony Persia. Persia took every opportunity to proclaim his retirement from the rackets.

Sam Turre chimed in, "he's spending most of his time on the yacht or in that place he's got in the desert - where the hell is it Steve - Barstow, Needles? Well anyway, 90% of the time we can always ring his bell on the water or in the desert, and when he's not in either, then its the apartment on Echo Park or the card game at the Friend's Social Club."

"Who's coming and going," asked Lang.

Turre thumbed the pages of his notebook.

"Joey Dancer. Maybe the old man's got points in some of the things Joey runs out of Acme Specialties. Johnny Fixx. The mouthpiece. That's all."

"That Fixer is gonna' shit on his own feet one of these days," breathed Lang.

Dave Hendricks interjected, "he's too smart, boss. Besides, Persia has well advertised tax troubles - there's a big civil penalty case with the Government. That's more than enough reason for his lawyer to be holding his hand. Nah, I think it's a waste of time crawling up Fixer's ass."

"Listen," said Harry Lang indulgently, "Johnny Fixx is too smart for his own good. Persia owns him and even Fixx don't know it yet. One day Persia will call it in and then we'll see another wise guy take a fall."

Sam Turre fumbled through his pockets and fed a tape cassette into the recorder on Lang's desk.

"The counsellor is becoming a radio personality boss. Thought you'd get a kick out of this."

Turre had caught the tag end of some electric Miles on 'Honky Tonk'. Johnny Fixx came on after the record played out.

"We were talking the other night about great Americans. Leaving out the 'founding fathers' - Washington, Jefferson, and then Lincoln - and taking a hard look at the last fifty or so years, who do we come up with? Sure FDR saved us from the Great Depression, Hitler, and Tojo, and Harry Truman held the line against the 'red menace', and maybe JFK was the real item, and who could leave out Martin Luther King but moving away from politics, who would most of you put on their list? Albert Einstein. Jonas Salk. Well, I've got a personal pair of favorites for you - how about Miles Davis and John Dillinger. Think I've flipped my lid. Hell no, folks. Miles is the Mozart of jazz. A one of the kind artist and innovator, he's everything an artist should be - always searching for new plateaus, never content to rest on his laurels. Every time he reaches the top, he moves on to find another notch up. Maybe the only other artist in the twentieth century to travel the same turf was Picasso. And how about Johnny Dillinger. Murderer? Nah. There's no proof Dillinger ever shot anyone in cold blood, let alone killed them. And he might not have been ambushed by the FBI outside the Biograph in July of 1934. Dillinger might have had the last laugh, feeding the coppers a double and riding off into the sunset south of the border. And who else more embodied the common man's outrage and backlash against the banks whose greed helped create the crash and bled the middle class dry during the Depression than the Indiana bank robber. Too bad we're not in a 'talk radio' format. I'll bet there's some interesting opinion out there on my choices. Well you might not be able to call, but how about dropping us a line. And now, back to the sounds, two from the late great Gil Evans, 'Las Vegas Tango', and the 1961 Impulse recording of 'La Nevada' - a/k/a 'Theme'."

"John Dillinger and Miles Davis? This guy is a real beaut," groused Harry Lang. "He's dirty. I feel it - and I'll prove it one of these days."

Dave Hendricks still wasn't buying it. "I don't know about Miles and Dillinger - Fixx is probably breaking balls to get people to listen. You know - say something outrageous. Hell Morton Downey makes a living doing that."

Lang growled, "Miles and Dillinger - bullshit. Fixer's an arrogant smart ass and like I said he's gonna' find out the hard way that you can't wade through shit without getting dirty."

Hendricks wouldn't back off. "Hey I don't know the guy personally other than to write him up when I'm tailing him.

He's eccentric alright. That penthouse in San Pedro isn't quite the normal digs for a mouthpiece. But dirty? I think that's a stretch. Fixer's a decorated war hero in the Nam. Silver Star, Purple Heart."

Hendricks recited from memory the portions of Fixer's police dossier that dealt with his war record.

11

Steve Dawes was himself a decorated Nam vet.

"Fixer's active in the Veteran's Outreach group. I picked up a rumble a while back that he was gonna' take one of the Agent Orange cases."

Sam Turre broke in. "None of that squares with Fixer bearding for Joey Dancer and that pilot - what the hell's his name?"

"Sonny Bamboo," answered Harry Lang. "They were all in the service together. Dancer's been in on every major heist in the Southlands for the past ten years. I know he's got dough in that air surveillance company run by Bamboo. Can you believe that? A convicted heist man - a second story man - in the security business! Fixer incorporated them and put up some of the money. They're selling downtown building owners their afterhours chopper surveillance package and what I think they're really up to is learning about building security and scheduling in blue chip businesses so that Dancer's crew can take down scores."

"Can you prove it, boss?" asked Dave Hendricks.

"Maybe I won't have to," explained Lang. "I tipped the Grievance Committee of the Bar Association and they're into Fixer's shorts. They've grabbed his account records and tax returns. If he left any financial tracks to Dancer, they'll find 'em. And when they do, we'll have the boy's ass."

Hendricks hated to take issue with the Lieutenant's legendary intuition but said nonetheless, "don't think so boss. But what the hell. Who knows?"

Harry Lang abruptly adjourned the meeting of his troops. "Okay men. Enough good and welfare. Get on Jimmy Doyle - like a fucking blanket. Stay on his ass tighter than two coats of paint."

## C H A P T E R   T W O

Jimmy Doyle was ringside at the Pink Panther. Cigarette smoke waffled up into the Japanese lanterns strung around the perimeter of the room. Waitresses took orders for brand name liquors in mixed drinks and bartenders poured well stock for the customers who were otherwise occupied with the table dancers.

It was a half hour shy of closing time and Doyle was feeling no pain. Baby Doll was on stage, her back to the audience. She squatted before him, wearing only heels and a blush, and wagged her tail as she looked lasciviously back over her shoulder. Doyle ran his tongue over his lips. Baby Doll pursed hers and giggled, then settled in to grind her five foot frame, all tits and ass, into the fur coat she used as a rug for her floor work. Doyle downed the double shooter of vodka and smiled contentedly.

It was funny how things happened. He'd been scouting a warehouse. They were moving hot appliances. Doyle figured it would be easy pickings to hijack one of their trucks. A nice piece of change - and better still, since they were dirty, who could they call? Then it happened. The clientele began changing. The buyers were no longer just plain folks or minor league fences. Big hitters in the local drug trade began showing up. Something big having nothing to do with appliances was about to go down. Doyle watched and waited. There were afternoons in the dirt bag bar down the street. Finally, one of the boys shot his mouth off.

The buy was set for the Coliseum - the afternoon of a Raiders game. Doyle had been watching long enough to know the whole cast of characters. They were smart. One man would bring the drugs into the stadium - an innocuous Chicano carrying the dope in a shopping bag. The rip was ridiculously simple. Doyle hustled the courier into a crapper after half time, sapped him, and walked out into the mid afternoon sunshine with the dope. The way he'd first figured it, Doyle would reach out to make a sale to other interested parties. But then Jimmy Doyle had an inspiration. Why take the chance? He decided on a ballsy play. Walk right into the warehouse. Tell them "the old man" didn't like independents taking down drug scores on his turf. Then tell them this one time there'd be no guns. All would be forgiven if they laid off dope trading in the future - and paid a territorial gratuity for their transgression. A half million wholesale. Doyle wouldn't be a pig. Leave them enough and odds were they'd reject a play to burn him. He'd take 20% for the boys, they'd get their dope, and all would be forgiven.

Even now Doyle rolled his eyes at the audacity of it. If Tony Persia ever tumbled to Doyle using his name to shake down drug dealers, there'd be hell to pay. He'd done some business with Tony 'P' over the years, but the old man seemed to really mean it when he preached that drugs were bad for business. Unauthorized drug deals could earn the offending party a one way ride in the channel in a 55 gallon drum. In a sense it wasn't fair. The big guys took points in big dope scores - brokered the deals while the machos and blacks took the street risks.

That was 'ok' - but a made guy or an associate didn't dare show any enterprise on the streets. As far as Jimmy Doyle was concerned, it was all bullshit. There was a tense moment in that warehouse when the boosters thought that maybe they could beat the location of the dope out of him and save the 20%. But Jimmy Doyle hung tough and bluffed it out, and in 24 hours he'd lead them to the dope - but only after his 20% was squirreled away.

"Hey big boy - Jimmy, Jimmy."

Doyle smiled. Baby Doll was sitting beside him. Her scent was thick with perfume and perspiration - down and dirty, just the way he liked it. She read it in his eyes. Maybe she could spring it on Doyle now. The dirt bag who ran the club had just held out on her again. She got $25 for every show. The price was right, but the bastards always found a way to take it back. Some girls ran heavy bar tabs, or paid a dope dealer for blow who kicked back to the club owners for the privilege of working their turf. Then there were the 'fines' imposed by the owners. Be late for a show and there was a fine. Fail to show up on time to work the bar in between shows, and more bucks were held back. Baby Doll couldn't eat it this time. She'd quit and needed a protector while she was between drinks.

"I told Solly that I was through."

The Big Fall

"He held out on you again?"

Baby Doll nodded "yes".

"Fuck that piece of shit. I'm goin' good kid. I can take care of you - until something comes along. Baby Doll reached under the table and kneaded Doyle's thigh.

"Come on big boy, let's blow this joint."

Baby Doll went by Bette Jones in her off hours, and Jimmy Doyle's personal nickname for her was "Jonesy".

"Cop whose joint, Jonesy," he quipped as he folded his five foot five banty rooster frame into her full figure to prance arm in arm with her out of the club. Doyle had a room in the old Century near Echo Park and Jonesy had to fight him off in the hall to at least preserve a modicum of the proprieties. She was as horny as he, and there were no preliminaries as he tore at her clothes and got down to "serious screwin".

Jonesy protested, "gimme a break Jimmy" but he knew she was farther gone than he at the moment and never let up.

"Here it comes," he screamed at his first orgasm, then a half hour later, "not bad for an old fuck", after his second.

Doyle laid out lines of coke on the end stand and he and Jonesy snorted the blow and took up where they'd left off. An hour later Doyle was still buried in her buttery flesh, now unable to pop, but enjoying it too much to let go of the possibility that he still might. Jonesy finally pushed him off and used her talented mouth to cop his joint.

"Yer the greatest, babe," groaned Doyle, as he lay back to light a cigarette.

"Where'd that come from," asked Jonesy, pointing at the blow on the end stand.

15

"A sample, doll," quipped Doyle.

"I shook down a bunch of cowboy machos. I'll be six figures richer in a day or two."

Doyle groaned contentedly.

"Let's go to Vegas Jonesy. What do you say?"

"Let's get married, Jimmy," she answered. "You know I'll give you all you can stand.

I'll dance.

When you're between drinks, there'll be money."

Doyle smiled vacantly and remained silent.

"Come on Jimmy.

We've been talkin' about it for years," she said hopefully.

"Ah shit babe - it ain't that simple. Sure, you love me and I love you. And the dough 'ill bail me out with the kids. It'll get Mary Margaret off my back too. But it's not enough to bury the past."

There was a cutting edge to Jonesy's tone. "Why don't you take the divorce and be done with yer' Virgin Mary?"

"She won't give me a divorce," lamented Doyle.

There had been a time when Jonesy would have bought that line. But now she knew better. Busts at the Pink Panther had introduced her to several lawyers. She'd asked how tough it could be to get a divorce. The answer was always the same. If you pay the tab - even sweeten the pot, nothing can stop you - not even a spouse who wouldn't let go. Jimmy Doyle was about to be in the chips.

He had to know that his Mary Margaret couldn't really stop him if he wanted to divorce her. Yet here he was again bullshittin'.

"Jimmy," she snapped, then noticed that he'd dropped off to sleep. Jonesy flushed with anger. The bastard would never change.

His Irish wife would have her house and respectability - and a rosary for her frustrations - and Baby Doll got to spend her nights under Doyle in flea bag boarding houses. A trip to Vegas was the juice this time to keep her in line.

"Fuck you, Jimmy," she breathed as she went through his pants pocket and wallet. The address was written on the inside of a matchbook cover. It meant nothing to her. But maybe the cop who turned her out on the threat that he'd violate her parole would pay something for it.

Jonesy wriggled into her dress in the dank darkness. Shivering, she mouthed the words, "all I'm good for is an all night fuck, eh, stud? Well, let's see who gets fucked now!"

Her upset flashed to a white hot rage. Jonesy slipped out of the room and into the hallway. A bare ceiling hung light bulb coated nearly black with dust was the only night light. The pay phone was wall hung at the end of the hall around the corner at the top of the stair landing. Jonesy had two cards to play. She'd need work, then maybe blood money for her tip on Doyle might tide her over.

She rang up the Condor Club.

Manny Cesar ran the roadhouse. It was after hours but there was always somebody on the phone when an all night card game was in session. Jonesy hoped the gamblers had come out to see in the dawn. Cesar himself picked it up. "We're closed," he rasped.

"It's Jonesy. I need to talk to Felix."

17

"Yeah, okay Jonesy," said Manny Cesar. "I'll get him for you."

Felix Masters always seemed to be hanging around the Condor. He watched the place for Manny Cesar and along the way had developed a crush on Baby Doll. She now hoped to exploit that crush to con Felix into offering her a job hostessing at the Condor.

Masters came on breathless, "hullo Jonesy. Long time no see."

"Hi Felix. I just quit the Pink Panther and . . ." Her voice broke, on que, and Masters asked "you okay kid . . . Jonesy . . . you okay?"

"Sure, sure, Felix - it's been a bad night. Well, I'm out of the club and - oh this isn't easy for me." Her sigh was audible, then she blurted, "I'm up against it for money. Any chance you can get me something at the club - it won't be for long. Just to tide me over until I get back on my feet." Masters hesitated not at all. "Sure Jonesy. You know better than to have to ask. You shoulda' just come over. There's rooms upstairs. I'll put you up. Shit, you can hostess. Okay?"

"Oh jeez, Felix. I really appreciate this," she answered working hard to put a little extra into the implied promise in her tone.

"I'll be around later this morning. You're the best Felix."

Jonesy took down two deep lungs full of air. The next call was one that always cost her - one way or another. She punched in the number.

"Lieutenant Lang," she asked.

"Who wants him," answered the dispatcher.

"I work for him. He'll want to talk to me."

"He's in the car. Hold on. We'll patch you through."

18

# The Big Fall

Jonesy nervously shuffled her feet and peeked around the corner down the hall. Doyle was still out.

Lang was taking too long. It would be just her luck that Jimmy would come to and miss her. Then the pre dawn call would be major trouble. If Doyle smelled it he had a mean streak that would take over until he got the answers he wanted. Another minute would be all she could dare holding for the Lieutenant. She counted under her breath. At 'forty-six', Lang's gruff "hullo" sounded.

"It's Jonesy," she whispered. "I've got something if the price is right."

"Harry Lang snapped, "if I bite, you stay out of the can a while longer. If there's a pinch, it's $500. You know the drill. Now stop jerking me off before I send a black and white to haul your ass down here. Give!"

There was no percentage in hassling with Lang. Jonesy coughed, her voice catching, and croaked, "Jimmy Doyle's about to do a big drug deal. Six figures is his end."

"When and where?"

"I don't know. He said the next day or two."

"Where?" repeated Lang impatiently.

She read him the address.

Lang asked, "anything else?"

"That's it."

He chuckled, "what got you pissed, doll - he pull out before you made it?" Jonesy spat, "fuck you, Harry."

Lang's laughter peeled out as Jonesy slammed down the phone.

She padded back to the room, throwing back her shoulders and raising her chin. They were all shitheads, but she'd be around when all of them were dead and buried. Jonesy turned the knob, then hesitated.

The hallway ended with a window that opened onto a fire escape platform. A shredded cheesecloth that passed for a drape flapped in the breeze in the window opening. She leaned into the opening, her hands on the sill. The horizon was a charcoal gray haze, the new sun a still shadowed promise over the foothills that brooded beyond the city.

Jonesy breathed deeply and stared into the beginnings of the new day. Doyle made no sound as he came up behind her. He chuckled and ground his hips into her buttocks, his hands roughly caressing her breasts.

"Mornin' darlin'," he whispered, as he bent her forward over the sill, his hands pulling up her dress.

"Jimmy," she protested half heartedly. In an instant he slid into her.

"Always ready, eh doll," he groaned as he slapped against her.

She moaned, "stop, you goddamned fool," but there was no snap to her admonition, and she began throwing it back at him, feeling terrible over what she'd just done.

He clasped her hips, forcing her to stroke him just so. Finally, it was only his pleasure that mattered as he rammed her roughly. There was pain, but pincers of pleasure burning to her core washed away the discomfort. She moaned her love for the man she'd just betrayed, a confessional an instant away from articulation. His hands kneaded her belly, and he twisted her head around to thrust his tongue into her panting mouth. Finally, he exploded and pulled his lips away.

"You do like your work doll, don't you?" he gasped.

His smart mouth brought her back.

"You're gonna' find out, lover," she whispered.

\* \* \* \* \*

Harry Lang personally worked the stakeout at the Sierra Bonded Warehouse. It was the night of the second day when Jimmy Doyle finally showed minutes past 10:00 p.m. His hands were empty. The door swung open, and a man twisted off the light bulb above and patted him down. The doorman said, "stay put Doyle and keep yer' hands where we can see them," as a confederate stepped out, demanded "keys", and then moved to search Doyle's car. In seconds he yelled, "nothin", and the doorman ushered Doyle in - the booster obviously light of the coke that was his end of the deal.

Lang squinted at the shadows, running a mind picture of what was going on inside. There would be no long wait. In ten minutes, Doyle emerged trailed by a Chicano. The pair entered Doyle's car and Jimmy did the driving. Harry Lang dropped low beneath his window line. A second car loaded with the Chicano's pals rolled out from behind the warehouse and then sped onto the street in Doyle's wake. Lang fell in behind them.

Lang radio'd the three cars that coordinated with him in the rolling tail. They'd stay with them on the parallel streets and close only if Lang signaled the password. With Doyle the target, Lang had selected "Irish" to close the net on him.

Harry Lang was pleased with himself. One of his bimbo snitches had come out of nowhere to prove him right about Doyle. Rudy Kutter's court order wasn't necessary. And with it went the duty Lang could most do without - kissing the ass of the politically motivated DA. The car ahead maintained 30 mph and in twenty minutes rolled into the lot at Union Station. Doyle and the Chicanos had parked and were walking toward the terminal when Lang signaled his troops to seal off the parking lot.

Harry Lang kept his distance and drifted through one of the arcades off to the side of the grand concourse. Across the way, Jimmy

Doyle and his Chicano pal paced before a bank of lockers. The Chicano gestured to the men who had been tailing them.

One stepped forward and placed an attaché case at Doyle's feet. Jimmy scanned the clusters of people in the station - an expected once over before giving in to his curiosity concerning the attaché case. Doyle knelt, popped the clasps, and grinned at the contents. He pointed to a locker and flipped the key at the Chicano. Jimmy Doyle nodded, picked up the attaché case, then stepped aside and began walking in a slow measured step to the doors. The Chicano's pals shadowed him, waiting on their bosses' signal that the exchange had been made. The main man dug into the shopping bag that had been in the locker. It passed muster and he waved off his boys. Jimmy Doyle was free to leave and he did just that, never looking back.

Harry Lang's crew waited until the whole bunch were in the parking lot. Then they efficiently closed in, flashed their tin, brandished an assortment of sawed offs and M-15's, and pinched the whole lot of them. Doyle sank to his knees, cursing. It had all been too easy. The Chicanos screamed their murderous intentions at the booster with big ideas who they were convinced had sold them out.

Harry Lang wasted no time at headquarters with the task of breaking down Jimmy Doyle. Doyle's hands trembled as he smoked and sipped black coffee. The dope bust had unnerved him. Being a thief in a sense placed him a cut above the scumbags even inside the walls. But dope meant hard time and every indignity that went with it - a gauntlet Doyle wasn't certain he could stand anymore.

Sam Turre sat in the corner watching for the signal from his boss that would energize him into action. Harry Lang paced beside the small painted over conference table that with its chairs were the only furnishings in the 15' by 20' room.

"We're recording this, Jimmy," said Lang. "You understand?"

Doyle gestured that he did. Sam Turre prompted. "We need your words Jimmy - for the tape - understand?"

Doyle's voice broke as he chugged the coffee. "Okay, okay. So you're taping. What the hell do you want from me?"

Lang eyed him. "You signed a Miranda waiver pal. I'm asking you again. You're entitled to a lawyer. You wanna' make a call. If you can't afford one, the court will appoint a mouthpiece for you. You know the drill Jimmy. So what do you want to do?"

Doyle nodded "no", and Turre again prompted "say it Jimmy."

"I'll get my lawyer when I'm ready - okay?"

"Sure, sure," said Lang. "Anything you say, Jimmy. After all this is your party - right?"

Doyle pulled a handkerchief from his pocket and mopped his brow.

"Jesus Harry. How the fuck did you know? Those macho cowboys think I was shillin' for you. They're gonna' cut me a new asshole. How'd you know?"

Harry Lang raised a foot to the chair beside Doyle and leaned forward to eye the booster.

"You've got bigger problems than the Chicanos Jimmy. We've got you down and dirty doin' a drug deal. This is Tony 'P's' town, boy. Peddlin' shit freelance don't cut it in these parts with the greaseballs. You're a two time loser to boot. This deal can put you away for life. That'll mean fifteen to twenty inside the walls."

Doyle's adams apple bobbed as he struggled to swallow the cotton drying out his mouth. He swiped futilely at the perspiration beading into rivulets that dripped down his cheeks into his collar. Lang dropped into the chair beside him and extended his arm around the booster's shoulders.

"I don't think you'll do fifteen Jimmy. Hell, I don't think you'll do a year. The way I see it, when Tony 'P' finds out you broke the rules on

23

drug dealin' - hell boy, it's even money he'll give you to the spics and they'll open you up with a shiv within a month after you arrive as a guest of the state."

Doyle's desperate eyes asked the question his parched lips couldn't quite form. Lang grinned in recognition.

"You bet your bad ass I will boy. Hell yes! By tomorrow this time I'll have the word to Tony 'P'. Shit, you know the wise guys even run the joint. Hell, maybe they even got a guy inside PD. I got no choice Jimmy. You broke the rules - you get no quarter from either side."

Harry Lang let the realization of the death sentence sink in, then hissed, his mouth a scant inch from Doyle's, "unless . . . unless . . ."

"Christ, I can't do that Harry. My god. I can't . . ."

"Scumbag's honor, eh Jimmy? Then pal you'll be remembered as a standup guy who got cut down in his prime. End of story."

Lang regarded the booster. The bastard looked puke gray. Good! Hurt, and hurt hard, pally, and maybe you'll see the light and give Uncle Harry what he has to have.

Lang signaled Sam Turre. "Let's get some sleep Sam. This hard guy, Jimmy Doyle here, he don't need our help. He can take care of himself."

Lang reached for a buzzer to ring the turnkey to let them out.

Doyle was calling his personal roll. There were a hundred petty crimes he'd been in on but none was enough to buy out of this mess.

"What gets me off the dime Lang," he blurted. "Like what exactly?" Lang returned to his seat.

"Who are the Chicanos distributing for?"

"Christ, I don't know," groaned Doyle. "I was casing the warehouse for a rip." Lang guffawed, "so really there ain't no honor among thieves and all that good shit, eh boy?"

"That's it exactly. I was gonna' hijack the assholes. Who could they call? That's how I stumbled onto the dope deal. I dealt my way in."

"And I'll bet I know how you pulled that one off Jimmy. Probably told the greasers you were Tony 'P's' man come to see to his cut."

Doyle's expression was answer enough. Lang shrugged.

"Well that does it then Jimmy."

The Lieutenant pushed the phone toward Doyle. "Ordinarily, I'd tell you you've got one call and to ring up a shyster. But since we go back aways, pal, I'm gonna' double the normal ration - and throw in some advice, gratis. Maybe you should use your first dime to ring up a mortuary. You've got a family. The arrangements . . . ."

Doyle slammed his fist into the table. "Okay . . . okay," he screamed." If I give you something worth your while, can you guarantee my safety. My wife and kids. Can you get us all into the program?"

"Listen Jimmy, I'll have you and your whole family out of here and on a military reservation in less than an hour."

Jimmy Doyle dropped his head into his hands. He had one chance and he knew it. If he sang it was a one way street - no way back, ever. If he didn't . . . . The words began as a reluctant trickle, then burst into a torrent. ". . . well . . . you know I did more than make a living as a booster. There were some insurance jobs."

"Buy backs," asked Sam Turre.

25

"No, torch jobs. I did some matching for the boys."

"Who, when, where, like exactly," barked Lang.

"The new Passeo Motel on Sunset."

"Stop jivin' us," groaned Lang. "That place is sitting there doing a land office business."

"I know," agreed Doyle. "But it's rigged to blow. I set it up."

"Why?"

"They couldn't open it. No certificate of occupancy. They cut corners and paid off the building inspector. The guy got canned. His replacement didn't buy so easily. So now the place doesn't come up to code and they can't open."

"Who put you on the job?"

"The place had a silent partner who paid me $25,000 to rig the motel for an electrical explosion that would burn it."

"Who?" Jimmy Doyle slumped back in his chair, his shoulders sagging with the weight of what he was about to reveal.

"Well," prompted Harry Lang.

Doyle sucked it up. He breathed deeply and leaned forward, his elbows on the table top. His manner was now cock sure. He even managed a thin grin. He held in place extra seconds because Lang was obviously losing his patience. Finally, he said, "Tony Persia!"

## C H A P T E R   T H R E E

"John Fixx, Attorney At Law" was stenciled in thick black gothic letters on the frosted glass insert in the door. Six ancient scarred oak chairs were arrayed on the landing, four to the right, and two to the left of the entranceway, the waiting room.

The freight elevator clanged to a halt on the eighth floor. John Fixx pulled the cord that tripped the mechanism to separate the top and bottom folding doors. The landing was lit by a single bare light bulb. Fixx peered out from the elevator and ran his eyes over the landing. Satisfied he was alone, Fixx stooped to pick up the pilot's map case that doubled as his attaché case when there were extra thick files to transport. His lower back answered to the motion with a sharp ache and Fixx straightened out his stocky five foot ten inch frame to shake off the discomfort. The elevator was large enough to handle an automobile, which had been exactly its function when the late Milt Glasser had owned the building and operated the Mid-Town Garage on the first six floors.

The freight was the only means of access from the street to the eighth floor loft in the re-christened Brisbane Building, John Fixx's office and city apartment on the waterfront in San Pedro. Law School had preceded two tours in the Nam. After the ordeal there had been a year and a half of aimless odd jobbing in the Southlands. Then a job in a legal clinic that specialized in budget criminal defense work. John Fixx quickly graduated to private clients with more serious criminal problems and deeper pockets. By the mid-eighties, Fixx was one of the handful of name criminal defense lawyers in the Southlands. His client list came to comprise the "who's who" of organized crime figures in Greater LA. Fixx hadn't planned it that way but when it happened, he found the fast track to his liking.

Along the way, John Fixx acquired the moniker "Fixer". He was the man to see in most insurance by-backs in the Southlands and his indicted clients aways seemed to land on their feet. There was a fair percentage of acquittals after trials, but plea bargains were Fixx' specialty. John Fixx knew his way around the back alleys of the criminal justice system and made no apologies for his knack for always pressing the right button at precisely the right moment to buy out for a client on the best terms available. Certain members of LAPD would volunteer that "Fixer" was more than just shorthand. But John Fixx knew better. He went to the wall for his clients and came to tolerate and even take a kind of perverse pride in the connotations of the epithet that had been hung on him. There was an element of uncertainty thrown off by the handle. And Fixer came to understand that his business interests were best served if clients, police, and prosecutors did not know quite how to take him. It was that maverick quirk of character that compelled Fixer to buy the abandoned garage and warehouse in San Pedro from Milt Glasser's estate and rehab it for his office and city home when most of his brethren found it difficult to breathe outside the glass curtain walled monoliths of downtown LA.

Fixer pulled the cord that would return the freight elevator to the ground floor. The city inspectors threatened a lawsuit if the cord wasn't replaced by a standard switch plate. Thinking about safety and things original, Fixer muttered, "damned few of us left," as he let himself into the loft. Max Gale was due any time.

Dusk. Shadows painted toward him. Brick veneer on the outside wall had given way to a plate glass curtain wall that overlooked San Pedro Bay. Mercury lights were heating to illuminate the Standard Oil Tank Farm and the endless ranks of tractor trailer depots. The moth ball fleet - bulbous gray presences waiting to hatch their long hidden fighting ships rocked on the swells beyond the quay. Two switchers whined assembling a freight train in the massive yard below, and derricks and cranes loudly throbbed to load three freighters scheduled to sail in the morning. And beyond, the rush and roar of flames atop the petroleum cracking towers in the refineries - San Pedro's unique signature on the nocturnal canvas. Moonlight suddenly freed from the overcast poured through the skylights. Fixer hit the switch for the overhead chain and hook winch for no other reason than to know he wasn't alone. He'd left the winch in place and delighted in activating it to scare the pants off unsuspecting clients. He shut down the motor and dropped into his desk chair.

Rusty Tannis had left him a note. Tex Tannis had been a flyer with him in the Nam. Rusty suffered through his withdrawal from the horror of the war that unfortunately never ended for Tex. Tex fell from flying commercial to working backwater freight operations. He'd finally blown his license and now his whereabouts were unknown.

Rusty and Tex had been separated for years and Rusty worked at making like Tex' location was of no importance to her. Their mutual friends knew better and Johnny did what he could to help her keep it together. Rusty had settled in to coming in twice a week to catch up his correspondence and filing. She was the only woman of Fixer's acquaintance whose scrawl was less intelligible than a physicians. He squinted down at the note. Rusty had hastily written, "a pair of stiffs from the Bar Association Grievance Committee were in grabbing at your files for Surveillance Silhouettes. You said to let them have them, so I did. You sure about being that nice to those creeps?"

The elevator motor kicked in below. Max Gale.

Fixer moved through the loft, hitting switches mounted on the facia of the massive mushroom pillars that dotted the floor to support the roof. Overhead track lights came on and open bladed fans swished above. The far end of the loft was partitioned off into two large rooms, one Fixer's living quarters, the other his recording and video studio. He closed the door to his personal domain and returned to the desk. Max Gale let himself in.

"Evening counsellor."

Fixer pulled the bottle of Jack Daniels and a pair of glasses out of his lower desk file drawer. "Drink, Professor?"

Gale nodded "yes" and Fixer poured the glasses a third full.

"Max, I thought this was your night to play film professor at UCLA?"

Gale was a Professor on the law faculty. Law was his life, but old films were his passion. Freedom to teach as he wished in the Film Studies School was his price to remain on the law faculty. Gale

29

believed in practicing what he preached, and his alliance with Fixer was a natural outlet. The clients were attracted to the flamboyant Johnny Fixer. Fixer tried the cases, and Max Gale did the law work and argued the appeals. And then there was the other something that held Max in the game: he was able to indulge his fascination with Fixer, a man who seemed to have it all on the line every day. Whether to save him from himself, or perhaps to change places with him, it didn't really matter to Max Gale. He and Fixer had become opposite sides of the same coin.

"I gave my class the night off so I could catch up with you Johnny?"

"What's on your mind Max?"

Gale took a long pull from the tumbler of whisky and growled as he swiped futilely at the liquor that dribbled off his beard onto his vest. Fixer chuckled, "fucking academic!"

"The Surveillance Silhouettes thing is heating up again, Johnny."

Sonny Bamboo was a pal of Fixer's from the Nam - a helicopter pilot, his name was really Streaks but after a daring rescue from a hot LZ in a bamboo grove, Sonny was for evermore christened Bamboo. Bamboo had come up with the idea to sell high rise owners airborne after-hours surveillance. Fixer put up part of the money and Bamboo put three choppers in service to patrol the rooftops of the commercial canyons of greater LA after hours. Bamboo drew a paycheck and Fixer had already gotten out half his seed money. None of that was the problem. Lieutenant Harry Lang suspected that another Fixer associate, Joey Dancer, who had also served with them in Viet Nam, was a silent partner in Surveillance Silhouettes. Dancer was a convicted felon with a robbery rap sheet a mile long. The Beverly Hilton jewelry caper and the Wells Fargo armored car heist were milestones on Dancer's dossier. Lang believed that Dancer was using information generated by Bamboo to case robberies in client businesses that believed they were being protected.

"The people at the Grievance Committee won't give me the source of the complaint, but it must have been Lang who whispered in their ear. They're half convinced you're fronting for Dancer. If they can prove it, you're in for a rough go, my friend."

"It's bullshit Max. I did Sonny Bamboo a favor. That's all. I'm not bearding for Joey Dancer."

"Johnny, they're going to subpoena all of Bamboo's books and records, and all of yours. If there are any money tracks from Dancer through you to Bamboo, we're in trouble. Is there anything I should know?"

"First, pal, you're a tad late." Fixer pushed Rusty Tannis' note across the desk in Max' direction.

"They were here this morning. No subpoena, just a request for my books for a couple of years. I left instructions with Rusty to let them have whatever they wanted. That was my message to them - 'nothing to hide'."

Fixer paced his side of the glass wall that held back the San Pedro night, his friend's apprehensions a persistent playback in his mind.

"Nothing, Max, not a thing. And if they want anything else, you tell 'em all they have to do is ask."

Max knew better than to doubt Fixer. He always seemed to be one step ahead of them. Still . . .

"It could be a flying squad, Johnny. You know how they operate. They'll swoop down on you and cart everything off before you can take any cover."

"Come on Max. What is this bullshit. This is Johnny Fixx you're talking to. Let 'em do their worst. I'm clean."

"Okay, okay, Johnny." Gale nodded solemnly and winced at what he'd next say. Fixer was nearly fanatical about the privacy of his personal life - and that mantle of privilege extended to any close personal friend.

"Johnny, Joey Dancer is a bad actor. If I were you I'd . .”

Fixer cut him off. "Dancer and I go back a long way, Max. It's blood, not money."

Gale exhaled audibly, raised his eyebrows, and nodded in agreement despite suspicions that wouldn't quite quit. "Anything else Max?"

"I ran into some of your Nam pals at the Veteran's Outreach Center. They're asking about the Agent Orange suit. You said you'd help them. If you can't, I'd tell them. They're hanging on your getting involved."

Fixer gestured at the stack of boxes against the far wall.

"Shit, Max, there's six months work in those papers. I just haven't had a chance to wade through it. But I will . . . . I will."

"Okay, pal. I'll let them know."

Gale finished his drink and picked himself up to leave.

"Hey John. I was in here night before last and Sam called. You been avoiding her? Her tone seemed a bit put out with you."

Samantha was Fixer's 'ex'. Since the divorce she seemed more right for Johnny than ever before. It was obvious to anyone who knew them, but of course neither Sam nor Johnny could see it.

Fixer showed the quizzical sad little expression that was his reaction to any mention of Samantha. "I'll call her, Max. Thanks."

Gale changed the subject. "I'm doin' an Alan Ladd retrospective with my class. We're putting together a video tape of commentary and film clips on 'the voice'. You interested in going through some of his oldies?"

"Sure pal. I always was a sucker for Veronica Lake's peek-a-boo hair do."

"I'll let you know when all the films have been collected."

Gale turned. "I'm out of here Johnny. I'll send up your elevator so you're secure."

Max Gale chuckled at his deference to Fixer's well known paranoia, and walked out.

\*   \*   \*   \*   \*

Fixer shut the office lights and retreated to his sound studio. A personal audio hobby with heavy emphasis on Jazz had mushroomed into an FM broadcast facility subsidized by Southlands University.

The University owned the campus FM station, and its most distinguished alumnus did the Southlands "late show", one a.m. to four in the morning, three times a week. The University somehow had recently freed up some grant money to increase the wattage of the station so that its broadcasts now reached an audience beyond the twenty five mile radius from the center of Greater Los Angeles. Mostly Fixer did the radio show live, mixing heavy doses of modern jazz with occasional interviews and personal reminiscences and opinion on long gone musicians and movies the way they used to make them. This night it would be a tape programmed to play in the midnight and later slot. Fixer interspersed some commentary, but a taped show was nearly always mostly music. There was another hour to complete for the taping. The show was another in Fixer's series on the "acoustic Miles" - the 'dark prince's' seminal period, perhaps his best.

The phone rang.

"Hullo boss," said Mark Nider, the student station manager who was Fixer's producer.

"Hey Mark. How's the boy."

33

"Jeez, the phone's still ringing on last week's show. 'Miles Davis' and 'John Dillinger', two of the greatest Americans of the Twentieth Century - if not ever? If we were commercial, I'd be rolling in new advertisers. Boss, you sure know how to give 'em something to chew on. You just jerking chains to get 'em to tune in?"

"From the heart, Mark. From the heart."

"Live or tape tonight?"

"Think I'll cool it for a day or two. I'll finish the tape in an hour. Can you pick it up? I'll leave it in the lobby in the lock box."

"Sure boss, no sweat."

Fixer hung up and in seconds the Miles mood was on him again as he spoke an introduction for the taped selections. They were in the room as he talked about them. Fixer knew it couldn't be, yet they were. It was thirty years before and Fixer breathed easy at being in a time when he couldn't be under any heat - just him, the magnificent Miles, and mostly dead jazzmen, and their music that put on a just so glow. Some of today's cats called themselves 'neo-classic' quintet players and strained to recreate the old days. That was the rub - 'recreate' - the 'gods' of the era invented the style and when you listened to them, you knew it.

Fixer mixed in the Prestige sides with Miles, 'Trane, Red Garland, Paul Chambers, and Philly Joe, with the immediately following Columbia sides, the sextet that included Canonball Adderley and substituted Bill Evans for Red Garland, and Jimmy Cobb for Philly Joe. All of it culminated in the absolutely magnificent 'Kinda' Blue' album. Fixer finished the tape after eleven and didn't know whether to laugh in exultation or cry because the music touched him so deeply. He belted down a double shooter of 'black jack' and ran the tape down to the lobby where he dropped it into the lock box for Mark Nider's pick up. Miles and friends had cleared his mind. He needed a night's rest, and by 11:30 p.m. Johnny Fixx was dead to the world.

But it wasn't meant to be.

It began as the tinkling of a chinese mobile in a light breeze then developed the sharp edges of a bosun's bell. But it wasn't any exotic port of call, only the end stand beside the bed that Johnny Fixx groped for. The phone was ringing.

"Yeah," he gasped as he worked to bust an opening through the cobwebbs.

"Yeah yer ass Fixer. You sound like you're half asleep. You planning a caper. I saw a movie once where this old bird is gonna' do in this dame with a shotgun and covers his action with a tape of a radio broadcast that puts him nowhere near the dames' place."

"What the hell are you breakin' my balls for in the middle of the night Dawes?"

Steve Dawes was a charter member of Harry Lang's personal flying squad. He had also done two tours in the Nam where he served four months with Fixer. That created a bond that entitled Fixer to an occasional advance whisper on one of Lang's bombshells. Fixer returned the favor when he could.

"Thought you'd want to know counsellor that Jimmy Doyle is now in the Witness Relocation Program."

"I never represented Doyle."

"That's right. But you do represent Tony Persia from time to time. And Tony did have points in a certain motel that couldn't get a permit to open. You followin' this counsellor?"

"Keep goin'."

"Well there isn't much more to cover. The motel was rigged to blow. That would have been a real good deal for the old man. Not so good for the insurance company. I think you can figure out

35

the rest. Bet you don't catch any more 'z's counsellor until after the sunrise."

Jimmy Doyle, a bush league booster, and Tony Persia didn't compute. Still, Fixer couldn't afford not to play through Dawes' tip. Tony 'P' paid him far too well to suffer any carelessness. Fixer rang up Acme Specialties. At two in the morning the place was shut down. The answering service was off and the phone figured to ring forever. An exercise in futility. Fixer hung it up, then impulsively grabbed the phone again to punch in the number one last time. The boss picked it up.

"Yeah."

"Morning Joseph. I was lonely."

"Sure Johnny Fixx. And I'm the King of Siam. What's up?"

"Your phones okay?"

"They're swept twice a week by the same outfit that does yours, or did you forget."

"You ever hear that the Old Man had points in that motel that couldn't open? Joey Dancer made no reply, and Fixer prompted, "you still there?"

"The answer to both questions is 'yes'."

"Then I've got to get to him on the double."

"Why?"

"There's some talk that a matcher spilled his guts and that tracks maybe lead to Tony."

"No way," exclaimed Dancer.

"Probably - but just the same, I'm gonna' follow it through."

"He's on the boat. You want me to send Bamboo?"

"The pad upstairs is finished and legal. They issued the permit yesterday."

Dancer again went silent. "You still there Joey?"

"Yeah, yeah. Say Johnny, I'm into a freight deal air freight - south of the border. I need a pilot who can fly heavy stuff with his eyes closed. You wouldn't happen to have a fix on Tex, would you?"

Tex Tennis, with Sonny Bamboo, as far as either one of them was concerned had been all the air force they'd ever needed in the Nam.

"Rusty was in here this morning, Joey. There's still no word on Tex. There's other buttons to push, though. But you know the guys not right - you're not gonna get him into anything, are you?"

"Shit no, Johnny. Just some bucks for fly time. Everything's on the legit. Really."

"Why is it that I just can't quite swallow that, bro' - but what the hell, I'll see what I can do."

Fixer showered and paced his bedroom. One wall was floor to ceiling bookshelves. Another was lined with sound, video recorders, and a projector television. Scabbards and swords of Fixer's Japanese katana collection hung from the pillar in the corner. He had a session scheduled for seven with his instructor. Things had changed. Fixer rang him up and made his excuses to the sensei's recording machine.

He straightened his clothes and her eyes touched him. Her portrait hung at the head of his bed. Samantha. They'd married and divorced, and finally settled in to be friends and sometimes more. Her light brown hair was tossed mostly off one side of her face, her lips barely parted in the hint of a smile. Those high cheekbones gave her a haughty air, but there was little of the patrician in her. It was her sad eyes though that you remembered, wide and so deeply green that they showed as ebony pools, wise and now beyond his secrets.

The Big Fall

*   *   *   *   *

Access to the top of the building was up a set of stairs that Fixer had camouflaged in a 'closet' on the landing next to the freight elevator. There was a cutting edge to the night wind that swept across the roof and Fixer clasped the pipe railing that ringed the top as he waited on Sonny Bamboo. Below a freighter sounded its horn - a resonant lonesome lament - as it crawled to a birth beside Seaside Avenue. The running lights flashed in from the northwest before the engine noise reached him. Bamboo was a good half hour earlier than he'd figured. The pilot must have been working the shopping plazas he'd recently acquired as clients in the Valley. The chopper hovered above the elevated platform that filled the center of the rooftop, rocking just a bit in the gusts, before Bamboo gentled her down and killed his engine. Sonny Bamboo stepped out of the bird and gingerly let himself down from the platform. His leg buckled as he hit the roof and Fixer jumped to give him a hand. The big black man flashed his teeth and waved his friend away. It was one of life's supreme ironies that Bamboo had come through countless fire fights in the Nam without a scratch only to have his legs begin giving out a decade later. The black man's curse - sickle cell anemia was eating away at his hip joints. The lethal cell, a blood cell elongated in the shape of a sickle, was found only in blacks. The cell lacked a certain amino acid which in equatorial Africa made it effective in fighting malaria.

Transplanted to the western hemisphere, the sickle cell created blood blockages in its hosts which killed red blood cells, caused jaundice, and created excruciating pain in the back, bones, and abdomen, and usually ticketed the infected for early death. One in four hundred black babies drew the short straw. Bamboo learned he was one of them as he neared the fourth decade of his life. Hip replacement surgery was inevitable for him, but Bamboo made do with medicines and acupuncture in his conviction that a man's constitution might not change his fate but well might postpone the inevitable.

"How goes it Johnny boy?"

"Not bad, pal. I need a ride to Tony Persia's boat probably north of the Catalina channel."

38

"We should be able to find him, Johnny. I gassed up on the way. Come on, let's do it."

The turbine coughed once, then caught, the roar and whine of the engine punctuated by the whir and whump of the accelerating rotors. Then there was the unmistakable taste and diesel smell of being in a chopper again. Bamboo called off their heading and course but Fixer had already begun drifting off in a thousand yard stare. Sonny Bamboo flew the chopper off the roof and out over the Bay, then north along the Palos Verde shore line. Bamboo glanced over and picked up on Fixer's expression. He shook his head grimly and yelled over the engine noise.

"Yer goin' back, eh, motherfucker?"

Bamboo poked at Fixer.

"It was dog shit there, pal. Why you wanna' go back there?"

Bamboo had it right and Fixer knew it. He grinned across at his friend, "just drive Sonny. Just drive."

"Joey's lookin' for Tex Tannis. You hear anything about where he might be?"

"Nothing, pal. Maybe the guys at the Mission - Buddha and his bunch - maybe they know."

In ten minutes Catalina was a shadowy blip in their wake. The moon was nearly full and the sea glistened in the wash of the rotors. Bamboo raised 'No Luck' on the radio. "She's twenty miles, north, northwest. Ten minutes, Johnny."

Two pin heads in the distance blossomed into the yacht's stern running lights dead ahead. Bamboo was below 500 feet, skimming the white caps. 'No Luck' was nearly dead in the water in preparation for Bamboo's approach from astern. A crewman guided Bamboo in over the landing pad with hand held beacons and jumped clear at the last instant as the chopper softly hit the pad. Bamboo shut down the engine and crewman efficiently scrambled up to the pad to tie down the chopper's skids. The yacht surged forward and adjusted its course.

"I'll be in the galley," said Bamboo.

"Okay pal. I'll find you there after I see the man."

A crewman directed Fixx to the main deck salon under the bridge. Johnny Fixx pushed through the mahogany doors with leaded glass inserts. A small man, wiry with a thick head of silver hair, wearing a navy sweater over gray slacks acknowledged him with a nod. Tony Persia. He wasn't alone. Dermot Spillane had earned his spurs working the police blotter before graduating to editor of the editorial page for the Trib. Whippet thin, balding, his face all eyes and mouth, Dermot Spillane projected a nervous energy that touched anyone in his presence. The editor leaped to his feet and clasped Johnny Fixx' hand.

"Counsellor, how are you?"

"Okay Dermot. And you?"

"I'm on holiday Johnny. My old friend Tony invited me out for a couple of days. There's nothing like being on the water. Not a care in the world."

"That's right Dermot," chimed in Tony Persia. Persia smoked a long Havana and pushed his glasses up into his hair. It was a cue for Spillane to take his leave.

"I'll leave you two to your business. But before you leave Johnny, be sure I know it so we can toast in the dawn with a taste of the 'holy water'."

The newspaperman's presence was one of those out of the ordinary things that Tony Persia might eventually explain. Persia read the unstated question and shrugged his shoulders letting his lawyer know that in due time he'd let him in on it. For the moment there was other business to be resolved between them. Persia smiled thinly and paced.

"You know Johnny, I'm comfortable out here. When I moved here from the east, before you were born, I spent time on the 'Rex'. She was a gorgeous old dame, too much makeup, over dressed, but still with snap in her hips. Neon signs on top, rubber rafts lashed to her sides all the way around. Nothing else on top except a chopped down bridge and a forest of ventilating stacks. And oh how the suckers loved her. There were water taxies swarming around her like bees."

"Those were the days Tony."

"You know I was on her the night Earl Warren's boys closed her down. He was attorney general out here then. Tony Cornero held 'em off for hours with the fire hoses. You're right kid, those were the days."

Persia moved to the bar and poured two glasses full with red wine.

"You know Johnny, my people were sailors in the old country. We were from Marsala, only a hundred thirty five miles across the Straits of Sicily from Africa - Tunis. I travelled to Bizerte, west of Tunis, many times as a boy. There were coastal plains, then the desert."

"Not unlike the Southlands - eh, Tony?"

"The sea of sand, and the ocean - and civilization sandwiched in the middle - yah got a point kid. All I knew back then was that we were heading to Africa to do some business. Bizerte was on a promontory right out in the Mediterranean. We'd trade fish for goods, then sail home in the twilight. In the summer the warm sirocco blew and we'd swear it carried the scent of african wild flowers, even though we knew it couldn't be so."

Persia emptied his glass and poured himself another.

41

"Drink Johnny, drink. The wine makes everything else better - food, life. Everything."

The gospel according to Tony. The sea maybe was in Tony's blood. And to hear him tell it, he parlayed his early years on the fishing boats into a career as an oceangoing rum runner during prohibition off the Jersey shore, then on the Great Lakes. Out west from the beginning of the Second World War it was the water again, the gambling ships that ran from LA down to the Baha. Persia stayed with gambling in Reno, then Vegas. He engineered Bugsy Siegel's takeover of the Transcontinental Wire Service and outlived his mercurial boss. When Jack Dragna declared war on Mickey Cohen, Persia somehow found a way not to antagonize either side and to survive the battle for the Sunset Strip. And he seemed to land on his feet in LA in the sixties with an import-export business and a fishing fleet that ran the coastal waters.

Colorful was the adjective Persia tolerated, but retired was how he characterized himself as the clock ran down in the eighties. Harry Lang didn't quite see Tony Persia through such rose colored glasses. Smuggling was Tony 'P's' game alright. Maybe it did begin with liquor, but all too quickly Persia shifted gears to move heavily into narcotics smuggling. That brought with it money laundering and even murder when the integrity of the narcotics pipeline was in jeopardy. Persia vehemently denied all of it. There were no incriminating tracks. Lang had no proof. In Persia's view, Harry Lang was a rogue cop who had lost his perspective, fallen into more than one man's share of bad habits along the way, and become little better than the hard guys he hounded.

Johnny Fixx sipped his wine and wondered whether there'd be answers from Persia.

"Well Johnny, what brings you out here in the middle of the night?"

"Jimmy Doyle," answered Fixer as he stared into Persia's expressionless face hoping for some read from his reaction. There was none, and Tony 'P' asked, "he's a booster, isn't he Johnny?"

"That's what I thought Tony. But maybe he was more than that. The police have him in custody. He confessed to rigging that new Passeo Motel to blow - you know, the one that couldn't get an occupancy permit to open."

"It didn't, did it, Johnny?"

Fixer's expression questioned.

Persia smiled, "blow, kid. It didn't go up, did it?"

"No it didn't. But that's not where it ends. Seems this guy Doyle was working for one of the owners. Not the paper owners. One of the real owners who had points in the place."

"You got a name, Johnny?"

"Doyle fingered you, Tony. He says you paid for the job. That makes it conspiracy to commit arson even though the place didn't go up."

"You got this on good authority, Johnny?"

"The best. One of the guys on Lang's personal crew. So as far as it goes, it's the gospel."

"Is there a charge now?"

"I don't know. I'll put Max on it to see whether Kutter's got a Grand Jury sitting."

Fixer dropped onto a sofa. Persia faced him as he paced.

"Tony, I've got to know what we're up against here. Do you connect with the Passeo Motel? And more importantly, are there any tracks through Jimmy Doyle to you?"

"I never knew that Doyle was a matcher. Like I said, far as I knew, the guy was a minor league thief. As for the motel, I personally never put a nickel into it."

43

The Big Fall

With Tony Persia you had to listen carefully, take what he gave you, and wait for the right moment to fill in the blanks. Persia had outrightly denied any direct investment in the Passeo Motel. He always chose his words carefully. What he'd left open was the possibility he'd backed someone else who had points in the motel. There was no need to press him at the moment.

"Well Johnny, I think it's our old friend Harry Lang trying to fit me into a frame again. I heard he was so bad into the sauce a while back that they had to take away his gun and put him into communications to dry out. Can you beat that. And this piece of shit still keeps coming. You can take care of it, can't you Johnny?"

"Count on it Tony."

# CHAPTER FOUR

Rudy Kutter had wasted no time in making his presentment to the Grand Jury in the Tony Persia case. He'd made the more or less mandatory courtesy call to Persia's lawyer, Johnny Fixx. Kutter offered a felony plea to attempted arson, a charge that carried a ten year max on sentencing. That in Kutter's view was quite a concession since a conviction on the conspiracy to commit arson charge could bring with it a jail term of up to twenty years. Persia was already past seventy. A ten year stretch in practical effect meant actual jail time of from three to five years allowing for time off for good behavior. A conviction on the conspiracy charge meant for all intents and purposes that Tony Persia would die in jail.

Johnny Fixx hedged on the deal and asked first to interview Kutter's star witness, Jimmy Doyle. It was an extraordinary request and Fixer knew it. Fixer indicated that he had information that would establish that Doyle not only had acted alone in the attempt to blow the Passeo Motel, but also had run an arson for hire business locally that had taken at least two lives in the past five years. Fixx wanted to confront Doyle face to face, in the presence of Kutter and even Harry Lang if necessary, with his incriminating evidence.

Rudy Kutter was having none of it. In his view Johnny Fixx was attempting to subvert the Grand Jury process in order to take the spotlight off his client. The plea deal was on the table. Take it or leave it. Fixx had passed, and that suited Rudy Kutter just fine. A quick indictment would be just what the doctor ordered in kicking off the DA's run for the vacated Senatorial seat.

Kutter notified Fixx by letter that his client Tony Persia was the target of the Grand Jury investigation and offered Persia the opportunity to testify before the Grand Jury. As expected, Johnny Fixx elected to withhold his client from the Grand Jury, and Rudy Kutter went forward.

Kutter questioned Doyle repeatedly. There was no margin for error. The stakes were simply too high. Each time the essential facts were identical in the telling. The Passeo Motel had been rigged to blow by Jimmy Doyle. Doyle had retained his sketch of the wiring and explosives positioning and the bomb squad found everything in place just like Doyle said they would. Then Doyle came up with the clinching piece of evidence. The price had been $25,000 cash which Persia had paid personally by handing over an envelope. All but $5,000 had been spent, but Jimmy Doyle still had the last five grand and the envelope in which the money had originally been paid. Forensics raised prints belonging to Tony Persia on both the remaining bills and the money. End of story. It was a full house indictment, 23 to zip in favor. Now Rudy Kutter *was* about to savor making the charge public.

There was a media full house spread out in his office. Every TV station and both newspapers were represented. So too were the pair of radio stations that specialized in continuous local and national news. Kutter faced the cameras from behind his desk, with Mary Donlon sitting to his right, and Sam Turre acting as Harry Lang's surrogate, to his left. Kutter began by brandishing the Indictment. Cameras zoomed in to focus on the caption.

"People of the State of California -v- Antonio Persillato, a/k/a Tony Persia".

Kutter then read from a prepared statement: "The Grand Jury has charged Tony Persia with conspiring with one James Doyle to rig the Passeo Motel with explosives and to thus destroy the motel as part of a scheme to defraud the insurance company that wrote the fire insurance policy. Fortunately, the scheme was aborted, but not before the explosives were installed by Mr. Doyle. Our investigators found both wiring and traces of the explosives still on the premises. Mr. Doyle is a cooperating witness and will testify at the trial. We view this as an example of the most wanton disrespect for the public safety imaginable. I am not exaggerating when I tell you that ten, twenty, a hundred, even a thousand people could have been killed or injured had the charges detonated. We intend to prosecute Mr. Persia to the full extent of the law. With me today are Mary Donlon, my first assistant, who handled the presentment to the Grand Jury, and Sergeant Sam Turre from the organized crime task force of Lieutenant

Harry Lang. Lieutenant Lang broke the case and Sergeant Turre is here to answer any questions on the investigation."

Bob Ward from the Tribune asked, "Mr. Kutter, what was the motive for this plot to blow up the Passeo Motel?"

Mary Donlon raised her hand and Rudy Kutter nodded, "go ahead, Mary".

"Bob, we have evidence that the defendant was a silent partner in the Passeo Motel construction and operating syndicate. When the building permit was revoked and a certificate of occupancy rejected, the investment of defendant and his partners was at risk. It is our belief that they turned to Mr. Doyle to perform his specialty to bail them out of a bad situation at the expense of the insurance company".

Crystal Lee moved on camera and leaned forward holding her hand held mic under Rudy Kutter's nose, an altogether unnecessary technical move since Kutter was already mic'd, but a tactic that placed Crystal nicely front and center on camera as she asked her question.

"Mr. Kutter, has Mr. Persia been arraigned?"

"Not yet Miss Lee. We expect to have him appear in the morning before Judge Minton."

"Is Mr. Persia in custody?"

"No he isn't. His attorney, John Fixx, has agreed to produce him in the morning and that is acceptable to us."

"What kind of bail will you request?"

Kutter deferred to Mary Donlon.

"In view of the seriousness of the offense, it is our intention to request a substantial bail. We are not at liberty to discuss the amount just yet, but it will be our position that the amount should be sufficient to guarantee Mr. Persia's appearance in a proceeding that could put him behind bars for twenty years should we obtain a conviction."

The Big Fall

The cameras again cut to Crystal Lee.

"Mr. Kutter, we talked less than a week ago on camera about the Escobar scandal. Do you recall that conversation?"

Kutter worked at maintaining his pleasant expression. Crystal Lee was setting him up for a going over on the absent Harry Lang and his possible_complicity in roughing up the named defendant when the Escobar narcotics busts went down. Kutter had anticipated the anchorwoman getting into Escobar and it was for that reason that Kutter decided against having Harry Lang on camera.

"Miss Lee, Escobar remains under investigation, but I will say this. At this date we have not found any evidence to warrant departmental charges or criminal prosecution. Now in fairness to all involved, I really believe we shouldn't pursue the subject any further. The investigation is ongoing. And unless the evidence shows probable cause that some departmental rule or law was broken - which it has not shown to date - there will be no basis for departmental charges or criminal indictment."

"Does that mean that Lieutenant Harry Lang is in the clear?"

"I really can't comment further on Escobar, Miss Lee".

"Perhaps the nomination for the Senate seat is something you can talk about Mr. Kutter?"

Rudy Kutter chuckled.

"One of my favorite subjects Miss Lee. I have been advised that the Nominating Committee concluded its meetings in Sacramento and that their recommendations will be presented day after tomorrow."

"Are you the candidate, Mr. Kutter?"

"I hope to be, Miss Lee, but until the Committee speaks, the party designation is still up for grabs. I guess both of us will have the story in a few days."

Simon Johnson from BZ Radio asked, "Mr. Kutter, what can you tell us about Mr. Persia's ownership interest in the motel. It was our information that Passeo Ltd. owned the hotel. The certificate of incorporation doesn't list Tony Persia as a shareholder, officer or director. How do you square that?"

"Well I think that question really gets into matters of proof at trial but I can tell you that we believe we can connect Mr. Persia with one of the principals of Passeo Ltd. That is how the defendant happens to have money in the deal. As we said before, the proof will show that Tony Persia was a silent partner, but most assuredly, a principal in the project."

Crystal Lee again. "I'd like to address this question to Sergeant Turre. Just what exactly did you find on the premises of the motel that convinced you that the place had been wired to explode. And, oh yes, just how was it that you knew enough to look?"

Sergeant Sam Turre leaned forward and eyed the anchorwoman. She knew how to needle the DA, so maybe she wasn't all bad.

"I'll take your second question first. We were tipped to take a look. I can't say who or when, or the circumstances, but we did get a tip. When we arrived, we immediately discovered that the explosives had been removed. They had been installed in the heating and air conditioning duct work and in the crawl spaces beneath the main floor and above the rooms. There were wrappings for C-4 explosives that had been discarded which we found. Also, there were traces of the explosive. It's a kind of plastic explosive that will adhere to a surface. Even if you're a pro in removing it, some traces will remain on the surface - more than enough to be discovered in a microscopic analysis. The wiring was all in place although the final connections had not been made. It looked to us as if what they had in mind was a connection into the phone system so that a call into the motel at a certain time would detonate the explosives and send the place up."

"Thank you Sergeant Turre," said Ruddy Kutter. "And thank you members of the media and press. We will be proceeding with the arraignment and as there are new developments, we'll get you releases or convene news conferences. Thanks again."

\* \* \* \* \*

The beach house was twenty miles north beyond Malibu off the coast highway. It was Johnny Fixx' second home. There was a wooden walkway down from the roadside parking pad to the shelf on which the front half of the cedar A-frame was constructed. The shelf ran out before the house did, and the rear half was built out from the shelf on stilts. Access to the beach was by ladder off the rear deck. Sea burnished boulders and tidal pools flanked the house on either side. It was as isolated a site as one could get on the shoreline within reasonable travel time to LA proper.

The ocean slammed up the beach, turbulent in the beginnings of a gypsy storm. In the distance, the lights of an oil drilling rig were barely visible. The wind gusted and howled, and Johnny Fixx paced his deck, sipping a scotch, and waiting on Joey Dancer. Complications were piling up in the Tony Persia case. DA Kutter had informed him that he would ask for $5,000,000 in bail. That was in Fixer's view outlandish, but the bail would be substantial. That was the immediate problem, but by no means the only problem for tomorrow. Max Gale had learned from one of Kutter's assistants that the DA intended to make a claim against any retainer paid by Persia to Fixer. It was Kutter's position that Persia had no visible means of support and that accordingly any money he came up with was the fruit of some illegal enterprise and as such subject to confiscation. Fixer wasn't particularly concerned about the outcome of that one. Kutter was on shaky ground. The case did not involve a scam where money changed hands and the defendant was unjustly enriched. Had the motel blown and the insurance company paid, then a conviction might bring with it the inference that the defendant was the beneficiary of dirty money as was his lawyer one step removed. But since the alleged plot to demolish the Passeo had been aborted, there could be no one to one relationship between dirty money received by the defendant and the payment of a retainer to his lawyer. Kutter had to know that, but he figured to press it anyway to give the defense one more thing to worry about.

"Gonna' be one helluva storm any minute, eh amigo?"

Joey Dancer's voice waffled up from the beach. Waves crashed onto the beach and washed up to the pilings under the house.

"If that's really you Joey, I'd get my ass up here pronto. What with the storm and high tide, you're gonna' be in it up to your eyeballs any minute."

Dancer climbed the ladder and pulled himself up the last two rungs almost vaulting onto the deck. Angular and wiry, his face more of the same, all lines and slants, planes and angles, like sculptures on Mt. Rushmore, Dancer projected raw energy barely suppressed on his five foot eight frame. Johnny Fixx led him into the house. A fire roared in the open hearth chimney that filled the center of the house, painting the burnished oak walls and floor a shimmering orange. Fixer poured two tumblers full of scotch and dropped into the middle of a mound of cushions before the fireplace. Dancer found a chair and settled in to sip his drink. He reached into his shirt and tossed a thick envelope at Fixer. It was unsealed and Johnny Fixx casually scanned its contents. The deal with Tony Persia was a hundred large for the defense, fifty upfront, the balance after the jury was picked. The envelope contained a draft for $50,000 as agreed. It also contained another $15,000 in crisp new hundreds, a performance bonus from Tony 'P'.

Fixer stuffed the envelope into his pants pocket and reached down for the remote that lay under a cushion. He pointed the switch at the amplifier for his sound system and hit the button. The tape player kicked in and the Miles Davis sextet, circa 1958, recorded live at the Plaza filled the room with "My Funny Valentine". Fixer downed his scotch and stared into the heart of the fire and muttered, "now that Philly Joe is dead, only the boss is left. What a fucking shame."

Dancer was talking to him, but only when his friend repeated yet a third time did his conversation register.

"Hey Johnny, do your drift on your own time, will you. It's the middle of the night and the old man asked me to cover his bail tomorrow. I'm gonna have to do some fancy dancing to raise the dough. You'd better not be far wrong in guessing what the Judge is going to want."

"Sorry Joey. Pour us another taste - okay. Judge Minton isn't a lunatic, but Kutter is surely going to go all out to put the Judge on the spot to clobber Tony. Kutter's asking for $5,000,000. It's crazy. They don't set bail that high for those scumbags in the Medellin drug cartel."

"So they don't," agreed Dancer as he handed Fixer a refill. "So mastermind, what do you see it coming down to."

"My best guess is a million. That's serious money. Maybe more really than even a publicity conscious Judge should set in a victimless prosecution. It's Kutter and his political aspirations that make the goddamned thing 'iffy'. He's always playing to the press and media. He'll make the trial a three-ring prime time circus. That puts heat on the Judge. Law and order and all that good stuff. Yeah, a million should satisfy everybody watching. You'd better line up a million cash. It's unlikely that the Judge is going to permit a property secured bond. They're going to want it green all the way."

"I figured about a 'mill'. I'll have it in bank drafts." Dancer chuckled, "yeah, bank drafts. Every one of them $9,999.99 to avoid the cash reporting requirements at the banks. We'll give 'em the odd change in silver. Shit, that'll piss Kutter off. What do you think?"

"Hey amigo, you forget we went to war together. What's another hand grenade when the bombs are flying, eh?"

"That's what we need Johnny. A real straight up shooting war to uncomplicate things - clear the head. What'd you say compadre, let's just do a disappearing act. We'll take the weapons, a fistful of cash and the fastest car we can find, and head south. There's always a war if you drive far enough south - right?"

"I've gotta' fight this one first, Joey, then maybe . . . ."

"You'll never leave it Johnny. Too many toys, and just enough white-collar danger to keep it interesting. Shit pal, this is your old friend Dancer. I know all about you, you motherfucker. In the Nam, Johnny, in the Nam! It's got to do with trouble, right. We're both fucking addicts. The good life by the shore. Bullshit. What would we do if we didn't spend half our time looking over our shoulders to see who's gaining on us? None of them really understand what it's all about, do they Johnny. Hell no! Trouble only finds those who need it."

"You're amazing, Joey. You deliver my retainer and make unnecessary my next five sessions with my shrink. Unbelievable. Encore?"

"I was getting to that compadre. I've been nosing around. There's some things you and Max should know before you go after that fink Jimmy Doyle."

Fixer moved away from the fireplace and paced before the glass doors that opened onto the deck. Rain beat down on the shore and blew in translucent sheets against the glass.

"You've got my undivided attention, Joey. What do you know?"

"Seems there's been a bunch of arsons - unsolved stuff - over the past five years. Mostly penny ante insurance stuff with buildings abandoned and about to fall to the wrecker's ball. Six in fact. Not the kind of stuff that ever gets any press. But two of them are different. A pair of derelicts were found dead burned to a crisp, one in each of the last two buildings that went up."

"Real human interest stuff, Joey. But how does any of it relate to friend Kutter and my client?"

"We've got a guy who will testify that Jimmy Doyle was the matcher. With two dead men, pal Doyle comes off as quite a bit lower than the gentleman explosives expert he's advertised to be in this case. I hear Kutter is going to attempt to sell Doyle to the jury as more than a snitch who bought his way out. They're going to try to paint him as a guy with conscience who pulled the stuff out of the Passeo on his own hook. Too many good folks gonna' get fried, and like that. It's all crap, pal. And we've got the pictures."

"Who's your man, Joey? Anybody I know?"

"A kid who was doing a stint at Pendleton. He stole the C-4 that Doyle was partial to. The kid's got a nose for the fast buck, but that's all. Nothing else bad on his record."

"Okay, that's promising. You get him together with Max Gale. I want the guy polygraphed. This has got to be iron clad. Nothing to chance, Joey. Understand?"

"Sure, sure, Johnny, every angle covered and on the legit. Right? And while we're at it, I thought that maybe you'd like to know they got you staked out. I drove past the house and parked a few hundred yards down. I worked my way down to the beach and nosed around down below. There's a car off the road across the street and a guy in the rocks by the water with a pair of binoculars. Shit, for all I know they might even have your place wired for sound."

"The joints not bugged. I'm careful about that. But they're out there in the dark watching. Shit - can you beat that."

"Naughty, naughty, eh. Shit compadre, you ponder all them imponderables while I slip away into the night to put together the man's bail money."

Dancer disappeared into the night.

Before the dawn, the storm was spent, and the surf subsided to a restless wail - the lonely lament of an errant gust trapped in a box canyon. And John Fixx watched and waited on the passing of the night.

## C H A P T E R   F I V E

The bail hearing was history. Judge Thomas Minton had set bail at $1,000,000 which was duly paid into Court at the conclusion of the hearing. Tony Persia was free without travel restrictions, and Judge Minton had set the hearing date for any Motions for five weeks hence.

Johnny Fixx had spent the past three nights in his office loft. The coast storms hadn't abated but it wasn't really the weather that had spooked him from the beach house. Being under surveillance had something to do with it. That and a fistful of other problems that were surfacing again to haunt him.

8:00 a.m. Another day without sun - the whole scene dull and heavy, like eyelids on a hungover drunk that wouldn't quite open to take that first look. Fixer sipped from a mug of coffee and considered his options. The phone rang.

"Hullo. Attorney's Office. The lawyers haven't come in yet. This is the answering service. Try again after 9:00."

Fixer's standard subterfuge when he didn't want to be bothered either before or after normal working hours.

"The service my ass," answered the familiar voice on the other end. Fixer chuckled.

"Just the guy I don't want to talk to. Jesus, can't you let a person get some sleep?"

Ron Goldstone had handled Fixer's finances for years. There were problems meeting calls for interest payments at note renewal times, and a blossoming mess with margin calls on Fixx' stock portfolio. Goldstone was a magician at juggling the books but this time it was going to take a healthy shot of cold cash to call off the wolves.

"Look Johnny my boy, I know you're ass over heels in that Persia case. I've been trying to get to you for two weeks. We've run out of room to maneuver. Now I know you don't want to hear this, but it's your money, so listen up and maybe we can find a way out of this. The banks don't want to know us. Combined it's going to take $65,000 in interest payments and some principal reductions to get them to renew the notes, and all I can get you is 90 days. They won't go for a year. Not even six months. So we buy the 90 days and see what it looks like then. Okay?"

"I can come up with the 65K Ron. Three days. Okay? So what else?"

The recent market crash and Fixer's stocks were the 'what else' that he really didn't want to hear about.

"Look Johnny, I'm liquidating what I can to keep the houses and banks off your back. But it's not going to be enough. Nobody could have anticipated what happened in the market. You got your horn caught just like half the other players in the market. So, we've got a problem. In your case it's a big one because your margin accounts are secured by your real estate. The bastards will not only sell you out, but they'll also grab your properties if there are any short falls after liquidation."

"How much Ron? And how long can you get me to work out of this?"

"You're looking at $150,000 minimum. Cold cash."

"You got any juice with the banks? When we renew is there the possibility that we can get a few bucks more from them tacked onto the notes?"

"I already tried that route, Johnny. The bankers say to a man that you're over extended. They're circling like a bunch of green eyed buzzards. I got you a week to come up with the money. That's the best I could do."

"Okay Ron. Let's compare notes in a couple of days. Can't say it's been nice to hear from you."

Fixer had been well aware of the squeeze even without Ron Goldstone laying it out for him. All of that was bad enough. But there was another piece. He'd spent three weeks in the past six months at the tables in Reno and Vegas. As usual the boys were accommodating with as much credit as the LA high roller required. And the luck hadn't really bit him in the ass all that badly. But the casino credit managers were beyond polite reminder letters to collect the fifty thousand dollar tab Fixer had run up. Dancer might call in some markers to buy him some time but going that route had more negatives than not. It was a sign of weakness that could bring with it a loss of respect. There was no way Fixer could risk that. He needed open lines of communication on both sides of the fence. Green would solve all his problems. The question was where could he raise the bundle in less than a week.

* * * * *

Max Gale had been busy over the past seventy-two hours. He'd personally taken the lead in digging into the background of Mickey Ferris, the marine accomplice who had pilfered the C-4 explosives that Jimmy Doyle used in torching a series of derelict buildings.

It was noon under black rain pregnant skies and Max Gale settled in to report what he knew to Johnny Fixx.

"The kid had a clean service record. Honorable discharge. He's been a civilian for eighteen months."

"You know Max," said Johnny Fixx, "even if this Ferris character pans out, we're not home. Too many holes."

Gale's expression questioned and Fixx explained, "let's say we pin down the disappearance of the C-4 from Pendleton . . .

Max Gale interjected, "I think I'm on the right track there. There's a Colonel who's an old pal. I've got Ferris' statement detailing what he says he took and when. I've given that to the Colonel to compare to their internal inventory records. If that works out, we find out whether the thefts that Ferris was supposed to be a part of actually took place."

"You haven't compromised the witness," asked Fixx.

"Hell, if he's telling the truth, there's got to be the possibility of charges under the Uniform Code of Military Justice. And that's only for openers. Our old pal Rudy Kutter will be laying in the weeds for this guy. Complicity in arson, especially where people were killed is damned serious business. Like I said, this Mickey Ferris might well dirty up Jimmy Doyle, but does he have any idea that in doing so he's probably going to be falling on his own sword?"

"As far as the Colonel is concerned," explained Max Gale, "he's a close enough friend that he'll search their records without pressing me for the punch line - at least not just yet."

"Okay, so we get past problem number one - did Ferris take the stuff - and we keep the heat off Ferris somehow even though at this minute, I can't see how the hell we can do that, that leaves us with the sixty four dollar question - so we establish that Ferris engineered the theft of C-4 from Pendleton, we're still left with putting Ferris together with our pal Jimmy Doyle. What have you got on that one?"

Max Gale grinned broadly. Johnny Fixx had seen that expression many times before. It was the master teacher telling his pupil that he was a jump or two ahead of where he figured him to be.

"I had Mickey Ferris tell his story while wired up to one of the Intertech rigs. He passed the polygraph with flying colors. I'm taking no chances. There'll be a repeat polygraph - I intend to put the questions to him in slightly different form. Then we'll be certain. But at least at this point, Ferris did have a one to one relationship with Doyle. Jimmy bought directly from Ferris and on at least two occasions, it appears that Jimmy actually pressed Ferris to grab additional C-4 that Jimmy needed for torch jobs he had to complete. So that part of it fits nicely."

"What about being able to prove that Doyle actually did those arsons. Obviously, Jimmy will deny it on cross examination. Is this Ferris any help there? Did Jimmy Doyle shoot his mouth off with Ferris - maybe tell him what buildings were going to go up, or better still, take him along on the jobs."

"Nothing that good, my friend. But Ferris can testify that at least twice, Doyle contacted him to get some C4 pronto because he had to take care of business. Each time, within a couple of days, Ferris read it in the papers. A derelict building went up."

"If that's the best we've got, I guess we'll go with it, but there's a hole in it big enough to drive a truck through. What about police records on the arsons."

"It could be a gamble, but maybe we've got an angle there. You know that Lang or one of his top boys will take the stand to lay out the police investigation on Tony Persia. On cross we can ask him to produce their files on the other arsons. Then you ask him the big one - the arsons were never solved, but who was their prime suspect. If it was Jimmy Doyle and if Lang and company don't lie, then we've got an admission from the coppers that just might stick in the jury's craw and dirty up the good Jimmy Doyle."

Johnny Fixx grinned wryly.

"Nothing's easy, eh Max. Stick with it. I assume there's nothing possible on a dismissal motion?"

"We'll go through the motions, but I don't see anything there Johnny. The charges in the indictment state the crime. It's a textbook indictment. So there's really nothing wrong on its face."

"What about physical evidence and Brady?"

"I've already demanded copies of their forensics reports and any exhibits. We should have whatever they've got on the prints on the payoff envelope and the money that links Tony Persia to Jimmy Doyle. Come to think of it, our buddy Rudy Kutter at least to this point - and you know how that can change - but for now he's being damned cooperative on all fronts. I guess he must figure the noose is pretty tight around our client's neck. As for Brady, he promised whatever they have within a week, but he also let me know that he didn't remember anything exculpatory in the testimony of the witnesses before the Grand Jury or the statements they took from people who weren't called. So Johnny, I think we're not going to get any nuggets here, and that my friend leaves the fate of Tony Persia squarely in your very skilled hands. You're simply going to have to work your magic in the pit and cut the legs out from under Jimmy Doyle so that the jury sees it your way."

* * * * *

It was dusk, three gradients of shadow creeping into the loft, when Johnny Fixx emerged from his audio studio. More Miles on tape, this time the years after the war when Charlie Parker adopted the trumpeter. Bop standards were the fare and Fixer sprinkled in later recordings of the same tunes by Miles with his late fifties quintet and sextet. That sextet was "the band", Martin Scorcese and a generation of rockers to the contrary notwithstanding. The phone rang. Ron Goldstone came on breathless, obviously agitated.

"They've frozen your accounts Johnny. I was an hour from making the transfer of the seventy five big ones to buy your note renewals. Goddamnit, if I had smelled trouble I could have done it yesterday or the day before. What's it all about? There aren't any tax liens, are there?"

Johnny Fixx ran his hand through his hair, once, then again, the second time in an almost ragged motion bordering on pulling. That mother Kutter had done his dance even though he damned well knew that the Courts would vacate any seizure within a day.

"I think I know what's going on Ron. It's nothing either one of us could have controlled. The DA seized my accounts because he wants to grab my retainer from Tony Persia. He's taking the position that any money paid by Persia is the fruit of an unlawful enterprise and as such subject to seizure. The 'feds' started the ball rolling on that one and our good state enacted parallel legislation. I'm a hundred percent certain that I can persuade the Court to vacate the seizure order. There really is no basis for it in this case. But that's going to take time. I'd like to say 24 hours, but 48 is more like it. That means you're going to have to stroke the bankers. I'm counting on you?"

"Christ Johnny, you're really making me earn my goddamned commissions, eh? Under the circumstances I don't see how the boys in three pieced suits and wing tips, can very well refuse. So we probably get by that one. I hate to be a pain

60

in the ass, but what about the other one – anything I can tell the brokerage houses? We need to show them some strength in paying down the margin calls, and fast."

"I'm working in it," answered Fixxer, less than convincingly.

"Okay partner, just don't be working on it too long."

The street level intercom sounded.

"Now what," groused Johnny Fixx. "Who," he asked.

"Harry Lang, we should talk," was the reply.

"My lucky day," muttered Fixer as he moved out onto the corridor landing to send down the elevator.

Lieutenant Harry Lang let himself in. Fixer had placed a bottle and two glasses on the corner of his desk.

"Taste, Lieutenant?"

Harry Lang dropped into a chair, opening his trench coat and nodding "no".

"What can I do for you Lieutenant?"

"You got it wrong Fixer, it's what I'm gonna' do for you. As time goes by, I seem to find your name coming across my desk more and more. And I say to myself, that shouldn't be. John Fixx, distinguished member of the defense bar, being caught on surveillance reports with the wrong people in questionable circumstances. Nah, that can't be right."

"Lieutenant, I'm busy. Get to the point or take a walk."

"Joey Dancer, Johnny, your good pal Joey Dancer. Now I know the standard spiel. You two were in the Nam. That makes you kinda blood brothers. Something. There's black and there's white, and as far as I'm concerned damned little in between. As big a hardhead as I am, even I give a man some room. But I keep my thumb on a situation when I don't quite buy it. And guess what, Johnny Fixx. You and your pal Dancer don't compute. You were mustered out six months before he was, right?"

Fixer nodded "yes".

"I'll bet Dancer never got into the circumstances of his discharge."

"His tour was over."

"The hell it was. The bastard was AWOL in the golden triangle and hooked up with the Shan army. He was ass over heals in narcotics smuggling. He was bagged in a raid up there and could have been shot. Because of his war record they booted him out and gave him a general discharge. He deserved a dishonorable and time in the stockade. But I guess your old buddy told you all of this, right."

"Even if you're on the money, all of that is fifteen years stale. Like I said before, Lieutenant, what's the point?"

"The point is Johnny Fixx that your partner - he is your partner in that surveillance scam your other pal Streaks or Bamboo, or what the hell ever his name is, is running - is no goddamned good. He'll bite you in the ass every time for a fast buck, and for my money, he'll sell out his mother if he has to to save his own ass. Now where does that leave a smart guy like you, eh, you tell me."

"He's not my partner Lang. You know I put up some of the money for Streaks service. That's the extent of it. Dancer isn't in the business. Chapter, page, and verse - end of story. Okay?"

"Why can't I buy you Fixer. You just don't add up. Yeah, guess I'll leave. I paid you a courtesy call. You're just not smart enough to see where it's all got to end. And you're such a smart guy. You just never can tell, can you. I'll be seeing you in court pal. It's gonna' take more than you to get Persia off this time. Airtight, Fixer. Not even a wise guy like you will be able to find any holes."

The elevator carrying Lang to the street had scarcely made the return run to the top when the phone rang.

"Must be my night for it," muttered Fixer.

Max Gale.

"Evening counsellor," he said pleasantly. "I got back on Mickey Ferris' case as soon as I left you. He passed the second polygraph. That in hand I figured I'd rattle Kutter's cage. I didn't say who and what but I told him we've got an iron clad witness who'll sink Doyle's credibility. Lang never batted an eye. He said Doyle's passed a polygraph and that Persia's going down. I offered to disclose Ferris' identity and even exchange polygraph tapes. Kutter just laughed at that one. Then he said the clock was ticking on the plea offer. I guess the sonuvabitch can smell it."

"I could have told you he wouldn't budge. Kutter is just marking time here."

"You do know about the seizure?"

"Yeah. Good news travels fast."

"I'll file the motion to vacate tomorrow. It'll be heard late in the day or first thing the following morning. Okay?"

"On the money, Max. Don't let Kutter rattle you. Rudy Kutter is running for Senator already over Tony Persia's dead body. And the guys who hide behind the tin, pal, Lang in particular, who work for Kutter are even worse."

"Like my friend John Fixx always says, different sides of the coin. I wonder. Cops and wise guys?

Fixer chuckled.

"One of these days you'll learn, Professor."

# C H A P T E R   S I X

Judge Thomas Minton had summoned counsel to Chambers for a pre-trial conference. District Attorney Rudy Kutter was represented by his first assistant, Mary Donlon. John Fixx appeared for the defendant.

Tom Minton was a middler, a cut above political hack pedigree, but a jurist whose tracks did not bode well for the defense. Minton never really practiced law privately. What little experience he had as an attorney was derived in a short stint he served in a 90 man law firm that specialized in putting together film and TV packages. From there Minton accepted an appointment as an assistant United States Attorney, his pay back for working in the trenches to deliver Orange County for then candidate Reagan. Two years later Minton was appointed United States Magistrate. He didn't quite have the political juice to swing the designation for Federal District Court Judge and when that plumb went elsewhere, Tom Minton threw his hat in the ring for a vacant seat on the California Superior Court. Minton was a winner. That was six years before.

In his years on the bench, Tom Minton gained a reputation for running a tough court. He was scrupulously fair during a trial, in criminal cases even bending over backwards to give the defendant every procedural break, but when the verdict was guilty, Tom Minton reverted to form. He was an absolute bear on sentencing. If Jimmy Doyle held up for the prosecution, that meant real trouble for Tony Persia.

John Fixx sat idly thumbing through papers in his file. He and Mary Donlon had scarcely exchanged the amenities as they were ushered into Minton's chambers. The office was high ceilinged and mahogany paneled, and with sufficient square footage to double as a hand ball court. Glass faced book cases lined two walls. Two large salt water aquariums covered the third, and Minton's desk backed up to the fourth. A leather covered sofa and two arm chairs in the same were arrayed before the desk. The counsellors Fixx and Donlon each sat opposite ends of the sofa, book ends working hard at not noticing the presence of the other. What remained of the office floor space was covered by a conference table and chairs. Numerous books and files were haphazardly opened on the table top that apparently was the Judge's personal work bench. There were no windows. Judge Minton was a relative newcomer to the Superior Court bench. It seemed that the truly important things came to jurists only with experience.

Judge Thomas Minton swept into chambers, a silver haired blocky six footer who still looked as if he could play guard for the University of California. Minton discarded his robes as he came and called to his clerk, "Gerard, I'd like you to sit in on this please."

Gerard was a slight young man, with a shock of red hair and ferverish eyes who seemed strung tighter than cat gut. Gerard fiddled nervously with the knot of his tie and slumped into one of the chairs.

Judge Minton eyed the attorneys and picked up on the icy silence between them.

"I'd like to think we can cooperate in moving this case along to trial. Are there any fact stipulations we can agree on to narrow the issues at trial?"

John Fixx eyed Mary Donlon. Mary Donlon watched Judge Minton and finally said, "I don't think so your honor. Of course if John would like to stipulate to Mr. Persia's guilt we can save the taxpayers considerable expense."

Fixx raised his eyebrows in an "oh really" gesture. "Counsellor, your levity is always appreciated. Seriously, I see three issues here that Judge Minton can perhaps help us with. The first is the Grand Jury minutes. Now I know that the letter of the law permits the prosecution to withhold those minutes from the defense until the trial is actually in progress and the person who testified before the Grand Jury is on the stand as a trial witness. However, we believe it is fundamentally unfair to subject the defense to the practically impossible task of having to review and digest those minutes in only a short time while the examination of the particular witness is suspended. It has long been a rule of comity in this County - and one which your office has usually followed to release the Grand Jury minutes prior to the actual swearing of the first witness. Your boss has advised us that he is not inclined to do that in this case. I would like the Court to make an order compelling the District Attorney to hand over those Grand Jury minutes at least seven days prior to the commencement of trial."

"What's your position on this, Mary," asked Judge Minton.

"Your honor, ordinarily we would not hesitate to accommodate the defense in this situation. However, the defendant is a senior organized crime figure of long standing in the Southlands."

"Hold on there," interrupted John Fixx. "My client has never been prosecuted or convicted under RICO. He has never admitted to being a member of an organized crime family, and I defy you to show me anything in the public record that proves the contrary. So, counsellor, let's not get lost in innuendo. It's not Tony Persia, the mobster, who's on trial here. Oh no. Your boss charged citizen Tony Persia, a man who has never even in your police files been associated with strong arm tactics, extortion, or influencing witnesses. Period!"

"Point to the defense," smiled Judge Minton. "But, Mr. Fixx, I believe the issue is one on which reasonable men, and women, can differ. Continue Mary."

"The point is your Honor that if the defense has access to the identities and testimony before the Grand Jury of the prosecution's key witnesses, there will be every opportunity for the intimidation and influencing of these witnesses by the defendant or by his known criminal associates. Now please, Mr. Fixx, save your breath on Persia's associations. We've got miles of surveillance tape that places your client with some very questionable people. For that reason, we simply cannot release the minutes in advance of the trial."

Judge Minton was still not persuaded that there was any clear and present danger of witness intimidation if the Grand Jury minutes were made available to the defense.

"Well Mary, unless you can document the likelihood that witnesses will be intimidated I'm not inclined to go along with you on this one. Do you have anything concrete that you can show the court?"

"Only police intelligence, your honor, but intelligence from usually reliable sources that we believe should be taken quite seriously."

"Anything else, Mr. Fixx?"

"I've had my say, your Honor."

"My ruling on Mr. Fixx' application for disclosure of the Grand Jury minutes is as follows: the prosecution will deliver to the defense not later than seven days before jury selection begins, the complete Grand Jury testimony of each and every witness to be called by the prosecution who also testified before the Grand Jury."

Judge Minton was running true to form. Let the defense win all the skirmishes, but then lower the boom when the issue truly was in the balance and throw the book at the defendant. Even at that Fixer was well aware that it sometimes came down to taking what you could get and maybe accumulating a sufficient number of tactical advantages to swing the outcome.

"Thank you, your honor. My next concern is jury selection. Will counsel be permitted to screen each juror?"

"I've always made it a practice to personally screen the panel myself, John. Otherwise, we'll be at this for weeks before we even get to the proof. We'll begin with a questionnaire. Then I'll personally question those who survive. I'll screen down that panel. What's left will be subject to your respective examinations and challenges. Acceptable?"

'Not really', thought Fixer, but this wasn't the issue to make a stand on.

"Yes, your honor," chimed the counsellors in tandem. "Anything else, counsellors?"

"Your honor," began Fixer, as he primed for the one that would surely elicit an explosive response from Mary Donlon, "the District Attorney, my esteemed colleague, Rudy Kutter, seems to be doing his damndest to try this case in the press. By my count he's already convened four press conferences the principal subject matter of which has been this prosecution. He's stretching the bounds of propriety and I believe he has already made it impossible for my client to get an impartial jury with all of the innuendo in the press. Under the circumstances, I do not believe Rudy Kutter should be permitted to ascend to the vacant Senate seat over the trampled remains of Tony Persia."

"Now just a minute, Mr. Fixx," snapped Mary Donlon, "you are completely out of line on that one. I'd be glad to provide the court with verbatim transcripts of Mr. Kutter's press conferences. Believe me, nothing improper was said concerning Mr. Persia."

"Well counsellors, I too have been following this case in the press, and while I don't believe the District Attorney has done anything improper to this point, his penchant for working with the press does open the possibility of something, however unintentional, happening in the future. For that reason I'm going to issue a gag order on both sides. No further mention of this case before the media - print, TV, radio. Understood?"

Both attorneys nodded their assent, Mary Donlon somewhat more glumly than John Fixx.

"Is that about it counsellors?"

"Just a couple of other things your honor," said John Fixx. "I received the latest trial guidelines from your clerk. You are requiring requests to charge the jury at least seventy two hours before jury selection begins. It seems to me that the law applicable to any particular case often crystallizes as the testimony develops. If we submit proposed charges in advance of the proof, we'll both surely want to make changes as the testimony enfolds."

"No problem counsellors. For good cause shown during the trial and before my charge to the jury, I'll be glad to permit you to supplement your proposed charges. Okay?"

"Fair enough," answered Mary Donlon.

"Last, your honor," said John Fixx, "but surely not least is our credibility witness. We have a witness who will show that Jimmy Doyle was directly responsible for at least six arsons before the Passeo Motel affair and that two persons were killed in those arsons. Further, we believe the police suppressed that information and did not make any of it available to the Grand Jury when Doyle was submitted to them as a reliable and credible witness - which in our view he definitely is not. We want a ruling from this court that our witness will be permitted to testify and also a subpoena directing the police to produce at trial all of their investigatory notes on those arsons and any loss of life in the fires."

"Your honor, how can this court rule in advance as to the admissibility of any testimony or the credibility of any witness. As for the disclosure of the police files, that too is clearly an extraordinary request, considerably beyond the bounds of what is reasonable."

"Well Mary, I tend to agree with you, but I'm more than a little curious about this character Doyle's past. So I'm ordering you to have all police files on the arsons Mr. Fixx referred to in my office next week. I'll review the material and if I deem it relevant, I will make it available to the defense in advance of trial."

Minton turned to his clerk.

"Do you want to add anything Gerard?"

"No, Judge."

"Well then counsellors," chuckled Minton, "there's the door."

"Give Rudy my regards," smiled John Fixx as he rose to take his leave. Mary Donlon said nothing and John Fixx barely stifled what he was thinking, 'humorless bitch'.

"Thanks your honor," said Fixx, as he pressed out of the door into the ante room.

\* \* \* \* \*

The Condor Club was on a promontory jutting into the ocean above Oscura Cove, ten miles south of Long Beach. The Condor came into the world in the twenties as a light house when a spur of the Great Western

Railroad ran down to the sea at Oscura to link up with a great wooden pier
that ran out into the ocean for two hundred yards. There was a time when
Oscura was in the running to become the Port of Los Angeles. It
became the preferred port of call for Baha rum runners sailing north
during Prohibition. Then shipping and commerce gravitated to San Pedro in
the thirties and Great Western and the Oscura pier both disappeared. But the
Condor endured, not as a beacon for errant shipping, but a watering hole for
errant souls atop the Oscura smugglers cove, as it came to be known.

The Condor offered music occasionally live and from records
and tapes played by the bartenders on the house sound system, and the
patrons from one of two ancient juke boxes at either end of the place.
Manny Cesar owned the Condor. He'd done a stint in World War II
with Pete Rugolo, the composer who became Stan Kenton's Billy
Strayhorn in the forties and fifties. Cesar made the Condor a
Kenton mecca and also was partial to the beboppers of the forties
and fifties. That suited Johnny Fixx who made the Condor his watering
hole of choice. The liquor was top grade, and the music even better. The
Condor also was the occasional hideaway of Tony Persia. It was Persia who
had summoned Fixer to stop by this night.

The Condor featured a long narrow main room, the bar running
two thirds the length of one wall, with cocktail tables covering the facing
wall. The end of the bar opened into an alcove for diners that faced the
rotunda under the spiral staircase to the top of what had been the Oscura light.
Manny Cesar used the light room as his office. The space under the rotunda
was the bandstand for the live jazz Cesar occasionally booked into the
Condor. Manny Cesar had a thing for the way it used to be. A rotating crystal
he'd rescued from a ballroom ticketed for demolition was centered above the
bandstand. A lighted checkerboard floor covered the bandstand, the lights
coming on randomly in lines or square by square. Wall sconces lit the rooms
and open bladed fans were placed strategically to ventilate.

Johnny Fixx made a bee line for the nearest juke box and punched
in his favorites. First selections from Miles Davis' collaboration with Gil
Evans on Porgy and Bess, then Canonball Adderley working with Evans'
orchestra and arrangements on a set of classic jazz standards. Fixer settled in
at the bend in the bar farthest from the entrance and the bartender served him
a tumbler of Jack Daniels, no ice, with water on the side.

The Big Fall

Felix Masters, Cesar's exec, materialized out of the kitchen. Felix was short and blocky, now in middle age nearly five by five. His pals called him "Heavy" and he took pride in some talents that were anything but. In close Felix had a dancing bear's feet and even faster fists. He was slow witted but blessed with a sense of humor and a fierce sense of loyalty to his pals. That made him the ideal manager for Manny Cesar. He'd never scam a pal and treated the Condor as if it was his personal preserve.

"Jeez, Johnny, where the hell you been? When Miles kicked in on the box, I knew it had to be you. Que pasa, amigo?"

"The law business has my full attention lately, Heavy."

"Oh yeah, that's right. Yer gonna get Tony off, right. Shit, I been reading in the papers. That Jimmy Doyle was always a cry baby motherfucker."

Bette Jones walked in and moved directly behind the bar. Her eyes moved all over Heavy doing what he wished her hands could. The fat man nearly blushed and Fixer nodded wryly. Jonesy ran the tip of her tongue over her scarlet glossed bee sting lips.

Fixer chuckled, "look, enough you two. I'll do a stint behind the bar, but I don't have all night, you'll have to make it fast."

Heavy grinned proudly at his pals perception of what was obvious and retreated into the kitchen.

"Freshen up," asked Jonesy. Fixer pushed his empty glass her way, and Jonesy poured him another.

Fixer nursed his third drink, waiting for the man. It was edging up on 10:00 p.m. when Tony Persia walked in. He was accompanied by a man Fixer hadn't expected to see, Joe Bayonne, one of the big men from Vegas.

Bald but trim, Bayonne wore a navy double breasted suit and steel gray turtleneck.

71

"Johnny, how are you," said Bayonne as he moved to embrace him.

Persia breezed past, calling, "come on boys, let's sit a table in the back."

Heavy personally served a round of drinks and the trio settled in around the table. Bayonne had studied classics in the old country decades before and carried with him the moniker "Dottore" in recognition of his academic achievements, both real and imagined. There were rumors that Persia and Bayonne had arrived from the old country at about the same time in the late twenties and had cut their teeth in the rackets in Montreal and Toronto on the St. Lawrence rum routes during Prohibition before migrating west to find their places in the sun.

"How goes it in the desert, Dottore," asked Fixer.

"The resort business is on an upswing Johnny. You know there was a time two, three years ago when the Atlantic City thing looked like it was taking a piece out of us. But that must have been a one time and out kinda thing for the high rollers. They're back, and we're doing what we can for them."

Dottore showed a quizzical little look, the one that normally preceded an insider's wink, then continued, "as a matter of fact, we laid out a lot of credit for our friends and we even look the other way if they're temporarily embarrassed - it can happen to the best of them."

Joe Bayonne smiled broadly, "I know. Hell, I been there often enough myself. We go to the wall for our steadies. Hell - it pays off. They keep comin back."

'Unbelievable' thought Fixer. Message delivered!

Dottore knew about his tab. It didn't figure that Persia got wind of it and brought him to the Condor just to assure Fixer that there was no rush. Fixer nervously swilled the liquor in his glass. Persia picked up on it and touched his finger tips to the top of Fixer's extended hand.

The Big Fall

"You get your money freed up, Johnny? I seen what that prick Kutter did to you. Max took care of it, didn't he?"

"Yeah Tony, a couple days ago. Kutter knew he couldn't make it stick. But he had to jab me in the ass."

"How long before we start the trial Johnny?"

"I was with Judge Minton this morning. I think we'll be in Court in less than thirty days. They're in a hurry. If that doesn't fit with your schedule, I might be able to jockey a day or two either way, but a real continuance is probably out of the question. Judge Minton gave me most of what I asked for in pre trial this morning. And he did that not out of any deep seated appreciation for a defendant's predicament in taking on the power of the government and the law enforcement establishment. He wants to move the case along, steamroller it to the court room on a velvet carpet."

"This Minton," asked Dottore, "he a stand up guy?"

"He's okay. I've been in his court before. There'll be no surprises. Don't worry about him. It's the jury that counts."

"And you're the best there is there, right," smiled Tony Persia, a strange light showing in his deep set eyes.

Fixer tipped his glass in recognition of the compliment.

Tony Persia then changed the subject.

"I asked you here tonight Johnny to let you know that Joe and I will be working on a deal shortly, something we want you to handle. My case is first priority - of course. But when I get acquitted, we're moving right into another deal. I'm moving some things around now. It's an international purchase. You're gonna have to handle the contracts and work with Joe on the financing."

"Glad to," said Johnny Fixx. "I'm your man, Tony."

"At's my boy," grinned Persia. "I knew we could count on you."

73

"Joe's gotta catch a plane back to Vegas, Johnny. I'm driving him to the airport."

"I'll be seeing you soon," said Dottore, as he moved to follow Persia out.

Dottore reached into his jacket pocket and came out with an envelope. "Here's twenty to spike the deal, Johnny. We'll be in touch."

Johnny Fixx hefted the envelope full of cash. Fixer grinned and muttered, "a new venture - christ, Tony, who the hell do you want me to kill?"

# C H A P T E R   S E V E N

As the clock ticked down to Tony Persia's trial date, Johnny Fixx began getting the feeling that the Prosecution believed they were playing a pat hand. The Grand Jury minutes were duly delivered, not a week, but ten days before the expected jury pick date. Rudy Kutter was on the phone as his messenger arrived at Fixx' office to advise his opposite number that the plea offer was officially withdrawn. Judge Minton continued to reserve decision on the production of the police investigation files for the series of arsons that Jimmy Doyle allegedly committed prior to the Passeo Motel wiring.

John Fixx couldn't quite put his finger on it, but his instincts told him to buy some time to reassess Persia's position and maybe get a handle on just what exactly the prosecution had. But an eleventh hour effort to obtain a continuance failed and Judge Minton moved the case up on the trial calendar so that jury selection began exactly one month to the day after the pre trial conference in Chambers. It wasn't that Judge Minton was totally unreceptive to some delay but the case had taken shape so simply around the testimony of informant Jimmy Doyle and the forensic evidence concerning the prints on the alleged pay off envelope and money that the defense really was hard pressed to come up with some half way credible hook on which to hang the continuance application.

There was some indication that the defendant might have a medical condition which conceivably could make him unfit, at least temporarily, for trial. But then Tony Persia just as suddenly became uncommunicative about his condition, despite the repeated pleas of his lawyers, and the defense tactic died as Johnny Fixx was left out on the end of a limb with nowhere to go. Without the medical basis, the defense motion was left to be predicated on basically unsubstantiated generalities.

Judge Minton was courteous but direct in denying the defense motion for a continuance. No platitudes about justice delayed being justice undone. Just the direction, "let's get on with it counsellors."

"We'd like to renew our application, your Honor," said John Fixx, "to receive and be able to review before trial the police investigation files for the series of six arsons in which we believe Jimmy Doyle was the perpetrator."

The Judge deferred the defense application to review the files "unless or until either the police or Jimmy Doyle takes the stand at trial."

"Half a loaf, eh," whispered Fixx to Max Gale as he returned to counsels table.

Both John Fixx and Max Gale shared the feeling that the absence of an outright denial from Judge Minton probably meant that he would rule in their favor when the matter again was raised during the taking of proof at trial.

And so it was that Johnny Fixx began the process of jury selection with an uncharacteristic sense of uneasiness. Rudy Kutter had declared publicly that he would personally prosecute Tony Persia, and true to his word, he was handling jury selection. Judge Minton had screened the panel of potential jurors down to one hundred twenty warm bodies. The Court increased the number of challenges each side could use to knock jurors off the panel for unfitness perceived only in the eye of the examining attorney - peremptory challenges having nothing to do with "cause" - to twelve, and by noon of the second day, the prosecution had used eight of its peremptory challenges, the defense six.

Finally, the attorneys agreed on the suitability of the first juror, and as was often the case, five more followed her in short order. The six jurors duly took their oaths and were seated on the permanent trial jury panel. A black female grade school teacher, aged fifty six. A black construction superintendent, aged sixty. A Chicano hairdresser, aged thirty four. An Italian accountant. This guy was a close call for Fixer. The ethnic factor obviously in his favor, but the profession normally not one sympathetic to the imputation of fraud in business dealings. A middle aged housewife, mother of two, fairly well preserved. Fixer liked her voice and the way her eyes seemed to follow him around the court room as he shifted position to ask his questions. Maybe a glib dandy in the courtroom was her cup of tea. Fixer would try to fill the bill. The last was a disabled Nam vet who made his living repairing computers. Fixer was surprised that Kutter failed to use a challenge to drop him off, especially in light of Fixer's war record and occasional involvement in veteran's organizations.

Fourteen jurors sat the box as both counsel took turns questioning. Fixer studied the clip board on which were placed the seat position and name of the fourteen candidates for the remaining seats on the jury. He took a mental snapshot of that clip board and instantly committed the names to memory. It was an acquired skill, but one that Fixer believed scored points with the jurors. They appreciated an attorney's ability to lay down his name list and chart, stare them in the eye, and address them by name.

Fixer dropped off a retired IRS agent. He noted an objection that a retired government employee should have been removed during the court's preliminary screening, rather than by one of his precious peremptory challenges. Rudy Kutter dropped off two ladies, one a career executive, the other a home maker, but both of the Jewish persuasion. It seemed that Kutter wanted no part of the stereotyped liberalism of any Jew regardless of their answers to specific questions concerning the case, and their professions of open mindedness and impartiality.

A Chicano union executive passed muster by both sides and was sworn and seated. A retired librarian was a gamble, but Fixer left her on. There was some snap to her answer that she didn't presume anything simply because the police pointed the finger at a defendant. A lady college professor, newly appointed to the USC faculty for marine studies, and transplanted from Utah. Her background was so improbable considering what she specialized in that Fixer decided to give her a chance. Also it was possible that living in Mormon country made her relatively unblemished in terms of mafia watching in the press and media. A lady veterinarian who specialized in horses was a shot in the dark. She looked a bit dykish but her preoccupation with horses, an avocation she unknowingly shared with Tony Persia for entirely different reasons, might in some secret psychic sense make her sympatico with the defendant, at least that's how Fixer rationalized leaving her on.

It was minutes past five and both lawyers kept at the three remaining jurors, each with only one peremptory challenge left. A voluptuous blonde interior decorator, her severely cut hair and business suit doing little to hide her attributes, passed muster for impartiality and intelligence. Kutter seemed taken with her. Fixer wasn't sure, but finally said "acceptable" and quipped under his breath to the prosecutor as they bumped elbows, "you owe me one Kutter."

The Big Fall

A gay interior decorator, an unabashed flamer, and a jewish matron, were the remaining pair.

Johnny Fixx took Kutter aside.

"Look Rudy, I sense that you're about to knock off Mrs. Spindleman. I'll give you John Anthony there as the last juror if you leave Mrs. Spindleman as first alternate. What do you say?"

Kutter had been at it too many hours to still be contentious.

"You got it Fixx. All we need is one more alternate."

Four candidates were led into the court room. Judge Minton took the stand in anticipation of the process of jury selection being completed. It came down to a rotund bartender recently transplanted from Bakersfield. Walt Williams had been a marine in Korea and earned the silver star. He looked to have seen it all come down the pike in triplicate. Human frailty figured to be something he could understand up close and personal. Fixer said "acceptable". Rudy Kutter finished his questions and paced before the jury box grinning vacantly at Walt Williams. "Okay," he finally said, and Judge Minton congratulated the attorneys for expeditiously completing jury selection, then addressed the twelve jurors and two alternates.

"Ladies and gentlemen of the jury, we will be starting day after tomorrow with the opening statements of the attorneys and the first witnesses. I'll tell you then in detail exactly what you can expect and what is expected of you. For now let me admonish you to refrain from reading anything in the press or listening to any media broadcasts involving this case. Also, you should not discuss this case with your fellow jurors or anyone else, friends, family, co-workers. Is that clear? The object here is for each of you to keep an open mind so that you can function fairly and impartially as jurors in this case."

Max Gale had witnessed the final hours of jury selection. He paused with Fixer in the massive marbled corridor outside the courtroom.

"Twelve souls, hardy and true," quipped Gale.

"I think we did all right," answered John Fixx, his expression remaining uncharacteristically solemn.

"What's the problem, John?"

"I've got a bad feeling about this one Max. Maybe it'll pass once we sink our teeth into whatever Kutter's got. What did you think of Doyle's Grand Jury testimony?"

"No surprises there John. They asked him the minimum necessary to hang Tony and when he'd said enough, they hustled him off pronto. I'll put his testimony together with what Mickey Ferris told me. It might give you some points to hang your cross on."

"Max, did you get a chance to talk to the Judge about the use of those magic words during the trial? I know he ruled that we could ask about 'mafia', 'la cosa nostra', 'organized crime', whatever, during jury selection, but I really believe he's got to bar the use of those words at trial as descriptive directly or indirectly of Tony Persia."

"Your absolutely right, John. And the Judge feels that way too. He agrees that since this is not a RICO case or a mob prosecution, but rather a straight arson case, that any mention of the magic words would be severely prejudicial to the defendant. He will issue a written order before we begin the trial barring both sides from using those words unless the proof or an admission opens the door."

"Well, there you are Max. You set for day after tomorrow?"

"Hell, I'm as ready as I'll ever be. You've seen the requests to charge. Judge Minton has them. I've also put together a trial brief in anticipation of certain issues being raised. I think we'll be okay."

"You're probably on the money, Max."

But still Johnny Fixx had reservations.

\* \* \* \* \*

79

Fixer pulled in to park under his building, then moved to the elevator. His hand was on the pull cord to open the doors when movement sounded behind the nearest pillar.

"Who?" snapped Fixer.

A massive black man with a mane of wild curly hair, a nose guard in another life, stepped into view.

Eddie Ebony.

Eddie was always close to Tony Persia. Persia called him his driver. Ebony was that and more. And recently he'd become a fixture around Joey Dancer's digs at Acme Specialties. As far as Fixer was concerned, whatever Eddie Ebony was into was none of his business.

Ebony's voice was as big as the rest of him. It resonated in the empty space of the garage.

"Hullo counsellor. Mr. 'P' said I was to give you this."

Ebony handed over a thick envelope.

"Tell your boss it's appreciated Eddie."

"Any time," said the black man as he turned to lope out of the garage.

Fixer stepped into the elevator and thumbed the contents of the envelope. Another draft for $50,000. As agreed. And $15,000 cash again. Tony 'P' was doing his best to keep his hired guns happy.

Fixer let himself in, dropped his briefcase, and tiredly shrugged off the overcoat where he stood. No lights. The dark equaled the quiet he needed just then. But the message light was flashing on the answering machine. Fixer hit the playback switch.

Ron Goldstone, sounding extremely agitated.

The Big Fall

"It's urgent, John. You've got to call me tonight. We could be out of time tomorrow."

The tape continued.

Rusty Tannis. Fixer had asked her whether she had a line on Tex.

"Hi, John. It's Rusty. I haven't heard from Tex. Not a clue. Sorry. Will you need me end of the week? I'm free. Give a call."

Ron Goldstone twice more. Then a dusky voice, all lipstick and cigarettes.

Samantha. His ex. A slight slur to her voice with some afternoon drinking.

"Johnny, I'll be at LeBistro drinking myself into oblivion. Stop by and I'll stop drinking long enough to buy you diner."

Fixer breathed 'I just might do that babe' as he dialed Ron Goldstone.

"Jeez Johnny, where you been?"

"I'm in court on Tony's case. You can't hold them off anymore, eh?"

"They're gonna sell you out tomorrow, and then put the property foreclosures in the hands of their attorneys."

"Oh shit Ron. I'm a lawyer. They've got to know I can tie up any foreclosure until we all die of old age."

"Maybe so pal, but what about your stock. They can make that disappear with a couple of phone calls and computer entries. You've got a half a million there and it's gonna be gone in the blink of an eye."

"I've got fifty large for you now. Stop by Le Bistro. Use it to buy me another couple of weeks. I'm about to pop a deal that will bail out my empire."

Fixer worked at sounding convincing even though additional money was purely in the mind's eye.

"I don't believe you Johnny boy, but I'm your loyal servant. I'll do what I can. See you in about an hour at the restaurant."

Le Bistro backed up to Marina del Ray and its forests of mastheads, lanyards snapping reassuringly against sundry mizzens and mainmasts. The hostess' station and checkroom opened directly into the lounge and bar, with the dining room beyond, cantilevered over the water.

Ron Goldstone sat at the farthest corner of the bar. He was basketball tall, gangly, all hands and legs. He looked uncomfortable carrying the beginnings of a paunch. He sported a toupee combed in a pompadour and his massive nose seemed to weigh down his face in a perpetual slouch. Fixer smiled broadly and extended his hand. Goldstone was having none of it.

"Gimme the bread, Johnny. My reputation is at stake here. Come on, none of your bullshit."

Fixer endorsed the draft. Goldstone gave it the once over, slipped it into his inside jacket pocket, and skipped off the stool.

"You look like an unmade bed," quipped Fixer.

Ron waved him off and gestured wildly in the direction of the dining room. "Yer ex is in there fella."

Samantha sat a table at the far end of the room set against the glass wall that overlooked the water. She'd let her hair grow long in the month and a half since last they'd seen each other. She puffed on a cigarette and sipped a martini. Her eyes were on the running lights of a yacht crawling out to sea. Then she turned and spotted Fixer.

"Hi doll," said Fixer as he sat beside her. She was partial to black and this night was no exception.

The dress was cut off one shoulder and hemmed just above the knee. Her tan was magnificent as usual, and her crossed legs caught Fixer's attention. No stockings.

Johnny Fixx had always been partial to Rubenesque women. Short and well rounded. Then he'd met the cool slender Samantha Forbes. Their romance had been whirlwind, an absolutely wonderful love affair for both of them. Even now as he raked his eyes over her, his attraction hit him dead center, a warm glow in his middle that could build easily into the white heat of desire. That would always be there. It was life that had done them in, in particular John Fixx' life, or more appropriately, life style. Samantha Forbes was free spirited and given to personal contradictions. Her passion for running and tennis would never square with her taste for alcohol and tobacco. But on one point she was adamantly consistent. John Fixx kept bad company. A lucrative legal career was too easy for him. Maybe Viet Nam put the curse on the man. Whatever it was, the wound went deeper even than his love for her. He had to spice it up with return engagements with half the hard characters in the Southlands.

Samantha was convinced John would eventually take a step out of line that would take him down. They'd had two children, Andrea, who was interning in Spain to complete her language program at UCLA, and Stephen, who had just graduated from Stanford. It was the children and their security, and her own, that compelled Samantha to break it off with John and in the process tie up beyond the reach of any creditor or governmental agency most of his money and assets. He'd fought the settlement, but really his heart wasn't in it. It was as if he knew that what she was doing was the right thing for the family. He'd remain his own man, and in the process come very close to losing her. Both were aware that time was against them. Neither would change very much. What was left to them were occasional overtures, one from the other that usually ended badly when their fundamental differences inevitably reared their heads.

83

"So sweetheart, you had to get a buzz on to crank up to calling me, eh," he quipped.

She smiled warmly.

"Don't do that Sam. I don't like coming face to face with my own stupidity."

"You said it, genius. Not me."

Another round of drinks was served. A martini for Samantha, a margarita for Fixer, his preferred drink of choice at any festive occasion. He raised his glass to toast her.

"I must have been nuts to let you get away from me."

She raised her eyebrows and retorted, "you're full of shit as always, Johnny my love."

"Still?" he asked.

"Sad to say - sometimes."

She turned to things of family to take the heat off their proximity.

"Have you talked to Steve in the past week."

He nodded "no".

"Well then you don't know the latest. He's talking about enlisting in the navy before lawschool. That's your doing, isn't it Johnny?"

Fixer never concealed his contempt for the profession that was his life's blood. The difference between law and lawyers for Fixer was akin to his views on religion and the clergy. Clerics were in his view weak useless con men who fed on the genuine need of people to believe in a hereafter. It was the same with lawyers. The law as an idealized code of conduct simply overshadowed the mere mortals who turned its practice into a business in its venality one step removed from street walking.

Steve was pretty much sold on getting a law degree. Fixer knew it was useless to try to talk him out of it, but that didn't prevent him from selling his son on taking a deep drink of life in the service beforehand in the hope that another alternative might jell when the boy was a bit older and wiser.

"I did talk to him, but the service thing is his idea. I didn't discourage it. You're right about that. But what the hell doll . . ."

Sam chugged down the martini, the liquor helping some to restrain her from snapping at Fixer. She changed the subject.

"That DA is really going to the mats with you over your pal Persia. Can he really tie up your fee like that?"

"Not really. He was just breaking my balls, a little reminder that you can't fuck with the sovereign. But don't worry kid, the checks will be in the mail - maybe a day or two late, but nothing serious."

"I didn't mean that, Johnny," she chided. "Maybe they're trying to tell you something. You lay down with dogs long enough . . ."

Fixer grinned as he interrupted "and you get rich, babe!"

"You're hopeless Johnny. An absolutely lost cause. I don't know why I seek you out." That smile again. "I guess down deep I must want to do social work."

Fixer reached to clasp her hand. He'd rolled $5,000 in hundreds into his palm and pressed the bills into her hand.

She gasped, "you are a bastard Fixx. It's a good thing I know you or I'd slap you with these bills."

With great exaggeration, Samantha dropped the money into her purse. "Thought I'd return it on principle, eh. Hell no. At least in my hot little hands it'll do some good."

He clasped her hands in his and bent forward to kiss them.

His eyes were riveted to hers. She leaned across and touched her lips to his. He ran the tips of his fingers over her cheek.

"My place?"

She smiled sadly.

"The flesh is so weak. Us good looking dames get so many bad offers - how can we say 'no' to all of them."

They departed Le Bistro his arm around her waist possessively.

*   *   *   *   *

Fixer prowled the loft, turning on the tape player and fixing them drinks. A sadly burnished trumpet and throaty tenor caressed the line of 'Round Midnight'.

"For all the sad young men, eh - and at least one middle aged one?" she quipped, finishing her drink and waggling her glass for another. Samantha fired up a smoke, inhaled gratefully, and accepted her refill.

Johnny Fixx nodded solemnly. "You drink too much. And those goddamned cigarettes . . . ."

"You drove me to it."

"Bullshit. You were a lush and smoked like a chimney when I met you."

"Did I? And here I've been blaming you for my bad habits - it plays well with my friends - especially after you dumped me."

"Dumped you?"

The Big Fall

She put out her cigarette and placed the empty glass on his desk, then stretched, her arms extended over her head. Fixx picked her up, "you're coming with me", and walked into the bedroom. Their undressing became a slow ritual dance, their pleasure something to be savored.

"It's been a while," she breathed.

"Your dentist pal's a little slow on the trigger?"

Her eyes flashed, and then smoked over with the beginnings of pleasure.

"Sorry," he whispered.

"Shut up," she snapped, as she kissed him deeply.

Suddenly they were out of time. "Now," she moaned as she opened herself to him grasping the ends of the headboard as he pressed her legs back onto her breasts to enter her. There was fury to his lovemaking but as he approached the end his thrusts became gentle caresses, his orgasm a sweet flooding that filled her.

He lay on his back, half asleep.

Samantha propped herself on pillows and smoked a cigarette, eyeing her portrait on the opposite wall.

"Did you resurrect that just because you figured you'd get me in the sack."

"Not so, babe," he rasped dreamily. "You're always with me."

"Sure I am - even when you're with some other sweet young thing."

## CHAPTER EIGHT

Day One. District Attorney Rudolph Kutter would begin the proceeding with his opening to the jury. The People of the State of California -v- Anthony Persillato a/k/a Tony Persia, had been selected as one of the test trials for periodic live television coverage. John Fixx had his suspicions about just how random had been the selection process for the Persia case, but decided against making an issue of it. Judge Minton permitted the reporters and cameras in for the openings, and Rudy Kutter seemed to be enjoying every minute of it. His suit was charcoal gray, his shirt a pale shade of the same, cravat scarlet.

Kutter pranced before the jury box, smiling often and working on the folksy 'I'm taking you into my confidence' tone that he believed most effective before a jury. Mary Donlon served as his trial assistant, furiously taking notes, perhaps to permanently memorialize every brilliant utterance of her boss. Beside her sat Sam Turre, Harry Lang's designee to work with the prosecutors and coordinate witnesses and exhibits generated by the department.

"Ladies and gentlemen of the jury," ponderously intoned the DA, as he lapsed into a sing song cadence more in keeping with a Gregorian chant than a legal argument, "this is a case about one man's arrogance - his wanton disregard for human life - and his all consuming avarice that drove him to pay a man to blow up - quite literally, to set explosive charges, to demolish the Passeo Motel."

Kutter deliberately turned to face the defendant and pointed a finger at him, his tone more reprimand than declaration.

"We will prove beyond any reasonable doubt, that Tony Persia paid Jimmy Doyle twenty five thousand dollars to place explosives throughout the Passeo Motel and to wire those explosives to explode when a certain incoming phone call was made. Make no mistake, ladies and gentlemen of the jury, about what we're saying here. The amount of explosives hidden about the Passeo Motel was sufficient to demolish a city block of downtown Los Angeles. These explosives were rigged to explode when an incoming call triggered an electric impulse that would act as a detonator. Miraculously that call never came. But while those explosives remained in the Passeo, literally hundreds of persons, workers, patrons, guests, used the facility, and were potential victims had the explosives been detonated."

Kutter nonchalantly strolled to stand before the defense table. Tony Persia wore a black suit, white shirt, and black tie. John Fixx sat next to him. He too wore black, but his shirt was blue, tie black with blue speckles in it. Max Gale flanked John Fixx. The Professor wore a three pieced gray suit, blue shirt, maroon tie. He alone was dressed for maximum visibility for the television viewers.

Kutter spoke slowly, dragging his words across his adversaries like so much unwanted sandpaper.

"Jimmy Doyle will testify for the prosecution that Tony Persia sought him out and paid him to install the explosives and rig them to go up. Jimmy Doyle did what he was paid to do. There's no question about that. But then Jimmy Doyle began thinking about what could happen. The destruction of the Passeo had become more than just an insurance fraud. The motel was in use. Hundreds of persons used it, dined there, slept in it, all believing they were entirely secure. Doyle knew there could be wholesale slaughter if the motel went up. Jimmy Doyle, not Tony Persia, on his own hook, and in peril of his life from Tony Persia . . . ."

John Fixx was on his feet, gesturing at the bench.

"Your honor, I'd like to extend counsel every latitude in presenting his intentions to the jury. But his last statement is pure fancy and clearly inflammatory. This is the first time we've heard anything about Jimmy Doyle, a career arsonist, being in fear of anything, human or otherwise."

"Sustained," said Judge Minton.

Rudy Kutter sipped some water and continued.

"It was Jimmy Doyle who removed the explosives to prevent a possible catastrophe. He will tell you what he did and when. You can judge his motives and credibility. We believe that when you've heard all of the testimony you will agree that the defendant did indeed pay Jimmy Doyle to destroy the Passeo Motel in order to recoup an investment in the then closed motel from the proceeds of an insurance settlement. You will hear the defense make much of the fact that Jimmy Doyle has avoided prosecution in this case by his agreement to give truthful testimony about his relationship with the defendant. Yes, in a sense, Jimmy Doyle is an informer. But we are satisfied that his statements have been truthful and that he will give truthful testimony during this trial. It is for you to weigh what you hear, to consider every piece of evidence, not in isolation, but as parts of the whole, and to render your verdict. We trust to your ability to see the truth, and to find the defendant, Tony Persia, guilty as charged."

"Mr. Fixx," directed Judge Minton.

John Fixx strolled to the jury box, then quipped, "I'll stand just about here for most of this. With the cameras grinding away, I think my left is my best side."

Laughter, barely suppressed, rippled across the jury box.

Fixer had decided it would be useless to attempt to cut away the forensic proof linking the envelope and bills to Tony Persia. His prints were plastered all over both. Rather than fight the connection, Fixer began by attempting to exploit it.

"Sure this is a case about money that changed hands between Tony Persia and Jimmy Doyle, but that money was paid by Tony Persia as a loan to help Doyle begin an electrical contracting business. It had nothing to do with any flight of fancy concerning any alleged plot to blow up the Passeo Motel. Jimmy Doyle was down and out. He went to Tony Persia and asked for his backing in a new electrical contracting business. Doyle had worked for Persia in wiring both his boat and also his home. Jimmy Doyle had been in and out of legal trouble for years. Doyle as an electrician often had access to a number of residences and places of business. He used that access to operate a lucrative business as a booster, a thief who stole furnishings, appliances, jewelry, you name it, he'd take it, to order. Doyle had been arrested several times as a thief, and twice done time on larceny charges. Tony Persia knew this and was only acting to help a friend whom he was convinced wanted one more chance to straighten out when he loaned him the twenty five thousand dollars as operating capital for his business. That was Tony Persia's sole motive in this case. Friendship, and trust. But Jimmy Doyle had something more in mind. He took Tony Persia's money, betrayed his trust, and continued to act as a booster. But worse than that, and unknown to Tony Persia, Jimmy Doyle also ran a lucrative arson for profit business in the Southlands. It was Jimmy Doyle who was responsible for the Quant Building fire and the Hegedorn Plaza fire three years ago. Do either of those fires ring a bell with you ladies and gentlemen of the jury. Probably not. But they were more than fires in derelict buildings. Two persons were killed in those fires, indigents, street people, bag people, the lost and forgotten of the City of Angels. I doubt that the prosecutor ever heard of them before today either. This then is the prosecutions' star witness. Jimmy Doyle. Thief, arsonist, and murderer. A person who when trapped by another charge he couldn't beat decided to invent a story to implicate Tony Persia in a purely fictitious scheme to blow up the Passeo Motel. Remember that Jimmy Doyle has betrayed a man who believed in him, who loaned him money when no one else would, to buy his freedom. He is in every sense of the word a paid informer. Listen carefully to what he will tell you. I can't believe that persons of your good sense will believe him. When you see through his lies, it is your sworn duty to acquit the defendant. We're holding you to that duty. We expect you to acquit the defendant."

Fixer returned to his seat.

Tony Persia whispered, "nice job counsellor."

Max Gale leaned in to say, "they were hanging on your every word, Johnny. I think we're off and running."

Bill Durning, a Federal Alcohol, Tobacco, and Firearms agent, was the first prosecution witness. Graying and grandfatherly, Durning used a folksy tone in detailing his inspection of the Passeo Motel several months before and his forensics work up. There were traces of C-4 found in the air conditioning ductwork and in the crawl spaces both above the rooms and under the motel. Pieces of the oiled wrap common to the explosive were also found.

Durning then testified to his findings concerning the electrical wiring in the motel. Ghost circuits had been installed that ran to parts of the motel where traces of C-4 had been found. The wiring then tapped into the telephone circuit board. Durning also testified that there was a dry cell sitting in the circuit panel box beneath the wiring.

Rudy Kutter then asked, "Mr. Durning, if the wiring you discovered was connected at its far end to a charge of C-4 and in the panel box to both a telephone circuit and the dry cell, could the connection have acted as a trigger or detonator for the explosives?"

John Fixx was on his feet.

"Objection your honor. There's been no testimony of any such connections. All of this is purely speculative. There are a million and one uses for a dry cell. Telephone wiring is just that. A circuit could have been mid stream in the process of installation. How can this witness tell us anything more than what he observed? The rest is a pure flight of fancy?"

Rudy Kutter responded, "I've qualified Bill Durning as an expert in explosives. He's had twenty years in the military working as a demolition engineer. He's a combat veteran. When he took his retirement he joined the ATF and has been with them for ten years. He works every day on matters like the one in question. He's eminently qualified to share with the jury his conclusions based upon what he observed?"

Judge Minton ruled, "I'm going to let the question stand. The witness may answer."

"The wiring if connected to a telephone circuit and the dry cell would, when that circuit was activated, produce an electrical impulse sufficient to detonate the packet of C-4 on the other end."

"And just how would the telephone circuit be activated, Mr. Durning?" asked the District Attorney.

"All that would be required would have been an incoming call on that line. Just dial the number. When it rings, bang. The whole damned thing goes up."

"Your witness, Mr. Fixx," said Rudy Kutter, as he returned to his seat.

"Good morning, Mr. Durning," began John Fixx. The witness nodded in reply.

"How did you come to be involved in this case? I guess what I'm asking you is who directed you to take a look at the Passeo Motel?"

"LA PD."

"Who specifically in LA PD?"

"Lieutenant Harry Lang?"

"Did you meet personally with Lt. Lang?"

"Yes I did."

"What did he tell you Mr. Durning?"

"He said they had a tip that the Passeo was wired with explosives. He told me that they believed the charges had been removed, but to take every precaution when we did our workup just in case some of the stuff was still there."

"Did Lt. Lang tell you who his suspects were?"

"No."

"And you didn't ask, is that right?"

"That's right. I didn't ask?"

The Big Fall

"You ever met the defendant, Mr. Persia, before seeing him today in this court?"

"No."

"When you did your inspection of the motel, was that wiring you've been talking about connected to anything?"

"No it was not?"

"Could that wiring have been laid in for a new telephone line or for telephone repairs?"

"Sure it could, but . . . ."

"No further questions Mr. Durning. Thank you."

Next up was Amy Browne, an FBI print expert. She detailed the prerequisite chain of custody for the alleged pay off envelope and the bills found in it. Harry Lang had personally handed her the envelope and its contents and instructed her to perform a laboratory analysis of both for prints.

Rudy Kutter showed her prosecution exhibits 3 and 4, a plastic bag containing a brown manila envelope, and a larger plastic bag containing $5,000 in hundred dollar bills.

"Can you identify these exhibits, Miss Browne?"

"Yes. These are the envelope and its contents handed to me by Lieutenant Lang that day when he asked me to check them for prints."

"Now, Miss Browne," continued Rudy Kutter, " did you perform that print analysis on the envelope and the hundred dollar bills that comprise prosecution's exhibits 3 and 4?"

"Yes I did."

"And what were the results of your analysis?"

94

"I found two complete sets of prints on the envelope including a right palm print. Also, there was a thumb print, a right thumb print on one of the bills, and a full right hand set of prints, including the palm, on another hundred dollar bill."

"Did you mark the bills that had the prints?"

"Yes. If you'll look at Exhibit 4, the two top bills are clipped together with a paper clip."

"And did you run those prints through your files?"

"Yes, I did."

"Were you able to find a match in your records?"

"Yes. All of the prints I found were those of the defendant, Tony Persia  the gentleman seated at counsel's table."

"No further questions."

John Fixx smiled amiably as he approached Amy Browne for cross examination. She was pale and thin, her dirty blonde hair closely cropped. There was no make up apparent. She was probably working on an ulcer on the short side of thirty. The lady definitely took her job seriously. Her expression showed nothing, but the eyes closely followed Fixer's every move. They were one step removed from a glare.

"You said Miss Browne that you found the defendant's prints on only two bills. Is that correct?"

"Yes."

"Were there other prints on the remaining bills?"

"No there weren't."

"None?"

"None, Mr. Fixx."

"Isn't that a little strange, Miss Browne. Money does tend to get around?"

"Not if it's new."

"Ah, then these bills looked like freshly minted green stuff, right."

"That's right."

"You folks do anything to try to track down the bank that maybe packaged up this money?"

"No. We weren't asked to."

"Thanks Miss Browne. I have nothing more."

It was mid afternoon and Harry Lang was slated to be Rudy Kutter's next witness. Due to the lateness of the hour, Kutter requested that the Court adjourn for the afternoon and take Lang's testimony in the morning.

Kutter explained, "we'll get him in in one sitting, your honor."

The DA then handed two packets of paper to John Fixx.

"Your honor, let the record show that I've just served Mr. Fixx with James Doyle's immunity agreement and also with LA PD's investigatory file on the series of arsons in the prior four years, all as required by the Court's prior order. I believe the adjournment, if the Court is disposed to so rule, would also afford the defense an opportunity to review these documents prior to the testimony of Lieutenant Lang, and Mr. Doyle, who we anticipate calling after the completion of the Lieutenant's testimony."

"I believe it would be to the benefit of both parties if we were to take the remainder of the afternoon off. So ordered."

The Big Fall

Judge Minton then addressed the jury.

"Ladies and gentlemen of the jury, I would again remind you that you are not to discuss this case with anyone. Also, you should not watch any media coverage concerning this trial, or read any accounts or editorials about the trial in the newspapers. Finally, I've permitted you to take notes during the testimony as a means of keeping your attention and also assisting you in recalling each witness and the sequence of testimony. However, those notes are for your use only in this courtroom. Your notebooks will be collected by the bailiff as you leave and returned to you tomorrow morning. Any questions? If not, thank you for your time and attention and we'll see you in the morning."

Max Gale escorted Tony Persia out of the courtroom. John Fixx was about to catch them when Crystal Lee stopped him.

"We're not on camera John. I know you're under a gag order, but is there anything you can tell me that might get me going in the right direction to develop a story?"

Crystal pointed at the sheath of papers folded under Fixer's arm.

"Any way I might get a look at the immunity agreement and the arson report?"

Fixer knew he was center stage both with Mary Donlon and Sam Turre who remained at the prosecution table shuffling papers while their eyes followed him.

Fixer looked Crystal squarely in the eye and winked, saying in a stage whisper, "sorry Miss Lee, you'll just have to wait until these things go in as exhibits. Judge Minton prohibited us from discussing the case in the press or media and I read his order as restraining us from making any exhibits available in advance of their introduction into evidence. Sorry."

Fixer huddled in the hallway with Max Gale. He thumbed the immunity agreement.

"Anything special," asked Gale.

"Nah. Just the usual whitewash for every crime the guy ever committed. The only hook is his agreement to give truthful testimony at trial. If he doesn't, he's still open to a perjury charge."

"What about the arson investigations?"

"You take them Max. I think you should get together with our pal Mickey Ferris. See whether his recollections concerning the C-4 rip offs coincide with these fires. If so take it as far as he'll let you. Maybe there's a way to trip up Doyle in there."

"I'll call you later," said Max Gale as he moved to the elevator.

"Hey Max," called Johnny after him, "that new money is jabbing my ass. Think about it. Is there a way to find out about shipments of *new* currency to banks? If we can pin down when and what bank, then maybe we can locate a teller with a long memory. I don't know just what that will do for us, but you never know. Give it a shot."

"Will do, John."

# C H A P T E R   N I N E

Dusk settled inexorably over the basin. Harry Lang would be on the stand in the morning. If the Lieutenant ran true to form, he would try to cut to the quick, but his obsessive commitment to bringing down Tony Persia also could be his undoing in the courtroom.

Johnny Fixx drove toward the sea, giving in by inches, inexorably nonetheless, to the pull from a dark corner that began on the other side of the world twenty years before. Whether a fatal flaw or the release valve from his pressure cooker existence, it really didn't matter. Lang would have to keep.

It was a shop in a row of like looking shops in a suburban mall. "Natural Foods" crackled from blue neon above the entranceway.

There were stalls off a main aisle where red meat, fresh fish, nuoc mam, fish paste, dried squid, fruits, and vegetables were offered for sale. Chicken claws hung from the walls. Pots and jars of herbs and spices rested on counters. There was ancient music, shrill and discordant. Viet women tended the stalls and nodded knowingly as Fixer walked to the rear door that opened into the back room. Then a passageway, dimly lit, with dragons and buddhas, and female figures with tentacle like arms, gracing counters and pedestals. And beyond silken curtains, hanging beads, and the sweet smell of bach biens. Within there were rolled sleeping mats in colorful weaves, with rectangular head rests, and hammocks strung around the perimeter of the room.

He sat in the center of the room, a balding blocky man, clad in black pajamas, legs drawn under and crossed in the lotus position. He offered a bowl of rice wine and turned to assemble what Fixer had come for. The pipe and its contents were wrapped in a silken white cloth. Fixer pressed the money into his hand and bowed stiffly from the waist.

Beyond midnight, Fixer was naked in his bed, dull light from a full moon slithering in through the skylight, a bladed fan swishing above. His eyes were riveted on her portrait. She became a mandarin yellow woman, her hair shiny black, cascading to her waist, knelt before him, fixing the forgetfulness. The pipe was long stemmed, its bowl an inverted door knob, teak on the outside, brass in the fire pot. She kneaded the

99

The Big Fall

opium with a metal tool and rolled it into a thick brown tar before pressing it into the hole in the center of the bowl. She passed the bowl over a kerosene flame and nodded reassuringly when it was time. Fixer inhaled, held the pungent smoke, then quickly blew it out. There was rice wine, then the pipe again as he exhaled lazily and vacantly waved a hand to touch the molecules of smoke.

There were four pipes in all, then a stillness beyond quiet. And finally images in the hazy brush strokes of water colors in pastel tones at dusk. It had been a place of festering sores, and open sewers, of dust and heat, and tin roofed reality, a place of perfumed rivers, and singing streams, of luxuriant mists, latticed paddies, and quenching downpours, of lush tropical gardens of brilliant purple and red bougainvillea, jasmine and mimosa, a place of pestilence, torture, and lang-tri, the death of a thousand cuts, a place of soft winds dancing lotus blossom ballets through trembling trees, of mystic sunsets, and thunderous dawnings, of endless webs spinning, and lunar 'eyes' in fragrant pools, a place of pagodas and cathedrals, of needlepoint Buddhist gravestones, and the round stone tombs of long ago dynasties, a place of gothic blockhouses and watchtowers, inscrutable and inexplicable, like Easter Island Monoliths, passed by, but not passed over, a place of saints and soothsayers, of bells tinkling, incense burning, and fruits and flowers offered in ageless temples, of fate and inevitability, a place to listen to the earth, a place where midnight dreams washed away in the glare of the morning after.

Saigon before the fall. The Caravelle in the rose light of late afternoon. She moved through a party for staffers of the U.S. Information Agency who were going home. Johnny Fixx sipped gin and tonic and took in the panoramic view of the City. The great bend in the Saigon River. Wharves buzzing with the comings and departures of fighting ships and transports. Beyond, vagrant rice paddies, a patchwork quilt flanked by palm groves and bamboo shoots, green on green, an expanse of luxuriant jade rippling in the wind. Artillery barrages far distant flashing across the sky, evening vespers for the City.

She brushed past, her hip touching Fixer's shoulder like a wisp of silk falling from a woman's bosom. She made an apology. Her eyes were knowing, her smile dusky.

"Join me," he said.

100

The guns finally fell silent as the tropical sky deepened from rose to violet, then gave way to the ivory pincers of the moon dancing on the inky horizon.

She was regally attired, a flowing ao dai in black and gold, a gold crown atop her head, spiraling to a point like a temple chidi. All jasmine and jade, her dark almond eyes flashed the promise of what was yet to come. Smoke swirled in serpentine paths through dappled night light that floated lazily from the sky light above. She smiled lasciviously, mimicking the wai sign as the ao dai fluttered to her feet. He was naked, craving her intoxication. But then she moved away. He was numb, the effort to sit up nearly beyond his capacity. She turned to him, her teeth snarling, a pistol in her hand. 'VC' slammed home but Fixer was beyond caring and slumped back into the bed to await the inevitable. She hesitated to savor her moment, and that saved him. Joey Dancer crashed through the door, firing his .45 as he came. Two slugs tore through her breast bone lifting her off her feet, slamming her into the bureau.

"You'll never learn, asshole. Never learn . . . ." cried Joey Dancer.

The wash of the bladed fan above became the roaring rotors of Hueys ferrying the dead and soon to be dying. And then they were still, the choppers bloating and decaying hulks, rotor blades lazily turning in the wind, bodies hanging from the blades, rotting in the equatorial heat.

"No, no!" he screamed, snapping back, flailing at the sweat soaked sheets. Time and place dully registered.

"Lie back," she whispered, sponging him, then loving him again.

Her ebony hair caressed his chest, and he ran his finger tips over her face.

Crystal Lee.

He passed out and suddenly was awake again. Samantha watched him from her portrait, her disappointment filtering through the dark. There were sounds from the office. Fixer moved to the door. Crystal Lee had gotten what she came for as Fixer knew she would. She copied Jimmy Doyle's immunity agreement and Lang's arson report then replaced them in Fixer's brief case. He moved back to the bed. She dressed and let herself out, now with a story to write and a dawn broadcast deadline to meet.

*     *     *     *     *

Johnny Fixx stepped out of the cab and Max Gale collared him at the curb.

"Have you seen the sunrise edition?"

Fixer knew what was coming, but there was no reason to share the prior night with Max. He nodded "no" and Max Gale slapped the first section into his chest. Fixer scanned the headline.

"Police Informant, Jimmy Doyle, a Serial Arsonist?"

"Crystal Lee broadcast the story on the early show and then its in the papers a few minutes later when the sunrise edition hits the stand."

"Understandable, Max. The same holding company owns the TV station and the newspaper. The spirit of cooperation, and all that."

"I was sorting through some papers in the courtroom waiting on you to show up, Johnny. Judge Minton's clerk came in and invited us to a conference in chambers 'asap'."

"So let's go see the man, Max," grinned Johnny Fixx. When Gale's sober expression failed to lighten, Fixx said, "it wasn't me Max. The dame must have found a way to grab what she needed. I didn't give it to her."

Rudy Kutter and Mary Donlon preceded them into the Judge's chambers. Max took a chair behind the sofa. Fixx found the end of the sofa, beside his opponents.

"I don't have to tell you why I asked you in here," said the Judge. "This is serious business. A clear violation of my gag order."

Rudy Kutter glanced at Fixer, then said, "your honor I hope you don't believe that my office had anything to do with this. Crystal Lee's broadcast and the story in the papers are the inflammatory stuff we certainly do not want out there available for the jurors should they turn on the TV or glance at a paper. We had nothing to do with it."

Judge Minton turned his attention to Johnny Fixx. Fixer did not hesitate.

"Your honor, I did not discuss this case with Crystal Lee or any other reporter. I did not give her any documents out of my file."

Fixer cut short his explanation to exclude any disclaimer that he was the source of the story. Judge Minton seemed satisfied.

"Well I can tell you this gentlemen and lady, I intend to press that reporter for her sources. We've got other business to attend to but this matter isn't closed by a long shot."

*   *   *   *   *

Rudy Kutter faced the jury and said, "the Prosecution calls Lieutenant Harry Lang of LAPD to the stand."

Harry Lang was sworn and launched into his elaboration of the investigation that led to the indictment of Tony Persia.

Lang was subdued and succinct. Rudy Kutter apparently had succeeded in persuading him that 'less' would be far more in the context of the trial.

Fixer whispered to Max Gale, "what the hell did they do, feed this guy a horse tranquilizer?"

Lang spoke easily to the jury.

"We discovered that Jimmy Doyle might have been involved in a scheme to hi-jack stolen property from a warehouse. We staked out the warehouse and caught Doyle in the act. He had a long record as a petty thief, two prior convictions. If we succeeded in convicting him on this one, he could have received a twenty year sentence. We interrogated Doyle and finally he agreed to give us truthful testimony about the Passeo Motel in exchange for our agreement not to prosecute."

"Why did you offer Doyle immunity, Lieutenant Lang?" asked the Prosecutor.

"The Passeo Motel situation was particularly aggravated. Hundreds of persons could have been killed had the motel been destroyed. All of them were innocent bystanders. And we were convinced that Doyle had reconsidered what he had done in returning to the Passeo to disconnect the wiring and remove the explosives. It was the man who hired Doyle who we believed should be our target."

Lang glared at Tony Persia.

"That man was willing to trade lives for a few dollars. That kind of person doesn't deserve to be free. If a deal with Jimmy Doyle was the price of putting his boss behind bars, that was a deal we felt we had no choice but to make."

Harry Lang hesitated, then continued with conviction, "It's a deal I'd make every day in the week."

Rudy Kutter turned Lang over to the defense for cross examination.

Fixer regarded his old adversary, then turned to the stenographer, "may I have prosecution exhibits 3 and 4." She handed them to the defense attorney, and Fixer passed them over to Lieutenant Lang.

"Will you please identify these documents, Lieutenant?"

104

Lang cursorily thumbed through them and placed them on the railing before him.

"Exhibit three is the immunity agreement for Mr. Doyle. I witnessed it and Mr. Kutter signed it for the People. Exhibit 4 is the LA PD investigatory file on several arsons."

"What crimes did you believe Mr. Doyle could be charged with after you brought him in for questioning?"

"We had discovered that Jimmy Doyle planned to take down the warehouse I mentioned on direct."

"Tell us about that warehouse, Lieutenant Lang. What went on there."

"They were selling appliances, televisions, vcr's, stereo equipment, cameras, jewelry."

"Were they in the yellow pages, Lieutenant?"

Lang made no response.

"Lieutenant, just what kind of operation was conducted at that warehouse."

Lang cleared his throat, and said, "it was a fencing operation for stolen property."

"And you had information that Jimmy Doyle was going to rip off his partners in crime?"

"Objection to the characterization," said Rudy Kutter.

"No," said Judge Minton, "the Lieutenant has already testified that he could have charged Doyle with a crime arising out of his plan to hijack the warehouse. I'll let the question stand as asked."

"Can you read back the question," asked Harry Lang.

"I'll rephrase it," said Johnny Fixx. "What I want to know is just this, how was it that you knew or had reason to know that Jimmy Doyle was about to take down this warehouse?"

"We were tipped," answered the Lieutenant.

"By whom, Lieutenant. When and by whom."

"I don't think I can tell you that Mr. Fixx. It was a confidential informant. If I disclosed his identity he could be placed in considerable danger, even at the risk of his life."

"Your honor, we want that name. The informant could shed considerable light on the motives and actions of the informant Jimmy Doyle. Doyle's credibility will be a vital issue in this trial. The Lieutenant's source could give us invaluable information on just why Doyle acted to save himself."

"Confidential informants are always protected in our courts," answered Rudy Kutter. "Besides, I don't believe counsel has made any showing that information he might elicit from the Lieutenant's source is or can be in any way relevant to the issues in this case."

Judge Minton ruled directly.

"I'm going to sustain the objection, but permit you Mr. Fixx to renew your request at a later time if you are able to demonstrate relevance, that at least to this point, I do not *see.*"

A tactical defeat on a point that Fixer initially made perfunctorily. Lang and Kutter fought it a bit too hard. Fixer smelled an opening, but couldn't quite piece any of it together just yet. It would come.

"Lieutenant Lang, let's get back to those crimes you were willing to absolve Mr. Doyle of in order to solve your Passeo Motel case. Tell us again what crimes you thought you had Jimmy Doyle for."

"Well Mr. Fixx, as I said, there was the hi-jacking at the warehouse. Also, there obviously was complicity in the scheme to blow up the Passeo Motel."

"Anything else?"

Lang should have snapped the answer. When he didn't, Fixer knew there was something more, perhaps the reason why the Lieutenant resisted disclosing his source.

"Nothing else, Mr. Fixx," answered Lieutenant Lang.

"Let's talk a little bit about your Passeo Motel case, Lieutenant, okay?"

"You're asking the questions," quipped the Lieutenant.

"Now you had been investigating a scheme to blow up the Passeo, and Jimmy Doyle surfaced out of nowhere to point you in the right direction to bag his boss, right?"

"No. I didn't say that. We had no open investigation concerning the Passeo before Jimmy Doyle began talking to us. He told us where to look for the explosives and he gave a statement that identified his boss and the terms of payment."

"So you had Jimmy Doyle down and dirty for the warehouse hi-jacking, and when the cell door is about to clang shut, pal Doyle suddenly gets religion. Isn't it possible that he invented the story in order to buy his way out?"

"Anything's possible, Mr. Fixx. But I'm convinced in this case that everything Mr. Doyle told us was the gospel."

"Were you surprised Lieutenant to learn that Jimmy Doyle was an explosives man and an arsonist? I mean, as far as you knew, Doyle was a booster - a thief, isn't that correct?"

"Human nature being what it is Mr. Fixx, nothing much surprises me. But to answer your question, we'd never charged Mr. Doyle in any arson case."

Another cute hedge. Lang was sitting on something, and Fixer decided to probe in another direction.

"Lieutenant, let me show you prosecution's exhibit 4 again. Now, that's your department's internal investigatory report about six arsons that took place in the past four years, correct?"

"Right."

"And two of those arsons, the Quant Building and the Hegedorn Building involved the loss of a life. Correct?"

"That's correct. Two people were killed."

"Were any arrests made in those arsons, Lieutenant?"

"No, we never made any arrests."

"But you did have suspects, didn't you."

"Well, we ran the files of known arsonists. Pulled them in and asked them to explain their whereabouts on the nights when the buildings went up. We did that sort of thing, but nothing more. We had no proof pointing in any particular direction."

"Was Jimmy Doyle pulled in for questioning concerning those arsons?"

"No he wasn't."

"Those arsons and the deaths remain open files in your department, right?"

"Yes they do."

"And nowhere in your files - I mean if we were to ask you to bring in all the back up files on these arsons - nowhere in those files would we find any reference to Jimmy Doyle, correct."

"Well I don't think so. No, not that I can recall, Mr. Fixx."

"Now what if your recollection was just a bit off. What if Jimmy Doyle had been questioned or mentioned as a possible perpetrator. And let's take it even a step farther, what if Jimmy Doyle was the character who torched or blew up those six buildings and in the process roasted two innocent persons."

"That's a big 'what if', Mr. Fixx, but it's your examination."

"Right, Lieutenant Lang, it is my examination. So if Jimmy Doyle was responsible for those fires and loss of life, six arsons, two murders, would you have been so quick to grant him immunity so that he could hand you his boss on the Passeo job on a silver platter."

"I can't answer that Mr. Fixx. We never arrested Jimmy Doyle on those arsons or murders."

"Now I notice, Lieutenant Lang, in reading your files, prosecution exhibit 4, that there were some similarities between the Passeo and both the Quant and Hegedorn arsons. You might say the 'modus operandi' was the same. For example, both were triggered by a phone wire. Also both were explosives jobs, C-4 to be exact. Isn't that correct?"

Harry Lang reexamined the files. "You're correct about the telephone detonator and the C-4, Mr. Fixx. But I think you have to go quite far afield Mr. Fixx to conclude from that that the same man was the arsonist."

Fixer grinned broadly at Lieutenant Lang.

"Harry, my friend, I never said that Jimmy Doyle did all those torch jobs and murders. But I think you just admitted the possibility that friend Doyle just might be your guy. No further questions."

## C H A P T E R   T E N

An electrical storm crashed over San Pedro Bay, the thunder penetrating the loft as dull thuds. John Fixx was walled up in his studio - a million miles from the pit of the courtroom. The subject matter was the night's broadcast. Charlie Parker in California after the war.

Bird had played with Diz in the Apple and followed him to bring be-bop to the west. The Southlands wasn't quite ready for the new music and Dizzy soon returned east. Bird remained in California and fortuitously his young friend Miles Davis turned up. After the pyrotechnics of Gillespie, Bird always seemed to prefer the warmer sounds of mid range trumpet virtuosos, Miles and Red Rodney among them. It wasn't that they couldn't hit some of the high notes. They simply seldom heard the new music in that register and perfected their sounds an octave lower.

A club in Little Tokyo became home base. Howard McGhee shared trumpet duties. There was no liquor license and McGhee's wife did double duty, taking the cover charge at the door and selling set ups behind the dry bar for the patrons who brought their own. Soon however Bird's connection through Moose the Mooche dried up. Parker drowned his regrets in alcohol and finally totally lost his equilibrium. He disappeared and was found wandering naked on the street after setting fire to his bed in a rooming house. Bird spent the balance of his west coast tour in Camarillo, fighting to cleanse his blood of dope and booze. He'd win that one but Parker wryly commented that removing the demons from one's head was quite another matter.

For Miles, the west coast with Bird was really the beginning of his trumpet style and a window to eventual immortality. The music was mostly air shots on Savoy and Prestige. Fixer finished his tape, threaded the machine, and set the timer Mark Nider had recently installed that would interface his equipment with the studio's and kick on the broadcast at midnight. He figured to do the intro live, but the timer was a fail safe just in case he dozed off.

A hot wind whipped rivulets of rain against his glass wall. The street level intercom buzzed.

"Who," called Fixer.

"It's me," answered Max Gale. "I'm coming up."

Max breezed in and dropped onto the sofa. Fixer pointed at the bottle of Jack Daniels. Max nodded "yes" and Fixer poured two glasses half full. They sat silently sipping the brown fire as nature's light show flashed outside.

"I think we're doing all right," said Gale.

"It's a standoff, Max. We're holding our own. But if this guy Doyle turns out to be a good witness, Tony's got a problem. Mickey Ferris might be our ace in the hole."

Max frowned.

"What is it?" asked Fixer.

"I've been baby sitting the guy, just like we planned, but he's nervous as hell. I was just with him. Kutter smells it but I'm pretty sure he doesn't know about Ferris yet."

"So where does that leave it?"

"The guy doesn't want to testify without full immunity. He says if we subpoena him and he doesn't have immunity, he'll just take five and claim the privilege against self incrimination."

"I guess you can't really blame Ferris, Max. But we've got to have him. Get to Kutter before court tomorrow morning. See the Judge if necessary. Kutter's got to grant this guy immunity. The Judge has to back us up. Hell, if Kutter can dish out immunity baths for a scum bag like Doyle just to throw the blocks to Tony Persia, then why not grant Ferris immunity so we can all get to the truth."

"The logic is compelling," smiled Max Gale, "but . . . ."

"I know, Max. I know."

The Big Fall

*  *  *  *  *

It was past one when the phone rang. Fixer was half out and knocked the receiver to the floor as he thrashed across the end stand to retrieve the phone.

"Hullo, hullo . . . ."

"Morning, John. Say thank you," answered Joey Dancer.

Fixer followed the phone to the floor and sat with his back propped against the bed.

"What have you got," he asked.

"You remember that new money that fink Doyle turned up with - the dough that had Tony's prints on it?"

"Sure, sure."

"I know Max is working on it, but we've got some pals in the banking business. I called in some markers to get them to find that currency shipment - you know the date and amount, the bank, anyone involved. They came through, Johnny."

"Lay it out, Joey."

"It was half a million in fifties and hundreds delivered to First Trust on April 10th, last year. One of the guys in First Trust does some business with me and he went over his employee rosters and came up the names of anyone who touched that dough."

"What does it sugar off to?"

"We got lucky. Persia's got accounts in that bank. One of the tellers remembers Tony coming in a week later on the 17th of April and asking for twenty five thousand in large bills."

The Big Fall

"Christ, Joey, you're helping to dig Tony's grave. That only pins down what Kutter's been saying about the money changing hands."

"Ah but there's more old buddy. Seems this teller remembers Persia and has a recollection of what he said that day when he picked up the dough. Persia told him that he was going to lend the money to help put a friend in business."

"Joey, this better be on the legit. It might come down to Tony's only chance to beat this thing. Did the guy remember anything else?"

"Nah. I tried to pin it down even better. You know, ask him whether Tony mentioned anybody's name - I was fishing for the guy to say Jimmy Doyle. But I didn't feed him the name and he couldn't remember anything more. So I left well enough alone."

"Give me his name. I'll have Max take his statement and then I'll file a statement of intent to use him as a witness in Tony's defense. Kutter will send some of his boys to rattle the guy. If he stands up, we'll put him on. With any luck, he just might break Doyle's back even if Jimmy puts on a good show tomorrow."

"Chuck Mercer," said Dancer, who then rattled off his work hours, address, and phone number.

*     *     *     *     *

Max Gale's glum countenance said more than words as he met Fixer for coffee before the morning court session.

"No dice John. Kutter won't recommend immunity. The Judge won't order it. He says we'll have to make an offer of proof if and when we want to put the witness on. Then he'll rule. I can't read his inclinations. It's fifty-fifty."

"That's about what I figured. Dancer came up with a bank teller who says he's the guy who gave Tony 'P' the twenty five large. The guy

113

apparently remembers Tony telling him the money was ticketed for a pal who needed the loan to start a business."

The fit was almost too perfect. Max Gale raised his eyebrows.

"I know, Max. But if it checks out we're gonna' have to run with it." Fixer glanced at his watch. "Come on pal, let's do it. We wouldn't want to keep Jimmy Doyle waiting."

Jimmy Doyle was tanned and collected on the stand. He wore gray slacks, and a black sport jacket over a rose colored shirt. Life in the witness protection program apparently agreed with him.

Rudy Kutter wasted no time taking Doyle through his testimony. Doyle never missed a beat relating in a measured tone his acquaintance with Tony Persia and Persia's proposal that Doyle wire the Passeo Motel to blow.

"The Tony Persia you are referring to, Mr. Doyle, is he in this Court?"

"Yes he is."

"Will you point him out?"

Pointing to the defendant, Jimmy Doyle said, "Mr. Persia is the person sitting between the attorneys at the defense table."

"Let the record show," solemnly intoned Rudy Kutter, "that Mr. Doyle has identified the defendant, Tony Persia."

"Did Mr. Persia say anything to you about his reasons for wanting to destroy the Passeo Motel?"

"He said he had a lot of money tied up in the place and that since it couldn't open, he figured to drop a bundle. He told me, 'better the insurance company than me'."

"How much did Persia pay you for your services in rigging the Passeo Motel to blow?"

"$25,000 in cash."

"I show you prosecution exhibit 3 and ask you whether you can identify it," said Kutter as he passed the manila envelope to Jimmy Doyle.

Doyle handled the envelope, ran his eyes over it, and answered, "Yes, this is the money envelope he gave me. The twenty five thousand dollars was in this envelope."

Doyle pointed to a check mark on the corner of the envelope and said, "I marked the envelope there. That's my mark, so I'm positive this is the envelope."

"I show you prosecution exhibit 4 and ask you whether you can identify it?"

"Sure, sure, that's what was left of the money that was in that envelope. I turned it in to you when I agreed to testify. I made those check marks in the corner of each bill in your presence. You told me to make those marks so that there'd be no mistake as to the money later on. So that's what I did."

"Now by my count there's only five thousand dollars there Mr. Doyle, is that right."

"Yes. I turned in five thousand dollars. That's all I had left of the twenty five. I bought myself a car and blew the rest in a week in Vegas."

"When did Mr. Persia pay you this money?"

"Middle of April, last year. I'm not a hundred percent sure, but my birthday is on the 19th and I was in Vegas to celebrate and I had the dough. So he must have given it to me sometime around the 15th. You know, a day or two either way."

The Big Fall

Johnny Fixx leaned around his client to whisper to Max Gale.

"Maybe we're gonna get lucky here Max. Jimmy's recollection is on the money with that guy Dancer found at the bank."

"Now Mr. Doyle, what did you do after Mr. Persia gave you the twenty five thousand dollars?"

"What I agreed to do. The wire job on the Passeo. I planted the explosives and ran the wire to the telephone circuit board. I also wired in the dry cell. Tony said to do it on a weekend when the construction crews had pulled off the job. So that's how I figured it. But then I began watching the place. Persia never told me that they'd gotten their occupancy permit. The place opened and there were people coming and going. My god, I couldn't just let it go up. Bricks and mortar are one thing, but when I saw all those people in the place, I knew I had to pull the plug on the deal. So that's what I did."

"What exactly did you do, Mr. Doyle?"

"I got back into the place. That was no easy order. I'd planted the stuff when the motel was closed. With the staff in there and guests, it was harder to move around and not arouse suspicion, but I managed to do it. I wore coveralls and told them I was working on the air conditioning duct work. That permitted me to remove the C-4 and kill the wire job."

"Where did you get the C-4?"

"I ripped it off." Doyle chuckled. He winked at the jurors. "What can I say. I'm supposed to tell the truth here, right. So I grabbed the stuff at a construction shack in Anaheim. It wasn't a problem."

"What did you do with the explosives you removed from the Passeo?"

"I figured the best bet was to put the stuff back where I'd found it, so that's what I did."

116

"What did Mr. Persia have to say about your decision to abort the Passeo job?"

"He was steaming. I offered to give him back his money, but he threw the envelope at me and said I'd better keep it for my funeral."

Kutter handed Jimmy Doyle his immunity agreement.

"Mr. Doyle, please describe the circumstances that preceded your signing this immunity agreement."

"I was casing this warehouse in the barrio. See I had information that they were running a cash and carry operation there, big time. At any given time there might be a half million dollars in appliances there. Hell, street price on the stuff was six figures, maybe more. And they were dirty. I figured to cowboy it in there and load up a tractor trailer and leave it high and dry. The place was always dark after three in the morning. Nobody ever showed before nine. That gave me half the night to break in and take what I wanted. They were wise guys themselves so they didn't figure anyone would dare take them down. There were no alarms, no dogs, nothing. All I had to do was drive up, pick the door lock and help myself."

"What happened?"

"Well everything was going like clockwork. I got in and started moving merchandise. Then all hell broke loose. Half of LA PD was there. Lieutenant Lang grabbed me. I guess the police had the place staked out for weeks. They were going to take down the whole operation. When I showed up, they had to settle for me."

"What did Lieutenant Lang tell you?"

"He told me that I was a two time loser and that he had me dead to rights for burglary and larceny. Another conviction would put me in the joint as a persistent felon for ten to twenty minimum."

"Did the possibility of doing time turn you?"

"Look I'd be lying to you if I said I wasn't concerned about doing that kind of time. Hell, I'm in my forties. That takes out the last good chunk of my time. But that alone didn't do it. To tell you the truth, the thing that really pushed me to do the deal was what Persia had said to me. I really thought he'd get me. Sooner or later. Those old timers can take their time on squaring an account, but they never forget."

John Fixx rose and gestured at the witness, "objection, your Honor. 'Old timers', their propensities, and their 'memories' are not in issue here. Move to strike that part of the witnesses' answer. We would also ask the Court to instruct the witness to be responsive and to stick to the information asked for."

"Objection sustained. The witness will refrain from an editorial comment. Just stick to what Mr. Kutter is asking you."

"Sure, your Honor. Sorry," said Jimmy Doyle. "Well, what was I supposed to do, keep my mouth shut and become a clay pigeon. I insisted that my family be protected. When Lieutenant Lang said he could structure it that way, I agreed."

"Mr. Doyle, has your testimony today been truthful in every respect."

"It has Mr. Kutter. It happened just like I said it did."

"Your witness."

Johnny Fixx strode directly to the witness stand. He grinned broadly.

"Nice suit and nice tan, Jimmy. The program must agree with you."

"Objection, your Honor," roared Rudy Kutter.

"Sustained. The witnesses' dress and tan were not opened up on direct." Judge Minton smiled despite his resolve to remain stone faced.

The Big Fall

"How are you Jimmy, long time no see," said Johnny Fixx, beginning again.

Doyle grinned and reached for his water glass.

"Okay if I call you Jimmy?"

"Sure."

"Jimmy, you were a professional thief, right?"

"You might say that."

"Well how was it that the defendant came to buy your services to blow up the Passeo? Now what I'm getting at is that Tony Persia, being in your words one of those old timers with a long memory, must have known about your talents as a booster, right. So how was it that he hired you as a wire man and demolitions expert, even conceding here that you could be telling the truth."

"I don't really know, Mr. Fixx. He came to me with the job, outlined what he had in mind, and I needed the money. So I said I was his man."

"Well Jimmy, your immunity agreement covers everything from the beginning of the world until the moment you stepped into this court room, isn't that correct?"

"Yes. That's my understanding."

"So if you had some previous on the job training in being a matcher or demolitions man, or wire man, you could tell me about it and the police couldn't charge you, right?"

"I think so, Mr. Fixx, but I'd never done anything like that before. I worked odd jobs on construction over the years. So I had a lot of opportunity to see how guys handled charges, things like that. But the Passeo was the first time I ever actually placed charges and wired a place."

119

"That trigger - you know what I mean - wiring in that dry cell to a telephone line and setting off those charges with an electrical impulse when the phone rang, that's pretty exotic stuff, wouldn't you agree?"

"Yeah. I'd have to say you're right Mr. Fixx. But again, it was one of those things I picked up. As a matter of fact you can check it out for yourself. I got it out of a book on terrorism in the LA public library. Bernard Fall was the author. It's right in there."

Doyle chuckled. "The two stretches I did gave me a taste for books. Nothing like them to get you through. That's why I spend a lotta' time in the library. You'd be surprised who you see there. Remember Bobby Fisher, the chess master? He's there all the time."

The sonuvabitch was holding up, just like Fixer feared he would, and he was glib and articulate to boot, with just the right combination of street smarts and sincerity.

Fixer reached for the prosecution's exhibit on the arson investigation and passed it to Jimmy Doyle.

"Mr. Doyle, have you ever seen that report before?"

"No."

"Take a read through it."

Doyle read the report, then looked up.

"Now that report details the police investigation on three arsons, is that correct?"

"Yes."

"Take them one at a time. Did Lieutenant Lang or any other policeman, or prosecutor ask you about any of those arsons?"

"No."

The Big Fall

"Take a good look at those dates, Mr. Doyle. In particular the Quant Building, and the Hegedorn Building. Did you ever purchase explosives, C-4, at or near any of those dates?"

"No I didn't. I don't know anything about these fires. I'm sorry people lost their lives, but these are nothing I had anything to do with."

"Let's return to that twenty five thousand dollars you say Tony Persia gave you. You'd been in and out of trouble for years, right?"

"That's a fair statement."

"And Tony Persia was an acquaintance. An old timer as you put it."

"That's right."

"And Mr. Persia had a certain reputation for generosity, didn't he?"

"Well I don't know that I'd put it quite that way, but Tony was known to help a friend."

"And if that friend had done time, once, maybe twice, and gone to Tony for a loan, a large loan, say twenty five thousand dollars, would Tony consider giving the man that kind of money to start a business, you know what I mean, for one last chance to be straight."

"I couldn't say Mr. Fixx. But that wasn't why he came to me."

"Did you go to him for money?"

"No. He found me. That's on the straight."

"Now when Lieutenant Lang pinched you at the warehouse, what did you tell him."

"I tried to talk my way out of it. I had a phony bill of lading for the stuff. I told Lang that I was just making a pick up."

121

The Big Fall

"So you lied to Lieutenant Lang, right?"

"Yes."

"And you didn't volunteer any information on the Passeo to him at that time, right. That was kind of a half lie, wouldn't you say."

"Your words Mr. Fixx, not mine."

"And you've made your living for years as a thief, right, a professional thief."

"You're right."

"So your life has been based on consistently breaking the law and lying when you had to, isn't that a fact."

"There were times when I lied. I had no choice. But not always."

"So when Lang had you dead to rights for the hijacking, he told you he had to have somebody, right, you had to give him somebody he really wanted so that you could save your...."

"Not in so many words."

"But that was the deal, wasn't it Mr. Doyle."

"I agreed to tell him what I knew about the Passeo, to be truthful. That was the immunity agreement."

"Now you lied in the warehouse that night. You stole for a living. You held back what you knew about the Passeo then, and when finally you were trapped like a rat in a corner, then you came clean about the Passeo, right."

"It didn't happen that way. I had no choice."

"When did you stop lying, Mr. Doyle?"

122

"My testimony has been truthful."

"Really! No further questions."

* * * * *

Johnny Fixx sat on a bench with Max Gale in the hallway. "The bastard held up, Max. I'll make the offer of proof on Mickey Ferris first thing. Have both of them in court at 9:00 a.m. Be sure you take Chuck Mercer through what happened at the bank that day. The date is vital."

"Will do, Johnny," said Max.

Harry Lang emerged from the crush of spectators filing out of the courtroom.

"Fixer, you're a fucking marvel. We've got your boss dead nuts, and you're gonna' make it close just because you're one slippery bastard. If you ever decide to go straight, give me a call."

"I'll do that Lieutenant, when they finally catch up with you. Count on me, I'll take your case gratis."

Lang chuckled, "I bet you'd do that, pal. Sure you would."

## C H A P T E R   E L E V E N

Sonny Bamboo hovered getting the tempo of the slashing wind, felt a lull, and touched down in the temporary vacuum on the building top. Fixer sprinted to enter the helicopter before the wind picked up again. There was an explosive feel to the night, dry heat and something more.

Johnny Fixx pulled himself in and screamed "go". Bamboo lifted off and flew south over the Bay and down the coastline.

"Those tight asses from the Grievance Committee were in to see me, Johnny."

"You do like I told you?"

"Sure, sure. I let them take a look at the checkbooks, invoices, receivables - shit, I told them while they were at it, why didn't they do my annual audit, seeing like they already had done half the leg work."

"Thanks, Sonny. They'll get tired of it sooner or later."

"What about Tony. How's it going, Johnny?"

"It's a horse race Sonny, but I'm uneasy. I called you to get away from it for a while. Am I screwin' you up tonight?"

"Nah, I'm done with my rounds. I figured to sneak under the military radar to have me a looksee at some goins on down the coast."

"What's happening?"

"They're putting on a show near El Toro Marine Air Station. Some kind of night flight training in F-18's. You game?"

"Hey Sonny, I said I wanted to get away from it, not get blown away in the wash from a bunch of supersonic jets. That's restricted air space isn't it."

"I'm not gonna' violate their airspace, just kinda nudge it and hang there to catch the show."

Bamboo kept at it in a southerly direction, skimming the white caps until the shoreline was a hazy pattern of light pin pricks.
Bamboo gained some altitude to give himself a cushion should he have to ride out any turbulent down drafts from the jets.

"Here they come," he cried, feeling the company before Fixer could pick them up visually.

A formation of four F-18's night flying blacked out and radio silent screamed past them at 5,000 feet, heading landward.

"They gotta' be doing better than 700 mph. Ain't that something."

Before Johnny Fixx could reply a second formation of four roared above them.

"They're flying too fast to land, where the hell are they going?"

"They fly south a little, I think, through the El Cajon pass, then overfly the mountains and come back down through Banning before they peel down to land at El Toro."

"Those F-18's are too goddammed big. They should get back to the F-4's, light and quick. That's what a fighter plane should be."

"Maybe twenty years ago, my man. Hell no. If Sonny Bamboo was in the shit, he'd kiss ass to get those F-18's to fly in and blow the hostiles back to their ancestors. Come on Johnny, let's circle back north to tinsel town."

Bamboo flew a wide arc northwesterly giving the Burbank airfield a wide birth as he recrossed the shoreline heading inland above Los Angeles proper.

"Where the hell are you heading?"

Bamboo swooped down into Topanga Canyon dropping almost to its floor before pulling up to explode over the rim into the vista of greater LA.

"There she is, Johnny. All plastic blondes with credit card eyes. Ha, ha. My kinda' girls."

Black faces, blacked out, the high rise monoliths of downtown LA were before them. To the left a light flashed then went out but there was movement on one of the rooftops.

"What the hell is that," cried Fixer.

"Damned if I know," said Bamboo as he bore left to take a closer look.

Bamboo hovered and watched and the lights came on again. This time they stayed on.

"Can you beat that?"

A shelf was cantilevered out over downtown LA from the building top. A film crew worked its perimeter filming a dance troupe performing at the very edge against the panorama of the city at night. The wind was holding as the dancers whirled ever closer to the edge.

"What the hell are they doing, Johnny?"

"They're in Japanese costumes. It's their usual morality play. See over there," called Fixer as he gestured wildly at the action on the roof.

"Yeah, yeah. That guy with the spear, what's his bag. He's a sentry or something, right."

"You got it Sonny. He probably went to sleep at his post and all the hysterics now are about the inevitable. His honor's gone so he's got to do the right thing."

"Those fucking slants ...."

126

The Big Fall

Bamboo pulled off the building and dropped down to head into East LA. A switcher labored at the head of a fifty car freight on the main line along the viaduct of the LA river.

"Take her down Sonny, I want to see that train."

Bamboo descended to 500 feet as the train clacked past a grade crossing, its whistle sounding a mournful lament, the industrial age beast of burden crying at the night for respite. The red flashers held back the traffic, the clanging warning bell lost in their blade wash, and Fixer stared hard into the core of the flashing reds. He was naked to their pull and he blinked at the lanterns clanging atop the massive horse drawn snow plow thundering down at him.

"Johnny, Johnny."

Bamboo's voice finally cut through to him.

"Look at that, will you."

The wait at the grade crossing had been too long for the patience of the occupants of two of the cars. Six youths piled out and were slamming each other around. One ran to his car and came back brandishing a baseball bat. Another reached into his jacket and came out with a knife.

"There's gonna' be blood," groaned Bamboo. As he said it, the knife slashed across to lay open a boy's belly. "Jesus," he cried. "They ain't never gonna' learn." Police cruisers closed in on the grade crossing. The combatants' cars were trapped in the line of traffic as the freight continued to rumble on through. With nowhere to go they ran on foot into the industrial maze of east LA. Their odd man out staggered and collapsed near the flashers, flailing wildly to hold his guts inside his torn belly.

"What a fucking world," lamented Bamboo as he climbed away from the carnage. "I need some fresh air, man - can you believe that?"

"Yeah, Sonny, fresh air," agreed Johnny Fixx.

\* \* \* \* \*

9:30 a.m. Judge Minton took the bench and instructed his bailiff to hold the jury in the anteroom.

"Mr. Kutter, do you have any other witnesses?"

"No your honor. The prosecution rests."

"Mr. Fixx?"

"We will proceed your honor and reserve our rights to move against the prosecution's case."

"That's acceptable," said Judge Minton. "Will you be calling your first witness?"

"I have an offer of proof, your honor."

"Proceed."

"Your honor, the defense has a witness who will testify that he personally over a three year period sold quantities of C-4 explosive, illegally obtained on a military reservation, to Jimmy Doyle. The witness will testify as to the dates of each sale to Mr. Doyle.    Those dates are each within one week, three within two days, of each of the arsons set out on the investigatory report of LA PD which is a trial exhibit. This testimony is vitally relevant to the credibility of the only prosecution witness to impute any criminal conduct to defendant, Tony Persia. Jimmy Doyle has testified that he has absolutely no knowledge of the arsons on that list, that he wasn't a suspect, that he had nothing to do with them, and that he never handled C-4 prior to planting the charges in the Passeo Motel."

"All right, Mr. Fixx, you may call your witness."

"Your honor, you are aware that I am unable to do so.

He is in this courtroom and available to testify, but since he may have illegally obtained the explosives he sold to Jimmy Doyle, he cannot testify without a grant of immunity from prosecution. We

128

are renewing our application to the Court to order a grant of immunity for our witness. Without immunity, we will be unable to present vital testimony which will show that once again Jimmy Doyle has perjured himself."

Rudy Kutter stepped to a lectern.

"We have previously considered Mr. Fixx' application your honor. Without hearing the testimony and being able to judge its probative value, its relevance, we simply cannot recommend immunity. It's purely speculative. Let them call their witness. After he testifies, assuming his revelations are as devastating as Mr. Fixx believes they will be, we will consider immunity."

"I'm afraid, Mr. Fixx, that I must agree with the prosecution. You may call your witness, but there will be no grant of immunity going in."

"Your honor, it is in my view fundamentally unfair to permit prosecutions, this one in particular, based upon the District Attorney's prerogative to grant carte blanche immunity to known criminals who can help make the People's case, but then to restrict immunity when the subject matter is testimony for the defense which is clearly exculpatory. We must except to the Court's ruling. The witness has declined to testify without immunity, and we will proceed to our other witness."

"Bring in the jury, Mr. bailiff," directed Judge Minton.

"Call Charles Mercer," said John Fixx.

Mercer was stocky and balding, thirtyish, ruddy complected, and wearing a rumpled beige suit, blue shirt, and maroon tie. Chuck Mercer took the oath, and dropped into the witness chair. He was perspiring and Fixer knew his work would be cut out for him.

"Morning, Mr. Mercer. Can you tell us your name and address for the record, and your place of employment."

Mercer stumbled through his address, but clearly stated "I'm employed by First Trust, at the Sunset Branch in Santa Monica."

"How long have you been with First Trust, Mr. Mercer?"

"This is my eighth year."

"What are your duties?"

"It's my job to retire old currency. To catalog it and bundle it for shipment to the mint. Then I also receive shipments of new currency from the mint. I do the accounting for the bank. I also handle large cash transactions for customers. I am familiar with the IRS currency regulations as well as those of the banking board, so it's also my job to file required reports, notices, those kind of things."

As Chuck Mercer got into it, he steadied some. He no longer nervously swiped at rivulets of perspiration that dripped down his cheek into his shirt line. 'Hang with it pal', thought Fixer. 'I'll get you through.'

"Did there come a time, Mr. Mercer, when you did a money transaction with the defendant, Mr. Persia?"

"Yes."

"Before we get into that, Mr. Mercer, do you see Mr. Persia in this courtroom. Will you point him out?"

"Certainly. He's the gentlemen sitting beside your bearded colleague at counsel's table."

"Let the record show," said Fixer, "that the witness identified Tony Persia, the defendant."

"Now Mr. Mercer, tell us about that transaction you did with Mr. Persia."

"Well, it was April 17th of last year. I was working on the paperwork for a shipment of new currency that had come into the bank a few days before. One of the tellers came into my office and said a customer was at her window and asking for twenty five thousand dollars in new currency. She said it was Mr. Persia. He was a good customer of the bank. I told her to send him into my office and that I would personally handle the transaction."

"And did you do that Mr. Mercer?"

"Yes I did."

"You gave Mr. Persia twenty five thousand dollars - a withdrawal from one of his accounts?"

"Yes. I did the forms for IRS with Mr. Persia."

"Did he say anything to you?"

"Yes he did. He and I chatted as I counted out the currency and finished the forms. He told me he was going to be loaning the money to a friend who needed it to begin a business."

"Now you're sure about that date Mr. Mercer, April 17th, 1987."

"Yes. That was the date."

"After Mr. Persia told you about his intention to loan the money to a friend to finance a business, did he say anything else to you?"

"Not that I recall."

"Your witness, Mr. Kutter."

"Did you take a vacation last year, Mr. Mercer," asked Rudy Kutter.

"Yes. It was a summer vacation. The end of July, the beginning of August."

"And you were in Los Angeles, working at First Trust on Sunset in Santa Monica all through April and May. Then June. Is that right?"

"Yes."

"Now you're sure about that?"

"Yes I am."

"No further questions, Mr. Mercer."

Max Gale whispered to John Fixx, "he's setting something up, John. Do you have any idea what's coming?"

"Not a clue. Grab Mercer and check it out with him."

Judge Minton summoned counsel to the bench.

"Mr. Fixx, do you have any other witnesses?"

"No your honor."

"Will Mr. Persia be taking the stand?"

"The defendant will not be testifying, your honor."

"What about you, Mr. Kutter. Any rebuttal testimony?"

"Yes your honor. We'll be calling one more witness, but we've just learned she cannot get here before late afternoon. Would it be possible to adjourn for the day and take her testimony in the morning?"

"All right. I was hoping to get this case to the jury before the weekend, but I'll accomodate you."

Judge Minton addressed the jury.

"Ladies and gentlemen of the jury, we will be taking the rest of the day off. As always, do not forget my warnings not to discuss this case with anyone, or read newspaper accounts or see or listen to accounts on the radio or television. Also, when you return tomorrow morning, bring toiletries and an overnight bag. We should be concluding sometime Friday afternoon, and your deliberations will begin then or on Monday. I'm going to order you sequestered for the duration of the trial beginning with adjournment after tomorrow's session. You'll be staying at a hotel, compliments of the County until you reach your verdict. So make your arrangements today, and we'll see you in the morning."

Max Gale huddled with Assistant District Attorney Mary Donlon as Johnny Fixx escorted Tony Persia out of the courtroom.

"What do you think, Johnny?"

"It's hard to say Tony. Doyle did better than I'd have liked him to, but we scored some points. If this guy Mercer holds up, I think we've got a chance."

"And if he doesn't . . . ."

"Tony, I've got to see Max."

"I've got Eddie bringing the car around, Johnny. Why don't you ride with me after you and Max have your meeting."

"Okay, Tony."

The crowd had dissipated outside the courtroom. Max Gale placed a cigar between his lips, grabbed his lighter, then remembered the smoking ban in public places in the County.

"What's it all about Max," asked Fixer.

"She said they've got somebody who's going to blow Mercer out of the water. She seems confident as hell. I believe her. She said we'd be nuts to let it go that far. Kutter will consider offering the plea deal to attempted arson again, with a recommendation for no more than five in sentencing. They think the Judge will go for it. Christ, Johnny, that's a helluva deal when we're looking at maybe twenty if the verdict is guilty."

"I'm riding with Tony. I'll lay it out for him."

Persia's limo was parked at the curb before the court house steps. Eddie Ebony lounged against the hood. Fixer skipped down the steps and Ebony held open the door for him.

"Where to, Mr. Persia?"

"Just drive Eddie," instructed Persia.

"The car is clean, Johnny. What do you think?"

"Kutter apparently has a witness who will cut up Mercer. If that happens, our alibi story that you withdrew the twenty five to finance a new business for Doyle falls apart. That's the last thing the jury hears before the closing arguments and the Judge's charge."

"You don't like it then, kid, right?"

"They're offering a deal Tony. They'll let you plead to attempted arson. They even sweetened it a little from before the trial. This time there'll be a sentencing recommendation of no more than five years. You know what that means. If you're not a problem prisoner and they max you out, you won't do more than 36 to 42 months. And you'll never be a problem prisoner. I think you can find a way to spend your time in the prison hospital at Springfield. That'll put you out in less than three years. I know that's serious time, Tony, but you're looking at a possible twenty if the verdict is guilty."

Persia was stone faced. He rolled his eyes, then nodded in the negative.

"A few years back kid, maybe. But I'm too old now to do a stretch, even in the prison hospital at Springfield. Besides, I'm working on one last deal - you know, a kind of retirement grand slam, so I gotta' be around."

Johnny Fixx stared Persia square in the eye. Persia's expression brooded, then hardened into a glacial drift.

'Case closed', thought Johnny Fixx.

"Okay Tony. We'll give it everything we can."

Persia grinned thinly.

"You like old movies, don't you kid. So do I. I seen one the other night. Cornel Wilde was the copper, Richard Conte the gangster. Every chance Conte got, he'd say 'first is first, second is nothing'." Persia chuckled, "we got no room for seconds, kid."

\* \* \* \* \*

It was standing room only in the courtroom for what promised to be the final session where testimony would be taken. Max Gale huddled with Mary Donlon in the hallway and delivered the defendant's decision not to take the deal.

"He's a fool," said Mary Donlon, as she turned to deliver the news to her boss.

Rudy Kutter nodded to Johnny Fixx that the 'message' had been delivered, then called his witness. A middle aged matron, nicely dressed, silver gray hair, the vision of everyone's mother, took the stand.

"Will you state your name for the record," asked the District Attorney.

"Alice Madden."

"Where are you employed Mrs. Madden?"

"I'm a ticket agent for Trans-Continent Airways."

"How long have you had that position, Mrs. Madden?"

The Big Fall

"Twelve years."

Kutter reached down to the table before the court stenographer where the prosecution's exhibits rested. He came up with two airline tickets.

"These tickets are marked prosecution's exhibit 23, Mrs. Madden. Can you identify them?"

"Yes, Mr. Kutter. I issued these tickets to a Mr. C. Mercer last April 1st, in 1987."

"What was the destination on these tickets, Mrs. Madden?"

"Round trip Mr. Kutter, from Los Angeles to Mexico City and back."

"And when were these tickets used, Mrs. Madden?"

"The first flight departed Los Angeles on April 5th, 1987. The return flight from Mexico City was on April 28, 1987."

"And were these tickets used, Mrs. Madden?"

"Yes they were - on the dates stated on the tickets."

"Now Mrs. Madden did you personally see to the mailing of these tickets to the customer."

"Yes I did. I have a specific recollection of this because the time was short to the 5th of April. I attempted to talk him into coming into the airport to pick them up. He insisted that I mail them."

"And where did you mail them Mrs. Madden?"

"To Mr. C. Mercer at the First Trust branch on Sunset in Santa Monica."

You could have heard a pin drop in the crowded courtroom. John Fixx was numb as Rudy Kutter said, "your witness."

Charles Mercer was a phony. Dancer must have known about it. The banker's false testimony could be the final nail in Tony Persia's coffin.

"Mrs. Madden, let me ask you this, do you have any recollection as to the identity of this 'C. Mercer'. I mean, could you pick him out of a crowd if we asked you to."

"No sir. I have absolutely no idea what he looked like. It was a telephone transaction."

"Okay. Now what you do know is that someone used those tickets, correct?"

"That's right."

"In your experience in working for the airline, Mrs. Madden, have you ever run into the situation where a person buys tickets and someone else flies under his or her name."

"Yes. It's really quite common."

"So as far as you're concerned, anyone could have used those tickets purchased in the name 'C. Mercer'?"

"I just don't know, Mr. Fixx. It's possible."

"No further questions."

Judge Minton asked, "are the proofs closed gentlemen?"

"Yes they are Judge Minton," responded Rudy Kutter, and Max Gale speaking for the defense.

"All right. The jury will be sequestered and counsel should be prepared to sum up first thing Monday morning."

## CHAPTER TWELVE

The message from Tony Persia was on Fixer's answering machine sandwiched between two each from Ron Goldstone and Crystal Lee. Goldstone wanted money to buy more time with the creditors nipping at Johnny's heels. Fixer had none for the moment. That meant Ron would have to wait. Fixer returned Crystal's calls but the anchor lady was out on assignment.

Tony Persia said simply, "Johnny, I'll be at the Condor. We should talk."

It was another strange night in the basin, drizzle thick enough to cut and the air even on the coast after hours tasting not quite right. Manny Cesar greeted Fixer as he pushed through the Condor's front door. Cesar was the spitting image of actor George Raft and became 'George Raft' to his pals.

"Hey, George Raft, how have you been," said Johnny Fixx.

Cesar shoved an evening edition at Fixer and said, "what a fucking place we live in, Johnny. Look at that. A baby got dragged off by a coyote. Can you believe that?"

"Ah what can you do, even paradise has its tab. And why not an innocent?"

"You know Fixer, yer a real pain in the ass when you get philosophical."

'George Raft' chuckled, and pointed to the backroom. "Persia's in back with Spillane."

Eva Scott walked toward them. She and 'George Raft' were an on again, off again item. Eva was partial to Evita and Fixer embraced her as she pursed her lips, "long time no see big boy."

Evita was a generous woman, from her charms to her disposition. When she was on a tear from Manny Cesar she'd inevitably adopt a hard guy down on his luck and give him everything until she caught him down

138

and dirty with some sweet young thing. Then there'd be hell to pay. She'd been a feature dancer in Vegas and knew how to take care of herself. Even without the flame red hair out of a bottle and thick layer of make-up, Evita was a looker. Dames like her with full figures tended to go to fat when they stopped hoofing, but not Evita. Garish she might be, but the woman took care of herself. Manny Cesar had set her up in a health spa, and Evita led most of the aerobics classes herself. Cesar probably came as close to loving her as he did any woman. The problem was that both shared a street persons conviction that anyone without a hole card was a fool. Each expected the other to cheat, and they did. It really got lost in the wash whether they cheated because they just couldn't do without it, or to get even.

Heavy lumbered to meet them.

"Eh, Johnny Fixx, how's my boy," he said. Heavy was limping again. Last time around his gait had been measured and even. Masters had damaged the leg years before when he drove the getaway car for Joey Dancer after the Beverly Hilton job. Dancer had bailed out of the car just before Heavy totaled it. Dancer kept Heavy out of it when the police nabbed him for the heist. That afternoon driving for Joey Dancer came to be the penultimate moment in Heavy's life and his loyalty to the thief who had covered for him was legendary.

Heavy steered Fixer to the bar saying, "I'm gonna' get the man a drink, okay."

Jonesy was behind the bar and as Fixer sat a stool beside Heavy she reached for the bottle of Jack Daniels.

"No Jonesy, mix me a Margarita. I need a taste of south of the border."

Jonesy smiled lasciviously and ran the tip of her tongue over her lips. She hummed the line to Prez Prado's old cha cha hit, 'Cherry Pink and Apple Blossom White', and began to sway in tempo to the tune.

"Any time lover boy," she cooed.

"The hell you say, doll," grinned Heavy. "The guy can have the shirt off my back, but not the dress off yours."

The Big Fall

Jonesy took the hint and worked the boards at the other end of the bar serving customers trickling in.

"Hey Johnny, everything's gonna' be all right, isn't it. Yer gonna' pull it out for Tony 'P', aren't you?"

Fixer shrugged.

"Bull shit, my man. Your the best in the business. Just like the old days in the Apple. Remember when the Yankees had the 'Clipper'. They owned the bottom of the ninth, and so do you, right?"

"Could be, Heavy. Could be."

Fixer downed his drink and moved toward the back room.

"See you later Heavy."

Tony Persia sat a table against the back wall with Dermot Spillane and waved when he sighted Fixer.

"Evening gents," said Fixer as he joined them.

Persia showed a devilish expression as he summoned a waitress and ordered "double shooters of Bushmills, all the way around."

"Not for me, boyos," exploded Dermot Spillane. "If my sainted father who fell in the Dublin post office with Pearse in 1916 got wind of my drinking irish protestant rot gut, he'd sure as hell come back to kick my behind."

Tony Persia chided Spillane.

"Dermot, yer a bombthrower at heart masquerading as a newsman, now isn't that so?"

"Never mind what I am or I'm not," said Spillane.

"Come here darlin'," he called to the waitress.

The Big Fall

"We'll have double shooters all right. But not Bushmills. Jamesons all the way around."

"We'll be working with Dermot's 'Northern Aid Society', Johnny, just as soon as we get this trial behind us," explained Persia.

Fixer's expression questioned, and Spillane leaned forward to whisper confidentially, "my brothers fighting the Iron Butterfly's latter day 'black and tans' in Londonderry have need for the implements of war, my son. Tony tells me he has a connection with certain Asiatic gun dealers who are fully licensed to bring automatic weapons into the country. If that's true, my principals are willing to pay you a handsome profit for the shipment and take all the risk of moving them once they hit the port of Los Angeles."

"It sounds like an interesting piece of business, Dermot."

"Well that it is, boyo. And let's get to it, the sooner the better."

Spillane drank his double shooter and dropped a ten dollar bill on the bar.

"For the fair Dierdre, an Irish maiden if ever I saw one."

Spillane walked out and Persia chortled, "the waitress is French and Sicilian. I hope Spillane isn't color blind especially where green is concerned."

Fixer moved to the juke box nearest them. Persia loved the big bands and Manny Cesar had stocked one of the boxes with vintage Stan Kenton. Fixer punched in 'Love For Sale', 'Eager Beaver', 'Artistry Jumps', 'Machito', 'Intermission Riff', 'Dynaflow', 'Peanut Vendor', and 'Jump for Joe'.

Persia ordered a bottle of wine and settled in to listen.

"You know Johnny, the kid who arranged this music for Stan after the war was a Sicilian, Pete Rugolo. I think he's still out here doing TV and film scores. And that tune that just played, 'Jump for Joe'. I knew the guy they wrote it for years ago in Buffalo, a 'DJ' named Joe Ricco."

It went that way for an hour as Persia discoursed randomly and the Kenton brass played on. After the tenor sax solo on 'Artistry Jumps', Persia leaned back in his chair and said appreciatively, "that was Vido Musso. I got him a job playing in one of Joe Bayonne's lounges in Vegas years ago when his wife got on his ass and he had to come in off the road for a while. Those were the days."

When the juke box shut off, so too did Tony Persia's good humor.

Persia rasped, "we're in a tough spot, Johnny. You don't have to tell me. I'm not blind. But we'll do what we have to, right?"

"It's up for grabs on Monday," said Fixer, stifling the impulse to again pitch the plea deal. When the old man said 'no', that closed the book, and Fixer knew better than to risk inciting his temper.

"You know Johnny, why the hell should I be the fall guy for that goddamned DA who wants to climb over my dead body to the Senate. What the hell's goin' on here. I'm not public enemy number one. I ran booze during prohibition. So did Joe Kennedy. I never did dirty business. You know that. Somebody who works for me runs dope, I'll cut off his hands."

"Tony, you don't have to tell me what's happening."

"I'm glad you understand kid. When they're out to get you, a man's friends got to walk the extra mile for him, right?"

Fixer nodded in agreement.

"I think we've got all the edge, Johnny. Now don't you tell me any different."

Persia paused and intently eyed his lawyer. "I've got twelve chances to beat the rap, kid, numbers 'one' through 'twelve', now isn't that so?"

142

Fixer nearly gasped, "but Tony . . . ."

Persia placed a hand over Fixer's mouth, then moved around the table to face him as Fixer woodenly found his feet. Tony Persia was a reprimanding father clasping the shoulders of a wayward son who just needed a push to find his way.

Persia kissed Fixer on first one cheek, then the other, and said solemnly, there's no time for discussion, Johnny. We're family. I know you'll do what's right! And remember kid, it's a two way street. You think it's those tight asses who'll give you a break. Never! It's your friends who'll take care of you."

Persia had been gone for nearly two hours and Fixer had taken more than the top third off a bottle of Tequila. Heavy mentioned that Joey Dancer was on his way, and Fixer waited on his friend to appear. Dancer finally walked in and joined him.

"Yer buddy, Heavy, said you were just around the corner. That was nearly two hours ago."

Dancer grinned, "what can I say. Something came up." Dancer saw it in Fixer's expression and waited on his friend to get to it. The explosion wasn't long in coming.

Fixer poured a shooter to the brim, lifted the glass, then abruptly slammed it back to the table, splattering the liquor.

"The cocksucker wants me to fix the jury," blurted Johnny Fixx.

Fixer was painfully aware of choices made. He worked hard at never squarely facing the fact that increasingly his 'good life' was underwritten by Tony Persia and his associates. Not that Harry Lang's crew was any better.

Fixer downed the shooter and whispered vehemently, "different sides of the same fucking coin!"

143

The Big Fall

For Joey Dancer no situation turned on moral choices, only on identifying one's friends and enemies.It had been that way for Joey in the Nam. He soldiered, but also he worked his real profession, stealing, there for the black market. He'd gladly lay it down for his buddies, but not the 'cause'. It was a stinkhole, the slopes shit hole, and they could have it. His tours became exercises in survival and making a buck along the way. They caught him working a smuggling deal with the Shan United Army in Thailand. It became their problem. He was a war hero and a law breaker. What to do about Joey Dancer. The brass decided not to break him. In twenty four hours he had a general discharge and a ticket back to the States. Now Fixer was tearing his guts out over this little piece of business that Persia had to have. A waste of time in Dancer's opinion. Johnny Fixx needed straightening out.

"There's no cops, or crooks, Johnny boy. We're all fuckin' outlaws in one way or another. You know that bullshit, 20% 'do' so that the other 80% can tag along for the ride. They don't have it quite right. It's 20% all right, but the 20% who 'steal' in one way or another and get away with it, that makes the fuckin' thing go. It's personal, Johnny, you've got to draw your own line, pal - and if you cross it, then you've done worse than sewer a pal, or break the law, you've sold yourself out. Nobody can tell you where that line is, Johnny. Not Harry Lang, and his cops, not Tony Persia, least of all me. But I'll tell you this my friend, if it takes dirty business to survive, then don't be a fool. Dyin' is easy, it's staying alive that's the problem." Dancer chuckled, "and in style my friend."

It was the longest night for Johnny Fixx. False dawn painted the horizon when finally he found his way to his beach house. Fixer walked the spongy sand, his thoughts lost in the roar and crash of the awakening sea. But it was all dark, the sky, the sea - and his prospects. He climbed back up to the house and made directly for the shower. The pincers of scalding hot water focused his thoughts, but not the answer. Johnny Fixx reached for a bottle, then pushed it away. That hadn't been the right medicine earlier and there was no reason to believe it would be now.

Fixer dropped into the overstuffed chair that was centered before the television and vcr, grabbed the remote and turned on the system. He'd forgotten that "Out of the Past" remained in the video recorder from several days ago. The 1947 noir classic played through its final scenes.

144

The Big Fall

Robert Mitchum, the undone private eye, crossed his shady employer, gambler Whit Palmer, played by Kirk Douglas. Mitchum fell for Douglas' girlfriend, Jane Greer, but the lady played the black widow, finally murdering Douglas and blackmailing the implicated Mitchum to run away with her, or else. Mitchum played along, but while Jane Greer packed a bag for their getaway, Mitchum called to tip the cops. Jane Greer and Mitchum drove in the early morning hours through the mountains south of Tahoe, she thinking their destination was Mexico and freedom, Mitchum knowing that sure destruction was around the next bend. Police blocked the road ahead. Jane Greer realized that Mitchum had betrayed her and pulled a gun to force Mitchum to turn back. As he struggled to grab the gun, Mitchum lost control of the car. The police opened fire. Jane Greer was hit, but before the crash, she got off a shot that killed Mitchum. As the screen dissolved into static, Mitchum's epitaph echoed for Johnny Fixx, "build my gallows high!"

The phone brought Fixer back from a deep sleep. The sun bubbled over the horizon like a spill of pink champagne, bathing the beach house in shafts of gold. "Great day to be alive," he breathed as he picked up the phone.

"Guess you and me are connected, no matter what," said Joey Dancer.

"Yeah pal, two peas in a pod."

"Your line clean?"

"It's swept twice a week. Even for microwave stuff. We're alone. What gives?"

"It's your call Johnny. After you left, Evita came in and bought me a drink. Then Jonesy joined us. Seems she was in the courtroom the other day and recognized one of the jurors."

"Some poor slob she turned a trick with?"

"My, my, Johnny, aren't we dated," quipped Dancer. "Right church, wrong pew, pal. Heavy is sweet on the dame, so don't ever let him get a whiff of this. Jonesy goes both ways. She was on the prowl at some

145

dyke bar and happens to run into your juror number ten - the fucking lady veterinarian with a thing for horses. Well, that ain't all she's got a thing for. You didn't know she was married and socially prominent, did you. Well, your straight laced little quiff, Barbara Stanley has a tet a tet with our gal Jonesy."

'Your call Johnny' he'd said.

Fixer's instinct for survival kicked in. His voice dropped to a whisper. "Christ, they're sequestered. How the fuck do we get Mrs. Stanley the 'message'?"

Joey Dancer answered, "leave that to me. Meet me at the plant tonight - around 9:00 p.m.

\*   \*   \*   \*   \*

Acme Specialties was separated from the Toyota yards by a six foot chain link fence overgrown with oleander. The Standard Oil tank farm was on the other side. Across the street the flats ran down to San Pedro Bay. The facing wall was precast concrete slabs held together by steel bars placed every ten feet. There were no windows and except for the sign at the corner proclaiming "Italian Specialties", "Meat Packing" and "Vending and Game Machines" Acme was grayly nondescript. There were rumors that Tony Persia had points in Acme, but Persia's interest remained pure speculation. Joey Dancer was quite another matter. Dancer made no bones about hanging his hat at Acme, and weekdays there was a steady stream of vendors and buyers to see Dancer and do business with Acme.

Johnny Fixx rolled through the unattended front gate minutes past 9:00 p.m. Electronic surveillance cameras swiveled to follow his direction. Fixer circled the plant and pulled up at the loading docks in the rear. He pulled himself onto the dock and walked into the darkened building. Access to the innards of Acme was through a cold room on the mezzanine used for shipment and loading of meats. Sides of beef, freshly slaughtered and oozing blood, were painted an unnatural red in the frosted lighting and swayed to the drone of the compressors. The cold room opened onto a catwalk that ran the length of the clear span warehouse below. Aisleways were cut through stacks of cartons on the floor and a glass office booth filled the center.

# The Big Fall

Joey Dancer sat behind a desk talking to Jonesy who paced before him. Jonesy finally broke off the conversation and moved out of the booth in the direction of a side entrance diagonally across the warehouse floor. Johnny Fixx moved away from the coldroom and walked down the steps to the floor. He moved directly to the office booth and had his hand on the door knob when Jonesy reappeared from behind a stack of cartons. She showed a strange little smile and said, "sorry, Johnny, I thought I forgot something." Fixer held the office door open for her, but Jonesy turned away, "I found it, I guess I was mistaken."

Dancer was angered at Jonesy's move and snapped, "sometimes that broad's too smart for her own good. What the hell was that all about?" "Maybe she really did forget something. Maybe she's got nose problems. No use cryin' over spilled milk, Joey. What have we got?"

Dancer returned to his desk chair and fired up a Lucky. Fixer opened a filing cabinet and came out with a half full bottle of Jack Daniels. He drank from the bottle and then placed the bottle on the desk before Joey. Dancer took a long pull, wiped his mouth, and grinned, "what we've got Johnny is Carla Samuels."

"You've got the floor bro, tell me more."

"Carla Samuels is a deputy assigned to play gopher for the lady jurors while Judge Minton keeps them in stir. She also happens to be one of our part time employees. Carla and Jonesy are built about the same. Carla's gonna put Jonesy in one of her uniforms, lend her a wig, and give her the right credentials so that she can play 'room service' for Mrs. Barbara Stanley. The rest should be easy. Mrs. Stanley gets a reminder that she should do the right thing or Jonesy visits with her husband, and like that."

"Can Jonesy pull it off?"

"She'll do as she's told," said Dancer with finality.

It was strictly a crap shoot whether Barbara Stanley would take the bait and do what they hoped she would. If not, the finger would quickly point back to Johnny Fixx.

The Big Fall

It had gone too far and Fixer nodded to Dancer, "work it out," as he turned away.

CHAPTER  THIRTEEN

It had been more than fifteen years before when Fixer woke up in a hospital in Tokyo, his head swathed in bandages, his vision cloudy, a dull ringing in his ears. There were the foothills of the Annamese Mountains, then the eerie cinder mist, the 'crachin', clinging at 10,000 feet to the craggy tops of the high Cordillera. The helicopters dropped through to the valley floor below and the unit piled out. It was to have been a simple shit pick up for a pair of advance scouts. Bamboo shoots clacked, elephant grass rustled, and the rain began to fall. It was up and over one sand crested hill after another. Then into a bunker half filled in by sand whipped and wetted by the monsoon to wait it out. The scouts were overdue.

Johnny Fixx worked his way down the backside of the bunker. An elephant trumpeted, then a tiger growled a response from within a thousand yards. Then the dirt floor opened and Fixer fell through into a cavern below. He landed on his feet and swiped wildly at the sand pouring down from where he'd been. In an instant the gray sky disappeared. The opening closed and in the black Fixer clawed wildly at the walls and dug for handholds up and out, all the while gagging at the sticky touch of cobwebbs. The more frantic his efforts, the more dirt he dislodged. But then he hit something hard and porous. The dirt veneer dropped away from poured concrete. Fixer fired a flare and tossed it into the farthest corner of the cavern. Three walls of concrete, logs on one side and above, the top of the cavern at least ten feet high. A pile of rotted clothes layered the corner. Fixer sifted through the decaying fabric and unearthed a log book with mildewed leather binding clipped closed around the pages.

The book was a handwritten diary. The first page disintegrated, so too did the next seven, as if to say what was chronicled was over and done with, let it lay. He kept at it and finally midway found pages that had held together in the unlikely time capsule. Entries were scrawled in French. Early 1954. A contingent of French Groupement Mobile 100, an elite French blocking unit detached from their main forces hundreds of miles to the north in the Tonkin, in place in the Central Highlands to prevent the Viet Minh from closing Highway 19, An Khe to Pleiku, and cutting the country in half. But Groupement Mobile 100 sallied out once too often. The Viet Minh sprang a trap on Highway 19 at the Mang Yang Pass, and the Mobile Groupement was annihilated. All but one.

149

The Big Fall

The legionnaire crawled away into the jungle where somehow he found his base, chronicled his unit's last battle, and walked back into the night to find the enemy. The legionnaire's scrawl was the last thing Fixer remembered. North Vietnamese regulars surrounded his unit and zeroed in the bunker with mortars. Everyone topside was slaughtered. Direct hits caved in the bunker on the cavern, burying Fixer and nearly killing him. He had survived when there was no good reason why he should and a relief platoon of air cavalry dug him out and ferried him home.

Recovery was slow in Japan. The concussion had been severe. There was the possibility of subdural hematoma and permanent brain damage. Fixer slowly but surely healed and when finally he was ambulatory, hit upon his own therapy for reconditioning himself for combat. Kenjutsu, the Japanese martial art of swordsmanship. Times half way around the world distant, but an avocation he carried home.

The pagoda like structure sprang out from a shelf in the Hollywood Hills. It was a shinto temple and the home of Lu, his sensei and a master of the katana. The rain was a steady drizzle and Fixer shivered in the early morning chill as he changed in the open alcove that adjoined the practice area. Discipline and fury, unlikely bedmates, the precise combination of which distinguished the honorable masters of the art from clumsy students. 'Honor', muttered Johnny Fixx as he pulled on his kimono and tied back the sleeves. Then the 'hakama' jacket over the kimono, kept closed by a twisted band of cloth around his middle and fastened behind in a ten figure knot.

Lu worked the class collectively, then chose Fixer to square off with him one on one. Kenjutsu was serious business and 'bokken' were used, traditional practice swords of hard oak balanced like the razor sharp steel of real katana, not the bamboo sticks common to the bastardized practice of kendo. Bows were exchanged, then teacher and pupil circled each other probing for some advantage. Fixer abruptly pressed a ferocious assault, all vertical cuts and diagonal slashes, straight on and relentless, as if dispatching his adversary could somehow restore the honor he'd placed in harms way.

Lu coolly met every thrust, defending, then attacking, in the systole-diastole, hard-soft technique that in a master's hands eventually turned a less skilled opponent back on himself to his lethal peril. Sweat poured down Fixer's face as he mounted yet another attack. Lu parried and attacked, pushing him off balance, leaving him finally with no other move

150

than a straight on attack based more on the strength of his arm than swordsmanship.

Fixer blundered, staggering off balance and open, and the sensei dispatched him with a stunning touch to the neck that in actual combat surely would have been fatal. Fixer dropped to one knee, the raised bruise on his neck throbbing, his head spinning with turquoise and magenta disks that floated in his field of vision.

Lu dismissed the class and returned with ice for Fixer's neck. Fixer knelt, sitting back on his haunches, breathing deeply, clearing his head.

Lu smiled, "you are troubled today Johnny. Worthy pupil, you have perhaps forgotten that subtlety can be more lethal than the strength of one's arm. In your world, one creates an image to impress others. It is fashionable to be ever on the attack. But in Asia one creates images only to conceal. So it is worthy pupil with the fighting retreat out of which springs the counter stroke to overcome an opponent."

Lu departed leaving Fixer to the pelting rain. The exercise hadn't helped. The thing now proceeded with a momentum all its own, beyond any of the players to affect the outcome, an outcome Fixer considered with a strange sense of foreboding.

"Johnny, Johnny," she called. "I thought I'd find you here."

Crystal Lee.

Fixer picked himself up and led Crystal into the dressing area. He toweled off and dropped to the wooden bench. "Nice day to cut your throat, eh?"

"Maybe not," she answered. "I think I've got something you might be able to use."

"Shoot."

"Remember my story about Jimmy Doyle's immunity agreement and the arson rap sheet from LA PD?"

"How could I forget it?"

"I wrote it from the information at hand. The only crimes covered by the immunity agreement as far as anyone of us knew were the warehouse rip off and Doyle's complicity in the arson that he said Tony Persia bought and paid for."

Fixer picked up on her drift.

"Crystal, are you saying there's something else."

"That's exactly what I'm saying. I was contacted yesterday by a Chicano in the County lock up. Ruben Ruiz. I went to see him when he mentioned Jimmy Doyle. Get this Johnny. Lang and Doyle both testified that the only exposure Doyle had was for the arson and the warehouse hi-jacking. Ruiz was one of the wise guys who operated that warehouse, and guess what my friend, it wasn't appliances friend Doyle wanted. He'd dealt himself into a drug buy, a big one. Half a million, maybe more. That's how Lang caught him. Dirty with dope and the money he'd shaken down from the warehouse crew to buy back their drugs. Ruiz figures that if Doyle could cut himself a way out of hard time by turning, his story should be worth just as much."

"That lying bastard Lang. I'm gonna' see the Judge and get him to reopen the proofs. If the jury gets a piece of this they'll never convict Persia. I owe you one doll."

Crystal smiled. "I'll find a way to collect."

\* \* \* \* \*

His weekend had already gone to hell, the weather killing a round of golf and the second choice of sailing, when Johnny Fixx barged in on Judge Thomas Minton.

"It's not Monday counsellor. Too early for your summation," quipped the Judge who was less than amused by the weekend intrusion.

152

"My apologies, your honor, but I've just learned something that I must share with the court that bears directly on the conduct of the police and prosecutor in the Persia case."

"Before you proceed, Mr. Fixx, I assume you notified Mr. Kutter to meet you here. I'd rather not proceed with any discussion of the case without both counsels here."

"I did contact Mr. Kutter's office and his home. He's away for the weekend. His wife is trying to locate him, but she apparently has no way of contacting him."

"This is highly irregular Mr. Fixx."

"I understand, your honor. But what I've just learned is so aggravated that I must bring it to the court's attention or risk doing irreparable harm to my client's interests."

"I don't like it Fixx. I think you're asking an awful lot of me."

Minton led the way into his study, took his seat behind the mahogany desk and motioned Fixx to the chair that faced him to the side of the desk.

Minton exhaled audibly, deciding against his better judgment to let Fixx proceed.

"Go ahead counsellor."

"Harry Lang deliberately concealed the real basis for Doyle's immunity agreement from the court. Doyle decided to rip off a warehouse in the barrio all right, but appliances weren't what he had in mind. Doyle stumbled into a narcotics buy, dealt himself in, ripped off the drugs, and was caught down and dirty by Lieutenant Lang when Ruben Ruiz met with him in Union Station to buy back the drugs."

"How do you know all of this?"

"Ruben Ruiz is in custody in the County lock-up. He spilled his guts. And now we have to do something about it." Thomas Minton picked up his phone and dialed the County lock-up.

"Turnkey, this is Judge Minton. I'd like you to check on a prisoner for me and get him to a phone in private so that I can talk to him."

Minton gave the turnkey the name and waited on his return.

"What was that," he said. "Again."

Johnny Fixx was on his feet.

"What happened Judge Minton?"

"Ruiz made bail. He's gone."

"Lang!" exclaimed Fixx.

"Now that's pretty far afield counsellor."

"Oh no, your honor. It has his signature all over it. Ruiz contacted the reporter, Crystal Lee. The lock-up guards must have tipped Lang. The good Lieutenant didn't know what was happening but he wasn't about to take any chances. So he arranges for Ruben Ruiz to disappear. Your honor, you can't let him get away with this."

"Bring me Ruiz and I'll consider reopening the proofs. Short of that I'm not about to proceed on any of the rest of your beliefs. I don't buy it. Harry Lang is a good cop entitled to my presumption that he's discharging his duties unless or until someone shows me page and verse to the contrary. I'm sorry Mr. Fixx."

So there it was. Harry Lang sweeping his dirt bags under the carpet while the pristine wheels of justice ground on to take Tony Persia down by the book. Persia fought back from the same gutter. And Johnny Fixx was to throw himself over the concertina wire so that Tony Persia could run up his back and escape the mine field.

The Big Fall

"No way out now," muttered Fixx as he took his leave.

\* \* \* \* \*

Sunday was always the hardest duty for Harry Lang. Camarillo. Insurance money had run out two years before. Lang was forced to transfer Edith, his wife of thirty years from a private nursing home to the State Hospital. Their lives had revolved around Cindy, the teenaged daughter who was vibrant and alive and a sophomore at UCLA. It was six years ago to the day when Lang had been called in from a stake out. Cindy was in City Emergency. Edie was grief stricken in the waiting room. The doctors advised them that Cindy had overdosed on cocaine. Lang refused to believe it and compelled the doctors to take him into the operating room where the emergency team worked to bring back his daughter. He had seen the drill countless times before, but this time when the monitors shrilled their final monotone the most important thing in his life was gone.

Edie never did recover. Inexorably she shut out the here and now and gradually lapsed into a nearly comatose state that was punctuated by increasingly rare interludes of lucidity. And even when Edie was herself, her personal clock seemed to have stopped the day her daughter died. She spoke of Cindy in the present tense and Lang bit back tears as he played his part in her remembrance charade that was all the reality left to her.

The sun broke through in mid afternoon and Harry Lang helped his wife into a wheel chair and pushed her out onto a veranda. Her hair had gone from its natural chestnut to completely white, and her complexion was a ghostly gray. Her eyes had been a lively hazel, but showed now as deeply sunken and fevered black. Her head was bowed and her body lifeless. But then miraculously she collected herself, sat up, and recognized her husband.

Edie was suddenly herself, chattering about neighbors they hadn't seen in six years, finally saying, "Cindy will be home this weekend, Harry. You will try to get Sunday afternoon off, won't you, so we can have family dinner together."

"Sure honey. I'll be home. Just as long as you let me know enough in advance - I'll . . ." The words caught in his throat.

155

The Big Fall

The Lieutenant steeled himself and willed back the tone his wife expected. "I'll be home."

"You know Harry, she'll be taking advanced Spanish courses next year.

That means a semester in Spain. My god, what will we do without her?"

"It'll be me and you for a while doll, like in the old days. We'll write, and there's the phone. She'll be with us Edie - she'll always be with us."

Edie looked at her husband and Lang saw the deep psychic defense mechanism putting out the light in her eyes to protect her from the horror she couldn't face. In an instant Edie was gone again.

It was always the same for Harry Lang on a Sunday. By 2:30 p.m. he was back in the City, kneeling at the altar railing in the Cathedral. There were no lights on during the day and only the flickering candles of a thousand vigil lights bathed the statuary and cavernous interior with another worldly glow. Cindy was first in his prayers. Had she died in a state of grace? It was unthinkable to Lang that one so young and good could be doomed to eternal punishment for a single transgression, an innocent mistake. His good sense told him that Cindy was safe. He wept for Edie. There would be no tomorrows for her. Only hell on earth until mercifully she was taken. And then Harry Lang prayed for strength to take down the vermin who had killed his daughter, destroyed his wife, and wrecked his families' life. He prayed not to Mary, mother of mercy, nor could he bring his eyes to meet those of Christ suffering on the cross. It was the godhead of the Trinity that Harry Lang prayed to, the God of the Old Testament, not the long suffering Son of forgiveness, but the stern father who made the Commandments and exacted punishment for transgressions.

If the law permitted, Harry Lang would hesitate not at all in personally pulling the trigger on every dope dealer he could collar. But the law did not permit the summary justice they deserved. There were defendants' rights - indictment, trial, and the vagaries of a jury verdict. And that's when Harry Lang prayed for biblical justice - an eye for an eye - for Tony Persia and every rotten soul like him. Persia

156

was beyond the dirty dealing on the street. But he called the shots and took the rake. There was never any doubt in Harry Lang's mind that Tony Persia and his crew had killed his daughter. Tony Persia would pay. All of them would pay. And if the system failed, Harry Lang would exact his personal retribution.

Sam Turre was parked at the curb when Harry Lang emerged from the Cathedral. It had to be important for the Sergeant to disturb Lang's Sunday routine.

"The boys at Central Lockup passed me the word that Ruben Ruiz - the main man at the warehouse who was Doyle's connection - spilled to Crystal Lee. He's beating the bushes for a deal or else."

"Get him the hell out of there, Sam. I don't care how you do it. He's got family. Find them. Make bail and put the fear of god into the sonuvabitch. If I find him in Greater Los Angeles again, he's dead meat. Make him believe it Sam. Understand!"

The bosses tone left no room for discussion.

\* \* \* \* \*

Lang had beaten him to the punch. And Johnny Fixx knew that the Lieutenant and Rudy Kutter would stay scarce for the balance of the weekend. The records at the County lock-up showed only that Mrs. Ruiz had bailed out Ruben. Crystal Lee had nothing else they could follow up on. A phone canvas of the more than one hundred Ruiz' in the phone directory netted nothing that matched up. The rap sheet on Ruben Ruiz disappeared and for all intents and purposes, at least until the Persia jury began its deliberations, Lang would insure that neither Ruiz nor his files would surface.

Fixx attempted to raise the point again with Judge Minton before the convening of court on Monday morning. Minton refused to reconsider the matter asserting that unless Ruiz presented himself prior to the commencement of summations, the proofs would be closed regardless of the revelations Ruiz might disclose.

"Proceed, Mr. Fixx," directed Judge Minton.

Johnny Fixx paced and looked back into the gallery as he collected his thoughts. Harry Lang was standing, his back against the door, a thin smile playing across his lips.

Fixx turned to address the jury. He watched them as a group but shied from individual eye contact.

"Ladies and gentlemen of the jury you have heard a very thin case indeed presented by the prosecution. The prosecution contends that Mr. Persia paid Jimmy Doyle $25,000 to demolish the Passeo Motel. Yet Mr. Persia is not the owner of that Motel. The prosecution never presented any proof as to the ownership of the motel or the alleged financial interest of Mr. Persia in it. This is a detail that will merit your closest attention and thought. If Mr. Persia is not the record owner of the motel he could not have been the beneficiary of any insurance policy on the motel. If Persia is not the beneficiary, how then could he profit by the destruction of the motel? The proof is entirely silent on this point, and remember that the defendant is not only entitled to a presumption of innocence, but also it is the prosecution, not the defense that has the burden of proving guilt beyond a reasonable doubt. I submit to you that the prosecution has left a gigantic hole in their case, one big enough to drive a greyhound bus through. It is not enough for the prosecution to sidestep the vital question of motive through innuendo."

"Without motive, what are we left with. Jimmy Doyle, a man who traded false testimony for his freedom when he was caught red handed hi-jacking stolen goods from a fencing warehouse. Doyle is an admitted arsonist. He admitted placing the charges in the Passeo Motel. He admitted installing a very sophisticated wiring trigger to the motel telephone system. Do you believe Mr. Doyle when he tells you that he learned of the trigger from a book he read in the LA Public Library. This is a man adept at handling very dangerous explosives and then rigging them to blow with an exotic electronic trigger. What does that tell you, ladies and gentlemen of the jury? Plainly and simply, it is very unlikely that Mr. Doyle was telling the truth when he testified that he muddled through - he took on the job training - when Tony Persia told him to blow up the Passeo Motel. The very basis for Doyle's testimony is absurd. On the job training under the circumstances of this case most assuredly would have resulted in both Jimmy Doyle and the Passeo going up in smoke. But that didn't happen. Doyle says he not only installed the explosives but then removed them, and all without incident. This is not an amateur at work. Oh no, ladies and gentlemen of the jury. This is a professional and a very experienced one at that. More lies from Jimmy Doyle."

"Jimmy Doyle is not robin hood. He is a professional criminal with a long record of arrests and convictions. He is an informer - not from any pang of conscience but to save his own skin. This is America where an informer is the lowest of the low, a person whose testimony is utterly unworthy of belief. I urge you, ladies and gentlemen of the jury to search your individual and collective conscience. You cannot convict this defendant, an innocent man, on the testimony of an admitted arsonist, a man with a long criminal record, a man who admittedly has made it a way of life to lie, cheat, and steal."

Johnny Fixx had been avoiding it as if not to look would somehow insulate him from the possibility. But inevitably he was drawn to it. He made eye contact with juror number ten, Mrs. Barbara Stanley. She instantly averted his gaze. The message had been delivered! Fixer's stomach was in his mouth as if he'd reached the midpoint of a freefall. Would there be time for the rip cord?

Prosecutor Rudolph Kutter calmly and dispassionately outlined the unbroken chain of circumstantial evidence linking the arson money pay off from Tony Persia to Jimmy Doyle.

"Tony Persia's prints were on the envelope and the money. Jimmy Doyle was never in any business that required financing. Tony Persia never took the stand to tell us just what he did and why. But we did hear from a bank officer who told us that he not only handled Mr. Persia's withdrawal of $25,000 in cash that was ticketed for Jimmy Doyle, but also that at the time of that withdrawal on April 17th, 1987, Mr. Persia made it a point of telling him that he was going to loan the money to a friend to begin a business. That seemed like pretty strong stuff at the time, ladies and gentlemen of the jury. And it was until we heard from the airline ticket person who spelled out for us the very disconcerting circumstance that the bank teller used airline tickets to take a trip to Mexico at the very time when he was supposed to be in Los Angeles handling that money withdrawal for the defendant. And after that testimony, ladies and gentlemen of the jury, did the bank teller again take the stand to deny that he was away on vacation on those dates."

Rudy Kutter's voice built to a tone of righteous indignation. "Of course he did not! He could not because that conversation with Tony Persia never happened."

"The defense argues that there is no proof that Tony Persia had a financial interest in the Passeo Motel. I submit to you that they must not have been listening to the testimony of Jimmy Doyle. It was Jimmy Doyle who testified without contradiction that the defendant hired him to blow up the Passeo Motel so that he could get his money out of the place. How Persia planned to do that after the fact of the destruction of the motel and the insurance settlement is not relevant to the issues before you."

"What are we left with, ladies and gentlemen of the jury. Paid testimony, informant's testimony may be dirty business, but so too is the business of crime. This was not a so called victimless crime. Oh no, had the plot to destroy the motel succeeded, ten, twenty, fifty, a hundred, perhaps more than that could have been killed and maimed. Lawbreakers have ways and means of covering their tracks. Underlings are paid to lie and take the rap for higher ups. Witnesses are pressured to have lapses of memory or change their stories. Even worse, physical violence, and sometimes murder are resorted to maintain the bond of silence. The government has no choice but to work with admitted criminals to gather testimony that will convict those that pull the strings to direct them. Immunity may sometimes be dirty business, but surely, so too is the arrogance of the lawbreakers that literally sucks the economic life blood from society, sometimes over the dead and maimed bodies of ordinary citizens who get in the way. Jimmy Doyle has a criminal past. We admit that. But Jimmy Doyle gave truthful testimony about Tony Persia, a man who remains in the shadows while others take the risks. If you believe Jimmy Doyle, regardless of the rhetoric of defense counsel, you must, it is your sworn duty, to convict the defendant."

Judge Minton charged the jury and warned them in conclusion that "the only issue before you is whether the defendant hired Jimmy Doyle to blow up the Passeo Motel to facilitate an insurance fraud."

"Bailiff," directed Judge Minton, "escort the Jury to the deliberation room. We stand recessed until verdict."

John Fixx shook his client's hand, his eyes saying what he couldn't. Fixer moved through the crush of spectators who milled about the rear benches and door to the hall.

Samantha had attended the final session. She embraced him and whispered, "you did all you could."

"Sure I did, doll. More than you'll ever know," he breathed.

"I'll buy you a drink, John," she said.

"You're on, Sam."

Crystal Lee stepped to block their way, a mic in her hand, a cameraman at her elbow.

"Mr. Fixx, any final comments?"

"It's for the jury to decide now. I'm confident Mr. Persia will be acquitted."

Fixer pushed on through. Crystal showed an amused expression when her eyes touched those of Samantha. The wife knew. She always knew. And there was an instant, a feeling Sam believed she'd sublimated to near non existence long ago, when she considered clawing out the eyes of the oriental bitch.

Fixer called after her and she moved around Crystal Lee. They took the stairs to the curb arm in arm.

Harry Lang lounged against the front fender of his car. He grinned, "good job counsellor, but this time I think your boy finally ran out of room to wiggle free."

"Shame on you Harry. We've got unfinished business. Ruben Ruiz, remember him?"

Lang showed a quizzical expression. "Never heard of the man, John. Who's he?"

## CHAPTER FOURTEEN

The cab driver called, "where to, bud?"

"How about a cocktail at the Bay Pub," Fixx suggested to Samantha.

"Sure Johnny. Sounds like a good idea."

"Bay Pub," called Fixx.

"Already heard yah, bud," answered the cab driver as he hung a 'u' to head in the right direction.

Built on stilts to take in the blue collar grandeur of San Pedro Bay beyond the trademark chain link fences that separated one warehouse from the next, the Pub was a popular eatery with the locals and the military. But in mid afternoon, the luncheon crowd had thinned. They climbed the steps to the restaurant and the hostess greeted them at the door.

"A table for lunch?" she asked.

Samantha looked at Johnny.

He smiled, "your call."

"Let's sit at the bar for now."

"Two Margaritas," she ordered. "You should celebrate Johnny. I think you earned it. Even though you know how I feel about your clients. You're too good for them, and you showed it again."

"Now, now, kid. We're all hired guns for someone."

Fixer worked at a certain pleasantness. If he succeeded, Samantha would not probe for what was dragging him down. At one time or another he had confided nearly every foul thing he'd ever been involved with in her. But this was different. There had been dirty business, things he'd regretted. Somehow she'd gotten them out of him. There was a different feel to this. It was one of those things a person did alone. "Like dying", he breathed.

"What was that John?"

He smiled and leaned in to nuzzle her neck. Perfume and more.

She pulled away stifling a giggle. "Ticklish," she explained.

"My lady with champagne shoulders and eyes like lost lakes." He grinned broadly.

"My god you've either finally flipped or you're reading Philip Marlowe stories again."

Fixx chuckled.

"You making any serious money selling real estate?"

"Not bad, John, not bad at all. Fifty big ones plus last year . . ."

"What", he cried in mock indignity. "And still you take my money. I'm getting myself a lawyer to reopen this thing. Hell, you make a few bucks more and you can keep me in the style to which I've become accustomed."

"I just might do that, Johnny. But we both know there's no corral big enough to hold this cowboy - is there?"

Samantha had a point, and Johnny Fixx turned to things of family to get off the subject.

"My son and heir - has he made his decision?"

"I think it is the service. I could have kicked you where it would do the most good when he first came to me with the idea. It had your signature written all over it. But I've thought about it. There are a lot of new lawyers these days. You've told me that yourself. Most of them, I suppose, are well trained. I mean in the sense that a garage mechanic can diagnose an auto problem and fix it. But . . . ."

Fixer sensed her drift.

"It's 'touch' that distinguishes the really good ones from the also rans. Most of them settle into nondescript yuppie existences. You know - they become just another rivet on a lengthening wing span. And for them that's all right. But a few aren't content with that. They want to fly on their own. I think the good ones should take their time. Get around some. Breath as much of it in before they begin selling their advice and expertise. That's why I encouraged him to enlist. I'd have been in favor of his joining an expedition to climb Annapurna." Fixer chuckled and ordered them another round.

"How long do you think your jury will be out?"

"That's one you can never figure. Max has a theory he swears by. But I have my doubts. In a big case if you're fighting the government, a jury that comes in at the end of one day, or even early in the second, usually means the defendant is sunk. You've got to figure that they spend some time getting to know each other in there, electing their foreman, and then going over the testimony. Then I suppose they discuss their views and only after everyone has a say do they call it for a first vote. At least that's how it should work in there. So that first vote probably takes place mid-day or late in the first day. There are usually dissenters from any consensus who have to be talked back to the majority position. Remember this is a criminal case and conviction can only occur when there is unanimity. Now if they get late into the second day, or into the third, that probably means the defendant is in pretty good shape for an acquittal. It's easy to be lazy and buy the bull shit the cops and prosecutors cook up. But if they've churned it two or three days, they're struggling with reasonable doubt. So according to Professor Max, day three in a complicated case is definitely the defendant's day."

"And what if they don't come in on the third day?"

"Then my love it's definitely in the lap of the gods. They're probably getting tired and bored, especially if they've been sequestered. Anything can happen. Days four and five also according to Max are slightly favorable to the defendant. A verdict is still possible for him, but also he might skate if they get hung. A dissenter who holds out for acquittal, or a cell of dissenters hangs the jury. No unanimous decision means the Judge has to call it off, declare a mistrial and send everyone home."

"How do you feel about it John?"

"Me, hell, I always figure I beat the other guys brains in, but I'm uneasy about this one. That goddamned bank clerk - his testimony should have signed, sealed, and delivered it for us. And then Kutter cuts the legs out from under him with that vacation testimony. I don't like it."

The bar television suspended above kicked in and Crystal Lee appeared doing a studio interview with DA Rudy Kutter. Kutter had received the designation from the State Committee for the vacant Senate seat. He was elated at that turn of events, but there was more. The man who had hinted at a primary fight for the nomination had thought better of it and closed ranks with Kutter in a show of party unity.

Fixer grinned wryly.

"The bastard probably bought him off. Well I guess he's gotten what he wanted out of all this."

Crystal Lee was signing off when Samantha abruptly turned on her stool to face Fixer.

"Is she going to get what she wants Johnny?"

Fixer averted her gaze and nodded wryly.

"Come on Sam, let's hit the bricks."

Samantha downed her drink and squeezed his arm.

"Sorry, it's none of my business."

Fixer was in no mood to be alone, but if Sam was about to explode into a jealous tirade that could continue for hours ....

She read it in his expression.

"Poor Johnny. Don't worry. I'll be good."

He embraced her and kissed her full on the mouth.

"Let's get out of here."

It was dusk and Fixer paced before his glass wall watching the cracking towers in the refinery to the left of his building. There was a violet haze above the flashing flames.

Samantha handed him a Margarita, "it's a mix, but close to the real thing. That's all you had in your cabinet."

"Mind if I do some taping Sam. I've got a show tonight and I don't think I'm going to last long enough to do it live."

"Be my guest Johnny. I'm hungry. Do you have anything in your kitchen we dare eat?"

He grinned.

"Check it out. I know I've been to the supermarket this year."

The phone rang and Sam picked it up.

"It's your friend Ron Goldstone, Johnny."

Fixer rolled back his eyes. He'd been dodging Ron for days. Samantha had no way of knowing his predicament.

"Hello Ron. How's the boy?"

Goldstone picked up the uneasiness in Fixer's tone.

He chuckled, then said "you think I'm calling you to break your balls for some dough, don't you?"

"Aren't you?"

"Then you don't know?"

"Ron, what the hell gives here. Did you buy me a lottery ticket that hit?"

"Your pal dropped by to see me and paid your tab. He said you'd done a helluva job for him."

He knew then without asking but asked anyway.

"What pal, Ron?"

"Persia. Tony Persia. He wrote a check to your brokerage account for a hundred large. You're sound as the dollar now my friend."

"And bought and paid for."

"What," exclaimed Goldstone.

Fixer replaced the receiver. Persia was a better man than Jimmy Doyle any day of the week. Maybe it really wasn't guilt or innocence but people after all, just like Joey Dancer had said. The equation could become very simple. Persia simply shouldn't be sewered by a fink like Doyle. Saving the better man was the thing. The means then weren't that important. Then why was it so goddamned difficult to swallow. Killing gooks in the jungle had been a horror, but he'd slept every night. There was damned little sleep now. The possibility that they'd convict Tony Persia strangely tantalized. It was unthinkable for a defense lawyer to hold that hope. But only if that happened would there be any certainty that the heat on juror number 10 hadn't taken.

Fixer grabbed the phone and rang up Max Gale.

"Max, what do you hear?"

"I just got back. It looks like the Judge is going to put them to bed around 9:00 p.m. They've asked for testimony to be reread.

And his honor isn't about to do it tonight. So that means everything is on tilt until the morning."

"What testimony?"

"Chuck Mercer, Johnny." The bank teller!

"Can you cover it in the morning Max?"

"Sure Johnny. I'll be there. You hanging at the loft?"

"Here or the beach. Try here first."

Johnny Fixx retreated to his studio. Samantha called to him, "Fixer's surprise will be ready in about a half hour."

"Okay Sam. Give me a couple of minutes to tape an intro."

The music was always good and true. It took him away. And that's where Fixer desperately needed to be.

He fired up the tape console and pulled the mic toward him.

"I was in New York City in February and March of 1958 midstream at Columbia. It wasn't a bad time to be alive in the U.S. of A. Ike was still around. As long as his hand was still on the stick, nothing much could really go wrong. We were losing round one in space, and Castro was cranking up to kick us out of Cuba. A friend of mine had been on the road with Stan Kenton and left the band when Stan decided to stop touring for a time and go into residence at Balboa. My pal was in the Apple looking for a gig when he ran into me. He'd heard about a recording session at Columbia's 30th Street Studio. A young fellow named Teo Macero was producing. We decided to take a listen. It turned out to be the Milestones session by the sextet to end all sextets, Miles, Trane, Canonball, Philly Joe, Chambers, and Red. I'm going to play the entire album for you tonight and let you in on a little secret. Take a hard listen to Philly Joe. On some of the cuts he isn't playing the full set of traps. Philly Joe had himself a problem in those days, one he shared with a number of other music legends. Miles wasn't about to advance him any more bread and Philly Joe did what he had to. He hocked part of his drum set to get well. That was more than thirty years ago. Listen up now and marvel at the music and what an extraordinary drummer was able to do with less than all of his instrument."

Fixer shut down the mic and triggered the CD feed onto his tape to begin 'Milestones', then closed his lights in the studio.

Sam's voice sounded behind him.

"Thought maybe there was something you'd rather have than dinner Johnny."

She'd turned off the lights in the loft and was framed in sultry silhouette in the doorway against the hazy half light of San Pedro filtering through the glass wall.

Samantha was nude to the waist. She wore only her black panty hose and heels. Fixer hadn't succeeded in conning her. She knew something was eating at him, something he couldn't quite bring himself to share with her. There had been a time when that would have obsessed her. The years had wised her up. He'd get to it, eventually. And now she'd give him the respite of loving and a few hours of balmy exhaustion. He took her then and there, standing, tearing open the front of her panty hose, lifting her so that he could bury himself in her softness. He kneaded her buttocks as she locked her sweet thighs around him and laved his face and mouth with her wet tongue. She exploded first and in seconds so did he. Then she dropped to her knees and took him in her mouth prolonging the aftershocks of orgasm. He lifted her, cradling her in his arms and walked to the bedroom. She lay on him gently undulating and soon he was ready again. Samantha smiled "my treat," and lowered herself on him, sweetly torturing with short soft strokes until finally he bucked into her roaring his release.

"Do you have any smokes, big boy," she cooed.

"Try the end stand."

She fired up a cigarette and frowned.

"Don't mean to be a pest my love, but that pipe is in there. I thought you stopped that stuff right after Nam?"

He could have lied, but his brain was on a lean mixture, relaxed like every bone in his body.

"It takes me away, doll."

"But why Johnny?"

He grinned and pulled her down to him, "original sin" as he kissed her deeply.

She left a note on the end stand in the morning.

"My brother's flying in. Wish I could stay. Call me. Be good."

There had been a chance for the light with her. Now it was three shades of gray, the last charcoal as the black closed in. There was an inevitability to Johnny Fixx and the dark. Maybe he just preferred it that way.

Max Gale called minutes before noon.

"No surprises Johnny. Judge Minton permitted them to listen to Chuck Mercer's testimony and that bank teller, Alice Madden. They've ordered lunch. I guess they'll be off and running again in an hour or so."

"Any feel for it yet Max?"

"None whatsoever."

\* \* \* \* \*

Midweek. The Persia jury had been out for three full days. A banner splashed across the front page of the Tribune proclaimed. "Jurors Want To Hear Bank Officer's Testimony Again." Judge Minton ordered the testimony read to the jury for the second time and admonished them to get back to their deliberations.

"I have every confidence that you will be able to work to a just verdict," he concluded.

On Thursday morning, Johnny Fixx was summoned to a conference in Judge Minton's chambers. Fixx walked in and greeted the Judge.

Rudy Kutter eyed him and said, "there's been a note to the Court from the foreman. They're split. After five ballots yesterday and two this morning, it's nine to three for conviction."

Fixer was well aware that both Judge Minton and Kutter were waiting on him for a read on the defense' position on a mistrial. Ordinarily four days of deliberations and an indication from inside the jury room that there was a hardening split would be sufficient basis for a motion for a mistrial. But this was far from the ordinary situation. It wasn't quite ripe enough to show one's cards.

Fixx spoke to Judge Minton, "your honor, the defense believes that a consensus for acquittal is likely and would urge the Court to permit the jury to continue its deliberations and in fact to instruct them to do everything possible to reach a unanimous verdict, regardless of the outcome."

"How about you, Mr. Kutter," asked the Judge.

"I concur with Mr. Fixx. A mistrial serves no one. Hundreds of thousands of dollars have gone into the investigation, indictment, and prosecution of this case. We need a result that is fair and final."

Fixer quipped, "as long as the verdict is guilty. Right Senator?"

By the following morning the situation had further deteriorated. The jury had for the third time asked for Chuck Mercer's testimony and that of the airline ticket agent, Alice Madden, to be read to them. This time

The Big Fall

Judge Minton refused their request and admonished them that it was their sworn duty to reach a verdict.

It was three in the afternoon on Thursday when Max Gale located Johnny Fixx.

"Get in to court Johnny. The Judge has ordered us to appear pronto."

"Verdict?"

"I don't know. Whatever it is, it sounds final."

Judge Thomas Minton was humorless as he asked the bailiff to summon back the jury. The twelve filed back in and the Judge addressed them.

"Mr. Foreman, I have your note and would ask you to explain for the record."

The Italian accountant had been elected foreman. His voice was steady as he said, "your honor, we have been unable to reach a verdict. We are split nine to three to convict and that split has held for two and one half days."

"We will poll the jury," instructed the Judge.

Five votes to convict, then the first 'nay' from the lady college professor transplanted from Utah. Two more votes to convict, before the second 'nay' from the retired librarian. Another vote to convict, then the lady veterinarian Barbara Stanley calmly saying 'nay', and a final vote to convict. Barbara Stanley seemed to be up to it. She locked eye contact with the Prosecutor and he broke it off.

Judge Minton asked the defendant to rise.

"I must conclude that the jury is hopelessly deadlocked. Accordingly I will entertain a motion for a mistrial."

"So moved," said Johnny Fixx.

172

"The Prosecution reluctantly joins in the motion, your honor," said the District Attorney.

"The court declares a mistrial," declared Judge Minton.

Max Gale beamed and clasped Tony Persia's shoulders.

"Congratulations Tony."

Rudy Kutter gestured to Johnny Fixx and approached the bench.

"Your honor, this matter is not finished as far as my office is concerned. We will review the evidence and make a determination on a retrial as quickly as we can. In the meantime we would ask you to direct that the defendant not leave the jurisdiction."

"Your honor," answered Johnny Fixx, "that's nonsense. Mr. Persia has been free on $1,000,000 bail without travel restrictions. He's been here each time he was expected to appear. Under the circumstances we would request that bail be continued without restrictions until Mr. Kutter makes his decision. Also, we would advise the court that should Mr. Kutter take too long with this determination, we will move to dismiss the indictment for violation of the speedy trial act."

Judge Minton ruled "gentlemen, I am going to continue bail without restriction. There will be no special instructions to the defendant concerning his whereabouts and schedule. I am also going to require you Mr. Kutter to file a notice of intention with this court within thirty days concerning your intentions in this matter. Either prepare to go forward or join with Mr. Fixx in a motion to dismiss the indictment."

Television crews were set up at the base of the courthouse steps. Crystal Lee stepped forward and Johnny Fixx moved in her direction, Tony Persia at his elbow.

"Will you make a statement Mr. Fixx?"

"I do not believe the Prosecution's proof was of sufficient quality to be convincing. That's why the jury could not reach a unanimous decision. In my view the mistrial is tantamount to an acquittal. Frankly, I would be surprised if the DA moves for a retrial. I think my client is a free man permanently."

"And how do you feel, Mr. Persia," she asked.

"Like sleeping for forty eight hours, Miss Lee, and then having one helluva party. And I think that's exactly what I'm gonna' do."

Johnny Fixx stepped back from the circle of Crystal Lee's interviewees and turned into Harry Lang's path. Lang was purple with rage. He bared his teeth and went chest to chest with Fixer.

"Your client's dirty Fixer, and I'm beginning to think that you're in it with him. I'm gonna' find out what happened in there boy. Whatever it takes, and whoever falls, and that's a goddamned promise you can take to the bank with all the dirty money that bastard pays you."

Lang disappeared into the crowd. Johnny Fixx sucked in deep lungs full of air.

Dermot Spillane waved for him.

"Nice job in there Johnny. Put this one behind you. I saw Lang go after you. Be careful my friend. There's things between Persia and Lang that go back a long way. It's personal between them and anyone who gets in the way is likely to get burned. Watch yourself boyo."

## CHAPTER FIFTEEN

'No Luck' looked like a garish street walker, strands of festive lights strung from her stack to masts fore and aft, and twined around her radar dish. Water taxis buzzed around her like bees homing on a hive. Tony Persia was celebrating and it seemed as if he'd invited half the City of Angels to celebrate with him.

Johnny Fixx was attracting almost as much attention as his host. Heavy steered him to the main salon bar.

"Johnny, yer the greatest. I knew you'd get Tony 'P' off. Yah did a helluva job."

Jonesy was on Heavy's arm. She joined in the accolades.

"He's right Johnny. You did quite a job, didn't you."

Her inflection questioned and Johnny Fixx abruptly cut Heavy short.

"I'll see you in a little bit pal. There's somebody over there I should say hello to."

Crystal Lee was gliding among the guests, a vision in mandarin red.

"The conquering hero," she exclaimed. Fixer grinned, "hey doll, it turned out to be a great story, didn't it?"

"That was then, this is now. What do you have for me tonight?"

"Later," he breathed as Joey Dancer walked in.

"Joey, where the hell's the old man. They're making me play host. I can't stand the attention and I'm drinking too much."

"He's in the study with Spillane."

"What the hell's the deal between them? Joe Bayonne' in on it, but I think he's strictly playing banker."

"I don't know much more than you do Johnny," said Dancer. "Tony asked me to arrange for the transportation as soon as they work out the deal with the South Koreans."

"He's really got permits to import the guns, Joey?"

"I've seen them Johnny. I think it gets hairy once they hit the LA shore, but the importing is on the up and up."

Manny Cesar trailed Evita into the room.

"Hey 'George Raft'," called Joey Dancer.

Evita flew into Dancer's arms.

"Hi big boy. Buy me a drink?"

Evita walked arm in arm with Dancer to the bar. George Raft shook Fixer's hand.

"You came through Johnny. Shit, we were all pulling for the old man. You did a nice job man."

"Sure I did," agreed Fixer none too convincingly.

Dancer fed Evita two drinks and sought to escape her by calling to Fixer.

"Johnny, Johnny, come over here. I need to ask you something."

Fixer leaned into the bar beside Dancer.

"Shoot, amigo."

The Big Fall

"I need Tex Tannis. Remember I asked you about him Johnny. That freight deal is gonna' pop any day and Tex probably could use the work. You hear from him?"

Fixer had been uncomfortable with it when Dancer first raised the possibility of using Tex to fly freight.

Fixer exclaimed "Tex!" then said, "what the hell do you want with him - christ, he was a Section 8 coming out of the Nam years ago."

Dancer ordered doubles, "the brown whisky from the square bottle with the black label."

They downed the liquor and did an encore. And then another. Whether too much liquor, or the peculiar chemistry between them, when their eyes met the destination was the deathly attractive nightmare place of years before. Suddenly they were alone in the roomful of people, on a trail in the Central Highlands that deadened in a graveyard of sorts. Bullet riddled bleached stone French watch towers were ghostly sentinels for forgotten fields of fire, flanking burned out hulks of American, ARVN, NVA and French tanks and personnel carriers. Rusted concertina wire blocked the trail, a bleached skeleton entangled on its barbs, scarlet wild flowers growing through the bones where blood had flowed. The platoon hunkered down in the elephant grass.

The Sergeant heard it first and exclaimed, "I gotta be out of my head."

The gurgle, and roar, and wheeze of a straining diesel engine sounded as a battered school bus barreled down the track at them. The men spread out to open up. The bus braked and skid to a halt .He stepped out from behind the wheel. A blue bandana tied atop his head, his full beard red, flecked with gray. He wore a leather vest, and nothing more above the waist. Tattered fatigue pants and boots covered the rest.

He waved both arms, "don't get nervous boys. Billy Gears is the name. I've got what you want.

177

"It was out of the question that he could be freely travelling the trail, but the Nam was a place that made things out of the question commonplace. He kept coming and Fixer stepped out to take a closer look. Gears eyes were jungle green, with yellow spots. His complexion was burnt brown. But he was an American and that made him a friend.

"He's okay," called Fixer as the platoon broke cover to gather around Gears.

"I'm a peddler boys," Gears exclaimed. "What'll it be Cambodian red, buddha grass, how about a drink, '33', 'San Miguel Tiger', 'Swan Jager', I'm the local distributor. And that ain't all my friends. I've got Montagnard jewelry, gossamer Ao Dai's for your ladies, rings, watches whatever your hearts' desire."

The platoon was speechless to a man. Gears grinned broadly his fingers nervously picking at the gold loop earring he wore through one ear.

"'Fuck' women - right, that's it, ain't it. Come on out here ladies and show your wares."

Three women stepped down, each of them a looker. Gears picked up the nervous movement of the men's feet, the imperceptible tightening of their bellies, and pitched his merchandise.

"This is 'Baby Fat'."

The name fit. She was five feet tall, and all breasts, behind, and thighs. Her hair was tied back behind her head. She wore cut offs and a halter.

"Hi boys," she said with an easy smile.

Gears patted her behind, and nodded to the other two.

"Dani and Lana," he said, introducing two tallish slender girls who where deeply tanned, with long straight blonde tresses reaching their backsides. They wore gauzy red sundresses and could have passed for sisters. But their faces distinguished them - Dani's features were soft and sensuous, Lana's angular and regal.

The platoon had been too long in the open. NVA regulars worked in close and all hell broke loose as they braced the troopers with automatic weapons fire and a mortar barrage. Gears bus was incinerated and he cursed the troopers who had cost him his wares. Casualties were taken and for a few tense minutes the men feared they'd be cut off and worse. Then the 'whump', 'whump', 'whump' and screech of the rotors sounded. Tex Tannis led a trio of gunships in close raking the underbrush with M-60 door guns and finally settling the issue with a brace of 2.75 rockets.

Tex Tannis was all the air force they'd ever needed in the Nam. He'd been busted from flying F-4's for drunkenness that really was a breakdown in the making. He flew backwater transports and kept his nose clean until finally they permitted him back in the kill zones leading cobra gunships. He saved them that day, and more times after that than they could remember. Tannis used it all up in the Nam. Stateside was one long run of trouble and bad luck for the man.

Fixer snapped at the bartender, "the bottle," and poured their glasses full again.

"Here's to the sonuvabitch who'd fly through any amount of shit to save our asses."

Dancer raised his glass, shuddered and turned away.

Johnny Fixx was suddenly alone, the party passing him by. And that suited him just fine. He drank heavily and had a comfortable buzz on by midnight. Tony Persia never did show.

"Ah boyo, the curse is on you tonight." Dermot Spillane had slipped into the salon to stand beside him.

Fixer stood almost at attention regarding himself in the bar mirror.

The Big Fall

"Yah look like Cu Chulainne standing in the Dublin post office boyo with that black vulture perched on his shoulder ready to pick at his guts when he falls."

"So you think I've got something in common with a celtic god, eh. And I thought I was the one who was drunk."

Fixer grinned. "You goddamned micks have a way with words, Dermot. That and tragedy."

Spillane squeezed Fixer's arm, "and so do you boyo."

Manny Cesar walked to the bar.

"Give him to me Dermot. I think there's something downstairs that'll cheer him up."

"Where the hell are we going," complained Fixer as Cesar led him below decks.

"In here" directed Cesar as he pushed Fixer into the room.

"What the hell," he gasped as the scene registered.

They were on the private side of a one way mirror that looked in on a stateroom whose principal piece of furniture was an oversized circular bed. A 'v' shaped pedestal of candles lazily flickered near the far side of the mirror. Incense pots sculpted as reclining tigers hung from chains around the bedroom's perimeter. Charcoal embers flashed through eye and mouth openings, wisps of heavy smoke waffling out. Silken strands danced a drugged butterfly glide from bladed fans.

Crystal Lee was spread eagled naked on an orange red tiger pelt centered on the bed. Evita poured oils on Crystal's body, droplet by sweet droplet, and slowly ran her breasts along Crystal's bosom and belly and thighs and legs. Crystal moaned long, low animal sounds and wildly thrust her head from side to side. Evita rolled Crystal onto her belly and massaged her back, buttocks, and legs. Crystal extended her arms clawing at the tiger pelt. Then Evita began licking at the cleft of

180

Crystal's buttocks, finally burying her mouth deep between Crystal's legs.

"For christ sake, Manny, how can you...."

Cesar cut him off. "It's okay Johnny. Evita's straight when she's with me. Tonight just isn't one of those nights. Besides Johnny, to the victor belongs the spoils."Manny Cesar handed Fixer the key to the adjoining door.

\* \* \* \* \*

"No rest for the wicked," screamed Joey Dancer into Johnny Fixx' intercom.

"Come on up," rasped Fixer.

Dancer let himself in.

"Christ, who got me here last night?"

Dancer chuckled, "I did pal and 'last night' was yesterday. Between the booze and those broads you slept through a whole damned day."

Dancer handed him a paper container of coffee from the bag he'd carried in.

"Come on pal, we're goin' to the Mission. I've got to find Tex Tannis."

"Christ Joey, don't do this to me today."

"I'm runnin' out of time, Johnny. I need the guy."

The Vine Street Mission was two blocks off Hollywood, flanked by a used car lot and an empty lot where a balding chicano sold 'discount' luggage at the curb. The Mission was stucco and tile, slowly graying in the heat and smog. For blocks in either direction, a gaudy neon veneer barely covered the underside storefronts, the seedy bars, army surplus stores, and pawn shops and secondhand stores where anything was for sale. Fixer winced. Dancer clasped his shoulder as they stepped onto the curb.

"It's hell all right amigo, but they try to dress it up a little, like pancake makeup on the bloated face of a night lady who should have taken early retirement."

The entranceway of the Mission smelled of sweat and urine, vomit, and forgotten hopes. Fixer stumbled as he barely avoided a discarded bowl of soup. Dancer handled a satchel and sidestepped a shattered bottle of ripple. It was a place where dreams came to die. There were old people, stooped and pasty, and junkies who twitched and paced, their eyes pleading for the fix they couldn't afford.

"In here," directed Dancer, as he led Johnny Fixx into the chapel.

The room was dimly lit, filled with scarred benches, a lectern finished in peeling paint, and an organ covered by a tiger striped poncho. There were three of them sitting the front bench silently staring straight ahead. They wore threadbare dress khakis and red berets, their arm patches the lightning bolt and eagle insignia of an airborne ranger unit.

Sergeant Rogers turned to regard them and strained to pull himself up on half dead legs, painfully supporting himself on forearm crutches.

"Lo Johnny. Joey. We've been waiting for you." Rogers began coughing, his pallor graying, his breath coming in tortured gasps.

"I'm gettin' weaker all the time. They give me penicillin and valium. But I hurt all over. Everything is bad. I've got a hot band around my chest. I think it's a heart attack. They say 'no'. I can't breathe. My lungs burn. I can't eat. I get stomach cramps, then I get nauseous."

The soldier's voice built in desperation.

"You understand, don't you? I'm wiped out. Joey's medicine gets us through the night. But it never lets up. There's nightmares. I void. I'm afraid of the dark. Christ! I've got this rash down my legs. Blisters and lesions, everywhere. Even on my prick. I'm dyin' man, and I'm alone. 'Uncle' don't know me no more. Not even a two bit street walker will come near me."

Fixer stepped back a step.

"Jesus, Joey, they think I'm here to tell them I can make something out of their 'Agent Orange' case."

Dancer coolly regarded his friend, whispering "take a swing at it smart guy. It's only time - right? You're always complainin' about what we do to stay ahead of it. So maybe this'ill help square things, at least a little."

Fixer snapped angrily at the futility of it all, "do what we came here to do, and let's get the fuck out of this place."

Joey Dancer moved to the front of the chapel where the trio sat.

"Tex Tannis . . . ." was the last Fixer heard as he walked out.

Johnny Fixx breathed deeply at the curb. Dancer joined him.

"What was in the fucking bag?"

"Something to get them through the night pal."

"I can't make anything out of their goddamned case, Joey. The government already decided to pay them a fucking penny on the dollar. There's nothing I can do."

"You don't have to explain, amigo. They know they're already dead. Maybe all they want you to do is try so that when they're carved in black marble, somebody remembers. Me, I handle 'Uncle' my way, and

183

at a profit. I leave them some goods. They sell for me, and shoot up the rest themselves."

They had driven for nearly twenty minutes before Fixer was able to speak.

"What about Tex Tannis?"

"Rogers said he was working at a glider school at Kelso. You or me?"

"I'll take the ride," said Johnny Fixx.

\* \* \* \* \*

Fixer breathed "nothing's easy" as he drove east from Los Angeles on I-15 into the desert. He exited at the dusty desert town of Baker and picked up the unpaved Kelbaker Road into the 47,000 acre expanse of the Kelso dunes at the foot of the 6,600 foot Granite Mountains. Work wasn't the ticket after the Persia trial and searching out Tex Tannis in the middle of nowhere seemed the right duty.

Sweeping knife edged crescents of wind shaped the sea of sand into curves and currents, troughs and massive dunes, shaded a constantly shifting fuscia with the ever changing angle of the sun. Desert sunflowers, golden primrose and desert lilies bloomed in the midst of patches of creosote bush and dune grass. A golden eagle tracking a peregrine falcon rode the air currents screaming down from the Granite Mountains. The lonesome birds of prey had company – Tex Tannis, banished to the desert purgatory to survive by teaching 'wanna be' pilots the fine art of glider piloting.

Tannis was once more without a pilot's license. It had been alcohol again. A spot check of the strip where Tannis flew had caught him with a blood alcohol level that equaled intoxication under the law. Fixer could never quite shake the sense of foreboding that grabbed at him from the first time Dancer had suggested Tex to fly his freight. License or no license, drunk or sober, Tex could do the job. And the man was alive only when he flew. That's how Fixer rationalized making the pitch to Tex Tannis.

184

# The Big Fall

Tex was on a scaffold replacing the nacel plate on a bi-plane's engine. He'd been long and lean with a shock of brown hair that reached his shoulders. Now there was grease around the middle and thinning hair cut short. He jumped off the scaffold and greeted his friend.

"Lo Johnny. Long time no see."

Tex' skin was leathery from constant exposure to the sun. His eyes were watery and distant and Fixer began to wonder.

"How's the boy," he exclaimed in a tone of genuine affection.

"I'm down to this Johnny. The bi-plane's my air force. When I'm not towing kiwis who want to fly, I use her to do crop dusting."

Tannis rigged a tow line to the nose of a glider and called into the radio shack.

"Tommy, come on out here and fly the tow. I'm taking an old pal up."

Fixer climbed into the glider cockpit behind Tex as Tommy fired up the bi-plane and taxi'd off with them in tow.

Tex released the tow line at 5,000 feet and soared down in a graceful series of dives and rolls through dome clouds that descended to cover the tops of craggy plateaus. High tension towers stood mute guardians to brooding mountain passes, misted openings, like perilous pathways to dark niches in the mind, undiscovered - or best left unpursued. Tex split dagger sharp peaks, then swooped to 1000 feet to buzz a Santa Fe freight snaking through the shimmering mid day heat haze on the desert floor. The man came alive in the air. Joey Dancer might be right after all. Tannis screamed over the field pulling out of a steep dive, executed a sharp turn to the left and cut short his approach by taking her straight in.

Tex grinned at Fixer.

"It ain't quite an F-4, but I try to make do."

185

The Big Fall

"That you do, pal," agreed Fixer. "Joey's running freight down in Mexico. He can *use* you for a while to fly transport. Number one, are you interested, and two, how close will the federales look at your papers. Is that revoked license going to queer the deal?"

"Jeez, Johnny, that's great. Don't worry about the papers. I fly down there once in a while. I've got some pals on the other side. All you have to do is spread a couple of bucks around. Dancer wants me to fly some freight. How about that. Hell you just made my day pal."

"Dancer said it'll pay pretty good Tex. Get in touch with him at Acme Specialties in Pedro."

"Will do pard, will do."

"Yer okay now, aren't you, Tex", Johnny Fixx called to his friend.

Tex showed his boyish grin.

"I'm fucked up, pal. You and me both know it. But I'd rather be fucked up in the air than down here. So you tell me, Johnny, am I okay?"

Fixx nodded.

"Rusty still workin' for you?"

"Part time, Tex. Why don't you give her a call?"

"I will. I will."

## C H A P T E R   S I X T E E N

Max Gale's campus office was ordered chaos. Every inch of wall space, floor to ceiling, was covered with shelves crammed every square inch with books and magazines. The overflow was stacked nearly waist high on either side of the great man's desk. At random intervals blank pieces of paper were crammed between texts and periodicals, Max' personal bookmarks. Max sat at his desk swiveled around to face the credenza that was covered with a word processor, printer, vcr, video monitor, and stereo system. He turned hands full with a stack of vhs video tapes.

"I'm doing that Alan Ladd retrospective for the film studies project. These are some of his good ones in the forties."

"Shane?" kidded Johnny Fixx.

"No not Shane," said Gale with a trace of irritation in his voice.

"The tough guy roles that made him one of the biggest box office draws of the forties. The Veronica Lake films. 'The Glass Key', 'This Gun for Hire', 'The Blue Dahlia', 'Calcutta', 'OSS', 'Chicago Deadline', and 'Appointment With Danger'. You like these 'winner take nothing' films."

"Every one black and white, right. Not because they didn't have color, but because they just looked better that way. No happy endings?"

Gale chuckled.

"Damned near none, but 'the voice' always died with his boots on. Run them when you get a chance, mark out ten or twelve scenes, the dialogue that's indicative of the genre, okay?"

"It's gonna' be Professor Max on film noir, right?" "Just run the films Johnny." Gale shifted gears, "you up for tonight?"

The Big Fall

Fixer's manner had been rather obviously labored after the Persia mistrial. Gale had picked up on it. "Anything I can help with?"

Johnny Fixx nodded "no" and breathed "you don't want any part of this one, Max. I'll handle it, and like everything else, clients, cops, prosecutors, dames, and creditors, it'll pass."

There was a knock at the door.

"It's Jennie, Professor. May I come in?"

"Sure, Jennie. Sure."

"Oh hello," she said to Fixer as she moved past him to stand to the side of Max Gale's desk.

"I've done those Burt Lancaster films you suggested - for my paper. 'The Killers', 'Criss Cross', 'Sweet Smell of Success'. And I've developed an outline."

'That ain't all you've developed', thought Johnny Fixx. Jennie leaned forward, her scarlet glossed lips within inches of her Professor's. She was peaches and cream, all curves and valleys, ripe and obviously infatuated with Max.

"Slide it under the door, Jennie - if I'm not here. I'll take a look, and we'll go over it."

"Later tonight," she asked.

"Maybe. Let me see how my schedule plays out." Jennie brushed Fixer's thigh as she moved out of the office. The door clicked shut and Fixer grinned.

"Max, you old dog, you. Did I read that little slice of life correctly?"

"You did not, you degenerate. Not at all."

"Okay, pal. Whatever you say."

\*   \*   \*   \*   \*

The seminar room was at the base of the law school tower. The subject matter was criminal defense, and Max Gale introduced John Fixx to the fifteen students gathered around the elliptical conference table.

"For those of you who have led rather cloistered lives and may be unacquainted with John, he's one of the best defense lawyers anywhere in this country. I've had the privilege of assisting him on several cases. He's trapped now with us, so fire away and don't be shy."

Johnny Fixx waved to the students, and asked, "what is it with each of you, idealism or a living?"

No one volunteered and Fixx said, "okay, tonight you ask and I answer, but keep that one in mind. Where you draw the line between the two might be all that's left when you succumb to early Alzheimer's."

A young woman who sat farthest from Fixer at the other end of the table, asked, "what about representing a client who you know is guilty as charged. How do you square that with legal ethics and personal conscience?"

It was the expected first question, and one to which there really was no pat answer.

"Legal ethics . . . ." said Fixer, his voice trailing off. For an instant the student's face merged with juror number ten, Barbara Stanley. Fixer willed Mrs. Stanley away and continued, "in the first place, even an admission of guilt may not be what it seems. Defense lawyers really can't be certain that a statement or confession or a lawyer-client confidence is the gospel. I don't mean to meander into metaphysics, but guilt in a moral sense isn't necessarily guilt under the law. And isn't culpability under our system really no more and no less than what the jury says it is after listening to the facts and legal arguments made by prosecution and defense. And the jury speaks, doesn't it, only after the proofs are closed. So defense counsel, even with the apparently

189

guilty client, must see the matter through to the end of the proceeding."

The student interjected, "with all due respect Mr. Fixx, that sounds like a summation."

Fixer smiled. "Point for the soon to be counsellor. Let's get back to basics. The criminal justice system in this country is based on two fundamental principles without which we'd have nothing. One is the presumption of innocence. The second is due process. Never lose sight of the fact that the prosecution must prove guilt beyond a reasonable doubt. That's a severe burden but one that is entirely proper when civil forfeitures, incarceration, and even the loss of one's life are the stakes in the game. Most of you have no idea how lopsided the advantage is to the police and prosecutors in the typical criminal case. Remember that in the state system the police do the investigation for the DA. In the federal, it's usually the FBI or some other federal police agency. It can take as long as eighteen months and even longer than that with extensions, for the people to bring in an indictment. Millions of dollars are at their disposal and basically unlimited manpower and brain power. Now it's the morning after the defendant learns he's been charged. He's in a panic and even if innocent or if guilt is doubtful, the defendant is already playing catch up. Press coverage may cost him his livelihood. Then he's faced with the financial burden of retaining an attorney. This can cost him his life's savings - literally. I see some expressions of doubt on your faces. Again, this is not the representation of a corporate client with deep pockets for the criminal defense attorney. The defense lawyer if he's any good knows that at some point rather quickly, the case will close in on him and require 100% of his time twenty four hours each day. So the retainer will be substantial both because of the likely drain on the attorney's time and the fact that when he's engaged he isn't going to be able to generate any other income from his practice. If he's doing his job, there simply won't be any time. Then there's the matter of investigators to go over the facts and retrace the steps the police have covered. No LA PD or FBI for the defense. It's usually the lawyer himself or private investigators, and in this day and age 'PI's' don't work cheap. Last but not least, the experience of being the target of a criminal prosecution, even if there's an acquittal, usually breaks the defendant financially - I know there are exceptions - but generally, the defendant may take years to mend his financial fences. So, as his defense counsel, you must get your money in full up front. If not, you may be working pro bono."

The Big Fall

"What it comes down to people, in my view anyway, is that the defendant is entitled to every break he can get, even if he did it. It's civilized to do it that way especially when the system's going to break him anyway."

The student immediately to his left asked, "I suppose what you say in the case of the ordinary citizen who is charged with a crime probably makes sense. But what about organized crime, the professional criminal. Are these people entitled to every advantage the system affords them?"

Another student called out, "yeah, what about RICO? Isn't that the equalizer for the prosecutors?"

"I'm not a fan of RICO. Even if I was a prosecutor, I'd be troubled by it. I'm going to assume that you have a basic familiarity with the Act. The prosecutor must prove a criminal enterprise and a pattern of racketeering in advancement of that enterprise. The pattern of racketeering can be as few as two criminal acts, usually but not necessarily committed in the immediately prior ten years. This is where I think the Act crashes head on into the due process guarantee. The crimes in advancement of the criminal enterprise - predicate acts - do not have to be in the present, nor do they have to be acts that have gone unproved and unpunished. Take a person who was charged, convicted, and did time for grand larceny, say seven years ago. Even though he's paid his debt to society, that crime can be one of the predicate acts. Now let's say that today he's charged with bookmaking. Being a gambler is almost as American as motherhood and apple pie. We love the crap shooter - the odds maker gliding from phone booth to phone booth taking bets on horses or numbers doesn't get us very upset. In fact, Judges tend to let them off easy ninety-nine out of a hundred. And can you blame them? Sure it's breaking the law. But if state lotteries are legal, as well as off track betting, and Vegas, and Atlantic City, and Vegas nights and bingo at church bazars, the moral case against gambling is rather hard to swallow. And if you can't find the moral basis for the sin, the legal sanction is tough to rationalize. So our defendant gets convicted in the present under a RICO indictment of being a bookmaker. Now if he had been charged simply with bookmaking, what's he looking at? Even a repeat offender faces little more than a fine and token time in the lockup. Aggravated gambling seldom draws more than a year, and it's local - not even in the penitentiary system. But, and here comes the hammer, the defendant in the RICO case under the federal model and all the state copycat statutes is facing twenty years in the can for a crime he's already paid for and gambling in the present that standing alone would be unlikely to subject him to any hard time. So now how do you feel about RICO?"

191

"But if there's little doubt, Mr. Fixx, that the defendant is a made member of the mob, then what choice does the government have but to proceed under RICO? I mean sir, these guys are sworn to silence, aren't they? Their business is crime for profit. So aren't they really forfeiting some of their rights by taking that blood oath and leading that life?"

"Be careful with your generalizations. There aren't many classifications that pass muster under equal protection. If a professional criminal isn't entitled to the same bundle of rights as the rest of us, then who's next? The person with the strange religion or weird life style or different skin color. I believe that it's at the very frontiers of the system that we make or break our laws. RICO can look very right and proper in some situations, but in others it can be a hornet's nest for abuse. And our legislatures and courts are looking the other way."

"Organized crime," said Fixer. "Hmm," he thought out loud. "One thing more on that one. Pity the poor prosecutors. Blood oaths in shadowy basements never to betray one's criminal brothers. Omerta - the code of silence to the death. Not so anymore. There's the federal Witness Protection Program and state equivalents. Wise guys routinely rat each other out. Paid and protected informants are usually the basis for indictments against organized crime. That would be more than a sufficient edge for the people, even without RICO."

"How close Mr. Fixx can a lawyer get to his client? I mean when do you come close to crossing the line?"

"If you're doing your job, every goddamned day. It's a constant struggle. The lawyer client privilege is an enormous burden. The Professional Responsibility to keep a client's secrets and confidences goes hand and glove with the evidentiary privilege. The duty to do everything in your power to save your client is an enormous burden."

"But Mr. Fixx, what if you're backed into a corner and the only way you can save your client is to cut a corner or even break the law or look the other way at his lawbreaking. Then what do you do. Shouldn't you blow him in?"

Johnny Fixx sat back in his chair and groped for the right words. Seconds ticked past and the silence bordered on the embarrassing.

The Big Fall

Max Gale jumped in to field the question, "that one may be a question for legal ethics rather than trial tactics for the defense, but the answer is crystal clear - you never break the law. Period. You're sworn to uphold the law. Each of you will be officers of the court. That's the line you never cross!"

\*   \*   \*   \*   \*

Surf was blasting against the shore rocks and the horizon in late afternoon was gray darkening to inky black. The weather guru on KLZ had predicted sun and clearing after a few tense moments. The tense moments seemed to be lasting longer than expected. A fog bank rolled in and Fixer retreated from the deck to the great room. He fed a tape into the vcr and sat back as the opening credits of 'The Blue Dahlia' ran.

The service had taken Alan Ladd away after two smash hits in 1942 with Veronica Lake, the pint sized leading lady with the lush hips and peek-a-boo tresses that was his match, 'This Gun For Hire', and 'The Glass Key'. 1945 brought the end to the fighting and the public craved another dose of their pint sized tough guy. Raymond Chandler just happened to have a book in progress that could fill the bill and John Houseman at RKO persuaded him to script a screen play for Ladd and Lake. Chandler wrote them 80 fast pages from the novel text he'd already completed and shooting began immediately. Within three weeks production had caught up with Chandler's pages and the author confessed that he'd run into a writer's block in resolving the story. Ladd hadn't been discharged and was facing a deadline for reporting back to his unit. Cast and crew were idle, but the meter ran on their salaries and per diems. John Houseman got to his pal Chandler and talked him into attempting to finish the script. Chandler had been on the wagon but breaking through required extraordinary measures. He took a suite at the Chateau Marmont and embarked upon a controlled drunk. Doctors and nurses were standing by. So too were a round the clock battery of stenographers and typists. Chandler's binge worked. He squeezed out the script, Ladd finished his scenes before being declared 'awol', and the film became a post war hit and a cult movie ever after.

Alan Ladd was back from the service, the fall guy in a murder plot that revolved around his two timing wife, and her gangster boyfriend, Eddie Harwood who ran the 'Blue Dahlia' Club. When his wife was shot dead with a service .45, the police focused their manhunt on Ladd. Ladd went on the lam with new

193

girlfriend Veronica Lake, who just happened to be Eddie Harwood's 'ex'. Eddie Harwood, the slippery nightclub impresario, clearly was a hard case coming undone because of woman trouble that opened his murderous past. His partner in crime, Leo, early on attempted to warn him off his 'weakness' for the ladies. Leo told Harwood, "when a man gets too complicated, he's unhappy. And when he's unhappy, his luck runs out."

"Are you getting 'too complicated' Johnny?" asked Crystal Lee.

Fixer shut down the film.

"I thought you were cooking us up something," he asked.

"I've got our dinner cooking." She motioned to the blank screen. "No comment, eh."

"Let's eat."

Salad, fruit, and white fish.

"When the hell are you going to cook a steak lady?" he asked.

"Not healthful," she answered. "Ever read about yellow skinned people having a problem with the pump?"

"Nah. You all cash in from stomach cancer that flares up because of the mercury and other garbage the fish put into your system."

"Shut up and eat Johnny."

"Yer right kid. It's all irrelevant. Something's gonna' kill us - and that's about all you can count on."

They were through the food and sipping a final glass of wine. "My ears in the prosecutor's office tell me your pal Joey Dancer is about to fall to a RICO indictment."

"Nah, can't be Crystal. We haven't been notified that Joey's a target. And besides, it just doesn't figure. Joey's been clean for years."

"It's got to do with some things years ago, the Beverly Hilton job, and the Wells Fargo thing."

"But that stuff is dead wood, Crystal. Joey did time for both of them. It's not enough. They need to show a pattern of racketeering into the present - from then to now with another major felony in the here and now to anchor the pattern."

Crystal shrugged, "I don't know, Johnny, but the word is that the boys downtown seem to think they'll come up with it."

"Can you beat that," said Fixer.

"Brandy," he offered as he moved to the stairs to the bedroom loft.

Crystal offered and Johnny wanted to think he had to have her. But another hour of drinking and snorting the blow she'd brought with her slowed him down even more. By ten he was on dead stop.

"Sorry, kid," he said lazily as he rolled away. Crystal watched his breathing deepen, then even out. Fixer would be out for hours. She moved down the stairs and into the kitchen. The beach house had few walls. The kitchen was separated from the rest and it was there that Crystal placed her call. Chick Hill was her editor.

"Nothing yet on Joey Dancer," she whispered. "I thought my source would come through with the lead we need. He still might. I'll let you know."

*     *     *     *     *

The car in his drive was unfamiliar. Samantha couldn't sleep and made the drive as the sun was rising. She'd surprise him and maybe they'd make a day of it. The door opened and Crystal Lee stepped

195

out into the bright morning. Samantha cursed silently and kicked her accelerator.

She screamed, "damned you, Johnny," and slammed her fist into the dash board.

Surprise her ex? She should have known better.

She fishtailed around a curve and hit her brakes. He had materialized out of nowhere. The man was not ten yards ahead of her waving his arms to pull her over.

She hit her door locks and began steering around him. No way any woman in her right mind would pull over for a stranger on the open road in the Southlands.

He moved across the road to cut her off, still gesturing for her to pull over. Then he reached into his coat pocket and began waving the badge.

Samantha focused on his face. She knew the man. He was a policeman.

She pulled onto the apron and rolled down her window. He trotted to her side of the car and bent at the waist to meet her eye level.

She finally recognized him.

Harry Lang.

"Good morning, Ms. Fixx. I didn't mean to give you heart failure back there. But I thought maybe we should have a chat.

"I can't imagine why that should be, Lieutenant, but I'm here so what is it you want to tell me."

His eyes were fixed and cold. She stifled an involuntary shudder.

"Your ex-husband is in deep trouble. He's definitely going to end up in jail. But that's the least of his problems. He keeps the kind of company that just might get him killed before it's over."

"What Johnny does is his business. He's a criminal defense lawyer. Bad company is his stock in trade. He can take care of himself."

"I wouldn't be too sure of that Ms. Fixx."

Samantha was far from convinced herself but she resolved to keep her reservations to herself. Lang saw it in her eyes and smiled.

"You know I'm right, lady. Now I know you're his 'ex'. And he keeps company with that slant anchorperson. So maybe you don't give a good shit what happens to him. And maybe you just happened to be taking a drive today that took you past his beach house. But if you do happen to spend some time with the man, I'd try to wise him up. I'm the only game in town for him."

Lang handed her his card.

"You can reach me at those numbers twenty four hours a day seven days a week."

He had her off balance. Did the policeman think he could turn her to spy on Johnny?

"What do you think I am, Lieutenant," she seethed.

"A woman who maybe married the wrong guy and who doesn't quite have him out of her system. And let me tell you this Ms. Fixx, you keep dancing with him and he'll use you up and hurt you every time."

"I don't plan on seeing him," said Samantha. "Deliver your own messages, Lieutenant."

The Big Fall

"That's probably for the best Ms. Fixx - I mean, that you not see him. I think he might be too far gone for saving anyway. At this point, he probably doesn't give two shits for anybody or anything, other than himself, and I really doubt that he'd ever put it on the line for another person - you included - unless there was green involved of the six figure variety."

Her eyes flashed with anger.

"He is what he is, Lieutenant."

And as she rolled up her window, Samantha called back to Lang, "and you are what you are, Lieutenant."

"Aren't we all," said Harry Lang as he watched her disappear up the road.

*   *   *   *   *

"Crystal," he called coughing away the sleep and rubbing at his eyes. Bands of shadow and light crept across the room from the skylight. Early morning. He called for her again.

"Left me high and dry," he croaked. "Best to be hungover and miserable solo."

Fixer moved to the deck. The sea was still high, but the clouds had disappeared. The sun was a brilliant lemon ball dancing on a string beyond the mountains behind him that ringed the City. Long shadows rippled over the breakers and the seaward horizon was still darkened with the night that only slowly let go.

Fixer padded to the kitchen, stoppered the sink and filled it with cold water, then dumped in two trays of cubes. He immersed his face, shuddered and came up for air, then did it again, this time counting to a hundred twenty. The procedure was repeated twice more. Fixer's homespun hangover remedy. The phone rang. Fixer gurgled away the wet from nose and mouth. Crystal Lee was calling. "What's the matter with you Johnny?"

The Big Fall

"Just waking up. I thought maybe I'd get a personal wake up call."

"Sorry love. A story was breaking and I had to get in to the newsroom to cover it. That's why I called."

Fixer was now fully focused.

"How so Crystal?"

"A B-17 bomber was hi-jacked from an air show - you know, a World War II antique."

"What's that got to do with me," he asked.

"The pilot may be one of your friends from that Mission on Vine where the Nam vets hang out. The police think the flyer is a guy named Tex Tannis."

Fixer exclaimed, "christ!"

"It's more than just a joy ride Johnny," she explained.

"They were tracking the plane over the ocean beyond Catalina and were about to scramble some navy jets to catch it and escort it home. Then the B-17 disappeared off the scope maybe eighty miles due west of Catalina."

"My god," he breathed.

Fixer dressed and scrambled out of the beach house, burning rubber as he accelerated onto the coast highway. A half hour later he braked before the Acme Specialties gate. Electric eyes on surveillance monitors blinked 'on' and 'off' and the motor whirred as the gate slid open, triggered by some unseen hand inside the building who had made him as a friendly. Fixer parked behind the building and walked in through the cooler. This time the racks were empty. Half the warehouse floor was stacked with the usual neatly piled cartons, the other half covered by more vending and arcade game machines than he'd ever seen before. Joey Dancer sat alone in the office booth that was the single illuminated area in the building.

Johnny Fixx charged through the door slamming it against its stop, his anger barely restrained.

Joey Dancer swiveled in his chair to face him, grim faced, his hands outstretched to placate him.

"I know. I know. I never figured it to happen."

"What the hell did you get Tex into Joey," snapped Fixer. "A freight run - you lied to me goddamned it. I'd have never ...."

"Shit Johnny, so I dressed it up a little. You'd have never gotten to him for me if I hadn't. And he needed the dough. He had me take it right out to Rusty. He didn't want to even touch it. And in a manner of speaking it really was just a freight deal. I got a tip they were flying an old B-17 in for an air show. Then I found out the bomber had a Norden bombsight in its nose that still worked. They must have made a half million of those things during the War. You got any idea how many are left - that actually work?"

The clouds were parting. Fixer picked up on it.

"So you hi-jack the B-17 and need Tex to fly it. All for the Norden bombsight."

"Something like that Johnny. I pulled the bombsight and trucked it to the old military airstrip north of Irvine, where it's stashed. Tex was supposed to fly the B-17 north to a private strip near Vera Cruz, set her down, and walk away. I never figured the plane would have mechanical problems."

"Christ!" exploded Fixer as he leaped to grab Dancer's collar and pull him out of his chair. "You goddamned fool. You put Tex back into a fighting plane. It didn't snap. He did! The poor bastard never flew north. He just took her out to sea and went straight in. Jesus, Dancer ...."

Dancer's bodyguards appeared on the floor. Paulie Flange moved among the pin ball machines randomly putting them into play and laughing hysterically as lights flashed, pin balls clacked, and bells rang.

Eddie Ebony moved to the booth door. "Take it easy Mr. Fixer," he whispered. "There's no future in it."

Fixer dropped into a chair, the anger beginning to let go. "Call off your boy, Joey," he said. Eddie Ebony moved back onto the floor.

"Now what happens," asked Fixer.

"You know the drill Johnny. The usual. The insurance boys will get into it and they'll be more than glad to sell it back to some air museum, maybe even the Smithsonian."

"And all of it over Tex' dead body."

Dancer was about to alibi again but he knew Fixer was beyond persuading. "The old man catch up with you the other night?"

Just then Johnny Fixx wasn't listening.

## CHAPTER SEVENTEEN

The message light showed on the answering machine.

Fixer rewound and hit playback.

Samantha.

"You know Johnny, I'll never learn. It's me, not you. I drove by your beach place. I was going to stop in to cook you dinner. The news wagon was there, and just my luck. Your yellow whore was leaving and probably saw me drive by. Damned you!"

The intercom sounded.

"Johnny, it's me Tony. Send down the elevator."

Persia let himself in. Fixer moved to turn on some music.

"Okay, Tony?"

"Sure kid, sure. Something mellow."

That something was 'Charlie Parker and Strings'.

Persia smiled knowingly.

"I remember the guy. I really do. It was after the war out here. I think he got busted for drugs."

"Camarillo," agreed Fixer.

"It's a tough life bein' an artist - right? Nobody really appreciates you until you're dead and buried."

"Sometimes, Tony. Not always. But sometimes."

Persia helped himself to a snifter of brandy.

The Big Fall

"Drink, Johnny?" Fixer nodded "yes".

"Johnny, I wanted to talk with you the other night, but the crowd - it just wasn't the right time. Did Dancer tell you I wanted to see you?"

"He did, Tony, but that party finished me for 48 hours."

"Hell, no problem. You know I been spendin' some time with Dermot Spillane. You've got the general picture. I'm doin' some business with Spillane's pals, the micks."

"Now that we're out of court I was going to begin getting into that deal. Bayonne is handling your financial arrangements. Right? I figured that's why he was meeting with you a while back."

"You got it, kid. That's the place to start. If the money isn't guaranteed, I don't make a move."

"Then I'll hop a commuter to Vegas and talk to Bayonne about handling the pay off. How much can you tell me Tony?"

Persia's "you're family, Johnny," was intended as an expression of affection and confidence. It rang hollow for Johnny Fixx.

"Joey told me the guns were coming in from South Korea under legal importing permits. That's your end. But even at that, can't the thing boomerang on you Tony. The IRA attracts attention."

"It's telephone numbers Johnny. Don't worry about mechanics. That's my problem. I just want you to stay clean and make sure my end gets taken care of."

"You think you'll be needing someone to cover your back Tony?"

Persia grinned easily. "me . . . . Hell no! It isn't that I don't trust the micks. It's just good business to have your end safe and sound before you hand over the 'merch' right?"

"I can't argue with being cautious Tony, but have you really thought this through. Why take a chance with the bomb throwers. You don't need the gaff."

Fixer pressed, "besides, Tony, the 'feds' tend to take a hard line on guns and explosives - harder even than drugs."

Persia's pleasant expression hardened.

"Don't worry about it Johnny. You just cover my end. Bayonne's got some ideas about the dough. You know the ropes. Set it up. The sooner the better. And when my money's in the bank, the micks get the merch. I go when you signal me."

The Old Man's mood again softened.

"Come on Johnny. Do it for me. It's my retirement present a final grandslam. I know the risks. It'll work out."

"You got it, Tony," answered Johnny Fixx.

"While we're at it, kid, maybe now's the time for you to get to know the 'other' Dermot Spillane. He stops by Paddy O'Rourke's every day. If you've got the time, pay him a visit. Patience isn't one of the man's virtues - not when Mother Ireland and his Northern Aid are waiting in the wings. He'll probably light a fire under your can. Stroke the man some, okay. And get it done right for me."

* * * * *

Paddy O'Rourke's was a touch of Ireland on the Cannery in Huntington Beach. The bar entrance was graced by vendors' stalls where tea sets from Belleck, sweaters from Donegal, records from Dublin, and maps of Ireland and the Easter Rebellion Proclamations suitable for framing were for sale. There were pictures of Pearce, Rosaries from Rome, portraits of John

The Big Fall

Fitzgerald Kennedy, and badges of the Sacred Heart and the Virgin
Mary, all of which carried with them Plenary Indulgences. Inside,
Paddy O'Rourke's was set up for the business at hand, a fifty foot bar
covering one mirrored wall, opposite another wall mirrored from floor
to ceiling. There were tables in the back surrounding a small parquet
dance floor and a giant juke box stocked with fare of Mother Ireland,
'Irish Soldier Boy' by the Corkmen, 'Mother Malone' by the Liffey
Boys, 'Oh Danny Boy,' by the Irish Rovers, and 'God Bless America'
by Kate Smith Five bartenders, all six foot bruisers, with mick mugs to match
were busy keeping up with the trade that was three deep at the bar.

Dermot Spillane sat a table in back and motioned Johnny
Fixx to join him.

"What'll ye be drinkin' boyo," grinned Spillane in an
exaggerated brogue.

"A shooter of Jamesons, Guinness on the side." Spillane
summoned the bar maid, a plump carrot topped number in short
green skirt and tight ivory sweater.

"A man after my own heart," said Spillane as the drinks
were served.

"It's the money we'll be talking about, you and I, correct
Johnny?"

Fixer grinned in appreciation at Spillane's performance.

"It's always the money, now isn't it Dermot?"

"Well what can we do for ye John. You know we're
anxious to get on with it."

"It's got to be fail safe and not dependent on any third
party payers."

"We'd talked, Tony and I, about a letter of credit written on a
Swiss Bank. The Northern Aid's got some friends among the Swiss

205

The Big Fall

bankers. We'd put it in place before delivery and Tony could draw it down as he pleases."

Fixer showed a mildly reprimanding expression.

"Have I misspoke boyo?"

"No letters of credit, Dermot. I can't be sure who's on the other end. Too many eyes and ears."

"Well then, how about something with recognizable value - payment in diamonds, for example."

"I don't think so Dermot. Tony'd have to turn them into cash. That probably means a discount and jewelry brokers have too many eyes and ears."

"Well what then," said Spillane, now working on his pleasant tone.

"Cash or bearer bonds. And if its bearer bonds, we can't accept them until our banker checks the paper. Nothing personal Dermot, but there's too much bad paper floating around, and Tony is one of those serious minded people who wouldn't see the humor in being stiffed, even unintentionally, with forged paper."

Spillane reddened, but held his temper. He ordered another round and munched on a boiled egg.

"I understand your concerns, John - after all Tony is a client and a friend, and you're looking out for his interests, but this is a matter of life and death to my people in the old country. We've got to get this done. Do you have any idea John of what it is we're fighting?"

Fixer remained silent knowing full well that he was about to find out.

"Even language in the North is different. There's darkness, fear, and death. No life to the words, boyo - oh no, it's words spoken in a winter's gale. And with good cause. In Belfast the News Letter carries stories front page about Catholic women being killed by Provos. Innocents caught in cross fires, but that's not how they report them. Any woman killed in Northern Ireland must have had a bomb in her hand, and the press damned well puts it there rightly or wrongly."

"I understand," said Fixer. "I meant you no disrespect, Dermot."

"So you didn't," smiled Spillane. "I forgive ye lad, but do you really understand? The Catholics can't work in the North, John. But in the War, when the fooking Northern government opposed conscription, it was the Catholics that enlisted in the British army 10 to 1 over the Protestants. No secret why that happened. The poor bastards figured they had a better chance facing Nazi bullets than staying home and starving to death. Today yah walk down a street and see the Union Jack flying from every doorstep on the better streets. They keep you out of the slums where the bloody Catholic majority is kept - just like South Africa. My god man, they have a Minister of Housing who owns two hundred flats that he's renting for rates that would make our shylocks look generous. So how many new housing programs do you think the man backs? There's B-Specials and Glasgowmen with their plaid tammys riding armored personnel carriers. You look at them the wrong way and you hear 'piss on the Pope you Fenian fucks.' And still they can't destroy their spirit. They fight them with rocks and bottles. Kids facing Lewis guns! It's a horror twenty four hours a day. Petrol bombs blacken the streets. We won't lose, but we know we can't win either. Not unless there's bullets and weapons and bombs."

"You'll have your weapons, Dermot. Just see to arrangements."

"I will boyo, I will, but let me tell you a little story before we leave. There was this boy who was a son to me in the old days. We were in the old country and were to hit an armory for guns. It was Sean's job to fix the time of the watch change. We didn't want to hit them when both watches were on the post. Sean miscalculated the timing by only a minute or two, but it cost us a man. During the shooting Sean saved my life, and after, I thanked him."

Spillane's folksy tone lowered to an ominous timbre. "Then I shot the lad in the knee cap boyo. He'd betrayed us all by not doing
207

his job, and because he was one of us, I made sure he'd never bend that knee in genuflection again to receive the Sacraments of Holy Mother Church. I loved Sean like my own son, but we all take our business quite seriously, and there is honor among us, and with those we deal with. What I did to that boy wasn't personal, although there's been scarcely a night since when I don't see the look of horror on his face when my bullet shattered his knee."

\*   \*   \*   \*   \*

It was less than 72 hours later when an adjuster from Northwest Mutual caught up with Fixer. Danny Shane was waiting in the garage when Fixer pulled in after an afternoon in court. Shane had been a middleweight boxer of some reputation in the Southlands thirty years before. His hair was gone but he'd stayed hard. Danny Shane had worked with Johnny Fixx before on buy backs so it didn't surprise him when the anonymous call came in instructing him that Fixer was "the man to see" on the Norden bombsight buy back.

"How are yah Fixer," he said, stepping forward to vigorously pump the lawyer's hand.

"What can I do for you Danny?"

"I received an anonymous phone call that you'd be handling the negotiations on the Norden bombsight."

"Probably the same guy who called me, Danny. No name, no numbers yet. I'll be notified. The usual drill. But they did instruct me to talk to the company."

"Are you going to handle it John?"

"Yes, I think so. Hell, if I didn't, another attorney surely would. You and I can work this one out, don't you think Danny?"

Shane flashed a toothy smile. "Certainly, John. Surely. It's always a pleasure working with you. You've got my numbers, don't you," asked Danny Shane as he passed Fixer a card as a fail safe.

The Big Fall

"Any feel for the identity of your client, John?" Shane chuckled before he'd spit out the question.

Fixer patted Danny's shoulder. "Not a clue, my friend. Not a clue."

There were answers that only Joey Dancer could provide, but Danny Shane being on his doorstep meant that the police were only a half step behind. Phones were out of the question and Fixer waited until after midnight to make the drive to Acme Specialties. He drove past the building and parked around a corner two blocks away. A fog rolled in and street lamps were distant glows as he worked his way back to Acme. The gate was closed and but for mercury lights in the yard, the building was blacked out. Fixer waited before the gate for someone on the inside to notice him.

Eddie Ebony's voice sounded on an intercom.

"Nobody home, Mr. Fixx. No forwarding address either. I'll tell him you stopped by."

"I'm goin' to the beach," said Fixer as he turned away.

You got used to driving in the fogs that covered the coast highways. The idea was to maintain a steady, but not excessive speed and not to lose your nerve. The one route to sure disaster was to slow down or worse, stop. Fixer had covered half the distance when the car pulled up not a foot off his bumper and stayed with him. The driver was either a pro or a reckless fool. Fixer kept going and the tail finally blinked his brights on and off, once then again. Fixer pulled onto the apron to let him pass. The car accelerated to pull even with him, then dropped its passenger side window.

Harry Lang.

He shouted, "pull off Fixer. I want to take you for a ride."

Fixer did as instructed and jumped into Lang's waiting car.

The Big Fall

"What's it all about Harry? You taking the law into your own hands?"

Harry Lang growled, "that's your game wise guy. It's all getting out of hand. You're really not worth saving, but you might have your uses, so I'm gonna' show you something."

Lang drove north, turned into a seaside canyon, climbed up the rim out of the fog, and then left the road on a dirt track. Flares marked the spot where a large panel truck had been driven off the road onto a shelf.

"Come on Fixer."

The truck refrigeration unit ground on in slow motion, reduced to faltering battery power. Lang waved to unseen sentries and led the way to the rear doors. He worked the latch and opened them. Sides of beef hung from racks and hundred pound boxes of bacon were stacked on the floor down the center.

"I don't get it, Harry," questioned Fixer.

Harry Lang pulled a manifest from his inside coat pocket and shoved it at Fixer. The load of meat belonged to Acme Imports.

"So, Acme processes meat, Harry. I still don't get it."

Lang climbed to the tail gate and pulled Fixer up after him.

"Guys like you never get it until it gets them. I'm gonna' stick your nose in it wise guy - not that it'll do any good, but it's gonna' make me feel better just to see the expression on your face."

Lang reached into one of the swaying carcasses and lifted out a plastic packet with white contents.

"Christ!" gasped Fixer.

"At least two ki's of coke here wise guy. Check 'em all pal - try anyone you want."

Fixer reached into one, then another. Everyone was a carrier pigeon for another 'ki' of coke.

"It doesn't prove a thing Lang. Who knows where this stuff came from. And those manifests could be creative writing."

Fixer said it but knew better. And Lang wasn't fooled, not in the least.

"Your pals aren't trading in the commodities future market, you goddamned fool."

Harry Lang reached ever so slowly into his trench coat pocket. For an instant Johnny Fixx feared the man was going to actually pull down on him. Lang handed him two well worn smudged newspaper clippings dated six years before. One detailed the drug overdose of a teenaged girl, the second the nervous breakdown of her mother. The names were Cindy and Edith Lang.

Lang led the way back to his car and made the return drive. The fog had mysteriously disappeared and a half moon watched them from a cloudless sky. The apron where Fixer had parked overlooked the sea. Lang pulled off and let him out. He accelerated back onto the road, then hit his brakes and backed in. Lang jumped out of the car and confronted Fixer.

"I don't know what makes a guy like you dirty. Are you bored with your talent, and the good life?"

"Lay off Lang. You're out of order."

"No, wise guy. You tell me, because I'm really confused by characters like you who should be running the show but waste their time trying to outflank the system, until finally they shit on their own feet. What the fuck are you all about, Fixer?"

Fixer stared out to sea to a place beyond the horizon that he was painfully aware couldn't be far enough to dodge this bullet.

"Your pals are in the dirtiest business, Fixer." Lang brandished the news clippings. "Don't you understand you sonuvabitch. It gets personal, people die!"

"Enough, Harry," gasped Fixer.

Lang was relentless.

"You're more than their attorney. You crossed the line, Fixer. Are you prepared to take the fall, lose it all, and do the time?"

Harry Lang barely suppressed his rage.

"The noose is getting tighter, wise guy. I can feel it. You're going down, and when you do, yer' scum ball pals are going to want to punch your ticket, and guess what Fixer, Uncle Harry just might stay in the grandstand while you swim after your own head."

\* \* \* \* \*

There were fits and snatches of sleep, but no rest. The morning was little better. Still Dancer didn't call.

Johnny Fixx walked in the surf and knew to a certainty that any move he made would cost him. A kid on a bike on the road sounded his horn. The morning Trib. They carried it midway down the front page where serious news stories were covered. An armory on the Pendleton Military Reservation had been ransacked. Stockpiles of M-16's, grenades, ammunition, and rocket launchers had been taken. Permits from the South Korean government to import guns? Dancer's disappearance was explained. The deal was all the way dirty. Dancer and Persia were an entry. Spillane wasn't beyond a killing rage if he was denied his guns. And Johnny Fixx was the man in the middle. "And maybe the odd man out," he muttered.

212

## C H A P T E R   E I G H T E E N

After hours at the Condor. Jonesy left the bottle of Jack Daniels before him and came out from behind the bar to sit beside Heavy. Fixer drank the brown fire straight up. Manny Cesar had taken the last rake from the poker game that was breaking up and now danced cheek to cheek with Evita. Jonesy was leaning across to nuzzle Heavy. Her hand dropped to his thigh. The big man was in seventh heaven. Jonesy was performing. She had eyes for everyone at the bar. The card players were let out. A couple of the regulars and their ladies stayed on to dance. Manny Cesar lowered the lights and the mood was a smoky lipstick glow.

Fixx eyed his reflection in the bar mirror and idly ran his finger tips through the wet on the burnished mahogany. Tony Persia had gone for the price and Fixer had come cheap. Now Joey Dancer was painting him into a corner. "Never Dancer," breathed Fixer as he swilled down another drink. His image dissolved in the mirror and Dancer was with him again facing the end in that southeast asian hell hole.

It had been a fire fight for a temple ruin with no strategic value other than as map coordinates to test the wills of men battling to possess them. Smoke shells shrouded the place in an acrid blackish haze. Fixer was alone in the cauldron, cut off, his calls for help unanswered. He smelled him before he saw him. The flame thrower had made him a scorched shadow on the earthen floor. The NVA were closing in. Fixer frantically threw the three grenades he'd carried. Screams to the left said that one hit home. There was quiet, but only an instant. Then they were screaming his way again.

He ran and then stopped dead in his tracks as what he'd run into registered. He was tied, head down to an inverted cross. Fixer retched but couldn't tear his eyes away. They had gouged out his eyes and the eyeballs dangled from sinew and nerve like the pop out eyes of a Christmas spring doll. He had been castrated and his penis stuffed into his open mouth. Both feet were hacked off. His guts were laid open, intestines taken out, pulling with them pieces of his stomach, liver, and kidneys. He'd been in Fixer's unit, lost the day before. Fixer called his name, gagging on the terrible stench. Sweet Jesus. He had clenched his fist! Fixer pulled the .45 and shot away what remained of his face.

213

Flame throwers belched avenging fire in lazy arcs, a malevolent dragon's breath searching out luckless stragglers. Fixer groped wildly ahead and found a crypt entrance. He staggered down the steps. He wasn't alone. Then the NVA troopers closed in, one softly calling, "it's okay 'GI'. You come out now. Okay." An old man bolted for the entrance. The trooper poured in the liquid fire and the old man was incinerated, spasming for terrible seconds in his death dance. The fire light showed a woman cowering in the corner, wild eyed and screaming. Fixer gestured for her to be quiet but she was beyond recognizing anything but the fire death that would consume her. He crept across, clamping his hand over her mouth.

The NVA trooper slowly walked down the stairs. "Now you die 'GI'!" He aimed the nozzle and the line of fire leaped at Fixer. He did the unthinkable thrusting the woman before him as a shield. Her face melted in the crackling heat like so much wax running down cheesecloth. The .45 in his hand registered. Would there be an instant more for him to turn the automatic on himself? He eagerly took the muzzle into his mouth. Then the M-16 cut lose, taking out the NVA trooper.

"Come on, come on," cried Dancer as he threw him a discarded AK-47. An NVA trooper was about to blind side Dancer. Fixer spat a curse and cut him down. They locked arms and walked in a measured pace out of the ruin, firing their weapons at anything that moved before them.

A hand clasped his upper arm. It was the Condor, here and now, and Joey Dancer.

Dancer's expression spelled trouble and Fixer numbed at what must follow.

"For christ's sake, Joey, what are you and Persia doing to me? Gun importation permits from the South Korean government - all bullshit. What gives?"

"Not now Johnny. There's something more pressing."

Fixer's expression was disbelieving.

214

The Big Fall

"What could be more pressing?"

"Carla Samuels" breathed Joey Dancer.

The lady deputy who had worked the switch to permit Jonesy to get to Barbara Stanley - juror number 10!

Fixer clasped Dancer's shoulders.

"What happened?" he spat, as the bottom dropped out of his stomach.

"She's been arrested. She was in on a deal to take down the police property room downtown. It was pregnant with cash and blow seized from a bunch of TJ machos."

It sank in. Fixer's tone dropped to a stone cold whisper.

"How do you know all this Joey? Where do you come in?"

"The dame never met me, but she's workin' for me, understand?"

It finally registered.

"Jesus Joey, you really thought you could walk right into the police station and loot their property room. Christ man, are you crazy?"

Persia was sunk and so was he if the deputy dealt her way out. Fixer poured his glass half full and slid the bottle to Dancer. The brown fire burned home. Fixer tightened up.

"How good they got her Joey? Can she wiggle out of it?"

Dancer's sullen expression was answer enough.

"They were tipped. They followed her to a locksmith where she made a dupe key to the property cage. They caught her red handed after she let herself in and substituted milk powder for two ki's of coke. She was carrying the coke when she was busted."

Fixer slammed his glass into the mahogany. "Assholes!"

"I'll cover it Johnny. Don't worry. She'll stand up and keep her trap shut."

"Maybe pal," breathed Fixer. "Maybe."

The other hand in the game suddenly occurred to him.

"What about the Old Man?"

"He knows Johnny. He's not concerned. All he cares about is doing the deal with Spillane, even if everything else comes undone. He told me, 'have Johnny get it done'."

"Why Joey? He's holding back. What makes more money that he doesn't need from a maniac bunch of bomb throwers suddenly so goddammed important?"

"He's dying Johnny."

"What!"

"You heard me pal. Remember back before the trial when we were thinking about trying to buy some time and there was mention that Tony was in bad health. That was on the legit. He's got the 'big-C'. The lungs are filling up. He's taking treatment on the quiet, but the Doctors tell him his days are numbered."

"And still he wants to do this deal with Spillane?"

"It means a lot to him Johnny. Clear your head. Cover Tony's end. I'll try to plug any leaks on this Carla Samuels thing. We'll ride it out."

Fixer walked out into the night. It was even money, no better, on Carla Samuels taking the fall in silence. If she turned, that meant Jonesy was next to go. It didn't take a road map to track the rest. Fixer was suddenly stone cold sober.

The Big Fall

It was four in the morning - peaceful like a graveyard - when Fixer entered the elevator under his loft. At the top he pulled the plug on the intercom. If they wanted him they'd have to climb to where the stairs ended and then scale the building. He felt a step away from death as he dropped into his chair. The remote for the vcr was on the floor at his feet. He hit the switch and laughed sardonically as the credits for "Double Indemnity" played out.

Fred MacMurray was mesmerized by the anklet worn by Barbara Stanwyck who displayed her legs and teased the insurance salesman with the promise of more to come. MacMurray was all too eager to bet everything on a murderous insurance scam hatched by Barbara Stanwyck, with her husband the victim. All too quickly the plot exploded. As the walls closed in, MacMurray killed his paramour to cover his tracks. In the final frames, the unrepentant MacMurray, down with a slug in his shoulder, lamented to his boss and mentor, Edward G. Robinson, that if he'd had a few minutes more, he'd have made it out of the office to a clean getaway in Mexico.

"A few minutes more," breathed Fixer. But where to go. It really came down to nowhere to run.

\*    \*    \*    \*    \*

Day one ran down. Then a second. He left the calls to his answering machine. Tony Persia called at 5:00 p.m.

"Glad I caught you, Johnny. Bayonne's in Vegas. Can you get to him on our deal. I'm really anxious to close the show on this one."

Persia's tone betrayed no infirmity. The Old Man was in control as usual, moving the pieces on the board to work through a strategy he shared with no one else.

Fixer knew better than to think that Tony 'P' would get into the Carla Samuel's thing, but like a kid wishing for what he knew he couldn't have, Johnny Fixx held the line hoping that Persia would tell him everything had been taken care of. It didn't happen, and Fixer finally answered.

"I'll get to him tomorrow at the latest, Tony. Okay?"

217

The Big Fall

"On the money kid."

The phone rang again.

Samantha spoke into the tape machine.

"Johnny, if you're there please pick it up."

"Hi babe. How you doing?"

"You still disturb the shit out of me Johnny. But I'm not angry anymore."

"Pack a bag Sam and meet me at the airport. I've got to see someone in Vegas. We'll stay the night."

"I don't know Johnny."

"Don't think about it Sam. There's a million reasons not to. You and I can both call the roll. Just do it. Please."

She went silent.

"Sam, Air West leaves every even hour. I'll meet you at their boarding area for the six o'clock." The line went dead on her end.

Johnny Fixx rummaged around the loft packing a new shirt still in the wrapper and a sport coat. He cleaned his shaving gear and toiletries out of the bathroom and dumped them into the suitcase before closing it.

He was unshaven and in shirt sleeves when he skipped out of the cab at the Air West terminal. Samantha was nowhere in sight. He purchased a pair of tickets on the next commuter and dropped onto a bench against the glass facing wall. 5:45 p.m. They called the flight. 5:55 p.m. Last call. Fixer took one last look out the window. The cab screeched to a halt and she flew across the walk to the entry door.

"Thanks Sam," he breathed as he led her through the gate and into the plane.

She settled in beside him and traced her fingers over his cheek.

"Are you all right John?"

"Now I am," he smiled.

Bayonne had arranged a bungalow at the Desert Inn. There was a message at the desk that he'd meet them later in the evening. Fixer led her in and set down their bags. Samantha ran the water in the circular step down tub that doubled as a whirlpool. Fixer needed no prodding. He skinned down and climbed into the steaming hot water. Samantha sat at the dressing table and removed her make up. She kicked off her heels and unfastened her slacks. She felt him watching her, smiled, and turned her back as she removed her sweater and panties. He felt good just watching her. She sat beside him and kissed him lightly on the cheek. He clasped her hands in his and rested his head on her shoulder. He began drifting and her voice was distant calling to him.

"Come on Johnny. Come back. You need to sleep." She dried him and pressed her body to his. Something was eating away at him. He wouldn't talk and she knew better than to press it. All she could do was be there for him.

The phone jangled. Fixer grabbed it and rasped, "yeah, who is it?"

"Your wake up call, sir. 10:00 p.m."

Samantha was awake beside him, on her side, her head cushioned on the pillow she propped up with her elbow.

"I put in the call Johnny. I figured you could use the sleep."

Fixer took her into his arms and breathed her essence.

"Sam, it's been such a goddamned long way around."

219

The Big Fall

"I'd like to think that maybe there's still time for us," she said, the words leaving a bittersweet taste in her mouth.

The phone rang again.

Joe Bayonne.

"Welcome to Vegas Johnny. Bring your lady down for dinner. I'm waiting in the lounge."

Sam pulled out of his embrace.

"I'm hungry lover, and at the moment, not for you."

"Never the luck," he groaned as he padded into the bath to shave.

Joe Bayonne sat a table in the center of the dining room. Tables were occupied on either side of him, but none behind.

"Hello Samantha," he said, rising to seat her. "It's been a long time. You're lovelier than ever."

"Johnny, do you know what you have here?"

"She's a bundle of trouble Joe. She always had my number."

Bayonne ordered for them, a variation on Beef Wellington, and a vintage wine. Samantha busied herself with salad. Bayonne and Fixer passed on the preliminaries and waited on the entre.

"So how is our friend Tony," asked Bayonne.

"He's not well Joe and he's obsessed with finishing this transaction with Dermot. Why is that Joe?"

"I don't really know Johnny, and that's the truth. I'm told the payment will be bearer bonds issued by the Banco do Brasil."

220

The Big Fall

"That's correct. One of Spillane's people will bring them to you for authentication. If they pass muster, can you use them to Tony's advantage?"

"We are somewhat fortunate here Johnny. It just so happens that the Brazilian's have an interest in one of the casinos we have invested in. They would love to have those bearer bonds and would trade points in the casino. It's a deal that works for everybody. So my friend, there are loose ends but with some luck all the financial strings will work favorably."

Samantha asked, "I couldn't help picking up your drift. Isn't Tony Persia retired? Especially after the mess with that character Jimmy Doyle?"

"You might say this deal is his retirement present, Samantha," explained Bayonne.

Joe Bayonne finished his after dinner Sambuca.

"I'll leave you two to enjoy the evening. Will you be leaving in the morning?"

"Probably the noon commuter," said Johnny Fixx.

"I'll pick you up."

Sam played twenty one while Fixer shot craps. The gambling wore thin quickly and within an hour they decided to turn in. Fixer ushered Sam into the bungalow.

"Is this your last go round with Persia?"

"It looks that way Sam."

Fixer weighed it and decided to lay some of it out for her.

"He's dying Sam. No kidding. This is his last hurrah, and I've got to go all the way for him."

The Big Fall

Fixer was showering when the package was delivered. Sam called to him, "John, Joe Bayonne sent up a packet for you."

Fixer toweled off and sipped the Margarita Samantha had mixed from the makings in the bar. Bayonne had sent up a file of thirty year old news clippings.

"What's it all about?" she asked.

"I don't really know. I've been asking the obvious question - why is Tony Persia so interested in this deal. Maybe this ancient history has something to do with it."

The news stories had appeared in the late fifties when Dominic Farina had gone to meet his maker. Farina was the east coast mafioso who had dispatched Tony Persia west after the war to oversee a newly acquired west coast franchise. Persia had made his bones as a soldier for Dominic Farina in the late thirties. Farina was among the mobsters collared at Appalachian in 1957 and died the following year. Earlier clippings disclosed that Farina had been summoned by Senator Kefauver's Committee at the turn of the decade of the fifties, and before that had been arrested with Tony Persia in the 30's for Volstead Act Prohibition violations. Near the bottom of the stack was a clipping detailing a strange story that occurred in 1940.

A keg bomb filled with nails and shotgun pellets had been placed at Farina's front door, apparently ticketed for him by a rival mobster. Farina however had been called away and his younger sister, Angela, answered the door. The bomb was detonated, and Angela was blown to pieces. Her killers were never apprehended, and the case remained open as an unsolved mob murder. The last article appeared in 1947 and noted Tony Persia's move to the west coast to serve as Dominic Farina's surrogate to oversee his burgeoning rackets in California and Nevada.

"Anything interesting," asked Samantha, when Fixer discarded the clipping file.

"Only you," he grinned.

222

The Big Fall

Joe Bayonne was outside their door at 11:00 a.m. His car turned out to be a gray stretch limousine and Bayonne rode in back with them.

"A good night's sleep," he asked.

"I needed the day away from LA, Joe."

Fixer squeezed Samantha's hand. "It was a perfect day."

Fixer handed back the clipping file. Bayonne smiled and explained, "there is probably nothing there, but at times history can help shed light on what appears beyond explanation. Do you know who Dominic Farina was?"

"Other than what's in that file Joe, no I don't. Should I?"

"Dominic Farina was born a mafia prince in Sicily. His father and grandfather before him were mafia dons. Antonio Persillato, our Tony Persia, was a young boy when Dominic Farina was a teenager. They were from the same village and their families were related. When the fascist agents of Mussolini declared war on the mafia after the Great War, Dominic Farina was smuggled out of the country by his family. So too was the boy Tony Persia who was sworn to the service of Dominic Farina by his father. You know that Tony was Dominic's bodyguard. Eventually, Tony became Dominic's trusted friend and associate. He was underboss in 1947 when Farina entrusted him with the family's west coast interests."

"I'm still at a loss Joe," explained Johnny Fixx. "Does any of this connect up with the here and now?"

Bayonne shrugged in the ageless gesture of uncertainty.

"There was one thing more Johnny. Tony Persia was with Dominic Farina in 1939 and 1940 when Farina took over the docks in Montreal. Montreal was a major smugglers port of entry. Farina had made arrangements with refineries in Turkey and Sicily and his goods were shipped in through Montreal. Persia worked with the 'blue shirts.' Some of their members were IRA men. They were a pro nazi group, like the 'bund' on this side of the Atlantic

The Big Fall

- not so much because they thought Hitler had anything worth 'buying' but because they'd throw in with anyone who might take the British down. These people had connections in the Belfast shipyards and helped Persia organize the docks for Farina."

\* \* \* \* \*

Fixer kissed his wife and bundled her into a cab at LA International. He felt almost alive as he watched her disappear into the line of traffic. Fixer raised his arm to flag a cab. The unmarked car cut off the yellow checker and skidded to a halt before him. Harry Lang bent across the seat to open the passenger side door.

"Get in Fixer."

"You like old movies don't you Johnny. I hear you're partial to those old gangster flicks. I thought we should have a talk where you'd be comfortable."

Lang drove to the LA River Viaduct and pulled into one of the run off tunnels.

"What do you want Lang?"

"Get out Fixer."

Lang stepped out and snarled, "judgment day counsellor."

Fixer stepped down the sluiceway, sloshing through the light run off. Lang pushed him and Fixer spun to confront the cop.

Lang said only, "Carla Samuels" and swung from his heels, crashing a left hook into Fixer's face. Johnny Fixx dropped to all fours in the wet.

Harry Lang slapped him with an affidavit when Fixer looked up.

"Read it," he snapped.

Fixer spit blood from a lacerated lip and woodenly focused on the affidavit. Carla Samuels had spilled her guts. Jonesy too had turned. Jonesy was quoted as telling Lang that she had run into Johnny Fixx the night the jury tampering scam was worked out at Dancer's office.

"You had to know, you piece of shit. You were in on it."

Lang's manner abruptly turned. He smiled benignly and helped Johnny Fixx to his feet. Lang's smile broadened into a sardonic grin. He paced before Fixer, then turned to confront him his face not an inch away. Fixer turned from his acid gaze and sour breath. Harry Lang clasped Fixer's chin and wrenched his face around to meet his eyes.

"I own you now, wise guy. If I pull the switch, disbarment is the least of your worries. You'll do twenty, minimum, and when I pass the word inside the joint, you'll spend half your time on your knees. I guarantee it."

Fixer pulled away from the cop. For an instant he contemplated making a grab for the pistol holstered under Lang's arm. The Lieutenant read him and nodded, "you're gonna' wish you were dead before I'm finished with you asshole. Go ahead. Try for it."

"All you smart asses will sell out your mothers if you even suspect you're going down. Ain't that right, counsellor? I'm callin' it in Fixer, and if you play ball, maybe I look the other way for a while."

Lang held all the trump. Fixer shuddered under a crushing weight. His voice was wooden, his eyes downcast. "What's the tab?"

"Joey Dancer, wise guy," said Lang. "You give me Joey, and I give you some room, until the next time."

"Christ Lang, I'm Dancer's lawyer. I can't do that!"

"You blew that one when you played with a jury. You're nothing but a rat scrambling to stay alive, Fixer. You've got

The Big Fall

twenty four hours, then I give all of it to Rudy Kutter and you can swim in your own shit."

## CHAPTER NINETEEN

Mostly it was Tex Tannis' memorial service that did it. That and a night in the neon grind of Hollywood. Rusty Tannis was seated in front, her two teenaged boys beside her. Both had been born during Tex' Nam tours. His picture in dress blues was on a table beside the lectern, medals and commendations arrayed around it. A Minister who had been a Chaplain and knew about the 'shit' delivered the eulogy.

"Tex never came to terms with the Nam. Some men because their heart was bigger than others or their courage a bit more never did. The war, at the same time a cause worth fighting for and a horror beyond description, had a way of twisting the guts of men who were generous with their minds and bodies and didn't look out for themselves. The survivors all learned that a man couldn't make it unless he held something back and stopped feeling everything going on around him. That was the trick, see it, but not feel it. Damned hard to do that. Tex was one of those people who never developed the survivors' tunnel vision. He used it all up in the Nam. When he came home it was only a matter of time, painful days, weeks, and years. He was a hero, a father, a husband, and the best friend his comrades ever had."

The Chaplain presented Rusty with a folded flag. She kissed it, then stooped forward sobbing. That tore it for Johnny Fixx. He blinked as tears welled up in his eyes and ran out of the chapel.

There were no name bars in the low life dregs of the City of Angels. The no questions asked dives where a man could drink and puke and drink some more, and maybe even think some, with no questions asked. Joey Dancer never showed at Tex' service. Dancer used up what little Tex had left. And why? For a few dollars more! Dancer had painted Johnny Fixx into a corner. He'd been the pied piper who'd made possible the jury fix. And Dancer pulled the Pendleton raid to permit Tony Persia to complete his last deal, a deal Johnny Fixx knew to a certainty was a keg of dynamite likely to blow them all to hell. That was one way of looking at it. But Fixer knew he had gone along with the program every step of the way. Dancer or not,

227

The Big Fall

Johnny Fixx was a man on Tony Persia's string. And then there was the Nam. Dancer had been a comrade in arms. He'd saved his bacon time and again. But that was a favor Fixer had returned more than once. You did that in the 'shit', no questions asked. It came back around to Tex Tannis. The pilot cancelled out the Nam debt. Fixer groaned "no". Nothing could ever do that. But a man was a fool if he didn't hold something back. Even the padre had said as much.

Johnny Fixx prowled his beach before the sunrise. A gypsy storm slammed toward shore riding the howling wind. Salt spray stung his face as the downpour tattoo'd the deck above. No place to go, except maybe over and out. Fixer climbed back up to the deck and trudged inside. His Walther automatic rested on the burnished desk top beside his telephone. Harry Lang's card was in his pocket. He dropped the card on the desk and clasped the pistol, then abruptly slammed it down. There was a residue of salt on his lips from the sea spray. Coppers in Europe fed informers a mouthful of salt before they spilled just to make sure they had the bitter taste of truth. It was all a matter of perspective thought Fixer as he muttered, "betrayal." But a man was a fool not to survive. And there had never been a fix too tight for him to slip through.

Johnny Fixx punched in Lang's number.

The bastard rasped, "who?"

Fixer coldly whispered, "there's a quonset on a deserted National Guard strip north of Irvine."

Lang blurted, "Fixer, the B-17 job? Fixer . . ."

The lawyer disconnected.

* * * * *

Fixer holed up in his studio taping shows that maybe would never be aired. He enjoyed doing the intros and fills and stringing together the music. So it really didn't matter whether he went down, and the broadcasts with him.

228

The Big Fall

"Most of you would say that Charlie Parker and Stan Kenton inhabited different sides of the same planet - their music millenniums apart. Some truth to that, but they did have something in common, and more than once. You figure it yet?"

"'The Metronome All Stars' concert in '49 and 'The Festival of Modern American Jazz II' tour in 1953. For the '49 concert Stan's trumpet section was augmented by Dizzy Gillespie, Fats Navarro, and Miles Davis. The '53 tour featured Charlie Parker playing Lennie Niehaus' arrangement of 'My Funny Valentine' and Bill Holman's reading of 'Cherokee'. And Dizzy was in the band too lending 'Manteca' to the book with Candido. If those occasions rang a bell you guessed half the answer, but there was something more."

Fixer chuckled, "someone, is more like it."

"Stan Levey," said Fixer. "The drummer who gigged with Charlie Parker and Dizzy Gillespie in the Apple in the mid forties and later was playing with the Al Belletto sextet when Stan was reforming his band in 1950. Stan heard the sextet, liked what he heard and built his new band around them. Stan Levey stayed longer that the other members of Belletto's sextet but there were artistic differences with the boss. Levey was a be-bop drummer who sometimes had his own ideas about how the big bands' arrangements should be played. Finally, Kenton and Levey nearly came to blows and Levey left the band. Kenton had seen it coming for some time and was apprehensive about finding a replacement for the mercurial but incredibly talented Levey. But Stan really had nothing to worry about. Buffalo, New York took care of everything. Mel Lewis joined the band, and the rest was history."

"Oh, and there's one thing more for you be-bop aficionados. Clint Eastwood's music director for the filming of 'Bird' his Charlie Parker bio-pic was none other than the same man who arranged for Bird when he toured with Stan Kenton, Lennie Niehaus, himself an accomplished jazz alto saxophonist."

Selections were programmed in from the Parker/Gillespie/Kenton tour in 1953 and from the principal albums the band had cut when Mel Lewis manned the traps, 'Contemporary Concepts', and 'Cuban Fire'.

The phone rang and the answering machine kicked in. "Crystal Lee, Johnny. Call . . . ."

Fixer sprinted into the office area and grabbed the phone before she clicked off.

"I'm in residence Crystal. What's going on?"

"Kutter's office says Joey Dancer is about to be indicted under the state RICO act. The old stuff, and the hijacking of a B-17 to hold its antique bombsight for ransom. And that's not the worst of it."

The hi-jacking had been expected. Something more was a surprise.

"What else?" asked Fixer.

"They're apparently charging Dancer with complicity in the disappearance of the pilot who flew the B-17. The pilot's death during the commission of the heist is apparently. . . ."

Fixx picked up the recitation of the well known rule of law, "felony murder."

"Will it wash John?"

"It's heavy handed. No body, no witnesses. It's the kind of kick to the nuts that Harry Lang might talk Kutter into, and win or lose, murder makes for better headlines than any hi-jacking."

"Can a murder charge wash - if they had the body?"

"Any time someone is killed during the commission of a serious crime, a felony, even if it was accidental, it's murder under the law. So Crystal, it just could wash if Kutter pieces everything together."

Even though the tracks were painfully obvious, Fixer asked the reporter, "what have they got to back up the hijacking charge. They haven't found the plane, have they?"

"I hear they received a tip on the location of the bombsight and sent a flying squad down to bring it back. Apparently, there was something there to connect it up to Dancer."

"Thanks much Crystal. I owe you one."

As he made the statement, Johnny Fixx grinned. Crystal Lee was a lady who always collected, one way or the other.

Within an hour, Max Gale called.

"Johnny, Rudy Kutter contacted me. He says Joey Dancer's been charged. He wants a commitment that we'll produce him for an arraignment pronto or else. He's prepared to ask for a bench warrant. The usual drill."

"Tell him Max that I'll get Dancer in 'asap'. I don't want any bench warrant. There will be complications enough at the bail hearing."

"I think he's going to press hard for tomorrow morning."

"I'll put the word out for Dancer. But tomorrow morning may not be possible depending on when he gets back to me. Do the best you can Max. Tell Kutter to keep his shirt on."

"I'm meeting with our esteemed DA in an hour. I'll do the best I can to find out just why they're strutting around like they've got a pat hand."

"Call me as soon as you know anything."

Eddie Ebony was on the phones at Acme Specialties. "Eddie, this is John Fixx. There's an indictment out against Joey. The DA is about to issue a warrant for his arrest. You've got to find Joey and have him get in touch with me. There's no time to lose. Understood?"

The Big Fall

"I got the picture, Mr. Fixx. I got an idea where I can find the man."

"Okay Eddie. Do it."

The afternoon was basically spent. Fixer waited on Max Gale's call. The intercom sounded. Gale was in the garage.

"The five o'clock freight is on the way down Max," answered Johnny Fixx.

Gale came through the door and immediately summarized what he had learned.

"Kutter is playing it a little close to the vest but I was able to piece some of it together. The cops got a tip that the Norden bombsight was stashed in a Quonset on an abandoned National Guard strip a few miles north of Irvine."

"Who's the tipster?"

"Rudy's not saying. But I did learn the connection between Dancer and the bombsight. They lifted a print from the bombsight and it turned out to belong to none other than one Paulie Flange, one of Dancer's close associates."

Gale chuckled. "The reason I know this boss is that Paulie's already a guest of the County - they picked him up for trying to sell a load of bootleg cigarettes - and since he didn't call you to represent him, I've got the hunch that Flange is maybe considering cooperating with Kutter."

"Christ Max, Kutter's spinning a real web of circumstantial evidence to hang Dancer. What about the part of it that goes to felony murder for Tex Tannis?"

"That's all speculative as far as I can determine. But there is one hard piece of evidence. Apparently, Mrs. Tannis has been questioned, and she told the cops that a few days before Tex disappeared, Dancer showed up at her place and handed her an envelope with $2500

232

in it. I guess the cops are trying to use that money as evidence that Tex was flying for Dancer when he took the bomber in."

"It's thin Max. How the hell do they know what Dancer had going with Tex, if anything. Maybe he was just laying some cash on the guy's wife for old times sake?"

"Agreed, Johnny."

"Keep nosing around Max. I've reached out for Joey. His pals probably know how to find him."

"They better get the lead out, Johnny. The best I could get out of Kutter on the arraignment was forty eight hours. Then Joey swings."

There was a hitch in Max's tone that Fixer had heard before. Something else was bothering Max Gale.

"Give Max. What's eating at you?"

"Besides the fact that this whole thing doesn't quite feel right, if you know what I mean, there is another angle. There just might be something strange going on here. Kutter's being close mouthed about the search warrant. Every time I ask to see it I get another serving of double talk. Who knows - maybe Harry Lang and company fucked up."

"Look into the ownership of that quonset."

"Will do, Johnny."

The resurrection of Joey Dancer wasn't long in coming. Fixer had just dropped off to sleep minutes past 1:00 a.m. The phone rang. "Morning, Johnny."

"Where are you Joey? You know what's happened?"

Dancer snapped, "tell that prick Kutter that I'm gettin' a tan in the Yucatan and I'll be in no later than day after tomorrow to say 'not guilty'."

233

The Big Fall

"Do it, Joey. I don't want them to grab you and make a media event of the arraignment, cuffs and leg irons and the rest. Don't leave me out on a limb. I'll arrange for the bondsman to be there, but if you don't show, I've got the feeling that both of us are going to need a bail bondsman."

Dancer's tone was strained.

"Is that so, friend. Really?"

Fixer thanked god that they were not eye to eye. His expression surely would betray him.

"You taking the arraignment, Johnny," asked Dancer, his tone still not quite friendly. "Max will probably handle it. He's hanging around Kutter trying to find out whatever there is."

"Day after tomorrow, right?"

Sensing that it meant something to Dancer, Fixer assured him, "You know Max is the best, but I'll try to be there."

"We should talk beforehand Johnny. You and me, privately."

"Name it Joey."

"How about the old Wanderers Amusement Park tomorrow? I've got a lot of running to do. Mind coming out round midnight?"

"I'll be there."

Joey's manner instantly lightened.

"Hell, Johnny boy, we'll beat the assholes - just like always, right?"

"Yeah Joey," answered Fixer. "Just like always."

\* \* \* \* \*

Max Gale called at noon.

"We're set with the arraignment and bail hearing at 10:00 a.m. tomorrow morning. Everything okay on your end?"

"I talked to Dancer. He'll show. Anything new on the search warrant?"

It figured to be blind luck if Lang had screwed up, but if he had, fate might take a hand to take Fixer off the spot.

Gale's tone was perplexed.

"That 'sob' Rudy Kutter may have us by the balls. He says the quonset is on an abandoned military reservation. One that just happens to be State property - the National Guard. Nuff said?"

Fixer picked up on Gale's drift.

"So he's going to take the position that the quonset was on 'public property' and that no search warrant was necessary since the DA's office and the Guard Commandant in Sacramento are both kissin' cousins of the same 'dancing Bear' - namely the sweetheart that graces the flag flying over the State house."

"You seem to have perceived the argument, my boy," agreed Max Gale.

"Keep digging Max. Find out about the users of that quonset from Pearl Harbor to the present, if you know what I mean?"

"You got it John. Thought you'd want to know that Paulie Flange is apparently kicking up his heels."

"How so?"

"Kutter's got Paulie, and he's making noises like Paulie's talking. Paulie's got his lawyer doing a bail hearing this afternoon."

"Max, it smells like a patented prosecutor's power play with a wise guy. Kutter's got the word out that Paulie's singing?"

"You've got it pal. It's a strategy that can push Paulie over the edge to cut that deal with Kutter."

"Or get him killed," said Fixer.

\* \* \* \* \*

The Wanderers Amusement Park had been built at Sunset Beach in the twenties when it looked like the LA sprawl would keep crawling down the coast past Long Beach to Huntington and Newport Beach. Then the Navy settled on Seal Beach for its Weapons Development Station only a few miles away. Disneyland put Anaheim on the map in the fifties. And the combination of the massive theme park literally down the road and the constant overflights and weapons tests almost within sight range spelled the end for Wanderers, despite more or less regular attempts by overly optimistic fast buck artist developers to resurrect it.

11:30 p.m.

There wasn't much left of Wanderers the way it had been in its heyday before the war. The Carousel house still held out against the sea gales. So too did most of the roller coaster. Everything else had either been bulldozed or blown down by the persistent sea winds. The storm of the prior week had pounded through the grounds. Johnny Fixx slipped through a break in the fence. A formation of A-4's dropped out of the clouds and overflew the Park at less than 2000 feet, their turbulence raising sand from nearby dunes that danced crazily across the grounds. Then the winds gusted, and loose clapboards and tin facia flapped from the dying Carousel House. A downed power line snapped at the night and Fixer made his way to a stand of trees that survived between the beach and the grounds.

From the cover of a tree, he watched and waited. There was something eerie about Dancer's selection of the Wanderer's Park for the meet. Fixer had stood on the very same spot three years before, unseen he'd thought. Now he wondered.

The Big Fall

It had been another stormy night that began at the Condor. Sam Pitts was an independent gangster of long standing in the Southlands. He was tolerated so long as he kept to his own turf, but then he began muscling in on local gambling clubs and thumbing his nose at Tony Persia. It fell to Joey Dancer to straighten him out.

Dancer drank more than usual that night and was strangely subdued. Fixer kept out of his way. The phone rang behind the bar. Heavy handed the phone to Dancer.

"Yeah, Sam," answered Dancer.

Pitts was calling for a sit down.

"The middle of the night at the abandoned park - Wanderers Amusement Park at Sunset Beach." Dancer showed a thin smile.

The deal smelled set up, but Dancer squared his shoulders and drank up.

"You want company?" asked Fixer.

"I'll cover it pal."

Dancer walked out and Johnny Fixx watched from the window as he climbed into his pick-up. Dancer turned north onto the Coast Highway. He was going to play the lone hand with Sam Pitts. Johnny Fixx called for Heavy to pour him another.

Manny Cesar stepped behind the bar.

"Evening 'George Raft'," smiled Fixer. "Heavy was just here."

"Who the fuck knows with that guy," grinned Cesar. "What are you drinking?"

The Big Fall

Fixer nursed down another Jack Daniels. Dancer had turned down his invitation to cover his action. But the man should have his back covered even if he was pig headed.

"Ah, shit, I'm gettin' too old for this crap," breathed Fixx as he drove off into the night on Dancer's tail. It was less than twenty minutes to the Park. Dancer's truck was parked beside the Carousel House. Fixer worked down to the stand of trees and positioned himself to take a hand if needed. Then Joey Dancer and Sam Pitts stepped out of the Carousel House. Pitts gestured with his hands and their animated conversation soon degenerated into invective and a shouting match. The tarpaulin over the cargo compartment of Dancer's pick-up moved. A head then shoulders surfaced in silhouette in the darkness.

"What the hell," whispered Fixx as he strained to make out the intruder.

"Too dark," he muttered, returning his attention to Pitts and Dancer. And then in an instant it didn't matter. Dancer was moving toward the beach with Pitts trailing him by a couple of steps. Pitts suddenly leaped forward and hammered a forearm into Dancer's neck. Dancer went down, stunned, and Pitts kicked at him. Joey violently shook his head clearing the cobwebbs and rolled onto his back, all the while clasping at his ankle. Fixer was an instant from breaking cover to even the score. But Dancer didn't need any help. He'd worn a gun holstered to his ankle and came up shooting. Pitts grabbed at his belly, then threw his hands to his face as the second slug tore through his cheek. Pitts went down like a felled tree.

Johnny Fixx slipped out of the Park the way he'd come. Joey Dancer could clean up after the parlay that had gone wrong. Whoever had hidden in Dancer's truck became unimportant. He'd settled back in under the tarp when Dancer got the edge.

That had been three years before, and Johnny Fixx stared at the beach where it had all played out as he moved toward the Carousel House. A clump of clouds covered the moon, completely blacking out the Park. He touched the Walther he'd tucked under his belt. Too late. He stiffened at the pressure of the weapon in the small of the back. No bookmaker would touch his chances, but Fixer whirled, the Walther in his hand, to make the desperate play.

238

# The Big Fall

Joey Dancer slid into view, grinning sardonically.

"Seen a ghost, Johnny?"

He knew!

Dancer always knew.

He'd somehow made his presence three years before when Sam Pitts ran out the string. And he'd figured Fixer with fitting him into the frame for the Norden bombsight hidden in Irvine. Dancer had one play. But Fixer's finger froze on the trigger. Dancer dropped the stick he'd jabbed into Fixer's back.

"What's a matter, pal, can't you take a little joke?"

Maybe he hadn't put it together.

Dancer nonchalantly lit a cigarette, making a show of keeping both hands plainly in view. It didn't figure but it was almost as if the man was baiting him.

Fixer stepped back and walked toward the beach, working hard at nonchalance when all his defenses were kicking in.

Dancer followed.

"What do you hear about Paulie Flange?"

"Joey, I think Paulie is holding, but for how long, that I can't say."

They were at the water line and surf pounded up the beach to ebb inches away from their feet.

"They must have tailed that asshole to Irvine," said Dancer.

"I've only used that quonset once in the past six years."

239

The Big Fall

Dancer's eyes bored into Fixer. He smiled easily and reached into his jacket. Fixer tensed, but Dancer came out with a pack of cigarettes.

Fixer's nerves were showing and Dancer grinned, "easy pal. Have a smoke."

Fixer broke eye contact and said, "I need to know who fronted for you in getting the quonset."

"How so, Johnny?"

"If we get lucky, there's a possibility the search was no good. You know what happens then, everything that follows will fall."

"I like that Johnny. A fucking happy ending - everything will be made right."

Dancer grinned broadly, "that's my Fixer, always one step ahead of the pack. But then, pal, what are friends for?"

"Let's get out of here, Joey."

They walked out of the Park to the abandoned lot where they'd left their cars.

Fixer had his hand on the door latch when Dancer clasped his arm.

"It's been a long time between you and me, Johnny. The Nam!"

Fixer almost screamed 'cut the cat and mouse crap'. He snapped impatiently, "what's with you Joey, feelin' insecure?"

Fixer's anger seemed to disarm Dancer. The tension instantly evaporated between them. Dancer grinned easily. "A friend shouldn't have to worry about a friend - right - Johnny? And there's only a handful of us left - eh?"

The Big Fall

"Damned few of us left," answered Fixer.

Dancer moved off toward his car.

Fixer reminded, "Court tomorrow morning. 10:00 a.m."

Dancer waved that the message had been received, then called back "happy endings, pal. Hah, hah. Yeah, that's it, we're gonna' have a happy ending. Right?"

## C H A P T E R   T W E N T Y

Johnny Fixx stepped out of his freight elevator in a rush to make the drive to Superior Court. 9:30 a.m. Dancer's arraignment was scheduled in a half hour before Judge Magdalene Mansfield. He set the attaché case next to the car door and adjusted his tie.

"Johnny, Johnny," she called.

Bette Jones.

Jonesy was pale and disheveled.

"I'm sorry for what happened Johnny. I was alone. They scared the crap out of me."

Fixer regarded the woman who had linked him to the jury tampering for Harry Lang. The bastard might have put her up to this.

"You wired doll?"

"I . . . I wouldn't do that Johnny. Heavy made my bail. I'm gonna' stay with him at the Condor. I'll make it right. I called Lang and told him I was going to take back my statement."

"Recant?"

"Yes. Whatever it takes."

"Anything I can do to help?"

"No, no. I just wanted you to know."

\*   \*   \*   \*   \*

Judge Magdalene Mansfield took the bench as Johnny Fixx slipped into the courtroom. The Judge nodded to her bailiff and the exit door was locked. Judge Mansfield had a personal rule: be on time or suffer a lockout until the first recess. Then the price of tardy entry was usually a dressing down from the bench.

Fixx had just made it.

Magdalene Mansfield had been child bride to Bill Mansfield, a mainline lawyer in the Southlands who was twice her age. Before Mansfield checked out he made sure that Magdalene achieved both of her passions, playing on the ladies tennis tour, and becoming a Judge. Magdalene had just celebrated her fortieth birthday. She was a tall woman with angular features. She sported a deep tan that was the real thing and long hair bleached faded brown from long hours on the outdoor courts.

Johnny Fixx dropped into the chair he had vacated as Max Gale escorted Joey Dancer to stand before the Judge. Rudy Kutter spoke from a lectern on the right.

"Proceed, Mr. Kutter," said Judge Mansfield.

"Your Honor we call 'People of the State of California -v- Joseph Dancer'. Two counts under the State RICO act for hi-jacking an antique B-17 bomber, causing its destruction, and removing its Norden bombsight for insurance ransom, and one count of felony murder in the disappearance its pilot, Tex Tannis."

"I'm familiar with the Indictment Mr. Kutter. Does the defendant waive the reading of the full Indictment?"

"He does your Honor," answered Max Gale.

"How do you plead Mr. Dancer," asked the Judge.

"Not guilty to all counts your Honor."

Max Gale then asked, "we would request your Honor an immediate hearing on the issue of bail."

"Granted, Mr. Gale. Mr. Kutter?"

"Your honor, the defendant is a dangerous criminal with a record of serious past offenses. He has served jail sentences for the Beverly Hilton jewelry robbery and the Wells Fargo armored truck robbery. His hi-jacking of the B-17 demonstrated his total disregard for human life. Tex Tannis, the pilot who flew the plane for Mr. Dancer, a decorated war hero with a record of mental illness in the aftermath of the war, was killed when the plane crashed into the sea. It was Mr. Dancer who placed Tex Tannis in harm's way during the commission of felony larceny. That is 'murder one' in this State your Honor, and given the circumstances and Mr. Dancer's past criminal record, the People strongly oppose bail. Mr. Dancer is in the importing business. Concededly he has international connections. We believe it is entirely possible that he will flee the jurisdiction. For all of these reasons, we respectfully submit that bail be withheld and that Mr. Dancer be remanded to the custody of the Sheriff to await trial in the County Detention Center."

"Your Honor," responded Max Gale, "regardless of how blackly the prosecution now seeks to gild the lily, what we have here is a charge of larceny. Mr. Dancer paid his debt to society for any past transgressions and has led an absolutely lawful life for the past seven years. No arrests and certainly no convictions. The felony murder charge is entirely speculative. There is no proof linking Mr. Dancer to Tex Tannis. It is assumed that Tex Tannis flew the B-17. It is assumed that the B-17 crashed into the sea. It is assumed that Tex Tannis was killed in that crash. However likely any or all of these circumstances may be, all are assumptions, and we submit the defendant cannot be jailed by reason of a chain of entirely speculative assumptions. And finally we would take strong issue with the prosecution's argument that Mr. Dancer knows the international highways and byways and is likely to flee the jurisdiction. Mr. Dancer was in Mexico when he learned of this indictment. He returned voluntarily when we contacted him. He has nothing to hide and his past record indicates that he will appear at all court proceedings. He has enjoyed his freedom before under a bail bond and has never forfeited bail."

"Mr. Kutter, the Court is inclined to agree with the defense on the issue of bail. Bail is set at $250,000 cash or acceptable bond."

The Big Fall

Johnny Fixx pumped Dancer's hand. "Congratulation's pal. Round one is history."

Hymie Manush rushed past Dancer to collar the baliff. The bondman presented his paperwork and within minutes, Joey Dancer walked out of Superior Court a free man.

Fixer preceded Dancer out of the Courtroom. Harry Lang stepped out from behind a pillar. He glared at the attorney and his client, squared his shoulders as if to throw a punch, then stepped aside as the men elbowed their way past him.

Eddie Ebony pulled up to the curb to chauffer Dancer. Joey stepped into the car, then dropped the window to call to Fixer.

"The 'old man' needs to talk to you Johnny. He's in town."

Johnny Fixx found his car and dropped the top. The weathermen promised no abatement in the soupy weather, but the sun was shining. Tony 'P' kept an apartment on Los Feliz above Griffith Park. On a clear day the Hollywood Bowl, Dodger Stadium, the Universal Lot, and Forest Lawn were part of the scenic vista. Persia's place was part of the rehab programs of the fifties that preserved the spanish styled garden courts. His was the end unit and Johnny Fixx walked through the court past the fountain and rang the bell.

Persia answered the door and ushered him in.

"Good to see you Johnny."

"Come into the study," he said.

Fixer settled into a massive leather chair, and Persia moved to the liquor cabinet to fix him a drink. The study was dark, mahogany bookshelves on three walls, a desk in the same, and cordovan chairs and sofa. The blinds were drawn and only a Tiffany desk lamp was lit. Persia moved to his humidor and pulled out a long Havana. He crimped its end and lit up. Tony puffed contentedly, then nearly doubled over with a racking cough. Fixer moved to help him, but Persia waved him off.

"It's okay Johnny. I'm not supposed to do this, but what the hell, it's one of life's few remaining pleasures."

"Joe Bayonne authenticated the bonds, Tony. If Spillane delivered the rest of them, your end should be in place and you can run with the deal any time you like."

"Ah, that's what I wanted to hear kid. That's good. I've got to make a call. Pour yourself another taste."

Johnny Fixx did just that and paced the perimeter of the study. Persia was an avid reader. Classics, Hemingway, Britannica, everything Barzini ever wrote about the old country, and mysteries that included Hammett, Chandler, and Ross MacDonald. Then a section of the bookcase that was closed off by ornate glass doors. Inside were old photographs, yellowed and sepia, in gilded frames.

Fixer leaned in close. All were pictures of an attractive young woman, her hair black and piled atop her head in a bun. Some alone, some with a baby in her arms, and one posed next to her father. Centered among the photographs was a crucifix, and burial mass card. Tony Persia maintained a shrine to Angela Farina the daughter of his don and mentor more than forty five years after her death.

Persia returned and noticed Fixer's attention to the cabinet.

"Some things stay with you a lifetime, Johnny."

Fixer for the first time took a hard look at Persia. His face was gray, weight melting off, and eyes watery. The man was failing.

Persia picked up on his scrutiny and smiled, "I'll be around for the finish Johnny. You'll see."

"Spillane's at that mick pub he's partial to kid. You stop by and see him. If there's anything more that he should do on the bonds, let him know. Otherwise, tell him I'm ready to go as soon as he is."

* * * * *

Dermot Spillane sat alone in the back room at Paddy O'Rourke's. Johnny Fixx approached and tapped a barmaid for a Guinness. Spillane smiled contentedly, then tipped a shooter of Jamesons to his lips. Spillane sat under an Aer Lingus poster of the 'Cliffs of Moher', and a framed reproduction of Pearse's 1916 Proclamation of the Irish Republic. Fixer pulled up a chair beside him and read aloud, "for the Irishmen and Irishwomen, in the name of God and of the dead generations . . . ."

Dermot Spillane answered, "you'd better believe it boyo."

Spillane pressed a receipt into his palm. Fixer recognized the signature as Joe Bayonne's. Jersey Joe had acknowledged receiving the Banco do Brasil bearer bonds. "Bayonne's going to contact Persia. That takes care of my end of the arrangements."

"That was what Tony was waiting for Dermot. He asked me to tell you he's ready to go as soon as you are."

"Ah that's good boyo. My people don't like to be kept waiting. That's very good."

* * * * *

One week to the day later, Johnny Fixx and Max Gale filed their Motion on Joey Dancer's behalf to dismiss the Indictment. Judge Mansfield scheduled arguments that same morning.

Fixer argued for the plaintiff.

"I will be brief your Honor. Our position is as simple as it is compelling. The prosecution's case turns on a Norden bombsight allegedly found by the police in a quonset at the old National Guard airfield north of Irvine. The prosecution concedes that there was no search warrant for their break in at the quonset. They have not argued that they tumbled on a crime in progress down there and were forced to enter the quonset to stop criminal acts, or acts they had probable cause to believe were criminal. The quonset was private property. The police had no right to enter the quonset without a warrant. Since they did, what they allegedly found in the quonset must be suppressed. It cannot be used in this proceeding. Without the bombsight, we respectfully submit the prosecution has no case. There is no evidence to connect Mr. Dancer to the B-17 hi-jacking. Without proof of that larceny in the present, the prosecution cannot reach back for Mr. Dancer's past record, to crimes for which he has already paid his debt to society, in any RICO indictment. That Indictment accordingly must fall. Moreover, without any basis for the larceny charge, any claims by the prosecution of Mr. Dancer's complicity in any felony murder, likewise must be defective. We are therefore coupling our motion to suppress the Norden bombsight, your Honor, with a motion to dismiss the Indictment."

Rudy Kutter strode to the lectern.

"I too will be brief, your Honor. We do not dispute the fact that there was no search warrant. It's absence was not an omission or oversight. We did not obtain one because we did not need one. The quonset was located on a military reservation owned by the National Guard of the State of California. Concededly the military reservation was abandoned, but the fact remains that since instrumentalities of the State Government, my department and the National Guard were involved, each of which enjoyed implicit permission to search the other's facilities, no search warrant was required. Accordingly, the search was not defective and the Motion should be in all respects denied."

"Any rebuttal," asked Judge Mansfield.

"Yes your Honor," said Johnny Fixx.

"Even conceding Mr. Kutter's point for purposes of argument, the actual facts do not support his conclusions. The quonset may have been owned by the State of California, but it was under a valid lease to the Blackledge Corporation. That corporation was listed in the Irvine telephone directory and retained an answering service to take and forward messages. I am handing up to the court the complete logs of incoming and outgoing calls from Blackledge for the past three weeks. As the court can see, no person connected to the police department or Mr. Kutter's office ever contacted

Blackledge. Blackledge therefore did not consent to the search. What we are saying here is that it was not for the State of California to consent to the search, if indeed it did directly or as Mr. Kutter argues, by implication. The entity with the right to possess and enjoy the premises, the tenant under a valid lease, was the sole party that could have consented. It did not. There is no warrant. Under these circumstances there can be absolutely no question that the search was defective. Accordingly, we repeat: the suppression motion must be granted and the Indictment dismissed."

"Gentlemen, you have three days to submit any legal authorities you wish the Court to consider."

*   *   *   *   *

Fixer anchored the end of the bar at the Condor when Heavy switched the TV from a baseball game to the late news as was his 11:00 p.m. custom and shuffled across the room to ascend the stairs to the light tower. Pointing upward as Fixer watched him, he said "Jonesy".

Crystal Lee spoke pleasantly into the camera. Joey Dancer was her lead story.

"Channel 6 has learned that the prosecution may be in grave danger of having its case against alleged mobster Joey Dancer thrown out on a legal technicality. It is called in legalese the 'fruit of the poison tree'. What it translates to in the Joey Dancer case is simply this. In order for the search of the quonset to have been legal, the prosecutor's office and police, in the absence of witnessing a crime in progress, either had to have a search warrant or the permission of the owner to enter the premises. The DA concedes that he did not have a warrant. But he argues that one was not needed since he had an implicit permission to search the quonset from the National Guard, another instrumentality of the State of California. The defense has countered that the quonset was leased to a corporation that could have been contacted by the government prior to the search but was not. What that may mean is that the Norden bombsight was unlawfully seized by the Government. If that is so, then any evidence flowing from that seizure is likewise illegal. The print lifted from the bombsight, and the person to whom it belonged, and his possible testimony, all may be suppressed. If that happens, Joey Dancer is about to be a free man."

"Couldn't have said it better myself, Crystal," breathed Fixer as he drank up.

Heavy descended the stairs from the light room, Jonesy in tow.

"Looking better for Dancer, eh?"

Fixer nodded in agreement.

Jonesy stepped behind the bar as the regular bartender wound up her shift.

"This one's on me," she said as she poured Fixer's refill.

\* \* \* \* \*

A couple of strippers from the Pink Lady beat the Condor's closing time with a pair of sailors they'd picked up. Joey Dancer came in the side door. Evita had joined Jonesy behind the bar and both kept up with their customers drink for drink.

Dancer sidled up to Fixx, and leaned in confidentially.

"You know, Johnny, if it'll do any good, I got the goods on that prick Kutter. We got pictures of him meeting that cunt assistant of his - what's her name - Donally . . . ."

"Donlon," corrected Fixer.

"Yeah, Donlon. They've been making a regular thing of it, twice a week, at different motels. What do yah think about that. So how does it play. Can we use it. I mean this prick deserves a message. Right!"

"Don't think so, Joey," said Fixer. "What the guy does in the bedroom is off limits. Besides, if we tickled him with it, he'd probably slap both of us with an obstructing justice charge. I'll pass on this one."

Dancer grinned.

"I thought you would, pal. But christ. My ass is on the line here, isn't it."

"We don't need it, Joey," assured Fixer.

"And you guarantee it, right," quipped Dancer. Fixer stared hard into Dancer's eyes. Joey nodded solemnly, then broke into another grin, and moved down the bar.

Jonesy was a naturally flirtatious woman. When she overdid the drinks, she became positively unmanageable. First one sailor, then his buddy danced with her. Heavy hung on the fringe of the action but his pained expression said he was struggling with his girl's antics. The strippers paired off with each other and put on a show that definitely would have been banned in Boston even in the Combat Zone. Jonesy wasn't about to be outdone. She grabbed Joey Dancer and slow danced him, finally standing in place, legs apart in a slow grind that went on three minutes past the end of the song that played on the juke box.

Johnny Fixx found a stool next to Heavy and bought him a drink. The big man couldn't tear his eyes from Jonesy. She fed the juke box and Joey Dancer stayed on the floor. Jonesy plastered herself against Dancer and did an encore more raunchy than her original performance.

"What's he doing," blurted Heavy.

"Don't mind them Heavy. They've had too much to drink."

Fixer said it but knew it couldn't be more than half true. Joey Dancer never lost control. Unguarded moments in public were for the rest of the world, not Joey. He and Jonesy didn't figure, but Dancer had to be up to something. Heavy was doing a slow burn, eyes narrowing, his lips thinning in a scowl. Dancer was grinning ear to ear as he escorted Jonesy out of the Condor. She never looked at Heavy. He slammed his fist into the bar, and screamed, "what the fuck ...."

"Easy Heavy, easy," said Fixer. "It's nothing. You know Joey. It's always business with him - nothing personal, especially with a pal's girl. There's nothing between him and Jonesy."

The Big Fall

"Nothing! That wasn't nothing I was watching for the past hour. He shouldn't do that to me. I'd walk through fire for that man. How could he do it?"

"Take it easy pal. I'll talk to him. You'll see. He's playing some angle."

Heavy was beyond consoling. He stalked out of the Condor muttering, "I could kill him . . . ."

\*     \*     \*     \*     \*

Johnny Fixx barely beat the dawn to his beach house. He was wired from the action at the Condor and settled in to watch a film to relax. 'Criss Cross', the final film in Robert Siodmak's film noir trilogy was his choice. The German director who had been born in America during his father's business trip, was an absolute master of the dark genre. 'The Killers' had been first, followed by 'Cry of the City'. Flaws fatal and inevitable undoing were Fixer's preferred bill of fare.

'Criss Cross' did not disappoint. His eyes were heavy by the final frames, but he revived as Burt Lancaster rushed to Yvonne DeCarlo with Dan Duryea on his tail. Both men loved the same woman, and she played them off each against the other. The unlikely trio of Jonesy, Dancer, and Heavy broke through, but Fixer willed them away. Lancaster finally double crossed Duryea in an armored car heist in order to grab the loot and disappear with DeCarlo. Wounded and on the run, Burt Lancaster returned to the hideout where he had stashed both DeCarlo and the money. Yvonne DeCarlo immediately sensed a set up and packed to leave Lancaster high and dry. But before she could melt into the night, Duryea walked in, gun blazing. DeCarlo cowered in Lancaster's arms as Duryea murdered them both. Then as police sirens closed in Duryea deliberately turned to walk out to his fate in the glare of the headlamps of the police cruisers.

Johnny Fixx shut down the vcr and climbed up to the loft. He had just hit the sheets when the phone rang.

Joe Bayonne.

"Sorry to wake you Johnny."

252

"That's okay Joe. It's been a long night. I was just getting to bed."

"I just wanted you to hear it directly from me. Everything is in place on Tony's deal."

"I know Joe."

"Good. And there's one thing more. Remember that history lesson I gave you a couple of weeks ago. There was one thing more I'd forgotten. I'm sending it to your office."

"Okay Joe," yawned Fixer, as Bayonne's message barely registered.

## C H A P T E R  T W E N T Y - O N E

Heavy's voice was frantic with fear and something more.

"Oh hullo Heavy," answered Johnny Fixx groggily. "How're you doing?"

Fixer had done an FM broadcast until 4:00 a.m. and then stayed up to work through the papers for a case that could begin in three days.

"Johnny, I know it's early, but I had to talk to you."

"So you got me pal. I'm up and my juices are beginning to flow. What's the matter?"

"It's Jonesy, she's moved out and she's acting kinda strange."

So it had continued to go wrong between them after the episode with Dancer a couple of nights earlier. Fixer couldn't level with Heavy. He was too stuck on the wrong dame. Jonesy's problem was men. Plural. That would always leave the poor stiff who fell for her out in the cold. And there was more. The woman had nose trouble, and not enough sense to know that one day she'd turn up in the wrong place at the wrong time.

"So what happened pal," gently prompted Johnny.

"She took a place in Palos Verde at the end of Hawthorne. You know, those apartments that hang over the ocean. I run into her at the Club and she doesn't even look at me. I apologize and still she won't talk to me. Not that I did anything. But you know how it is with some women." Fixer wanted to ask what it was that Heavy thought he had to apologize for. But sometimes it was that way between a man and a woman. No matter who did the jabbing, one went into a pout or the cold treatment, and it was up to the other to break the ice by apologizing for something he hadn't done in the first place.

"She'll come around Heavy."

"I don't know Johnny. Maybe you could talk to her. Could you?" asked Heavy, his tone at once hopeful and pleading.

254

The Big Fall

That wasn't the best idea Johnny'd heard for a variety of reasons, but maybe not the worst either.

"Gimme her address Heavy. I'm not promising anything, but I'll try to catch up with her. Okay?"

"Christ Johnny. Thanks. I really appreciate it."

*   *   *   *   *

A messenger showed up at 9:30 a.m. with the letter from Joe Bayonne. It was handwritten and unsigned and obviously by someone other than Jersey Joe.

"Joe thought you should know that Dominic Farina had help in the old days when he made his move on the mob that ran the docks in Montreal. He struck a deal with the IRA. They had strength on the docks in the thirties. The deal was simple. They opened up the port for him and paid the right people to look the other way so he could ship in his goods from Turkey and the old country. He helped them smuggle in weapons and then turn them around to Ireland. The IRA used his empty bottoms on the return trips. It worked for a time, but then things began coming apart. The police smashed the local cell of the IRA and pretty much wiped them out. There was talk that the coppers had inside help in doing in the micks but nothing ever came of it."

*   *   *   *   *

The Palos Verde hills bottomed out to the volcanic shelf sheared out of the sea cliffs by an ancient comet. Minutes before the sunset. Charcoal ash shimmered ebony and the brick veneer of the apartments showed nearly iridescent in the amber rays.

Jonesy's unit.

A beige four door sedan was parked at the curb. He was past it before the alarm bells began jangling. There was a spotlight under the driver's side mirror. Hub caps were bottom of the line, County procurement cheap. Fixer backed up. The small antenna for the two way grew out of the rear deck.

255

The Big Fall

The police!

There was a garage, empty with its door up in the unit diagonally across the way. The apartment was blacked out. He backed into the garage and waited.

Each passing minute lengthened as his nerves began getting out of hand. The cop could be in any number of units for a variety of reasons. But when the door opened from Jonesy's unit, Fixer knew that his adrenalin rush had been on the money.

Harry Lang!

The bastard was hedging his bets just in case Dancer skated on the bombsight heist. Jonesy's attentions to Joey Dancer were now explained. The dumb bitch was working for Lang. And the statement she had recanted concerning Fixer, that too had been window dressing to perfect her cover as Lang's eyes and ears inside.

But why?

Should Joey Dancer be tipped. He drove north on the coast highway, then turned back, the issue unresolved. The message light was on when he walked into the loft. Max Gale's voice was ebullient, "Judge Mansfield ruled in our favor all the way. She granted the suppression motion and dismissed the indictment. Dancer's a free man. I've already contacted him."

Crystal Lee carried it front page during her 11:00 p.m. broadcast.

"Superior Court Judge Magdalene Mansfield ruled late today that the police search of the quonset in Irvine where the Norden bombsight was located in the Joey Dancer case was illegal. Judge Mansfield suppressed the evidence found as a result of the search and stated that without that evidence the prosecution had no case. She dismissed the indictment."

Footage of Rudy Kutter cut in. The DA said only that "my office has not had the opportunity to review Judge Mansfield opinion. There may well be an appeal in this case."

Crystal returned.

"We have not been able to locate defense counsel or Mr. Dancer for a statement. If it holds up, the dismissal of the Dancer indictment will stand as a crushing defeat for the crusade of DA Rudy Kutter against organized crime in the Southlands. Following as it does on the heels of the mistrial in the Tony Persia case, the government's defeat in Joey Dancer's prosecution will surely cause police and prosecutors to re-examine their methods and perhaps to re-order their priorities. We will stay with this story and expect to have more for you as developments unfold."

The whole thing was in a swirl, loose ends on loose ends. Too many voices in explanation were yet to be heard to piece together what was happening.

Joey Dancer.

Fixer decided to let it lay for the time being.

\* \* \* \* \*

The pagoda was shrouded in morning ground fog when Fixer arrived. There was no Kenjutsu class scheduled, but the building was always open to special students of the sensei. Fixer's footfalls resonated over the burnished oak in the deserted practice hall. Vapor drawings crawled out of incense pots spotted around the perimeter of the room. The master as was his custom had taken his exercise at first light. Ceiling hung mobiles tinkled delicately in the light breeze. Fixer dressed and worked through an exercise regimen with the hard oak practice sword. The idea was to find the serenity that usually came with the physical exhaustion of kenjutsu. Mind clutter seemed to drop away. An insight was possible, and Johnny Fixx desperately needed to know who was dealing seconds in the game he couldn't escape.

The Big Fall

Bathed in sweat, his breathing coming in ragged gasps, Johnny Fixx moved to the cabinet where the real katana were displayed. The sensei's prize, a katana of the Sagami School, the priceless centerpiece of the collection.

The pupil reached for the katana below it, unsheathed the sword, blooded his finger on its razor's edge, and repeated his exercises, this time with the renewed intensity that followed the tempered kiss of cold steel.

Cut! Step! Cut!

The sensei's commands now second nature. Fixer sank his hips, keeping his knees and elbows flexed as inexorably he reached for a killing rhythm. The master's voice "mastery of a thing comes at its own pace," and again and again Fixer repeated the exercises. His arms finally leadened, Fixer dropped to the lotus position before a shrine to the Buddha. Beside the icon rested the sensei's treasured photograph of his deceased wife. The incense soothed and he breathed deeply as burdens dropped from his shoulders one after the next. But there was no escaping the crush of the burden hardest to bear.

The wind raised sparks from the charcoal that fired the incense, the flame filling the circular opening closest to him, and Fixer saw the lanterns so many years before on the horse drawn plough rumbling toward him. Every snowflake, each crystal, he saw every detail. Then he started, the cords in his neck tightening.

He wasn't alone!

Harry Lang!

The Lieutenant's face distorted in a rage, veins purpling to explode from his neck, as he unholstered his pistol and walked to stand over Fixer. The words were a frenzied torrent.

"You piece of shit - you really think that your smart assed pal 'the professor' has saved Dancer's ass and gotten you out from under?"

Lang's voice was that of a madman.

The Big Fall

"You know where all the skeletons are buried. You low life, do you hear me?"

Johnny Fixx stared into the gentle face of the sensei's wife. Her face became Samantha's. She was there, then gone. And he was alone.

Lang pressed the muzzle behind Fixer's ear.

"Tell me you hear what I'm saying, smart guy."

Fixer deliberately raised his head to meet Lang's eyes.

"No more, Harry. No more!"

Lang backed away, training the pistol in a two hand hold on Fixer's head. He spoke with icy calm, "you'll give me what I want Fixer. Bums like you can't let go - you can't go the distance. Today, tomorrow, whenever, you'll buy out. But I'm callin' it in now you sonuvabitch!"

"You're crazy Harry."

His eyes raked over the Lieutenant's. "Maybe I am too pal."

Fixer turned away from Lang. His inattention galvanized the policeman into action.

"Goddamned you, Fixer!"

Lang's eyes narrowed, his fingers tensing on the grip and trigger. The first report shut down all sense and sound for Fixer. The slug slammed into the wooden floor inches from his folded knees. He never heard the second. There was a wetness on his neck, then a searing hot pain. The second slug had grazed him.

Fixer sprang to his feet, clasping the katana and finding the samurai's fighting stance, hips down, knees and elbows flexed, the sword held before him, imperceptibly swaying, a murderous extension of self.

259

The Big Fall

"What are you going to do Harry? Kill me? Everybody dies!"

Fixer advanced in mincing little steps, an instant from springing at his adversary. Lang's bullets would take him down, but not before he got in a killing cut. It was his entitlement - an instant of immortality to make it right. Lang stood his ground, deliberately sighting the pistol in a two hand hold on Fixer's middle. 'Just like they trained you, Harry, you dumb bastard! Shoot for the torso. Better odds to get in every shot. But that won't stop me Harry. Take the head shot. But you don't have the balls to risk a miss, and being sure of a hit is what's going to take you down with me,' thought Johnny Fixx.

"See you in hell, Harry," he breathed.

"No!" The sensei's shrill command stopped them both. A reprimanding glance and Fixer gave way sheathing his sword. The sensei pushed at Lang admonishing him, "this is a Temple of peace. You are not welcome."

Lang's shoulders sagged. He stuffed the pistol under his belt and ran his hands through his hair in increasingly frantic motions. He rolled his head and rubbed at his neck, a man whose life was paining him to the very core. Harry Lang walked out of the exercise room.

The sensei clasped his pupil's shoulders, his eyes probing to learn the wellspring of the unbending cold determination to kill even at the certain forfeit of one's own life. Could the master know? The step out of line that had been one too many, the trap unending with no way out.

\* \* \* \* \*

Fixer stepped out of his elevator and killed its power, isolating himself from the City of Angels. There were no messages. Dancer still hadn't surfaced. Fixer drank some, then drifted off. He awakened, his mind racing. He was going down without fully understanding the why of it. Jonesy and Dancer, Persia and Harry Lang, and Johnny Fixx, the City of Angels teaming around them, uncaring, and uncivilized. Fixer fed a film into his recorder, and dropped into his chair. The 1946 version of 'The Killers', with Burt Lancaster, Edmond O'Brien, and Ava Gardner, Robert Siodmak's

The Big Fall

noirish masterpiece. The opening scene at the diner, faithfully adapted from the Hemingway short story that inspired the film. Burt Lancaster stoically awaited his fate, his eyes riveted to the darkened door framed in the last light he'd ever see that filtered in from the hall, an instant before the killers burst in to shoot him to pieces.

Fixer fast forwarded to the final frames. Ava Gardner, the femme fatale who'd played black widow to every man in her life, coldly pleading with her dying husband to take her off the hook yet another time. Maybe answers weren't really the point. Maybe it all came down to just knowing when it was time to lay it down.

Fixer lost himself in a bottle.

It was Lang screaming at him that brought him around. But he wasn't really screaming, only calling, again and again. Fixer grabbed for the phone. It was dead. Still Lang called. It wasn't the phone.

The intercom.

Then another voice, "hey Johnny, it's Steve Dawes. I'm with Harry. Send down the elevator. It's important."

Steve Dawes chaperoning Harry Lang. Why not after yesterday.

Fixer got it in gear, "I'm sending down the elevator. Make sure you're both on it and come in with your hands in plain view. I don't know what your boss told you Steve but he pushed too far yesterday and I'm never going to let him get close enough to do that again."

Harry Lang led Steve Dawes into the loft.

Fixer snapped, "you got a warrant Harry. No? Then get the hell out of my face. You're a mental case. Get away, or so help me, I'll kill you."

"Show him Steve," said Lang coldly.

261

The Big Fall

Steve Dawes dropped the morning edition on the desk. The headline read, "Two Women found beaten and shot to death in a Shallow Grave at the Wanderers Amusement Park." Fixer looked up.

"Keep reading wise guy," snapped Lang.

The women were identified as Bette Jones and Eve Scott.

"Jonesy and Evita," blurted Fixer.

Steve Dawes pulled a packet of papers from his inside jacket pocket and handed them to Fixer.

"The 'ME's' report Johnny. It ain't pretty."

Harry Lang was fully in control of his emotions. "This tears it Fixer. You've got until Monday, pal, to give me what I want, page and verse. Forty eight hours, then I close the show on your short and crooked life, and on your murderous friends. Got it?"

Fixer turned away.

* * * * *

Johnny Fixx called the Condor.

"Heavy around?"

Manny Cesar recognized his voice.

"Hey Fixer, it's me, 'George Raft' - Heavy's been gone since they picked him up to 'ID' Jonesy. Can you believe that. What the fuck did those dames do to deserve that? Christ, Evita wasn't in to anything. I still can't believe it."

"You're right Manny. I can't figure it. Like the man said, 'the world's a shit sandwich and everyday you take another bite'."

"You hear anything Johnny?"

262

The Big Fall

"Nothing pal. And I sure am sorry for you."

"What a fucking world."

"You seen Dancer Manny. I need to talk to him."

"Nah. Nobody has for days. If he shows or if one of his guys comes by, I'll pass the word. Johnny, they're having a service for Evita day after tomorrow."

"I'll be there Manny. I'll be there."

\*   \*   \*   \*   \*

It was Miles again, after midnight. Johnny Fixx did the broadcast live.

"Any of you who tune in regularly know that I'm a goner for Miles - any Miles - but mostly the quintet of the mid fifties and the sextet that it evolved into. Sure, the quintet of the middle sixties, Tony Williams, Herbie, Wayne Shorter, and Ron Carter was about as good as you could get. But for me, Trane, Canonball, Bill Evans, Philly Joe, Paul Chambers, they were even better. I've got some transition sides for you that were done live in Stockholm in 1960. John Coltrane had decided to go his own way in March of 1960. Miles was more than a little distressed. Not that he didn't wish his already famous sideman well. Miles always nurtured talent and took pride in their later achievements. But Trane was different. He was just too damned special and too good a fit, hand and glove, with Miles. So the 'dark prince' was beside himself in the search for a replacement. Then along came Sonny Stitt. Stitt got the teenaged Miles Davis one of his first big band gigs. Miles never forgot that. And Sonny Stitt was an acknowledged master of the alto and tenor saxophones. Stitt toured with Miles for the better part of a year playing both horns. Fortunately, the tape machines were running during two of Miles Scandinavian gigs, in March of 1960 and in October of 1960. I'm playing those albums for you in their entirety tonight. Enjoy."

Sunday morning, and still the silence. Fixer was up with the dawn. A steaming hot shower. Then what? Fixer rang up Tony Persia's apartment. No answer. Same result with the radio telephone on 'No Luck'. The

263

The Big Fall

clock was ticking on Harry Lang's ultimatum. Now the stakes included murder of the cold blooded variety. It came down to Joey Dancer.

The phone rang.

Fixer grabbed it, his tone anxious, "that you Joey?"

"Sorry to disappoint you, Johnny."

Samantha.

"My one and only."

Fixer could see that bittersweet look of hers, humor and hurt, as she said, "at least some of the time Johnny."

"Talk to me Sam. Anything - just talk to me."

"You're finally in over your head, aren't you?"

"Guys like me were born for the 'shit' love."

"I know, I really finally do know that some men can't live without it."

"I can't live without you, Sam."

The line went silent on her end.

"Sam . . . ." he called, wishing for all he was worth that she hadn't hung up. And then she was back, her raw emotions nicely suppressed, her voice girlishly bright because she knew he needed her that way.

"If you provide the place I'll bring the Fourth of July picnic with me. Okay?"

'Christ', thought Fixer, 'the goddamned fourth of July weekend, and it hadn't registered 'till now'.

"Meet you at the beach house in an hour Sam."

The Big Fall

* * * * *

She wore a gauzy ivory coverlet, her black bikini showing through. "Come on," she prodded as she made directly for the deck and beach below, leaving the picnic basket for him to ferry down.

"There's sun, but who knows when those damned coast storms will kick up again."

Johnny Fixx sprawled on the blanket. She stifled her curiosity about the dressing on his neck, smiled, and served him fried chicken, baked ham, and chilled champagne.

"You know Johnny, you could be a real pain in the ass, especially if I didn't have this terminal fondness for you."

He was thoroughly enjoying himself.

"What the hell good is it Sam if you don't get it spoon fed."

"You just led with your chin lover boy. But this is our day so I'm going to let that gem pass."

Fixer relaxed. The sun was never quite so hot as when the sea was near. The chill of his predicament was suddenly gone. He'd do what he had to, and do it right, and Harry Lang could go straight to hell.

Samantha leaned over him, lightly running her fingers over his face, then kissing him, and shuddering, "can I help, Johnny?"

"You're a helluva dame Sam . . . the best!"

It was a day for living. He grinned and tugged her to her feet.

"Come on, let's swim."

265

The Big Fall

Fixer went in with slacks and t-shirt. Sam dropped the coverlet and swam beside him.

She had always been a bloody fish and soon she disappeared in the surf on course up the beach. Fixer swam back to shore and trudged through the spongy sand. Samantha came out fifty yards farther up and ran back toward him. He jogged to meet her, and grabbed her waist and swung her off her feet when they met.

"Are we on camera?" she giggled. "This has got to be a bad out take from a commercial."

Later, much later, they lay together before the fire. Fixer moved to turn on the late news. Samantha's eyes flashed. He nodded almost imperceptibly that he understood, and switched on Channel 10. A well scrubbed junior anchorman was subbing for the regular.

Joey Dancer again was the lead story.

"Police sources have advised Channel 10 that they have a new cooperating witness who may be able to link Joey Dancer to the murder of rival mobster Sam Pitts three years ago. Neither Dancer nor his counsel were available for comment. Police Lieutenant Harry Lang said that an arrest was imminent."

"Do you know what that's all about," she asked.

"I'm beginning to get the picture Sam. But at this point, until Dancer surfaces, I'd only be guessing."

Fixer killed the television. "Come here beautiful. All of it's out there. It can't touch us here."

"Don't leave Johnny."

"I won't Sam . . . ." he said, his voice trailing off.

"It's been years of Decembers, Johnny. Is it too late for us?"

266

His good sense, every nerve ending, screamed at him that it was twilight, the dark about to flood over him. It always came down to here and now with him, never any tomorrows. There was no way out. But with her in his arms, her breath on his neck, her eyes, those goddamned knowing eyes, pleading with him for one more miracle.

His was the voice of another person, another time, in another place.

He touched his fingers lightly to her cheek.

"It's a stacked deck, kid . . . ."

"Never for us," she breathed. "We . . . ."

His second chances were long gone. He knew it. So did she.

"We . . . ." He said it once, then again, his voice building in intensity.

"We!"

"All right. I'm done with it. We're gonna' crash out of here."

There was uncertainty in his tone.

"Sam, you will come with me . . . ."

Her eyes locked onto his. He kissed her, the lightest touching, then clasped her to him. Her heart pounded against his chest.

"You make anything possible," he whispered.

Now he was in command again. No uncertainty. Just a single minded desire to be free of it, to put all of them behind him, regardless of the cost - so long as she was with him.

"You pack a bag Sam. It might be for a good long time. We're out of here."

There was no good reason why they should be able to pull it off, but the way he'd said it left no room for doubt.

"All right, Johnny.  All right . . . ." She held him with all her strength.

"There's nothing here for me without you."

\* \* \* \* \*

It was after midnight. He was drowsy. Paranoia suddenly gripped him. He grabbed the Walther from the end stand drawer and placed it beside him on the bed.

She understood.

"Stay close, Sam. I'm drifting. Just a cat nap, and then we'll start moving. Okay?"

"I'm going to walk on the beach. A few minutes. I'll wake you when I come back."

"Take the gun," he said.

She smiled.

"I don't think I'll need it, Johnny. Sleep. I won't be more than a few yards away."

"Take it," he whispered, as the black engulfed him.

She kissed him and he floated off in the warm wash of a river of perfume.

The phone rang. Fixer came to, grudgingly, not wanting to let go of her touch.

1:30 a.m.

The Big Fall

She hadn't returned.

The phone kept ringing.

He picked it up, coughing away phlegm, rasping, "yeah, who is it?"

Joey Dancer.

"Public enemy number one, pal. How you doin' Fixer?

Can you come down to Acme. We should talk. You catch Crystal's broadcast. Jeez, I must of had company a couple years back at Wanderers. You got any idea who that might have been."

Fixer was instantly fully awake. The bastard was figuring him for the snitch on the Pitts shooting. Right church, wrong pew. No way Fixer wanted to walk into that buzz saw.

"Ah, my old buddy Johnny Fixx don't want to talk to the Dancer, eh."

Dancer's tone hardened.

"Well, Johnny, you got no choice. We got a very close friend of yours here."

"Put her on," snapped Dancer.

"Johnny, oh god, Johnny. I'm sorry."

Samantha!

They'd grabbed her.

"No!" Fixx screamed. "No."

Blood drained from his face. He was light headed, and then he understood.

269

The Big Fall

There was unfinished business with Joey Dancer.

'No way out', he groaned.

In control again, his tone icy calm.

"Okay, Joey. Your call. I'm coming. You hear me, goddamned you. I'm coming. You keep my lady safe, pal."

Dancer cackled.

"I love it, Johnny. Like I always said, 'if you're skating on thin ice, what the fuck, you might as well dance. Right."

## CHAPTER TWENTY-TWO

Johnny Fixx sat in his car a block past Acme Specialties. Two in the morning inched up on three. He zeroed in the yard in his rear view. A convoy of tractor trailers roared past and turned into one of the terminals near the piers. He watched and waited. No one showed. Harry Lang figured to be nearby, but the usual telltales for a surveillance were nowhere in sight. Fixer took a final look, put the Vette in gear, and hung a U-turn to backtrack into the Acme yard.

Discarded wrapping flapped in vagrant gusts. Johnny Fixx killed his lights and rolled slowly through the opened gate. The yard was deserted. The folding door on a loading bay was open, as if in invitation, and Fixer climbed up, checked his back one last time, and walked through. A bare lightbulb swung at the end of the corridor, painting shadowy crazy quilts over the damp masonry walls. Beyond that a catwalk and ladder down to the floor. And Joey Dancer, sitting in his office booth that was lit bright enough to be the star of Bethlehem atop a Christmas tree. It was too easy. Too inviting. 'Too fucking obvious', he thought, but Fixer walked straight in, just like he knew Dancer expected him to.

Two women executed with head shots dumped in a shallow grave, one on top of the other in a final naked embrace. A crew from Pacific Power & Light had visited the Wanderers Amusement Park to disconnect a power line that was torn down in the storm. The shooter had thrown in their clothes after them. A piece of Evita's slip somehow had not been covered. That tipped the crew. Had they not made the service call, the coyotes would have unearthed the corpses and dragged them up into a canyon, and no one would have been the wiser until the bones turned up years later, if ever.

And now the bastard was making war on his woman!

Fixer levered a round into the Walther's chamber, and dropped the automatic into his jacket pocket. He was on the warehouse floor, his footfalls resonating through the cavernous interior. Dancer swiveled in his chair to face him as Fixer emerged from the shadows.

Johnny Fixx had run it. Say little. Let it play of its own momentum. But the sight of his friend tore off the stops.

The Big Fall

"Where is she, Joey? I'm here. She walks. End of story."

"Maybe it ain't that easy sport," answered Dancer. Fixer exploded, "you are murdering bastard! You put down two women in cold blood!"

"You know Johnny, you've been makin' easy money too long," spat Dancer. "Jonesy would have blown in her mother. She was on Lang's string for years. No way I was gonna' give her the slack to make a move on me. No fuckin way! Evita shit, I feel bad about her, but she got tangled up with that cunt and I couldn't take the chance. Christ, the bitch probably had you in her sights, too."

"Christ, Joey. What about Tex? Doesn't anybody count with you anymore?"

Dancer sat there looking straight through him.

"Tex was a blood brother, Johnny. He needed the dough and I gave him a chance to die in his own kind of combat. I'd do the same for you."

"And what about you Johnny, my friend. What about you, counsellor? You knew about that quonset in Irvine, pal?" There was no point in any denial.

"So I did Dancer. I did what I had to, but I made it right."

"Now we're talking the same language compadre. Maybe I did too, Johnny."

Dancer was on his feet, his tone accusing. "Maybe the lowlife that blew me in at Irvine also whispered in Lang's ear about Sam Pitts."

"You're wrong, Joey."

"I don't think so, Fixer."

"I want my wife out of this, Joey. Now!"

272

"You'll get her, Johnny boy. But first you're gonna' do me and Tony 'P' a last good turn."

"What the hell are you talking about, Dancer," screamed Johnny Fixx, his emotions barely in check.

"We need a delivery made, pal. It might be a one-way ride. That's the price. Do it, and your lady walks. Be an asshole and she'll share a shallow grave with you."

Joey Dancer lit a cigarette and followed the smoke trail upward. He grinned and waved at the catwalk directly above. Eddie Ebony was covering his bosses' action.

"What do you think, Eddie?"

Johnny Fixx saw the Smith 459 in Ebony's hand. His brain screamed the caution, 'Ebony won't fire', but the message went undelivered as his fingers answered some primal survival instinct hot wired to his spinal cord by passing his brain. It was all wrong. The Walther was in his hand, but Eddie had the edge. "Don't do it!" screamed Ebony. Fixx never heard the round that tore through his side and slammed him into the wall. He snapped off a shot, more a pain reflex than by design. Joey Dancer took the stray round in the belly, staggered back a step, then sat slowly down against the far wall.

Dancer ran his hand across his middle, winced at the blood leaking from his belly, and waved at Eddie Ebony.

"Christ, no more! Goddamned you Fixer. Eddie, keep him covered," he gasped.

Fixx' hand numbed and the Walther dropped to the floor.

"Johnny, Johnny . . . ." groaned Dancer as he stared at his bloodied hands.

"You made a mess out of me boy."

273

The Big Fall

Dancer's head rolled to the side, but he willed himself back.

"Christ man, Persia's deal with the micks is going down. Now look what you've gone and done Fixer."

Johnny Fixx frantically grabbed for his hand kerchief, wadded it and pressed it into Dancer's middle in a futile attempt to stop the bleeding. His finger tips touched what his eyes hadn't seen and he tore open Dancer's shirt.

"A wire," he gasped. "For christ's sake, Joey. Who the hell is on the other end?"

Dancer's laugh became a ragged gasp from deep in his lungs.

"They had me good this time Johnny, but they gave me an out. If I gave them Tony Persia and the micks, I could take the dope and run to Mexico."

Dancer groaned as blood trickled from the corner of his mouth. His breathing became a halting rattle. He wrenched the words from his lips.

"And for good measure Johnny, they wanted you thrown in too. Shit, I figured you for fingering me for Sam Pitts."

"It wasn't me Joey."

"Can you beat that pal, and here I thought I had it all doped out nice and neat. Everybody had a price, but my way, only the Dancer would be around at last call to collect."

Dancer clawed at the tape around his middle that held the transmitter. Fixer grabbed it and threw the device against the concrete knee wall beneath the glass panels.

"The desk drawer, Johnny," directed Dancer.

274

The Big Fall

Fixer gingerly hefted a packet of explosives taped to a stainless trigger mechanism.

"What the hell Joey . . . ."

Fixer dropped beside Dancer and leaned in to hear his words.

"That's Tony Persia's little surprise for the micks. You never figured it, did you kid?"

Fixer's expression questioned. Dancer slowly articulated the story, the words coming in a halting cadence.

"It's not guns or money with Persia. Close to fifty years ago in Montreal, the cops got to Farina and told him he could have his docks, but he'd have to give them the mick bomb throwers he was working with. Farina made the deal. The micks tumbled to it and planted that bomb outside Dominic Farina's front door. But it was his sister who opened that door. Angela Farina took the blast for the don. I hear Joe Bayonne's been feeding the story to you piece by piece. I guess he figured even a dumb shit like you should know why he was being set up for a kill. But Jersey Joe and Persia were close Johnny, and Joe held back the punch line. Not me though compadre. Shit, we're shot to pieces, right. So what's the point of bullshitin' each other."

A coughing spasm doubled him up, and Dancer clutched his belly.

"I'm back compadre," he whispered. "Can't leave you yet Johnny - oh, no, motherfucker - not until we're square."

Dancer gathered himself.

"Maybe you already know what I've told you. What you didn't know was that Tony Persia loved Angela, but because he was sworn to protect the don, he had to keep his distance. Tony Persia knew where that bomb came from. The don did too, but he warned Tony off. The lid had to stay on the smuggling pipeline in Montreal. So Tony Persia bided his time. The man waited more than forty years to take his vengeance on the

275

micks. He knew he was dying - down to the last draw. So he cooked up the arms heist just to suck them in. Tony had Spillane bring in all the big guns. They're all on that boat."

Dancer touched the bomb and grinned. "I was supposed to leave his calling card after he left. And then I decided you should be my stand in."

"The old man's crazy. The people who killed his Angela are long dead." Dancer grimaced.

"They're all the same to Tony. Maybe he's on to something compadre - when it comes down to it, hatred is the only thing that lasts."

The pain was a red hot poker probing deeper and deeper into his middle. Fixer clasped his side. Dancer held out his blood soaked hands, then pulled at Fixer's lapels, his fists clenched in a death grip.

"You can have your lady, Fixer. But you're taking that ride for me. That's the only way it plays."

Dancer pointed to Ebony above them on the catwalk.

"You hear, Eddie. You bring the lady back to the beach house, just as soon as the word is out that the delivery was made by my friend, Johnny. Understood?"

"You can count on me, Joey," said the bodyguard.

"No delivery, no lady. You got that Fixer?"

"Deal, you sonuvabitch!" screamed Fixx.

Dancer laughed hysterically.

"If I wasn't feelin' so goddamned lousy, I'd be loving every minute of this. You were born for it Johnny, your fucked up genetic mojo is in those old black and white movies you keep watching. Those guys all go down in the end, don't they?"

276

The Big Fall

"Sometimes pal, but not before they do some damage Joey."

"The freighter's docked at Point Fermin, lands end in Palos Verde, Johnny. They're loading the guns now."

Dancer clasped Fixer's hand in his.

"I'm gonna' level with you Johnny. It was one fuckin' sweet deal. My end was a load of dope that came up from the Baha on the freighter. That part of the deal is signed, sealed, and delivered. Sonny Bamboo's got my end. He's supposed to pick me up at the old Seaside Motel in Balboa. And then south of the border. I bought me a piece of Mexico, cops included."

Dancer worked at the grin.

"If you get lucky, pal, Sonny's your way out. But I wouldn't count on it. It's a bitch, ain't it, pard."

Fixer was light headed as he struggled to his feet. He held the bomb before him.

Dancer cackled, "careful there pard. You wouldn't want to have an accident and take us both out."

"All you do Johnny is hit the switch on top, then ten seconds later, boom!"

"And pal, don't get any ideas. Once you walk out of here, you do the job. You make any move to come back here, you do anything to move on us, and the lady's dog meat."

Dancer began hyperventilating, his hands tearing at his middle.

"... just a pair of bad assed soldiers," he gasped.

"Joey!"

Dancer clawed his way back, one last time.

277

"No medics this time pal. Guess if a man's got a one way ticket, it might as well be a pal who punches it, eh, Johnny?"

\* \* \* \* \*

Dermot Spillane paced nervously before Tony Persia. The freighter rocked gently on the swells. Persia sat a chair in the radio shack sipping a glass of wine.

"You said Dancer would be here by this time."

"He should have Dermot. He'll be here any minute. Besides, the trucks got here, didn't they. Your cargo is being loaded, right? Everything checked out, didn't it. So why are you so edgy?"

"I'm not Tony. I sent Colonel Slattery below because he was asking too damned many questions. He's in this country illegally from Dublin. This stuff is ticketed for his boys on the other end. He's right to ask those questions, but what can I tell him? It's just that I want to finish this up and get under way. As long as we're here there's always the chance somebody will stumble onto what we're doing."

"Have some wine Dermot. It makes everything better."

A crewman opened the door.

"Mr. Spillane, there's something out there at the top of the hill. Take a look."

Spillane moved out of the radio shack and climbed to the bridge. Persia trailed him up.

Dermot took the glasses and crabwalked them up the darkened road.

"What is it," asked Persia.

"A car. A blacked out car."

"Police?"

"I don't know. . . ."

Spillane squinted into the eye pieces, then exclaimed, "no, its a sport car. I've never seen the boys in blue drive one, have you Tony? Take a look."

"You're right Dermot. Maybe you should send one of your boys up the hill to take a look."

Spillane called down to the deck.

"Pull those two cars across the road. Block it good. And you Jack, take a ride up the hill in the jeep. There's somebody up there watching. Check him out."

Spillane glared at Tony Persia. The old man sipped his wine and smiled easily.

"Put your daggers away Dermot. I'm here. I'm your guest. What could go wrong?"

The Vette slowly rolled down the hill.

"What the hell," screamed Spillane as the engine caught and the car began hurtling toward them.

"Turn the lights on him and get out here with the weapons, quick!" he commanded.

The deck and superstructure of the freighter were lined with armed men each sighting in the Vette.

"He's gonna' run the barricade, goddamnit, open up, pour it in!"

"Who the fuck is that running down there," cried Dermot Spillane.

279

The Big Fall

Harry Lang broke cover from the pallet of crates where he'd been conducting his one man stake out after Dancer's tip. Joey Dancer had said to come alone.

Dancer!

'Double crossing bastard', breathed Lang.

He stepped into the road as the guns cut lose from the freighter. And then he recognized the car.

"Fixer, you fucking lunatic," he screamed.

Johnny Fixx slammed through the car barricade. The stainless timer on the packet of C-4 gleamed in the spots from the freighter that now found him. A lifetime came down to seconds. He hit the switch and kept the accelerator on the floor. It was only an instant for a few yards more, an instant that had taken so goddamned long for him to end up where he always knew he would. Fixer focused on the bridge. Tony Persia seemed to be grinning down at him, tipping a wine glass. It couldn't be.

Harry Lang!

The cop calmly fired from a two hand hold, emptying his clip into the windshield. Then the Vette ripped into him, breaking his legs. Lang was catapulted up and onto the hood, his bloodied face distorted with a rage unfulfilled, his hands clawing at Johnny Fixx beyond the shattered windshield. The bullets from the freighter found their mark. Harry Lang's head exploded. His body slithered off the hood and crumpled under the wheels.

The micks riddled the Vette, but Fixer knew they couldn't take him out, not quite yet.

Persia breathed, "Johnny Fixx, can you beat that."

And then the Vette exploded as it leaped from the pier to slam across the gangplank and into the freighter. A blood red ball erupted skyward. The mangled chassis of the Vette settled into the water. The freighter lurched in the water, then a cracking and dull thud. Finally silence.

Dermot Spillane grabbed Tony Persia, shaking him. "It's done. He didn't make it. We're okay . . . ."

Persia smiled. An enormous roar, then a rush of white hot air, and the freighter disintegrated as the fire from the Vette explosion worked through the tear in the water line to find the powder below decks. The old man was falling, falling, the photograph of his beloved Angela floating down with him, just beyond the reach of his fingertips.

Johnny Fixx figured to ride it out, but instinct propelled him through the driver's side door. He gasped her name then resigned himself to the finish. 'I'm done, it's done, she's safe, so why fight anymore', he thought, but he beat the explosion by a second, maybe two. It didn't figure, but somehow the bullets and explosives never touched him. He swallowed water, choked, and swam, his head spinning from the concussions of the explosions, his side throbbing with razor stabs that intensified with every stroke. And then he touched bottom. Fixer gasped for air and thrashed in the shallows, finding his feet, and trudging through the slime onto the beach. The very top of the freighter's stack and the yardarm of one of her deck cranes were all that showed on the surface. The sun was up, a crimson beacon, and Johnny Fixx hurting from every pore, limped up the beach to home in on it.

\*   \*   \*   \*   \*

A Chicano trucker driving south to Chula Vista had offered a lift and asked no questions. Fixer peeled two 'C' notes from the roll that padded his pocket. They were damp, but Fixer managed a grin, "they'll dry amigo."

It was sadly backwater - the Seaside Motel in Balboa, four stories in cracking stucco, a tiled roof faded to rust hanging on a shelf, the sea below, fields above washed by giant sprinklers laboring to beat the salt spray and squeeze crops from arid soil. They brought up a bottle of Jack Daniels and extra towels. Fixer rang his beach house and kept calling. No answer! He made another call, then wrapped the towels around his middle. The sea

281

crashed over the breakwater. Fixer watched out the window, then floated a couple of steps on legs that weren't there and slumped into a threadbare chair before the television set. He was in and out, lucid, then dizzy, finally nauseated. He labored to turn on the set. Channel 6. Beads of perspiration dribbled into his eyes. He blinked at the burning. Crystal Lee reading the news. Samantha crowded her out. She loped toward him on their beach. Fixer willed her into his arms. But Crystal's insistent voice brought him down to the here and now. Fixer rubbed at the stubble on his face. 'Samantha', he breathed, but it was Crystal Lee saying his name. Then his picture on the screen.

"Police are seeking defense attorney John Fixx for questioning concerning the explosion that destroyed a freighter at Point Fermin in Palos Verde. Police also believe that John Fixx may have information concerning the death of police Lieutenant Harry Lang who apparently was killed near the freighter, and mobster Joey Dancer who was found shot to death in his office at Acme Specialties in San Pedro."

Crystal Lee's broadcast shifted to film footage of Felix Masters being ushered into a police car outside the Condor Roadhouse.

"There is speculation that Masters was the surprise witness that prosecutors promised would help make their case against Joey Dancer for the murder of rival mobster Sam Pitts three years ago."

'Heavy', gasped Fixer, as the pieces finally fell into place. Heavy had been the stowaway in Dancer's truck three years before when Joey shot Sam Pitts. Heavy would have died for Joey, but when Dancer killed his girl, Heavy made it right by blowing him in to Harry Lang.

Then Crystal again.

"In a related story, Channel 6 learned today that Rudy Kutter, the District Attorney of Los Angeles County will kick off his Senatorial campaign at a rally before the convention of the Police Benevolent Association scheduled for Parker Center next Friday evening. DA Kutter told us that he will delegate some of his daily operating duties during the campaign to his first assistant, Mary Donlon, but Kutter emphasized that he would remain in command as far as any policy decisions were concerned."

"Always hedge your bets Rudy . . . ." breathed Johnny Fixx.

A knock sounded at the door. He grabbed the Walther and said, "come." She was oriental, ebony hair, her eyes wide black marbles. She wore white shorts and a black halter top. The pistol registered but she walked in like Fixer was holding a drink.

"I'm Solitaire - from the escort service."

Fixer nodded, dropped the pistol beside the chair, and gestured at the bottle. Solitaire poured herself a stiff drink, downed it, and said, "we have to take care of business first."

"That's okay. Did you bring it?"

Solitaire opened her bag and showed the contents. "Okay?"

Fixer gestured at his pants that he'd discarded on the bed.

"The dough's in one of the pockets. Take it."

Solitaire rifled the pockets and came out with a wad of bills.

"It's only $300. You must have two thousand here."

Fixer smiled, "your lucky day doll."

Solitaire knew better than to ask a well heeled trick any questions. She dropped the money into her bag. Maybe it was her lucky day. She stripped, then knelt before Fixer, kneading the opium, then tamping it into the bowl. The towels around Fixer's middle were staining red with new bleeding. Solitaire worked at not noticing. She lit the pipe and placed it in his hands.

The Big Fall

He used the phone again. It rang and kept ringing as he dropped it to the floor.

"Samantha" he breathed, and Solitaire smiled, "yes", as she massaged his legs.

Fixer's cheeks hollowed as he inhaled the opium smoke, his choke reflex barely suppressed. Finally the pipe drew well and he ascended a high drunken peak. His world spread out to view, his life perhaps a thing that could be explained.

He walked the grounds of a decaying amusement park. Bull dozers and wrecker's balls demolished the rides. Children lined the beach, weeping. Carousel horses were shattered. The roller coaster exploded like a torrent of spent matchsticks, one section slithering intact into the sea, a hump backed sea serpent frantically fleeing a world bent on its destruction.

Crystal Lee broke into his world.

"Los Angeles County celebrated the Fourth of July today with a rally at the Coliseum . . . ."

"Shut her off," he asked, and Solitaire did.

His Fourth of July should have ended in a black marble monolith. The Nam! Napalm incinerated the perimeter. Flocks of Hueys hovered over the platoon's mad rush to safety. Door gunners raked the dust. Tracers flashed through the acrid smoke swirling up from the battlefield. NVA regulars screamed their hatred and sprang from tunnels to meet them. Bayonets found the mark. Fixer was at the dead run, Joey Dancer suddenly beside him. Firing as they ran, vaulting dead troopers. Mortar rounds slammed in, closer, and closer. Small arms rounds whizzed by. The wailing of the dead and dying. "Sweet fucking Jesus," groaned Fixer in amazement at still being alive. Then another round exploded lifting them bodily.

The crack and whump of hostile fire dulled. Alive. Dead. 'The deep within the deep', intoned the sensei. The rush and roar finally far distant.

# The Big Fall

Samantha was there smiling gently. Eddie Ebony crowded her out.

"You sonuvabitch, Dancer," he roared.

Samantha!

His eyes were glazing. It was the shabby seaside hotel in Balboa. He watched out the window. Police cruisers descended the track to the jetty, sirens blazing, flashers on.

The red lights accused. The indictment read 'a nearly honorable man who'd wasted his principles on the undeserving, for dirty money'. But what had been the gain when everything was ending badly. The lanterns jangled in a friendly cadence at the ends of the horse drawn plough rumbling to ferry him across, horses at the gallop, the teamster smiling, the snow coming down in wind whipped swirls. Live badly, die well!

"No, goddamnit," he gasped. "Not just yet. No!"

He dialed the number again. One ring, two, then four more.

"Hello, hello. Johnny, is that you?"

Sweet Jesus. She was alive.

"Is Ebony there?"

"No Johnny. No. I'm alone. I'm safe."

"Sam, stay put. I'll get there. Somehow I'll get there."

"Are you all right, Johnny?"

"I'll get there," he groaned.

The roar and whump of rotors. A cop talking on a bullhorn. "John Fixx. We know you're inside. Come out with your hands up. You have ten seconds."

The Big Fall

Again on the bullhorn.

"Get that chopper out of there. This is police business. Get it out or we'll open fire."

Solitaire helped him up. The chopper was on the beach not twenty yards from where he stood.

"Stay down," he told her, as he staggered through the door to the stair well.

He crashed through the rear door and limped through the sand.

Sonny Bamboo jumped down from the chopper, his bad leg nearly buckling.

"Johnny, Johnny. Hang on man. I'm coming. Hang on."

"She's waiting for me, Sonny. You've got to get me out of here. Don't let me die here."

"We ain't doin' no dyin' today John. Not you. Not me. Hang on to me. We're gonna' make it."

Sam Turre and Steve Dawe directed the police cordon around the Seaside.

Turre cried, "he's gonna lift off, and Fixer's in there with him. Open up on that chopper. Blow them to hell." Steve Dawe jammed his automatic under Turre's chin. "Let it be, Sam. They're all dead. Lang, Dancer, Persia. Leave Fixer be. We can pick him up anytime."

An officer escorted Solitaire to the command car. "She was in there with him, boss. Tell him what you told me."

"He's badly hurt," she gasped. "He's lost a lot of blood. I don't know whether he can make it."

"Let it be," Steve Dawe screamed.

He holstered the automatic. His voice implored. "Enough, Sam. Okay?"

Sonny Bamboo lifted off, Johnny Fixx strapped in beside him.

"Ah shit," groaned Sam Turre. "Hold your fire. You hear me. Hold your fire."

\* \* \* \* \*

Johnny Fixx clutched his middle, the pincers of pain clearing his head.

"Hang on, pal. Hang on. There's more money in back than either one of us can ever spend. Dancer's pay off. In thirty minutes I'll have us in Mexico. Hang on!"

"The beach house, Sonny. Sam's there. The beach house!"

"Okay, okay," called Bamboo as he turned up the coast.

Samantha filled the second ashtray, then downed another tumbler of Jack Daniels. He had to be close. "Damn it," she cursed climbing down the deck ladder to the beach.

The chopper skirted the waves.

"Johnny!" she cried.

Bamboo set down on the beach and hit the sand to escort Samantha into the chopper.

"Oh, my god," she gasped, as the blood around Fixer's middle registered.

Samantha knelt beside him, her arms around him, her head on his chest.

"Johnny, Johnny, oh god, I love you."

They were back over the ocean, minutes away from the border.

Johnny Fixx touched her hair then ran his hands over her face.

"No tears babe. We made it. No tears."

He began slipping away. His head sagged of its own weight, his eyelids becoming incredibly heavy.

"No, no," she screamed, willing him back.

"There's a doc near Dancer's place. He'll know what to do. No questions asked," said Bamboo. Sonny radioed ahead.

In fifteen minutes they were on the ground, an ambulance parked not ten feet away.

Fixer was bundled onto a gurney, Samantha running beside him. He was in and out, her hand squeezing his, the force of her will his lifeline.

The red flasher atop the ambulance.

Fixer grinned.

Concentric black lines in the blood red core.

Not the destination he'd figured.

The Doctor trotted beside them. Her eyes pleaded.

"He has a chance. We must hurry before he goes into shock."

The attendants inserted the plasma 'iv' into his arm.

He mouthed the words.

288

The Big Fall

"What," she cried.

"Don't let me go . . . ." he whispered.

It had been a long way down - the big fall - but finally he understood that none of it mattered. Her touch, her tears, his universe, her smile, sun enough. He had nearly lost her. But finally it was only the two of them, for one more breath, or another lifetime, it would be enough, as long as they were together.